HARLEY MERLIN AND THE SECRET COVEN

BELLA FORREST

Nightlight Press

Prologue

I froze, my back against the window, my whole body shivering as the beast in front of me shuddered with delight.

Another second and I would become its dinner.

Something inside me roared like thunder, unwilling to give in yet. The air around me thickened—I could feel it tickling my fingertips, beckoning me to wield it. I'd done it before, though not with the strength I would need to disable a fiend as savage as this.

But I had to try. There was no other choice.

I summoned all the energy I could muster, and, for the first time ever, I sensed the particles of Chaos flowing through me. My mind went into overdrive, and I thrust my hands out. The winds outside listened, rumbling and whistling as they crashed through the window.

I ducked as broken glass exploded everywhere. Shards cut through the beast's face and eyes, and it hissed from the pain.

With no other route to safety, I embraced the winds and leapt onto the windowsill. My breath hitched as I looked down at the sheer drop, and then I closed my eyes, abandoning myself to the air.

Chapter One

My eyes wandered around the poker table.

The dealer, a young man in his early twenties, had been fitted into a crisp white shirt and black silk waistcoat, his brown hair slicked back with too much gel. His dexterity as he shuffled the deck made me stare, before I went on to check the players.

Two women and three men. Three of them had skipped on the Gamblers Anonymous meetings—I could tell from their frayed nerves and shoulder-crushing guilt. It was written all over their faces. The other two, a man in his late twenties and a cute brunette who didn't look a day older than twenty-three, struck me as the coolest cucumbers I'd seen all evening.

This was a steady gig I'd gotten my hands on, so I had to do a good job. Three months in, and I'd already gotten fifteen people banned for cheating and counting cards. It wasn't an easy profession, though—for most people, anyway. It required a lot of psychology and the study of body language, along with excellent knowledge of the game itself. You had higher chances of success if you were a former cheater, preferably with some Vegas experience. But I had very little experience at all.

Then again, I wasn't "most people."

After betting, it was time for the "flop." The dealer displayed three cards in the middle of the dark red velvet table—seven of clubs, queen of diamonds, and a five of spades—while we checked our "hole" hands again. I had nothing to use, but I bet anyway. The casino supplied my betting cash, so it didn't matter if I lost. My prize came in the form of a generous percentage of the cheaters' relinquished winnings if I caught colluders at the table, along with my hourly rate.

Texas Hold'em was a favorite game choice for collusion, and with the amount of money involved in tonight's game, I knew I'd get some bold players this evening.

My instincts were pointing me to the "cucumber" couple. The other three were already sweating. One was clearly a veteran gambler, at least compared to the rest. With graying hair, salt-and-pepper stubble, and sweat stains on his peach-colored shirt, the man was nervously clicking two blue chips between his fingers as he stared at the three cards in view. He was going to fold soon.

I could feel it in my bones. There was nothing he could do with what he had in his hand, and what was on the table. With five crappy cards combined, and just two more to go with the "turn" and the "river," he wasn't *feeling* this round, at all. Sure, he had the gambling bug, but he'd probably lost enough over the years to know when to pick his battles.

He scoffed, and folded.

Hah, called it! Who's a smart girl? You're a smart girl, I mentally congratulated myself while my gaze wandered around the table. I was a smart girl. It was the only thing I'd learned from my father.

I flipped open my black satin clutch—which I'd matched with my dress—pretending to look for a tissue. I kept a small note in my card wallet. I pulled it out and examined it for a moment.

Harley, I am so sorry for doing this to you, but there is no other way. Stay safe. Stay smart. I love you. Dad.

That note was the only thing my parents had left me with,

before dropping me off at the orphanage when I was three. I was bounced around from one foster home to another after that. It was rarely a pretty picture, and my father's advice somehow helped me retain my sanity. Even now, as I glided into adulthood, I kept looking at that note for guidance, whenever a part of me wavered. As a foster kid, I always had to "stay safe" and "stay smart," though the two rarely went hand in hand.

When the turn was dealt, I glanced around the poker table again.

Each of these people had their stories to tell. They had first names and last names, parents and grandparents, uncles and distant cousins, social security numbers and student loans. In my twisted view of the world, they existed, while I was just a visitor of sorts. Always on the outside, looking in.

I had no identity. Just a name on paper. I rented an apartment in Park West and pinpointed cheaters in casinos for a living. Nobody knew anything about me or my... special skills, and I was okay with that.

"I'll raise you twenty," the male cool cucumber said, looking at the equally chilled female across the table.

In the eyes of everyone else, they didn't know each other. They were complete strangers exchanging pleasantries during a game of Texas Hold'em, where tens of thousands of dollars were at stake. But I could feel the physical attraction between them. The guy was head over heels in love with her. She was just as crazy about him. There was a familiarity between them, an intense emotion that they couldn't hide from *me*. That was the downside of being an empath; I felt every emotion as if it were my own.

I basically had the hots for both of them, as if we'd been together for years. *Ugh...*

When the river was dealt, I could almost hear the guy's heart thumping out of his chest. His excitement filled me to the brim, and, judging by the looks the couple exchanged briefly, unbeknownst to anyone else, they were ready to do some good old-fashioned whipsawing—raising and re-raising each other until they trapped another player in between.

And I knew exactly who their target was for this round. The other female, one of the compulsive gamblers. She was nervous, her eyes darting across the five cards now shown on the table: a seven of clubs, a queen of diamonds, a five of spades, a jack of clubs and another queen, of hearts.

My hand was weak. All I could offer was a pair of fives. I folded, clicking my teeth.

"Maybe next time," I said, leaning back in my seat.

As expected, the cucumbers started teasing each other.

"I'm thinking it's a good night," the guy said, then tossed a few red chips on the pile gathering in the middle of the table. "Thirty."

"Your overconfidence could be your weakness," the girl said, grinning, and raised him another thirty, her tongue passing over her pearly white teeth. The tight, jade-colored dress she wore was meant to arouse, and based on what I was reading from the guy, she was getting the desired results.

I shifted in my chair, slightly uncomfortable with feeling someone else's arousal, but stayed focused nonetheless. The girl's outfit looked expensive. They weren't here to play for pennies.

"I'm in," the female gambler replied, tossing her own share of chips, worth thirty thousand dollars, while the fourth player folded, shaking his head.

The cucumbers seemed to ignore the woman, and continued taunting each other, while the dealer watched, amusement twinkling in his eyes.

"Raise you another thirty," cucumber girl said, grinning, as the guy bit the inside of his cheek and added more chips to the pile.

"You're bluffing," he replied. "Thirty."

The female compulsive gambler frowned, but the energy coming from her echoed confidence. She felt like she had a good hand. A really good hand. My guess was that it had something to do with the queens. She raised them another thirty, then narrowed her eyes at her own cards.

"I'm not bluffing," the girl said. She raised an eyebrow and pushed forty thousand dollars' worth of chips forward. "Raise."

The guy scoffed, scratching the back of his neck as he contemplated his choices for a couple of seconds. The female gambler, on the other hand, had quickly sunk into despair. I realized then that maybe her hand wasn't all that good. If I wanted to confirm collusion between the cucumbers, I needed the lady to fold so I could then watch the guy fold as well, and let the girl win. It seemed like the natural way for it to play out at that point.

"Okay, now I'm pissed," the guy said, and raised her another twenty.

The female gambler cursed under her breath and folded, nervously counting the chips she had left, while the cucumbers pretended to glower at each other. It was getting a little too dramatic for my taste. Even a non-empath could tell they were slightly over the top.

"All in," the girl challenged the guy, and pushed the rest of her chips into the middle, prompting the others to stare at her in disbelief.

The pot was somewhere over $350,000, and it was time for the guy to shake his head in disappointment, then fold. My fingers gripped the edge of the table, my nerves anticipating the moment I'd get my proof of collusion. I *knew* they were hot for each other in ways no two people meeting for the first time would ever be.

He tossed the cards, facedown, feigning irritation as he gulped down his drink, then motioned for a waiter to bring him another one.

Bingo!

Once they got away with this, they were going to get more brazen. I *wanted* them to dig themselves into a hole as deep as possible. The bigger their winnings at the end of the night, the bigger my prize.

I straightened my back as the dealer collected the cards and shuffled them, while the girl raked the mountain of chips over to her side of the table. She stacked them quickly into groups of $20,000, between sips of her fruity drink.

Personally, I looked forward to watching that smirk get wiped off at the end of the night.

It was time to get security to pay attention. I fiddled with my onyx earring, giving the head of security a brief sideways glance. Malcolm the bouncer stood at the end of the bar, ten yards away, pretending to chat with the bartender. He noticed my signal and discreetly brought a hand over his mouth, communicating a message through the tiny mic mounted into one of his cufflinks.

"It's showtime," the dealer said.

I shifted my focus back to our table as cards were dealt.

Oh, you have no idea.

Chapter Two

One by one, four of the ten security cameras in the room slowly turned and zoomed in on our table. For good reason, too. We were at the turn of another game, and the cucumbers were busy signaling each other.

Had it not been for the guy's stretched nerves and my ability to sense them, the cheaters might have gotten away with it. A mixture of excitement and fear, guilt and desire rumbled through the couple, while the other three players were simply hopeful that their luck might turn around. I was getting a little angry at this point—it was bad enough that these people were struggling with an addiction. The cucumbers were literally preying on them while carrying out their little we're-strangers-at-the-same-poker-table charade.

I folded, then homed in on the familiarity between them. They'd been doing this for years, and, when they thought no one was looking, I could see the longing in their stolen glances. They got off on these thrills.

The air changed. I couldn't exactly describe it, but it felt different, as if it were electrically supercharged. A rush of tingles tickled my spine, and I slowly turned my head to get a better look at the rest of the room. I'd yet to learn how to fully detach myself from what I was feeling as an empath, so I suspected that whatever anxiousness the cucumbers were experiencing, it had been passed on to me, too.

I settled on a pair of deep green eyes that belonged to a tall young man, maybe in his early twenties, who took a seat at one of the booths, just ten feet away from our table. His hair was dark brown, almost black, curled and unruly on the top, and smoothly shortened into a fade on the sides. He wore a navy-blue suit—elegant but a little casual—paired with a black shirt, its collar unbuttoned. His facial features were clear-cut, matching his equally sharp gaze.

The way he looked at me made my back automatically straighten itself. I wasn't sure what that reaction was all about, but I quickly realized that he was responsible for the sudden flow of energy through the room. The intensity pressuring my shoulders and stomach seemed to radiate from within him.

A waitress came for his order, while my table got ready for the river. I caught a glimpse of the cucumbers signaling each other, before the girl folded. I had to give them credit: they were making an effort to be inconspicuous.

"Sparkling water with ice and lime, please," the electric dude said.

I couldn't help but turn my head to look at him again. His voice sounded like liquid velvet. *And who the hell comes into a casino and orders water?*

"Coming right up, sir," the waitress replied.

"A *lot* of lime, please," he added, then glanced at me.

Holding my breath, I shifted my focus back to the table. We were going into another round, after the cucumbers had just cleaned out the veteran gambler. He muttered a curse under his breath, then started walking over to the cashier at the other end of the room.

"I'm gonna go get some more chips," the gambler grumbled. "Don't start without me!"

The dealer raised his eyebrows at us. "Is everyone okay if we give the gentleman a couple of minutes to rejoin us?"

"Damn straight," the cucumber guy grinned, annoyingly overconfident. "I can't wait to clean him out again!"

The one thing I hated most about these confident guys was that, when it rubbed off on me, I got cocky and made dumb mistakes—like, really stupid, what-the-hell-were-you-thinking types of mistakes that either got me in trouble or, worse, hurt.

I watched the waitress return with the electric dude's lime water. He gave her a brief nod, then frowned at the highball glass.

"Can I get more lime, please?" he asked, his voice low.

The waitress gave him a perky smile and a wink, then rushed to the bar for more lime. She liked him. I knew that for a fact, because I was having a hard time taking *my* eyes off the guy. *Damn my empathy.*

She returned with a small bowl filled with lime wedges at the same time as our veteran gambler, whose energy and hope of getting a better hand filled me up with unwarranted optimism. Nevertheless, my attention was fixed on the electric dude, who stuffed more lime into his glass, turning its contents into an almost-limeade.

Only then did I notice the rings on his fingers—ten sterling silver bands, one for each finger. There were inscriptions engraved on all of them, but I couldn't make out the words from where I sat. His gaze found mine, and he lifted a curious eyebrow. My cheeks heated, and I slowly turned back to my table as the dealer started the next game.

The strangeness in the air didn't fade away, though. It lingered around me, and I couldn't shake the feeling that I was being watched. Something was... off.

As the first three cards were laid out on the table, I glanced over my shoulder. The electric dude had this look about him, a quiet but bone-rattling charm that reminded me of British rock stars—the tall, dark, and handsome type, not too bulky but not skinny either, who look good in whatever you make them wear. Except skinny jeans. Nobody looks good in skinny jeans.

He took out a tablet and absently swiped its screen for a couple of minutes. A tap on my table made me check my hand, then the flop. Once again, my cards were useless. I folded, eager to get back to what my electric rock star was doing. I just couldn't look away, and there was no perky waitress around to blame. *I* was the curious and interested one.

He stilled, slowly putting his tablet down as he looked up and around the room. He seemed to stare at something, and I followed his gaze to the top left corner of the ceiling. I caught a glimpse of something dark slipping into the vent… a long, thick black tail.

What the…

I figured it could be an oversized rat. *But since when do rats scamper across the ceiling?*

The hint of a bad feeling poked at my stomach, and I exhaled sharply. Maybe I'd imagined it.

I checked the booth, and… he was gone. Whoever he was, he was weird. Devastatingly handsome, but weird. I looked up at the vent again, but there was nothing there to arouse any suspicion.

"Miss?" The dealer's voice dragged me back into reality. He was talking to the cucumber chick, who pursed her lips, then briefly glanced at her mate. He was pretending to look at his cards, resting his chin in his hand, index finger tapping the tip of his nose. I'd learned by now that it was a signal for a good hand.

"I'll put in twenty," the young woman replied, pushing blue chips to the center of the table.

A large figure appeared to my right. I would've been startled, had I not recognized Malcolm's pale blue eyes and round, bald head. He was big and soft on the outside, kind of like the Michelin man stuffed into an Armani suit, but a damn brute if ever crossed.

It's showtime.

They'd probably seen enough through the cameras to confirm my suspicions, if they'd decided to send the big guy, directly. A wave of fear and panic hit me like a bucket of ice water—hard bucket included in the toss. The cucumbers were broiling, as Malcolm glowered at them. Their faces were pale, beads of sweat blooming on their temples. I had never felt anyone switch from giddy to petrified in just ten seconds.

"You two." Malcolm nodded at the couple, still separated by the three gamblers. "I need you to stand up and slowly step away from the table."

Malcolm never ordered anyone to do anything. He used his calm voice to simply tell people what they had to do, without a fuss. Nobody dared challenge him. What he said was going to happen... well, it always happened. With no exception. He told you to stand up, you sprang to your feet. No questions asked. This time, however, it didn't seem to immediately stick.

"Is... Is there something wrong, sir?" the cucumber guy asked, his voice a little pitchy, as the girl slowly stood up, gripping the edge of the table as if to stop herself from collapsing.

Their world was crashing down on them, and it hurt like hell. My stomach tightened itself into a knot, and my blood went on the race of the century through my veins. I broke into a sweat as my heart skipped a couple of beats. Of course, the legal implications were damning. If caught cheating, players were taken to a back room, where the police would later find them. What happened from the moment they left the table until the police officers got there, however, varied from one establishment to another.

Malcolm was big and scary as hell, and this couple seemed to have been through the motions before—otherwise, they wouldn't be so terrified. What they didn't know was that Malcolm only employed legal methods of detention. No one walked out with bruises or broken bones unless they assaulted someone, and security were forced to defend themselves.

"I'm not going to ask you again," Malcolm replied. He hadn't even brought backup with him. To be fair, there were two guards stationed by the main entrance, anyway. There was nowhere to run.

The guy stood and chuckled nervously.

"Seriously, what's going on here? What did we do?" he asked, while the girl pressed her lips tight together.

"I think you know exactly what's going on," Malcolm replied dryly.

The three gamblers stared at each other, then scowled at the couple. The old-timer was particularly pissed off. I could tell from how badly I wanted to shove my fist in the young guy's face, as he continued to laugh it off.

"No, I don't! I'm just here playing my game. I'm not bothering anyone!" he insisted.

"You really don't want to do this here, buddy." Malcolm was unfazed and nodded at the bouncers from the main entrance. They both walked over and flanked the couple. "We're going to go into the back room now."

"Nah, man, I'm not going to no back room." The guy shook his head, trying hilariously hard to keep his cool. I noticed a yellowish glimmer in his brown eyes but couldn't quite put my finger on what it was, exactly. It could just be reflections from the overhead chandeliers.

Fear clamped on my throat and stiffened my muscles. He didn't want to disappear into that back room. I thought I could maybe soothe him a little, tell him that nobody was going to hurt him back there, but that would mean revealing my identity as a casino employee. If I outed myself now, other players would learn about me, and my job would be compromised. So, I kept my mouth shut and tried to ride it all out.

"Relax, buddy," Malcolm retorted, rolling his eyes. "No one's getting kneecapped tonight. This is a legally compliant establishment, not a mobster movie."

The two security guards politely, yet firmly, nudged them away from their chairs and escorted the couple away as they both voiced their protests.

"Wait! My money! What about my money?" the guy cried out.

"You'll get your buy-in back, but all your winnings will be returned to the house, since you've been cheating your ass off," Malcolm shot back.

It wasn't over, though. The crippling fear didn't leave me. The farther the couple got from me, the lower the intensity of their emotions was supposed to be. That was always the case. No exception. My unique ability was subject to physical distance.

And yet, I was still terrified. I realized then that I wasn't experiencing the couple's feelings anymore. It was someone else. I glanced around the casino, catching glimpses of curious customers as they watched the couple getting escorted to the other side of the room.

The three gamblers left at my table were just… upset. They felt like idiots, and, by extension, so did I. But no one here was afraid. The games we'd played were going to be annulled, and they were going to get their money back. Those were the house rules, where cheaters were involved. At the end of the night, they were going to walk away as the winners, so to speak. Of course, we all knew they were just going to gamble their money away at another table an hour later, but still. It felt like a second chance for them.

Malcolm offered a warm smile to the remaining gamblers. "You're free to put your money into another game."

That's how a casino works, after all. They make their money from other people's vices. It wasn't Malcolm's place to preach or to judge. Our key responsibility was to drive revenue.

So, it was obvious that the fear making me tremble didn't belong to the gamblers. I made brief eye contact with the dealer, who looked away, and it hit me. It was him.

The dealer was absently shuffling a deck of cards, but his fear seeped through me. He was involved with the cucumbers. There was a whiff of familiarity that I hadn't caught from him earlier because I'd been too focused on the couple. But how? The couple had only seemed to coordinate with each other during the games, so how had the dealer helped?

A thought crossed my mind, and I opened my clutch and took

out a pair of small, yellow-lens glasses. I looked through them at his deck of cards and exhaled. They were marked. The yellowish glimmers in the cucumber guy's eyes weren't a chandelier reflection. They were contact lenses, crafted from a material that worked like my special glasses.

I quickly took my glasses off, chuckling. "I thought I could see better with my glasses, but the light really isn't helping," I murmured, flashing a smile to the other players.

I then gave Malcolm a discreet nudge and nodded at the dealer, who was nervously eyeing us both at this point. He'd caught on. He'd realized what I'd done. The guy was a new employee—otherwise, he never would've used marked cards on my shift. No one had warned him, either. *Good.*

"You," Malcolm said to the dealer. "We need to talk."

"A-About what?" he replied, his voice barely audible. His enclosed position at the specially designed table made *me* feel trapped. The dealer could have no access to people near the table during the games, to avoid foul play. Hence, he was basically plopped in the middle of it. To get out of there fast, he'd have to jump over the table and crawl to the edge.

He didn't give Malcolm a chance to explain, as he did exactly what I'd expected, and sprang on top of the table. It was time for more… drastic measures.

I held my breath, and thousands of cards burst out from the shelves beneath the table.

The dealer fell backward, dazed and confused by the flurry of playing cards swarming all around him, like crazed birds in a horror movie. He yelped and cursed as they fluttered frenetically around him, swatting him over the face, defying the laws of physics.

Gasps erupted from around the table and the rest of the room as the cards scattered in the air.

Malcolm lunged after the dealer, but he rolled over the table, pushing the other players away as he made a run for the main doors. There was no security on that side, and he could easily escape. The two guards were busy with the cheaters, and the others were farther back in the room, with not enough time to reach us.

"I don't think so," I muttered and set my sights on one of the empty chairs at the last blackjack table by the exit.

When I said I wasn't like most people, I wasn't kidding. Empathy wasn't my only unique... skill. Telekinesis, over which I had better control, was the second one—though I'd yet to understand its extent, and it often depended on my anger to perform properly. Straight-up weirdo.

It felt as if I had these invisible tendrils extending from my fingers, and I had to focus them on an object in order for me to take hold of and then move it.

The dealer had made me angry enough to focus and take control of that chair, twenty feet away from me. It slid across the room and tripped the guy. He stumbled and landed flat on his face, with a painfully heavy thud. I had a feeling he'd at least sprained something in the process.

Atta girl!

I was still working on improving my telekinetic ability, but I'd managed to move an object to a predetermined location without a fuss. Compared to my earliest attempts when it first began to manifest, around the age of seven, I dared to call it progress.

Malcolm ran over to the dealer and pushed his knee into his back, prompting him to cry out from the pain. Two other bouncers rushed in from the bar and got the dealer up on his feet.

"Take him to the back room, too," Malcolm barked, annoyed whenever he was forced to get athletic in his Armani suit. "We're pressing charges!"

They both nodded and dragged him away. They passed by me, and there it was again: the sheer terror. This guy had been in prison before. He clearly didn't want to go back, but hey, you commit crimes, you pay the price.

Malcolm got up as I collected what was left of my poker chips and bid my farewell to the other three players. Two waitresses and a new dealer quickly took over, inviting the players to resume their seats and offering plenty of drinks on the house. It was the least the casino could do, after one of its crooked dealers had shoved three of its clients away from the table.

"How did you do that?" Malcolm reached my side as I walked over to the cashier.

"Do what?"

It was time to come up with good excuses for my inhuman abilities. Fortunately, I had an entire arsenal of perfectly reasonable explanations. Malcolm was very fond of me, but he was also very curious. This wasn't the first time he'd caught a whiff. My "intuition" had been a subject of his fascination from the day he'd hired me.

"The cards, Harley," he replied, slightly irritated. "How did you do that?"

"Dude." I chuckled. "I rigged the drawers. It's an old-school carnival trick. I knew he was dirty."

Malcolm frowned. "How did you know that? How did you spot him?"

Ugh, digging deeper.

Malcolm had worked as a police officer for ten years before switching to private security. His detective skills had yet to simmer down.

"I noticed some signs, Malcolm. Nothing special, trust me," I said. "People are… well, they're people. Their emotions betray them, and you, my friend, are a very intimidating presence. You made the guy nervous; I could tell before we opened the doors tonight. So, I employed some good ol' mechanical tricks with the drawers, in case he tried to make a run for it. Which he obviously did."

"And the couple? How did you spot them this time?"

"It's my job, Malcolm. I'm not telling you my secrets." I giggled. "It's how I earn my keep."

"And the chair?" he asked.

He'd saved the best for last. I let out a long, tortured sigh as I returned the chips to the cashier with a friendly wink. She smiled briefly and handed over a receipt, which I slipped into Malcolm's chest pocket.

"I have no idea what you're talking about," I replied dryly. "Not my fault that boy has two left legs and can't even run without tripping over random objects."

"The chair slid and—" He stopped himself, then took a deep breath, closed his eyes for a second, and pinched the bridge of his nose.

He was frustrated. We'd been doing the same dance for three months now, since I'd started working here. I caught the cheaters. Sometimes I had to employ my unorthodox methods to stop them from fleeing. Then I had to explain the unexplainable. We'd both then shrug, I'd get paid, and we'd part ways until my next shift.

The casino didn't like drilling for information. As long as the cheaters were caught, and I got my bonuses, we were all happy. But Malcolm's detective intuition made it hard for him to let go.

"So, what's my bonus for tonight?" I grinned, eager to change the subject to what *really* interested me.

"Five percent, as usual." Malcolm shook his head, giving me the half-smile that labeled me as "incorrigible."

"Oh, that's..." I quickly did the math in my head and reached three zeroes, in the upper half of a decimal. "Hell, yes! I get to give my Daisy a new paintjob. Maybe a new exhaust, too!"

After a life spent with a handful of personal belongings stashed in a black garbage bag as I was carted off from one foster family to another, I'd recently acquired a car—a raucous, black 1967 Ford Mustang in need of improvements and lots of love. I'd named her Daisy, and she was my first purchase as a responsible adult. She was also the birthday present I gave myself upon turning nineteen. Naturally, I was eager to invest a little bit of cash in her upkeep, whenever I got the chance, since the casino job paid pretty well. Most of the bonuses went right into my future college fund. But I did spoil myself and Daisy once in a while. Regardless of what others said, adulting was fun.

Malcolm smiled softly. "I've got a good mechanic I can recommend, if you're interested."

I was filled with affection, a gentle warmth I'd always imagined felt like fatherly love. I'd only felt it once before, with Mr. Smith, from my last foster family—the *only* decent home I was put in. Malcolm was, indeed, very fond of me. I thought of a warm breakfast on the kitchen table whenever he looked at me that way, reminding me of Mr. Smith's maple syrup pancakes and freshly squeezed orange juice.

"That would be great, thanks!" I beamed at him, then remembered the cucumbers. "Just so you know, the couple you guys lifted—they know each other. They didn't think anyone would notice, but you know me. I think they're quite seasoned, too. You might want the cops to check with Nevada casinos."

"Good point. Thank you, Harley." Malcolm gave me an appreciative nod. "They'll get banned, anyway, and we'll put out a nationwide alert on their profiles. They didn't show up in our system when they came in."

"Ah, yes, facial recognition cameras. I keep forgetting we have those," I muttered, as I caught movement at the corner of my eye, then above us. Looking up, the flicker of a shadow in a corner by another vent made me still. I could've sworn I'd just seen that long black tail again…

I must be tired.

"They'll get arrested, too," Malcolm replied.

I shrugged. "Hey, man, that's what happens when you don't keep your nose clean."

In retrospect, I could've ended up a lot worse, as a foster kid. We were the discarded souls that nobody wanted. Most of the kids in the system ended up in juvenile detention centers and, later on, prison.

It wasn't really their fault. Nobody chooses to be a criminal at the age of twelve. Your environment pushes you. The lack of involvement from the authorities when you signal abuse from one foster parent, then another—it makes you lose any semblance of hope. The system doesn't believe you, and you grow up distrusting the system in return.

Nobody listens to you. Nobody cares. You do what you can to get by. That's how it usually goes down for us kids with black garbage bags.

I did good for myself. I stayed out of serious trouble, despite my often-troublesome abilities. Of course, the other foster kids didn't grow up with a note from their dad, telling them to "stay smart" and "stay safe."

As miserable as I was without parents to call my own, I still felt a little lucky to have had that handful of words to guide me.

It was better than nothing.

Chapter Three

Shortly after the incident, my shift was over, but the night was far from coming to an end, with about a dozen customers left at the poker and blackjack tables. Only one of them was walking away with more money than he'd come in with. The others filled me with a sense of disappointment, and, at the same time, hope—the idea that they'd try again next time, and maybe beat the house.

I wasn't a gambler myself, nor would I ever indulge. Given my ability as an empath, I'd already experienced the thrilling highs and the devastating lows from all the players I'd had to sit next to during my work hours. I could never get over the pit in my stomach after watching someone throw twenty grand right into the dealer's hands. Loss was one emotion I was already familiar with, and it wasn't something I needed more of. On top of that, at nineteen, I wasn't even legally allowed to gamble. Working there and pretending to be a gambler, however, was a different story, thanks to several legal loopholes that Malcolm had taken advantage of, in order to get me on his crew.

"You have to let me set you up on a date with Daniel," Malcolm said with a smile, watching me as I collected my clutch from the top of the bar, then put my leather jacket on. The jacket was one of my favorites, and I rarely parted with it, especially given these cool early spring nights we'd been having lately.

"Now, why would you do that to your own son, Malcolm?" I grinned.

"He's nineteen; you're nineteen. You're a good girl; he's a good boy. You're lonely, and Daniel sure could use a female presence in his life. I could go on," Malcolm replied, rubbing the back of his neck.

His wife died when Daniel was only five, so it had been just the two of them for a very long time. Shortly after he became a single dad, Malcolm put the police badge away and started working in security—a slightly safer line of work, since he couldn't put his life at such risk anymore. Not while raising a son, anyway.

Malcolm was being truthful, though. Daniel was a good guy, and I'd met him a couple of months earlier. I'd noticed the sweet looks he gave me, but I didn't think anything of it until Malcolm first suggested a date. This was his third attempt, and it was going to be a no, once again. Daniel was sweet and all, but he just wasn't my type. Not that I actually knew what my "type" was, but something inside me just didn't click with Daniel.

Besides, being in a relationship meant I'd have to eventually explain my weird powers, and I was nowhere near ready to have that conversation with anybody.

"Sorry, Malcolm, but it's still a no for me," I replied gently, careful not to let him down too hard. "I mean, I'm happy to go out with the both of you, since there's so much of San Diego I've yet to experience, despite growing up here, and you guys know all the good burger joints, apparently… But I'm not getting into the dating game anytime soon, and I'd hate to string Daniel along."

"Can't blame an old man for trying." Malcolm shook his head slowly as the shadow of a smile passed over his face.

"See you in a couple of days." I winked, waved him goodbye, and walked out through the back door. I'd parked my Daisy in the far-right corner of the employees' parking lot, away from the others, and I could see her from where I was standing as I searched for my keys at the bottom of the clutch. Customers parked their cars on the other side of the building.

The casino door closed behind me with a loud click, and my fingers finally clasped around my keys. My stomach seemed a bit upset, as if there was a little monster inside, gnawing away at it. *Leftover pizza for dinner it is, then.*

There were a few other cars in the lot, besides my Mustang, including Malcolm's black sedan. I walked over to mine, welcoming the cool darkness of midnight. The stars glimmered overhead, in the company of the giant pearl commonly referred to as the moon. I'd always been captivated by it, especially when it was so big and glowing so close to the Earth, though I knew its size was an optical illusion, the horizon tricking my mind and warping reality.

A shadow darted across the asphalt before me, but vanished somewhere behind my Daisy before I could see what it was. I ignored the sudden chill and kept moving, keys in hand, eager to sink into a hot bath at home.

"No, please!" a man yelped somewhere farther down on 55th Street, just where the parking lot ended in its shoddy wooden fence.

My heart hammered in my chest. I walked faster, my stilettos clicking across the asphalt as I reached my car.

"What... What are you?" The same voice grew louder, and I stilled, crippled with horror. But it wasn't my horror—it was his.

I squinted into the darkness, but couldn't find the man who had cried out.

Maybe he was just some dude who'd snorted too much of that "good stuff." But his emotions were far too powerful. I'd experienced drug-induced panics from other people, and none were as intense as the thick sheet of ice constricting my heart in this moment. Besides, my instincts were already telling me to at least find out what was going on, to see if I should call the police.

I walked around the car, toward the fence. I looked down 55th

Street, both ways, but there was nothing to see, other than dim orange lights cast by distant streetlamps.

"What the..." I muttered, catching movement somewhere to my right, just where the small apartment blocks started rising, lined with palm trees.

The man whose voice I'd just heard emerged from the shadows. He tripped and fell over, just twenty feet away from me and right in the middle of the street. Fear crashed into me in a second, much more brutal wave, paralyzing my muscles. *Oh, man, he's scared out of his mind.*

"Get away from me!" he shrieked, then stumbled to his feet and started running again.

"Dude, are you okay?" I called out as he got closer.

He was pale, paper-white almost, his face drenched in sweat and his crisp, Friday-night-out suit covered in dirt and cuts. He was pretty roughed up, his lip split and a purplish bruise blaring around his left eye. He stared at me for a second, then exhaled sharply with genuine relief. I felt hope bursting inside my chest—his, as he hoped I would save him. *From what, though?*

"No, I'm not! You've got to help me, call the police!" he said, his voice trembling. "I can't see... I can't see who it is... or what it is, but it just won't let me be!"

"Um, wait, what?" I got confused, fast.

My initial thought of a drug-related trip gone horribly wrong crossed my mind, until a shadow flickered across the ground. I looked down and saw the long black tail I'd seen earlier inside the casino. It lashed out from the shadows to my right, and coiled its tip around the man's ankles, sweeping him off his feet.

"What—" I didn't manage to finish my thought. The man fell hard on his back, screaming as he got dragged away. "No, no, no!"

I dropped my keys and clutch and jumped over the fence, my left heel slipping. *Not the best night for stilettos, clearly.*

"HELP!" he cried out.

I ran after him, slightly limping from the pain budding in my left ankle. His emotions were toying with my senses, and it took considerable mental effort for me to push it all down so I could focus on what was happening as I followed him.

Whatever had latched onto his ankles had a surprisingly long tail. *Snake, maybe? No, what kind of snake can do that?*

A large figure took form in the semi-darkness ahead, with light from a streetlamp offering me a better view. My stomach churned, then wriggled itself into a small, painful ball, as I came to a halt. This was not a snake. Nor was it a man.

Whatever this is, it's not human.

"Oh, God, help me, please!" the man bellowed, desperately scraping at the asphalt beneath him as he was dragged backward.

I tried to catch his hands, his fingers bloodied by his attempts to get away, but I missed him by inches. And then a bloodcurdling growl made me freeze in place. The creature taunting the guy came into view, its big black eyes fixed on me.

As it noticed me, it stopped dragging the man, enough for him to look over his shoulder and cry with exasperation. "What the hell is going on? What's happening to me?"

"You... You can't see it?" I murmured, staring at the horrible beast standing before me.

"See what? There's nothing! I don't... How is... Why is this happening?"

It hit me then that the man couldn't see the creature taunting him. I figured it was better that way. He was spared the visual horror.

I was standing face-to-face with some kind of... monster. It was huge, at least eight feet tall, with bulging, pitch-black eyes and two long, twisted horns that sprouted from either side of a crooked, asymmetrical head. Thick strings of drool clung to a pair of enormous fangs, and razor-sharp claws protruded from the ends of its lanky, ape-like limbs. Its skin was leathery, a dark and dirty shade of gray, with spikes erupting from behind its neck. A stringy tail trailed behind it, and, judging by the giant bat wings extending from its back, this thing could also fly.

It growled again, this time louder, as it continued glaring at me.

"What… are you?" I gasped, my own fear taking hold of my bones and joints, pushing my instincts into survival mode.

"You can see… it?" The man gawked at me, blood trickling from his temple.

"Yeah, but, trust me, you don't want to know."

It was a weirdly freakish hybrid, a cross between an ape, an overgrown lizard, and a bat, and it was looking way too intensely at me. Claws as big and as sharp as the monster's took hold of my heart as it let go of the man and smacked him over the back of his head with its tail.

He lost consciousness, and the monster moved over his body, its shadow nearly swallowing him. Every nerve in my body screamed for me to *run*. But I couldn't leave the man to die. If our situations were reversed, I knew I'd want someone looking out for me.

Given the disgusting amount of drool, it was dinnertime for the beast, and the dude was its main course.

"Hey! Leave him alone!" I shouted.

Whatever this creature was, it wasn't interested in meaningful conversation. The monster sneered at me, then shifted its focus back to the guy, its jaws parting with anticipation as it lowered its head for a bite. My fight-or-flight instinct kicked itself into fight mode.

I thrust my arms out to help concentrate my telekinetic powers. First, I had to latch onto it. For some reason, I needed a clear view and angle to "lasso" the target. Fortunately, given how preoccupied the thing was with its meal, that wasn't hard. I curled my fingers, focusing all my energy into its throat. The creature stilled, then choked as my hold on it tightened.

I was panting hard. I'd never performed such a precise grab before, and certainly not with a target this big. Nevertheless, I latched on and pulled the monster away, swinging my arms up as I tossed it over my head. It snarled as it was forced to part with its prey, sailing through the air.

My breath stopped as I saw where it was going to land.

"My car. Not my car!" I blurted out, then latched onto the creature once more, waving it away from my beloved Daisy.

It missed my Mustang by inches, and crashed into the fence. Wood splinters flew outward, and the monster groaned from the pain, then lifted its head to glare at me. Its anger flowed through me like lightning. I'd really pissed it off now.

The guy behind me came to and gasped, as all he could see were the creature's claws crushing the asphalt beneath it with each step it took toward me. *Think fast, think fast, think fast!*

The monster lunged at me, baring its fangs, its black eyes wide and filled with rage. I tried to swat it away again, but it darted to the right. I launched another mental lasso at it, and it jerked to the left. It had already figured out my telekinesis.

"Crap," I muttered, desperately trying to think of another way out of this mess.

"What?" the guy behind me croaked.

"Run," I breathed, as the monster veered toward me again.

I put my arms out, hoping I could at least nudge it away, but then a flash of fire exploded between us. The blaze pushed me back a couple of feet. It didn't hit me, but it certainly got the monster, forcing it into a rough landing on its back.

"What the hell is going on here?" the guy cried out.

"Why do you keep asking *me*? How the hell am I supposed to know?" I shot back, genuinely exasperated.

It was bad enough that I could see the thing, and still had no idea how to stop it. On top of that, I'd just nearly gotten myself blown up, somehow. All I wanted was a hot bath and a slice of yesterday's pizza. Was that too much to ask?

"Step aside, miss." A somewhat familiar voice caught me off guard.

Behind me, a young man emerged from the shadows of the residential building next to the casino's parking lot. The deep green eyes, the dark curls resting on his forehead, the smooth, dark blue silk of his suit—it was the electric dude I'd seen earlier during the poker game.

The monster grunted, shaking its ginormous head, then looked at us and let out a spine-chilling roar. The electric dude frowned at the creature, pursing his lips as if he were dealing with a smaller-sized nuisance, like a rat, and not the living nightmare slowly getting back up on its hind legs.

"You... You can see it, too?" the guy on the ground asked him.

"Seriously, why are you still here?" I rolled my eyes at the wounded stranger, then pointed at the end of the street. "Just run!"

"No, stay there," the electric dude replied, his voice low and eerily calm in spite of the raging monster shuddering in preparation for another attack. "You're a witness."

"Who are you? And what the hell is this... thing?" I managed, trying to wrap my head around the many unknowns that had gotten between me and my leftover-pizza dinner.

"I'm Wade. Wade Crowley," the electric dude replied, and only then did I catch the hint of an Irish accent he carried. "And that's a gargoyle."

I stared at him, then at the monster, for a couple of seconds, noticing the soot on its horrific face. The fire that had hit it earlier had burned through its thick skin, but hadn't managed to inflict significant damage. What the heck was it made of?

"A what now?" I blinked several times, my brain left behind for a moment.

"A gargoyle. Not sure what wasn't clear about that statement." Wade raised an eyebrow at me, as if I was the idiot. As if I was supposed to just know what that thing was. He'd made it sound as though gargoyles were as common as sewer rats.

"Well, pardon me for not knowing that gargoyles are real and not just creepy statues!" I shot back, slightly annoyed.

Wade opened his mouth to say something, but the gargoyle's

sudden movements made him put his hands up. The ten rings on his fingers lit up in an incandescent orange, and, to my shock, flames burst from his palms, hitting the monster right in the face. The creature yelped and covered its head with its wings, then growled and darted to the side, dissolving into the darkness behind a small building flanked by a Jeep, just outside the casino's parking lot.

The way the light fell over it made it difficult to tell whether the gargoyle was still there.

"Did you kill it?" I asked, craning my neck to get a better look, as the guy behind me got up and backed away slowly.

"Nope," Wade replied, scanning the building. I couldn't stop staring at his rings, which were still glowing a peculiar shade of amber.

The gargoyle jumped out and landed on top of the Jeep, the hood bending inward under its weight, as it snarled at us. It moved too fast for Wade to hit it with fire again, dodging the flaming balls as it zigzagged across the street toward me and the guy on my right.

"Stay down!" I shouted at him, then tried another telekinetic move on the gargoyle.

I managed to smack its shoulder but didn't stop it, as it took flight and shot right at me. Light flickered across its face, and I ducked as Wade's flames hit it hard. Whatever ability Wade had, it was similar to mine, but he was in much better control of his powers than I could even dream of being with mine.

The gargoyle landed on its side, but didn't give Wade a chance to hit it again, and bolted toward me and the guy once more. This creature was really persistent about getting its dinner.

I put my hands out and managed to latch onto its right wing. It gave me a panicked look, and I slapped the asphalt in a sudden crouch, as it was the only way for me to bring it down, given its considerable size. I felt like the puppet master in charge of a giant white shark, my muscles straining.

Wade watched as I struggled to keep the creature down. I noticed his frown, and scoffed.

"A little help here, *Wade*?"

"I figured since you ignored my request to step aside, and you're continuing to disrupt my operation here, I might as well see what you can do," he replied sarcastically. "Clearly, not much."

As much as I hated it, he was right. The gargoyle tossed and turned until it escaped my hold. *Dammit, I need more practice!*

"Your operation?" I snapped. "For Pete's sake, help me kill this thing!"

"No one's killing anything tonight," Wade replied, then brought his hands up again. The gargoyle dodged several fire pellets, then decided to deal with the source, directly.

In three wide jumps, it reached Wade and pounced at him.

"Don't let him get away!" Wade shouted at me.

"Let who get away?" I replied, then glanced over my shoulder and saw the wounded guy trying to run off.

"If he gets out there, the gargoyle will go after him before I get a chance to catch it. Keep him here!" Wade grunted as he tackled the gargoyle with what looked like Judo moves.

What in the world is he doing?

Nevertheless, I caught the guy by his sleeve, pulling him back and farther away from the middle of the street, where Wade was struggling to get on top of the gargoyle.

"Just stay here. He says it's safer if you don't run. Let him do his… thing," I said to the guy, then stared at Wade for a couple of seconds.

The beast got the upper hand and punched him so hard, Wade flew twenty feet to the right, then slid over the fence and slammed against the passenger door of my car. My heart hurt as I heard the metal dent on impact.

"My baby!" I gasped, as Wade quickly came to and frowned at me.

"Your baby?" he muttered.

"Ah jeez, not you! My car! Don't scratch my car!" I shot back.

The gargoyle didn't wait for Wade to get up. It rushed at him, and I knew that if I didn't do something quick, my Daisy was going to pay the price. Fueled by fear itself, I sprinted forward and found the strength to clap my hands and do something I hadn't done since I'd nearly destroyed the shed of my last foster home.

The friction of my palms coming together created sparks, and the adrenaline pumping through me provided the energy I needed to generate a thin sheet of fire, which I aimed directly at the gargoyle.

Wade froze, his eyes wide as he saw the blaze coming. Just as I'd manipulated the creature earlier with telekinesis, I employed the same arm movements to guide the fire sheet as it slipped right in front of Wade, prompting the gargoyle to come to a grinding halt, its knees scraping the asphalt.

"Hah!" I cackled, then brought my arms back, as if pulling two ropes, and the fire sheet moved closer toward the gargoyle. The creature scrambled backward as the flames licked at its back.

Wade jumped to his feet and ran around the beast, depositing small green crystals in a circle, before he stopped, dropped, and slapped the ground hard, muttering something. I stilled as the green crystals lit up from the inside, my fire curtain gone in a flash. Bright, greenish-white beams shot out from the gems, then became flexible and lashed around the gargoyle. The creature didn't know what to do, scared by my fire and blinded by the strange, flashing ropes that stretched over it in a net-like pattern.

Wade got back up, casually dusting himself off, as the now-incandescent-green ropes tightened into a trap and knocked the gargoyle down, forcing it into submission. The creature struggled and growled, but whenever it tried to stand, the incandescent ropes burned into its thick skin, far worse and deeper than any of the fires that had been thrown at it earlier.

Only then, as I managed to catch my breath, my knees and arms shaking from both physical exertion and shock, did perfectly reasonable questions start knocking the air out of my lungs.

What was that trap? How did it work? How could light be bent like that? How come Wade could use fire the way he did? Did it come from those rings on his fingers? How did he know what a gargoyle was? Why had the creature tried to attack the guy? Where had it come from?

Of the many darting through my head at this point, I figured I deserved answers at least to these questions. I shifted my focus to Wade, understanding right then and there that (a) I wasn't the only one with peculiar abilities, and that (b) he clearly had the answers I needed.

Answers that I'd been looking for since I was seven years old and first noticed how different I was from everybody else.

Chapter Four

"*What* is going on here?" I asked, my voice trembling with a mixture of concern and confusion.

On one hand, I felt a sense of relief in knowing that I wasn't the only one who could do what I did. After years of keeping my abilities to myself, out of fear of being labeled a freak or, worse, locked in a cage and dissected in some government facility, it was oddly refreshing to see someone else as weird as me.

On the other hand, this incident opened up a whole new can of worms, one drenched in questions I'd stopped asking many years back. Given my crappy childhood, I was never naïve enough to dream of some magical family waiting for me somewhere, in a faraway land. My abilities didn't come with an instruction manual, so I had to do my best with trial and error.

Five minutes after he'd managed to subdue the gargoyle underneath that strange, incandescent net, Wade didn't seem too interested in my presence. He circled the beast several times and took notes in a small pocket journal.

He stopped, then looked up at me.

"I told you to keep him here," Wade muttered.

"Huh?" I frowned, then quickly remembered the guy we'd just basically rescued.

I looked over my shoulder, watching the guy limp away.

"You. Stop," Wade called out, and raised his hand. The rings on his fingers lit up once more, this time blue, as he gestured to the guy to turn around and come back.

I held my breath as the man was compelled to do as he'd been asked. Judging by the horrified look on his face, he had no other choice. His body was no longer under his control.

"What… What are you doing to me?" he mumbled, his lips trembling with fear.

"Relax, I'm not going to hurt you," Wade replied, then motioned for the guy to sit down, which he inadvertently did. "Just stay there until I get to you."

He then made a couple more notes in his pocket journal, while giving me the occasional glance. Was I being mentioned in there? What was his deal?

"Dude. Seriously. What's happening here?" I asked again, raising my voice. His gaze found mine, and suddenly I felt genuinely irritated—that was his emotion, not mine. I annoyed him.

Really? I'm *the annoying one in this scenario?*

"You're very impatient. Not a good sign," he said, then put the journal back inside his jacket pocket. He walked over to the Jeep with its bent hood, producing a set of keys from another pocket. He opened the trunk and pulled out a Mason jar, narrowing his eyes as he looked at it for a couple of seconds.

He shook his head, then took another, larger jar out and walked back to the gargoyle, which had been forced to calm down, unable to free itself from the incandescent net. I took a couple of steps forward, getting closer so I could take a better look at the green crystals. They weren't fixed on the asphalt in any way, and yet they served as anchors for the luminescent ropes. No matter how hard the creature tried, the crystals didn't budge. This was one too many shades of weird, way past what I could do.

"What are these?" I asked, pointing at the crystals. I figured I could start small, as far as my many questions for him were concerned. Not that he'd been particularly responsive to anything so far.

"Put this down there, by the gargoyle's head. Take the lid off," he replied, bringing the Mason jar over, then handing it to me. "What do they look like to you?"

I glanced at the rescued guy for a second—he was still sitting on the edge of the road, trembling as he stared at us, and muttering to himself. I couldn't hear him, but, putting myself in his shoes, I imagined he was asking all the gods in the universe and beyond why he was stuck here with us. *Poor guy. Wish I had an answer for you.*

"Crystals, I guess." I shrugged, then placed the jar by the gargoyle's head and held on to the lid. The creature looked up at me, revealing its hideously huge fangs. It was difficult to properly quantify the amount of uneasiness I felt in its presence, but, given its physical restraints, I took comfort in the fact that it couldn't hurt me anymore.

"You are correct." Wade nodded, his green eyes measuring me from head to toe. His inquisitive expression made me feel way too self-conscious, but I could at least sense that his irritation was starting to subside. Instead, curiosity took over. He was trying to figure me out.

"Care to elaborate, at least? It's not every day that I bump into a freakin' gargoyle and a dude shooting fire from his fingers," I retorted, resting my hands on my hips.

The pain in my ankle reminded me that I'd sprained it earlier, and that I was still wearing a black cocktail dress, stilettos, and my grungy leather jacket on top. I probably looked like I'd just come out of a high-end thrift store. Nevertheless, I couldn't worry about my appearance, not with all the questions I had for this guy. Even out in the street, the air between us felt electrified, charged with intense energies that were well beyond my control.

Whatever I'd felt inside the casino in his presence was back, making my skin tingle.

"They're called entrapment stones," he replied, then sighed and nodded at the jar. "And that's a monster holder."

"For the… monster." I pointed at the gargoyle, basically voicing the conclusion to myself.

"You're quick." Wade purposely examined me again. "Not bad for… What are you supposed to be, a barfly?"

Ugh, the sarcasm, the arrogance. I could smack him.

"A casino employee," I retorted, gritting my teeth.

"That's what they call you these days. Okay. Now, step back," he said. "I need to put this bad boy away."

"I take it this isn't your first rodeo," I noted dryly.

"Of course not. Although, it is odd for this to happen in such a public space," Wade replied, concern drawing shadows between his eyebrows. "Gargoyles are never this brazen."

I nodded slowly and moved back. Compliance seemed like a better tool to employ if I wanted any answers out of him. He raised his hands over the beast, his rings lighting up red this time. His lips moved as the gargoyle growled and twitched, then instantly disintegrated in a puff of black smoke. The incandescent net also vanished, as if the light simply went out, leaving behind twelve green crystals.

A gasp left my throat as the jar glowed red, sucking the black smoke inside.

"Now, put the lid on tight," he added.

I did as instructed, then picked up the jar, staring at its contents. This was getting weirder with each moment.

"How… How does this work?" I mumbled, then watched Wade as he collected the crystals and stuffed them in his other jacket pocket.

"Gargoyles are, as you so eloquently put it, monsters," Wade replied. "However, they're not the regular fleshy monsters you read about in books. Judging by how confused you seem, I'm going to go ahead and assume you've never heard of witches, warlocks, or Purges."

"Wait, are you telling me that witches and warlocks are real?" I asked, suddenly understanding the magnitude of his statement. I'd heard the terms, of course, although mostly from books and movies. The thought that I might be one had crossed my mind, but with no specific literature to explain exactly how I was able to do the things I could do, it had stayed just that—a thought.

"You can't tell me you're surprised, based on your abilities." He sighed, seemingly bored with my obtuseness. But he wasn't bored at all. The tingling sensation in my throat and limbs was excitement, a curiosity—not just his, though. Some of it was mine. I wasn't alone in this.

"Not exactly. I've just never had a term for it." I shook my head slowly. "How is this possible?"

"That's a long story, and I strongly recommend that we clear this area before the rest of the casino employees and customers come out," Wade replied.

"Hold on," I said, stepping back before he could take the jar from my hands. "So, what you did… what you do… it's all magic? Actual magic? Like, wands and all?"

"Give me that." Wade snatched the jar back, then strode to his Jeep. I didn't leave his side, watching him put the item in a duffel bag inside the trunk and then walk over to the guy sitting on the other side of the narrow, dimly lit street. "Yes, actual magic. No wands, though. This isn't a children's book. This is the real world."

"So, what, you use rings? Did your witchy ancestors consider wands to be a fashion faux pas, or what?" I shot back.

"Hold that thought," Wade replied, then shifted his focus to the guy, motioning for him to stand up. The man was about as tall as Wade, but much thinner—though I was willing to bet he had sweated out about ten pounds just from tonight's events.

Wade snapped his fingers in front of the man's face as his rings lit up blue. "You. What's your name?"

"Jamie," the guy replied absently, a blue glimmer blooming in his eyes.

"Jamie, what were you doing out here tonight?" Wade asked.

Jamie blinked slowly a couple of times, then responded: "I had drinks with some friends. I was walking home."

"Okay, this is what happened, Jamie. You came out of the bar, where you had drinks with some friends. You were walking home, when two men tried to rob you. You don't remember their faces, but you got roughed up a little bit. You hit back and ran away. You're safe now. They're gone. There's nothing for you to be afraid of. You didn't see anything else. You didn't experience anything else. When you wake up tomorrow, tonight will seem like a distant memory, and you will be at peace. Everything will be okay, Jamie. *Obliviscor memoriam.*"

Jamie's eyes shone bright blue for a second, then returned to his natural shade of brown. He took a deep breath, then rubbed his face, as if just waking up from a deep sleep, while Wade put his hands behind his back, the light in his rings gone.

"What… What happened?" Jamie asked. The horror that had been blaring out of him and right into me was gone. Instead, there was confusion, with a tinge of shame, typical of the drunken man who'd lost his way. Whatever Wade had just done to him, it was a lot like hypnotic suggestion, from what I could tell.

"I don't know, mate." Wade shrugged, feigning disinterest. "You must be drunk or something. Why don't you go home? You're freaking my girlfriend out."

"Huh?" I mumbled, barely catching his lie, as Jamie stared at me.

"I am so sorry." Jamie frowned, then walked away, and vanished behind the corner into the main street.

"Your girlfriend?" I glared at Wade, my cheeks on fire.

"Part of the job. We lie, we deceive, we protect their ignorance at any cost," Wade replied, then turned back and walked over to his car.

"Wait, *we?*"

"You didn't think it was just the two of us, did you?"

"Come on, man, you've got to give me something more than half-answers and rhetorical questions!" I exclaimed, and caught him by his arm. The muscles beneath the soft fabric of his jacket were rock hard, and I found it hard to let go, even when he stopped and turned around to face me again. "Obviously, I have no idea what I am, what you are, or why there was a gargoyle out in the middle of the freaking city, hunting for dinner! You're the first person I've met who can do… stuff."

He breathed out, his shoulders dropping, and looked at me for a while, then swiped through his phone.

"Why did you hypnotize him? *How* did you hypnotize him?" I resumed my line of questioning.

"Humans can't know who we are and what we can do. It'll put both us and them in danger, for reasons that cannot be explained in the parking lot of a casino," Wade replied bluntly. "He's better off thinking he got mugged, believe me. I've got a cleanup crew to handle CCTV and other loose ends. As for the *how* part—here."

He took out a business card and handed it to me.

"What's this?" I asked, turning it over to find his name, phone number, and organization beautifully written in swirly, embossed golden lettering. "Wade Crowley… San Diego Coven. Coven? Seriously? There are covens?"

"I like how you're able to answer your own questions if I let you think," he said, and my throat burned the moment he raised his eyebrow again.

"What's this?" I shot back, my teeth gritting. My patience had abandoned me completely.

"Here's how it's going to go from here on out," he replied, all traces of sarcasm gone. "You are a witch. I am a warlock. Magic, Harley, is real."

"Wait, you know my name?" I gasped, my eyes widening to the point where I feared I'd feel them pop out of their orbits. He cocked his head to one side, amused that I'd even asked such a question.

Warlock, remember? The dude probably knows your blood type, too!

"Go on," I whispered, suddenly regretful that I'd interrupted him. Questions were good, but too many could deter him from giving me answers I now desperately needed.

"I belong to the San Diego Coven, and you need to come in soon and introduce yourself to us," Wade continued. "Witches and wizards rarely fare well on their own. We require the protection, the privileges, and the rules of a coven in order to survive and to thrive. Whatever answers you need, the coven has them, as long as you pledge your allegiance to us."

"Hold on—allegiance?"

It was my turn to raise both eyebrows at him. I was just getting used to my independence. There was no way in hell I was getting myself tied down to anyone or anything.

"Loyalty. Now that you've been discovered, you cannot hide anymore. I will have to report your existence to the coven," Wade replied.

"Can't you pretend that we never met?"

"Don't you want answers?"

"Can't *you* give them to me?" I asked, torn between my general wariness of the unknowns presented by a coven's existence, and my need to understand myself and my abilities.

"You want your cake, and you want to eat it, too, giving nothing in return?" Wade asked. "That's a tad naïve."

"So, what, I just walk into your magical coven, recite some pledge of allegiance, and poof! I'm yours to do with as you please?" I retorted, crossing my arms over my chest. His raised eyebrow made me go over what I'd just said, and I resisted the urge to smack myself for not thinking prior to speaking. "You know what I meant!"

"I do, but that's not how this works. You have powers, Harley. And with power comes a responsibility, as cheesy as that may sound. The coven doesn't just offer answers. You'll learn more about yourself. They'll teach you how to develop and control your abilities. You'll become part of a family."

I didn't have an answer. Just more questions, a growing pit in my stomach, and the feeling that I could be getting myself into a heap of trouble. Ever since I was a little girl, I had serious issues with authority. I simply could never stand being told what to do, and whom to obey.

My recent stride into adulthood had been an absolute blessing; I no longer had to get anyone's permission to do whatever I wanted. I followed the rule of law, I paid my taxes, and I kept my abilities to myself because that's what helped me survive. I didn't need a coven telling me what I could and couldn't do.

My knee-jerk reaction was to back away and pretend tonight never even happened.

And Wade could tell that I was thoroughly undecided. Chances were that it was written all over my face, too. "You don't have to answer right now. Think about it. You have twenty-four hours, after which I'll be expecting your call."

This guy is unbelievable.

"That's your idea of giving me time to think about making a life-changing decision? Twenty-four hours? I'm pretty sure the waiting period for adopting a dog is seven days!" I replied.

"You interrupted my capture of a very dangerous creature just now," Wade said, his tone implying much more than his words. "You're lucky I'm not hauling you down to the coven right now. Be thankful that I'm giving you a chance to come in by yourself and show good faith."

"Interrupted your capture?" I asked, struggling to contain my outrage while riding out the waves of frustration that Wade was experiencing. How was I the one frustrating *him*? "That guy was about to get eaten alive by a freakin' gargoyle!"

"And I was there, ready to intervene. There was no need for you to get involved," he insisted, mirroring my pose as he crossed his arms over his chest.

"Pardon me for not walking away from a man's cry for help!"

A taxi pulled up twenty feet ahead, on the street corner, and honked once, the driver persistently looking at Wade.

"Just…" He closed his eyes for a second, pressing his lips tight, as he carefully chose his next words. "Just think about it. And whether your answer will be yes or no, call me. You have twenty-four hours."

"What if I say no?"

"Harley. Just think about it before we continue this conversation," Wade said, then collected the duffel bag from the back of his Jeep and got in the cab. The engine roared to life, and the car joined the thin traffic stream on the main road, leaving me behind with a ton of questions and no reasonable explanation as to why the parking lot fence had been destroyed.

"Crap," I cursed under my breath, then nervously looked around. There were no cameras covering that corner of the parking lot.

I checked my watch. A quarter past midnight. I had maybe five minutes to get out of here before Malcolm and the others emerged from the casino.

I grabbed my keys and clutch from where I'd dropped them and slipped behind the wheel. I got out of there and drove straight home, my hands clutching the wheel so hard my knuckles turned white.

It was bad enough that everything I'd thought I knew about myself had been twisted and reshuffled to the point where I could barely think straight. I was being asked to join a coven I knew nothing about. I'd just witnessed a monster trying to kill an innocent guy, then the innocent guy getting his memory wiped by a dude whose sheer presence made the air around me feel heavier.

The streetlights flickered past me in shades of orange as I stared at the road ahead and wondered what to do. The events of the night kept replaying in my head, and I made mental notes of the key moments. At least I knew what I was…

"After all these years," I muttered as I reached my apartment and locked the door behind me. A heavy sigh rolled out of me, and I walked over to the living room area, dropping Wade's business card on the coffee table next to a pile of magazines.

As much as I disliked the thought, Wade was right. I could at least think about it before deciding anything. Sleeping on it sounded like a good idea, until my stomach reminded me that I'd barely eaten throughout the day.

I headed over to the fridge, where two slices of pizza awaited, next to a can of Coke. I scarfed down my leftover dinner, while standing in the dark and staring out the windows.

What was it that I wanted for myself? Where was my life headed?

Most importantly, what could I get out of that coven, and what did they want from me?

Chapter Five

I woke up the next day from a variety of absolutely mind-boggling and downright weird nightmares. The strangest creatures snuck into my subconscious somehow, from the gargoyle I'd seen the night before to fiendish beasts with serpent tails, wings, and fangs that seemed eager to tear me to shreds. Big, round yellow eyes haunted me wherever I went. Shadows hissed behind me, and whenever I turned around, there was nothing but darkness until monstrous shapes formed and I ended up running, desperate to save myself.

The sun was out, peeking through the wooden blinds of my bedroom windows. I was covered in sweat, my t-shirt drenched and stuck to my skin, shivers running down my spine. My heartrate was accelerated, my breathing uneven, as I tried to remember the ghoulish faces I'd seen in my nightmares.

It didn't take long for me to realize that it all had something to do with Wade Crowley and the events I'd witnessed in his presence. The image of that gargoyle hounded me well into breakfast, which consisted of coffee and a couple of slices of toast—anything else would've made me hurl—as I shuffled around the house in a permanent state of queasiness.

My instincts screamed at me to stay away from Wade and the coven, along with whatever pledging allegiance to them entailed. Sure, I was grateful to at least know what I was after all these years, but joining a coven was the last thing I wanted to do right now. I liked my freedom too much, and I'd gone through a lot of crap to get it.

I fished my father's note out of my wallet, sipping my coffee as I read it twenty times over.

Stay safe. Stay smart.

Maybe my parents knew something. Maybe my dad wanted me to stay safe from such organizations. I'd seen plenty of witch movies, and I'd read about the Salem witch trials when I was still in high school. Needless to say, the literature on the subject wasn't exactly encouraging.

After a couple of hours and a hot shower, I took Wade's business card from the coffee table and tossed it into the trashcan. It was all too creepy and unknown, and my stomach seemed to loosen up a little as soon as the card landed on a pile of torn-up pizza boxes. I was better off alone.

My phone buzzed with a text, and I glanced at the sender: Ryann Smith. Part of me had expected it to be from Wade, given his stalkerish tendencies, like how he'd known my name, but I was relieved to see my foster sister's name on the screen instead. Her text read, "Coffee at St. Clair's Café in 20?" I responded with a resounding "Yes!" The distraction would be nice. Plus, I had errands to run near her house—our parents' house, I should say—and I figured it would be a good time to catch up. Not that I could tell her about the whole bucket of weird I'd been dealing with, but she was a familiar, friendly face and had this way of soothing me like no one else could.

When I got to the café, Ryann was already there, waiting patiently beneath the signature red awning. Standing one head shorter than me, with long brown hair and gray-blue eyes, she was the all-American sweetheart. Class president and valedictorian with numerous debate trophies and one too many pantsuits for her young age, Ryann had dreams of one day becoming president. Until then, however, she was prepping for a bountiful career in law, followed by a seat in the Senate. The girl was extremely ambitious and was my best link to normalcy on this earth.

"Mom's asking if you want to come with us to Maui this summer," Ryann said, smiling as we sat down at one of the small, round tables outside. I hadn't seen her in a couple of weeks, but, every other weekend, Ryann made her way down to San Diego from UCLA. My heart filled with pride whenever I saw her—everything she'd set out to accomplish, she did, sooner or later. "One week, all-inclusive. They'll cover the hotel; you just need to pay for your flight," she continued. "I'm thinking fruity drinks, orchid garlands, gorgeous boys on the beach, and, of course, basking in the sun. You can't say no to that."

"It'd be stupid of me to refuse!" I beamed, deeply touched that Mr. and Mrs. Smith were so keen to spend time with me.

Out of all my foster families, the Smiths were the best—sweet and kind people who loved me like I was their own… like I was Ryann. I made a mental note to pay them a visit by the end of the month, and bring along a basket of Mrs. Smith's favorite baked goods. If you wanted her on your good side, all you needed were raisin scones and banana walnut bread.

"We're thinking end of August," Ryann replied, adding sugar to her latte. "Mom has these wonderful vacation package offers from her travel agent. We had to vote on *where* to go, in the first place! Dad wanted Peru, but Mom and I convinced him to do Maui now, then look at Peru, maybe for the next spring."

"End of August sounds good." I cradled my warm cup of black coffee in my hands, pleased to take in all the positive energies coming from Ryann. She was fond of me, and I could feel it. I wished I could tell her just how wonderful she felt to me, but I'd already decided to keep my abilities a secret from her. Ryann was better off not knowing—for her own safety, in case anyone in a black suit with a badge came after me. "I'll have a look at flights as soon as you guys decide on some dates. And I'll pop by the house sometime next week. I owe your mom a major hug."

"And scones." Ryann chuckled.

"Wouldn't dream of showing up without some," I replied, and we both laughed lightly. "How've you been, anyway? How's college treating you?"

"You know, it's even harder than I'd anticipated. But, hey, pretty sure that's the textbook definition of adulthood." She grinned, then sighed a little. "It's exhausting, and I don't get much time for social stuff, but it's okay. They say the first year is the toughest, just until you get used to the rigor and deadlines. Honestly, I'm loving every bit of it, and I'm so lucky that my parents actually saved up for this. Wish we were there together, though."

She turned sad as she said that, wringing my heart around. I covered her hand with mine and squeezed gently. "We both know I'm not law school material," I replied, smiling gently. "They'd kick me out of pre-law before the semester was over."

"Have you decided, though? I mean, on what you want to do? I understand the whole gap year thing. It's a wise choice and all, but it's already spring. Application deadlines end in July, if you're doing rolling admission," Ryann said, frowning slightly. I could tell that she was worried for my future, and I really didn't want her to clutter her mind with my inability to make a decision.

Frankly, I didn't know what I wanted to do with my life. I had these abilities that forced me to keep a low profile, given the fact that I was still learning to control them. College life didn't sound "safe and smart," as my emotions were still quite volatile and had a direct impact on my telekinesis, in particular. Not to mention the accidental fires, the sudden earthquakes, and the bathroom floods. Whenever I was distressed, my relationship with the natural elements suffered, and there were only so many excuses I could use before people started looking at me funny.

"Not yet." I gave her a faded smile. "It'll come to me soon enough! I'm stuck between anthropology and law enforcement. It's better than the ideas I had last fall, I guess."

"Last fall." Ryann narrowed her eyes, pursing her lips as she tried to remember. "Ah, yes. Psychology, right?"

"Yeah." I shrugged. "Honestly, I'm having a hard time finding my place in the world right now. I might take another gap year, but I'll make up my mind. Eventually."

"Well, you are ridiculously good at reading people," she said. "Whatever you go for, just make sure you get to make use of that skill, and that it involves quality footwear."

I burst into laughter; she reminded me of her mom. Mrs. Smith had this hilarious way of practical thinking where career choices were involved: don't become a firefighter unless you're used to forty pounds of equipment weighing you down at all times; don't become a mail carrier if you don't like dogs; don't become a chef if you don't like hair nets…

"I don't know, I think I'd do all right in a uniform," I replied.

"San Diego does welcome decent people on its force. I'm sure you'd make a great cop if you decide to go there," Ryann said, filling me with her familiarly warm affection. Man, the faith this girl had in me was almost impossible to quantify. "I'm just happy you ended up with us when you did. I know the foster system doesn't give you many chances, and that people somehow look down on kids like you. I plan to change that when I get into office."

Leave it to Ryann Smith to try to change the world.

I'd considered multiple career choices over the past few months. My empathy skills were out of this world, so I knew I'd have a leg up in any fields related to law enforcement or psychology. Reading people was basically already paying for my rent and food—why not turn it into a bona fide career? I liked it enough, even when some emotions were too strong to handle. I did get a kick out of unmasking cheats and thieves at the casino, after all.

I wanted to ask her for advice about my encounter with Wade

and his request for me to join the coven, but I couldn't exactly tell her the whole truth. Some omissions were necessary.

"Ryann, I wanted to ask you something," I said, and she raised her eyebrows in response, letting me know I had her full attention. "I'm just curious… I was watching this movie the other night, and it got me thinking. What would you do if, say, you had these… call them superpowers, and someone who also had superpowers came to you and told you to join their organization? Out of the blue. You don't know them, you don't know what they do, what they represent. But everything you know about these superpowers isn't very positive, and people like you have gotten hurt in the past whenever they went out in public."

Ryann blinked a couple of times, then giggled. "Have you been bingeing fantasy TV shows again? Lord, if there's one way to keep you indoors for days on end, it's to get you a streaming service."

"Yeah, I know." I chuckled. "But just… you know, just humor me. Would you?"

"Would I what?"

"Would you say yes? Would you join the organization?"

"Hm. Not without knowing what they do," she replied, shaking her head slowly. "I mean, who are they? What does their logo look like? Honestly, if the logo has snakes or spiders on it, it's a clear sign to just say no. Every comic book will tell you the same. And another thing that counts, at this point, is what kind of superpowers do you have, and what do you use them for? Are you a solo vigilante, or do you want to be part of a league of legends or… whatever?"

I couldn't help but raise an eyebrow at her, slightly amused. "Wow, and I'm the fantasy fanatic, huh?"

Ryann laughed, throwing her head back for extra flair, then took my hands in hers.

"I got it all from you! From the moment you walked into our home, Harley. Remember what was in your black bag?"

A lump formed in my throat as I remembered the look on her face when I first arrived at the Smiths. She was so eager to get to know me better. All I had were the clothes on my back, scars from my previous "families," and a black bag with more clothes, shoes, and several comic books I'd been carrying for years.

How far I'd come, thanks to Ryann and her parents.

I nodded, finding it hard to reply as tears threatened to work their way to my eyes. It was always so good to see her. Whenever I felt lost, Ryann had this way of bringing me back, most of the time without even knowing what I was going through.

"In the end, Harley, I think you just do what feels right," Ryann added. "Your instincts are never wrong, are they?"

I smiled. "No. No, they aren't."

She was right. My instincts were still in survival mode, and I had to pay attention to them.

As soon as I got back home and walked through the door, I felt as though I'd made the right decision by not following up with Wade Crowley. Besides, his air of superiority and arrogance kind of irked me. All the more reason not to—

"Weird..." I murmured as I reached the coffee table.

My stomach churned at the sight of Wade's business card, which was back on top of my magazine stack. I checked the trash can, then stared at the card for a long moment. Wade's name glimmered gold, along with his phone number and "San Diego Coven," making me retrace my steps prior to leaving the house.

"I swear I threw this out..."

I turned the card over and noticed the symbol on the back. With all the madness from last night, I hadn't even properly checked for other details. The coven's logo was interesting, to say the least. It was a stylized Ouroboros, the ancient image of a snake eating its tail. Needless to say, that amped up the creepy factor to eleven.

Muttering to myself, I ripped the card up and tossed it back in the bin. The more I looked at it, the more annoyed I got. I *really* didn't like being told what to do.

Unfortunately, the universe had other plans for me, as it so eloquently convinced me over what quickly became the three weirdest days of my life.

I tried to get on with things. My mornings were usually reserved for long walks with a home-brewed coffee, or a hazelnut latte if I was craving a special treat. The day after my meeting with Ryann, I went out for my aforementioned morning routine, after taking out the trash, Wade's shredded card included.

In need of a clear head, I took the long route around the neighborhood, gazing at the new spring/summer collections on display in fashion stores. A gorgeous leather jacket caught my eye, so I stepped closer to the window to see the stitching details on the sleeves.

I didn't spot it, initially, but there was a card in the window glass, just to the right of where I was facing it. Leaning over, I noticed the details, and froze. It was Wade's business card, with the same embossed gold lettering, his number and organization name just below.

"What in the world?" I muttered, then touched the glass.

It was in there. In the freaking window. It wasn't glued or taped to it. It was in the glass!

I gasped, then glanced around, as if expecting to see Wade somewhere nearby.

"Excuse me," I said to a lady passing by. She stopped to look at me, and I pointed at the window. "Can you see that?"

"See what?" she asked.

"The... The card in the window."

"What card?"

I looked at the window again, and the card was still very much there. Something clicked in my head, and I instantly understood that it was just for me to see, and no one else. *The dude's a warlock, after all. And he's basically trolling me!*

"N-Never mind." I shook my head as the lady walked away. "Sorry."

I stared at the card for a while, trying to figure out how Wade had pulled this off. Did he know I'd be walking past that specific store, at that specific time? How did he... Had he followed me?

After a couple of deep breaths, I decided not to let him get to me. If this was his way of trying to capture my attention, I was sure as hell *not* going to give him the satisfaction of knowing it had worked.

I resumed my walk past other stores, but my temperature spiked as I spotted the card again, in other windows. It was everywhere, its golden letters quietly glimmering in the morning sunlight. I walked faster, heart thudding as I turned the corner and came to a sudden halt.

Every single window down the block had one of Wade's cards in it. And I was the only one who could see them.

"That just makes me want to get as far away from you creeps as possible," I breathed, ignoring the shop windows entirely.

I resisted the urge to call Ryann just so I could get my fix of tranquility. She was probably busy making her way back to UCLA, anyway. Instead, I went home and enjoyed the rest of my day off with a solid TV binge about teenage vampires in Pennsylvania.

On day two, I didn't even leave the house. After a full breakfast and two coffees, I settled on the sofa and turned on my TV, hoping I'd get my mind off things. The more creeped out I got, the more determined I was not to give in. Who the hell was Wade Crowley to tell me what I should do with my life, anyway?

After just twenty minutes of pretending to watch a vampire flick, I flipped open my laptop and started searching the internet for anything related to witches, warlocks, and covens. Nothing popped up for the

San Diego Coven, of course, other than a message board for Wiccan practitioners, but they were completely harmless fifteen-year-olds with way too much free time on their hands. They riddled their posts with winking and heart-shaped emojis and lots of Xs and Os.

I'd gone through the motions before, as far as internet research into witchcraft was concerned. But I didn't have as much information then as I did now—though the difference wasn't exactly staggering. The Wade Crowley I'd met wasn't on any of the social networks, nor did I find any of his pictures online.

But when I started looking for ways to ward off magic, the search engine was overloaded with all kinds of websites. After some light browsing, I noticed some recurring patterns in the recommendations—lining the doors and windows with salt to ward off evil spirits and dark magic.

"Might as well," I muttered, then grabbed the salt shaker from the kitchen and lined the door and windows, as per online instructions.

I ordered a large pizza and was careful not to disrupt the salt line when the delivery boy brought it over. Armed with a can of chilled Coke and a gorgeous cheese pizza just for me and my ragged nerves, I switched to a romantic drama, putting my feet up on the coffee table.

I inhaled the first two slices as I absently watched the main character, a blonde-haired heroine with perfect natural makeup, awkwardly ask her love interest out on a date. Oh, the bravery—according to her goofy best friend. Ugh.

Something didn't taste right where my third slice was concerned. The more I chewed, the worse the texture became. It tasted almost like… paper.

"What the…" I mumbled, then looked down and nearly choked.

I sat up straight and used both hands to tear the pizza slice in two. Right in the middle, nestled between melted strings of mozzarella cheese, was Wade Crowley's business card. Well, half of it, anyway. I stared at it, unable to register the reality of what was going on.

"Seriously, this is some messed up—" I bit my tongue, then dumped the pizza pieces on top of the rest, before washing the taste of paper down with Coke.

I was equal parts angry and creeped out, wondering how much farther Wade would take things if I didn't call him. I had no idea what to do. Move to another city, maybe? Los Angeles or San Francisco could work. I'd always wanted to see more of my country, anyway. Why not start now?

But maybe Wade wasn't going to stop. Maybe the coven was going to come after me in the end.

"Jeez, listen to yourself!" I groaned, leaning back into my sofa, just as the guy on TV kissed the girl for the first time. I waited for my heart to flutter, as it usually did with kissing scenes, but nothing happened.

My mind was stuck on Wade and his stupid magic tricks.

Why was I letting him drive me out of town? I'd survived childhood in the foster care of some truly horrible people. There was no way I was letting that jerk scare me out of my own city. *Hell, no.*

On day three, I was still significantly on edge. I had a shift at the casino, which I hoped would help keep me focused on something other than that wretched business card.

The night started out smoothly, and I'd settled at a blackjack table, waiting to see if anyone was counting cards without the dealer noticing. The players were all excited, and my blood was pumping with the thrill of gamblers. Knowing the downfalls of such a road, I could only feel sorry for them. Chances were they'd be walking out poorer than they'd come in.

"Yeah, so I called him yesterday," a young woman told her male friend at the table, laughing as they clinked glasses and the dealer flipped another card. "And he was like, 'Who's this?'"

"No. You're serious?" The guy seemed shocked and amused at the same time.

Judging by the ache in the girl's heart, though, the laughter was just for show.

"Yeah." She giggled. "He'd deleted my number. What a jerk, right?"

"Absolutely! You're much better off without him!"

"Right? That's what I thought." She nodded, as if feeding off her friend's encouragement. I could feel the hope inside her, that maybe tomorrow would hurt less than today.

"Wade Crowley?" a waitress asked, as she stopped by our table.

"Wait, what?" I replied, not sure I'd registered the question.

"Wade Crowley. Five-five-five. Two-three-one-five. San Diego Coven," the waitress said, eyebrows raised.

I blinked several times, then looked around and laughed nervously. "Sorry, I didn't catch what you said."

"Wade Crowley," the brokenhearted girl repeated, frowning at me.

"Five-five-five. Two-three-one-five," the guy next to her added.

"Have you lost your minds?" I croaked, unsure of what was going on, since they were looking at me as if I were the crazy one.

"San Diego Coven," added the dealer.

"This is freaking me out, man," I managed, jumping to my feet and stepping away from the table, as all the players, the dealer, and the waitress gawked at me.

"Wade Crowley?" Malcolm came to my side, visibly concerned.

What is this?

Malcolm put his hand on my shoulder, squeezing gently, as if to calm me down. "Five-five-five. Two-three-one-five. San Diego Coven. Wade Crowley."

But the words coming out of his mouth had nothing to do with my panic attack. I was close to hyperventilating at this point, wheezing and breathing heavily as my heart kicked around in my chest.

"Wade Crowley?" the waitress asked from behind.

"Oh, for crap's sake!" I blurted out, and took several steps back, as more people turned their heads to look at me. "Can you not hear yourselves?"

"Wade Crowley. Five-five-five. Two-three-one-five. San Diego Coven. Wade Crowley," Malcolm said gently, trying to come closer.

"No way! I'm out of here!" I growled, then ran out of the casino.

The night was chilly as I rushed straight across the parking lot to my car.

"Wade Crowley?" a young man asked, as he passed by me and gave me a seductive wink.

"Go to hell!" I shot back, and darted to my Daisy, my heels clicking frantically across the asphalt. I got in my car and turned the key in the ignition, my fingers trembling and slick with sweat.

"This is too much," I murmured, my eyes stinging with tears.

The Mustang grumbled as its engine set it into motion, and I drove out into the main street, leaving skid marks behind. I flipped the radio switch on and turned the volume up, drowning in guitar riffs of alternative rock music. I needed all the noise I could get to drown out the echoes of what had just happened.

My favorite song came on, but it sounded weird.

"You've got to be kidding me," I breathed, as I realized that the lyrics were also reciting Wade Crowley's name, phone number, and organization. "You son of a… That's my favorite song, and you freakin' ruined it!" I shouted, then turned the radio off.

I ran a red light but didn't get stopped by any traffic cops on my way home. *Like I even care, at this point.*

What were my options? Clearly, Wade's reach was far wider than I'd initially thought. His powers were… fearsome, to say the least. I mean, if he could do all that with just a business card, what were the odds that I could keep living in San Diego, undisturbed?

Judging by the last few days, obviously zero. I had two choices, from what I could tell. Call Wade, or get out of San Diego.

. . .

When I got home, I threw all my stuff on the floor and took out my phone, jabbing my finger at the screen. With all the times I'd seen the business card, I'd memorized his number already. The line rang, and I did my best to keep a calm and composed voice. I couldn't let Wade know he'd reached the edge of my patience. My honor demanded that I keep my cool.

"Took you a while," Wade said from the other end of the phone, his voice smooth and low.

"What the hell are you trying to do?" I shouted.

There goes my self-control…

"I take it you got my message?" he replied dryly.

I will kick him in the nuts, I swear.

I took a deep breath, then closed my eyes for a couple of seconds. "More than once. You're quite persistent," I retorted.

"Well, you're stubborn," he shot back. "Be here at noon, tomorrow."

"Wait, be where at—"

He hung up on me. I exhaled, lingering somewhere between a fit of rage and a bout of hysterical laughter. He was deliberately messing with me, and I'd already given him too much satisfaction.

"Fine." I shook my head slowly. "I'll come see you, then. But where?"

The guy was so arrogant and self-assured, he'd forgotten to give me an address. It wasn't as if one could simply find the San Diego Coven on an online map. I'd already tried that.

I tossed and turned throughout the night, barely catching a couple of hours' worth of sleep, and as soon as I woke up, reality came back to smack me over the head.

I sighed, then got out of bed, eager to hit the shower. Hopefully, Wade was going to call back with an address. Otherwise, I'd have to do the most unpleasant thing I could think of at the moment—call him again.

Shivers rushed through me, and I shuddered as I walked toward the bathroom. I glanced down and yelped, jumping back a couple of feet.

"You crazy… crazy… crazy jerk."

On the floor, at the foot of my bed, were spilled coffee beans, carefully arranged into a string of letters, big enough for me not to miss them. My shoulders dropped as I reached a rather unpleasant conclusion.

There was no way out until I went to see Wade Crowley.

The letters on the floor were clear, as far as my destination was concerned: Fleet Science Center.

At least he gave me an address…

Chapter Six

A few hours later, still hopped up on caffeine and plenty of frustration, I drove up Park Boulevard to Fleet Science Center. I wasn't sure what I was doing there just yet, but I figured I'd meet Wade somewhere inside, so I parked my Daisy out front, then went around the building.

Balboa Park wasn't all that busy at noon, with only a few parents and their kids out and about. It was a school day, after all. The circular fountain caught my eye, as water gushed out, its murmurs soothing my nerves.

I walked through the main entrance and stopped by the reception desk, where two young ladies flashed me bright smiles, their name tags telling me everything I needed to know. Several school groups were touring the Center, the noise of children squealing and laughing prompting me to raise my voice to make sure Ellen and Jane could hear me behind their desks.

"Hi. I'm here to see Wade Crowley," I said, mirroring their sunny dispositions.

Ellen nodded, then checked her computer screen, typing in Wade's name. She frowned slightly, then looked up at me.

"I'm sorry, there's no one here by that name," Ellen replied. "Are you here for the archive and library job openings?"

"Um, no," I said, blinking several times. "I, uh… He told me to meet him here. Sort of. Hold on."

I pulled my phone from my jacket pocket, suddenly feeling a little out of place as I noticed the plethora of crisp white school shirts and neat black jackets worn by the Science Center employees. My tight jeans and leather boots and jacket didn't help me fit in much. I went through my call history and tapped on Wade's number… which was disconnected.

"Son of a…"

My frustration was rearing its ugly head once more, and I stifled a curse to spare the nearby kids my foul mood, while Ellen and Jane offered a pair of awkward smiles in return.

"You're late." Wade's voice startled me.

I turned around, then stilled at the sight of him, an inch too close for my comfort.

"No, I'm not. You said noon," I shot back.

"You're three days late." He kept his calm demeanor, though his voice cut through me like a knife. It was his intention to make me feel guilty, and, though I'd never tell him, he was succeeding in making me regret delaying the visit. I could've avoided all the weirdness with his "magic tricks" had I simply called him the next day.

Then again, hindsight was always 20/20.

"I didn't commit to anything, from what I remember," I said, crossing my arms. I wasn't going to give in, and, judging by his emotions echoing through me, he seemed to like that. The man was a walking contradiction, clearly.

"You'll learn soon enough what the rules are," he replied. "Anyway, you'll have to forgive Ellen and Jane—they're both new here. The Center is going through a restructuring of sorts, and they've just joined our team."

He gave them a polite nod, and they both blushed and fluttered their eyelashes at him in response. I resisted the urge to roll my eyes, by then well aware that Wade was eye candy to these girls. Ellen gasped, then covered her mouth with her hands.

"I am so sorry," she replied, as if suddenly remembering who he was. "You're from the Archive and Library Department, aren't you?"

"Mm-hm," Wade confirmed. "I'll take it from here, ladies. Thanks."

He motioned for me to follow him. We left the reception desk and headed through the main hall. I glanced at the wall-mounted signs and, based on the right and left turns we took, we were walking toward Kid City, the museum area dedicated to children under the age of five.

"So, what's up with that weirdo card trick?" I asked, stuffing my hands in my jacket pockets.

My gaze wandered around, occasionally settling on framed photographs of various space missions. The moon shots were particularly fascinating, dramatic black-and-white contrasts reminding me of how tiny we were, how insignificant our world was when compared to the rest of the universe.

"I think it deserves a bit more appreciation than that," Wade said. "It does require a certain amount of skill to pull off."

"Is that how you get girls to come see you?"

The sideways glance he gave me was a warning sign. Not that I took it seriously—after what he'd put me through, he was going to put up with this, and more. Wade Crowley wasn't going to be the one to knock me down, and I sure as heck didn't want him to even get the opportunity to try. It was what I'd learned to do whenever I was brought into a new foster home with more than one kid already on the premises—you acted tough; you held your ground; you showed them you couldn't be intimidated.

Otherwise, they trampled you worse than a herd of panicked elephants.

"What am I doing here, Wade?" I asked, noticing the Kid City sign ahead, in big, colorful letters, just above the entrance.

"I thought I made that perfectly clear the other night," he replied, looking ahead. "You're a witch. And the coven wants to meet you."

"In Kid City?"

The room was built to resemble an actual city, with building cutouts and a pretend road stickered onto the floor. There were plenty of kids crawling around, too. I counted at least three who seemed to enjoy chewing on the plastic scenery. The others were busy running around and giggling, playing with huge toy blocks and riding the red fire truck on the side of the road.

I could tell Wade was a bit embarrassed as we followed the cute little highway, dodging rogue toddlers while the parents watched from the sides. Before I could further tease him about his presence here, all the childish emotions from Kid City rammed into me with unexpected force.

All of a sudden, I was five kinds of excited, but also amused and angry. I glanced over my shoulder and noticed two kids fighting over a seat at one of the computers. They both wanted to play and had little respect for the wait-your-turn policy. I felt it all, and it was a little too much. Children were way more intense than adults. Their emotions were raw and amplified, often cutting my breath short.

I started walking faster, and Wade noticed.

"Don't like kids much?" he asked, and stopped between "The Factory" and "The Supermarket."

"Can you just tell me where we're going?" I snapped.

On the other side of the "road," there was a metallic board on which magnet letters had been mounted. Two kids were shuffling them around, and my attention was temporarily drawn to the letters' bright colors, before I realized what they spelled: *ordo ab chao*. The kids both looked at me, two smiling boys, while I rummaged through my scarce knowledge of Latin. Unlike many, I had the chance to study some during high school.

"From chaos comes order," I muttered. *Yup, add that to the list of weird.*

I didn't get a chance to ask Wade about the letters, as a four-year-old girl clamped on to my leg, giggling and refusing to let go.

"Play with me! Play with me!" she said, her curly brown hair framing her cute, round face.

For some reason, this little girl actually liked me. I gave her a smile, then shook my head, while Wade watched the exchange with glimmering amusement.

"I can't, sweetie. This guy here wants me to go with him," I replied gently.

She looked up at Wade, then frowned.

"Do you know him?" she asked, pouting.

"Not really, no," I said.

"My mom says to never talk to strangers. Not even if they give you candy."

The shadow of a smile flickered over Wade's face, and I shrugged in response.

"He didn't give me any candy." I sighed.

The little girl scowled at Wade, then got up and released my leg so she could ball her hands into little fists and rest them on her hips in a reprimanding posture. "You should give her candy!"

"I will, I promise." Wade nodded, trying hard to keep a straight face.

"Oh, wow. Call me crazy, but you two would look great in an AMBER alert, Wade," I said.

Wade shook his head slowly, clearly displeased with my comment, then walked toward the emergency exit door to our left. I followed him through, and we reached a small corridor with a secondary staircase. There was another door right ahead, and Wade stopped in front of it.

"I'm going to overlook the fact that you just basically called me a child abductor right now, and welcome you to the San Diego Coven," he said, his tone flat as he placed his palms on the door at shoulder height.

"We're in Kid City, Wade. Did you forget to take your medication this morning, by any chance?" I retorted, still not sure what we were doing. At least there were several more feet between me and the kids now, and my nerve center was no longer controlled by the emotions of four-year-olds.

"Aperi Portam," Wade said quietly, and the ten rings on his fingers lit up red.

He pushed the door open, on which there was a janitor sign, then walked through. There was nothing but darkness ahead. Things were getting weirder with each second that passed, but it was too late to turn back. I figured I could always kick him in the nuts if he tried something funny.

I walked in after him and quickly came to a halt, as I realized that everything around me had suddenly changed. The janitor door closed behind us with a loud clang, and I stood in awe, smack in the middle of a massive hallway. It stretched far and wide, with dozens of large, black wooden doors on both sides. The ceiling was high, beautifully composed with interconnected arches, neo-Gothic relief sculptures, and gilded details, in eye-popping contrast to the creamy marble walls and dark blue floor. It was an architectural masterpiece all by itself, and I could only imagine what the other rooms looked like.

One thing didn't make sense, though.

"Wade, what's happening here?" I murmured, gawking at the dragon-like sculptures holding up the arches. "I've been all over this place, repeatedly, and this… this wasn't here. It's not supposed to be here."

"It isn't," Wade replied, turning to face me. "This, technically speaking, doesn't exist in the real world. Welcome to the San Diego Coven, Harley Smith."

"This doesn't exist, yet I'm standing right in the middle of it."

"Call it an interdimensional pocket," he said with a shrug. "We couldn't exactly build our coven where the humans could see it or easily access it, so we devised these… bubbles that exist between dimensions."

He motioned for me to follow him, pointing at the end of the hallway.

"A world within our world," I breathed, trying to take it all in.

Fortunately, I'd been dealing with my otherworldly abilities since I was seven. I'd gone well past the stage at which something like this could shock me to the point where I'd crumble and lose my mind, simply rejecting this new reality. Nevertheless, it still wasn't easy to digest.

One too many questions fluttered through my head, but I held my tongue, knowing that I'd get my answers soon. Hopefully, I'd get them one at a time.

"You're probably wondering how this all works," Wade said. "Space is not linear, nor is it finite. It can be bent to fit our needs, if we know how to do it. Most importantly, achieving such feats requires tremendous amounts of energy. Everything you see around you, in fact, is energy solidified into matter."

I walked over to the wall and touched it. Its surface felt smooth and cold, and my skin vibrated gently in response. I pushed a finger forward, but the marble didn't budge. It was solid, indeed.

"This is incredible," I murmured. "So, you're telling me that this space here… it can't be seen at all from the outside. And no one can come in."

"Only those of us able to use magic. The coven is rigged to record and allow certain individuals in—those who belong here, those who belong to other covens, and those we approve to come in," Wade explained, then motioned for me to follow him. "Come on, I'll show you around."

I nodded slowly, my mouth open, and reached his side. We walked forward, watching as doors opened and people moved around—all of them young and dressed like… normal people. They all stared at me for a while, before going back to whatever business they had behind various doors.

"How does the coven recognize who's who?" I asked.

"Magic," Wade said. "There are spells in place."

"Okay, you'll have to be a little bit more specific than that."

"You'll find out more soon enough, don't worry. For now, just think of this structure as a massive, self-sustained organism that has a conscience and a memory. It knows who we are, what we do, and when we do it. It remembers our steps with photographic precision, and it can be set to deny access to those lacking the appropriate clearance."

We reached the end of the hallway, which split into two equally large corridors that went in opposite directions. On the wall in front of us, a giant plaque was mounted. It was made from stainless steel, and I could see myself and Wade reflected on its shiny surface. The words I'd seen earlier on the kids' magnet board were clearly engraved at the top in elegant, swirly letters. *Ordo Ab Chao*. Below it, a block of text followed, also in Latin.

"What's that?" I asked, trying to read and failing to understand about 90 percent of it. Other than the words "mystic," "courage," and "virtue," nothing seemed familiar.

"A pledge of allegiance," Wade replied. "It's the oath we take when we join the coven. A promise that transcends time and space. Words of great importance that we can never go back on. You'll learn it as well."

"Whoa there, buddy! I'm here to say hi, not join your weird cult. Though, I'll have to admit, it looks cool and all," I said.

I followed Wade down the corridor to our right, constantly looking around, admiring the dragonesque sculptures and sharp arches stretching overhead, the brass chandeliers and chiaroscuro paintings. These things were probably worth a fortune, but the aesthetic was pretty weird. The artwork was more classical, while the arches and architectural details were neo-Gothic, and the walls and floors were simple, downright minimalistic.

My two years with the Smiths had given me access to a private school education, and it was there that I finished high school. My teachers tended to look down on me, given my rough-around-the-edges attitude, but they had no other choice but to teach me the same as the ritzy kids in class—subjects that included art, architecture, and design. I was surprised to see I'd remembered some of it as I analyzed my surroundings.

It all looked beautiful, but eerily different. It felt that way, too. For lack of a better word, I decided to stick to "otherworldly" when describing the overall look of the San Diego Coven. People passed by us, most of them nodding at Wade. The ladies, in particular, seemed thrilled to see him.

"They're all, uh, witches?" I asked, making eye contact with some of them. The vibe they gave me was a mixture of curiosity and suspicion. I was a stranger on their turf, after all, so that didn't come as a surprise.

"Witches, warlocks, yes," Wade replied, then turned left into a stunning dining hall.

It was enormous, with three long rows of white marble tables in the middle, covered with white porcelain and sterling silver tableware. Globe-shaped light pendants hung from the ridiculously high ceiling, and another table was set at the far end, perpendicular to the others.

"This is the banquet hall," Wade said. "It's where we all eat. Designated staff handle preparation and service, of course. Some of our younger witches and warlocks are given part-time jobs here. Not that they need to pay to live here, but the human world can be expensive to navigate."

"You mean you people *live* here, too?"

"Most of us, yes. Rarely does the coven allow its people to rent their own places in the city. It's safer and easier to live here. It's not like we lack the space," he replied.

"What does the coven do, exactly?"

"A lot of things," Wade said, smirking. Then he walked back out into the corridor, with me not far behind. "Magic is the result of powerful energy manifested through physical bodies. We are born magical, and never made. The energy itself is Chaos, the founding force of the universe itself, the power that fuels the world. However, from Chaos comes Order. It's what we live by. There must be rules in place. We're heavily outnumbered by humans, and we are peaceful by nature. You're probably well aware of the fact that humans tend to destroy what they don't understand."

"Yeah, I guess. I've seen the movies," I said.

"You must've been called a freak more than a couple of times, too. Right?"

Flashbacks to the first couple of times that my powers manifested knocked me over the head. "Among other terms, yes."

I'd been called a monster, too. A weirdo. An abomination. I could go on, but there was no point in dwelling on the past. I'd survived it.

"Well, the covens are here to protect those of us through whom Chaos flows freely. Those of us capable of magic," Wade replied. "In return, we adhere to the laws, we enforce them, and we do our best to make a positive impact on the world. Humans aren't doing a very good job of taking care of this planet or themselves, which is where we come in—in moderation, of course. We're not superheroes, nor do we have a duty to serve them. Our main purpose is to keep them out of magical harm's way. There are things out there… creatures other than witches and warlocks, and phenomena that humans would never be able to understand. We keep them out of sight. We neutralize them, if needed."

Much like he did with the gargoyle the other night, I thought, nodding slowly.

We reached another hall, this one three times as big as the dining room. Its walls were smooth and black, and there was a plethora of obstacles and training dummies, targets and barriers. This was a training area and, judging by the burn, frost, and tear marks on the wooden puppets, this was where the witches and warlocks basically let loose.

A variety of medieval shields and weapons were mounted on the walls—swords in silver-plated scabbards with gemstones embedded into the hilts, bows and arrows of different sizes, lances and spears, hammers and hatchets, knives and daggers, and several clubs. This was a place for warriors. I was more of a Mustang and leather jacket kind of girl…

There were about twelve witches and warlocks training, holding their hands out as they launched fireballs at wall-mounted targets. An instructor in a black, military-style uniform walked behind them, barking orders and criticizing their stances.

"Spread those legs out, Rodriguez! If you're a good shot, you won't have to worry about someone getting close enough to kick you in the balls!"

"Wow," I breathed, feeling sorry for the Rodriguez boy, whose embarrassment was flushing my cheeks already.

"This is where we train, as you can see. That's O'Halloran, one of our instructors. You'll like him, I think. He's just as abrasive as you are," Wade said.

"If I'm abrasive, then that makes you what, exactly? Sulfuric acid?"

"You know, that smart mouth of yours won't get you anywhere good in this place," Wade retorted, then stepped in front of me. I moved back, but he followed, maintaining a distance of a few inches. His face was too close to mine, his irritation setting me on fire—or was it just his presence that had that effect on me? I wasn't sure, but his card trick still creeped me out six ways from Sunday, and his arrogance made me want to punch him. The farther I got away from him, the better.

"Crowley!" O'Halloran shouted, prompting Wade to look over his shoulder. "Is that the new girl?"

"Yeah," Wade replied.

"New girl? No. I'm just visiting!" I said, raising my voice to make sure O'Halloran heard me.

When he didn't respond to my statement, I tilted my whole upper body to the right, so I could see past Wade's broad chest. O'Halloran was tall and massive, the typical soldier type, his features rough, his chin square, and his bluish eyes narrowed at me.

Something about him made my blood chill—probably the fact that no emotions came through from him.

He was either a master of self-control, or an android. My money was on the mechanical parts.

"Bring her in later. I want to see what she can do," O'Halloran replied, completely ignoring me.

Wade looked at me, then exhaled sharply. He was genuinely frustrated, though I couldn't tell why, exactly. I felt what he felt, but the why part belonged to his thoughts, which I didn't have access to. Ironically, I'd spent half my life wishing I didn't have these abilities. However, as I walked out after Wade, I was wishing I had more power, enough to be able to read his mind, and maybe even disappear.

My conscience and my instincts were already at odds. Part of me was excited about this place. It felt good. It had a hint of home that I couldn't ignore. But my father's words kept blaring in my head. *Stay safe. Stay smart.*

"Let me show you the living quarters," Wade said, as we advanced through the corridor.

A set of double doors covered in elegant mahogany relief sculptures awaited at the far end. He touched the brass door knobs and muttered something under his breath. It sounded like Latin, but I didn't pay enough attention as I stared to my right, where an archway led into what looked like a courtyard, lush with trees and flowers. A small, round stone fountain stood in the middle, water trickling from a dragon's mouth into a fan of seashells.

The term "otherworldly" came back to mind, and I felt as though I'd left the material plane, sincerely fascinated by the courtyard's peacefulness.

"Come on," Wade said, snapping me back to reality.

The living quarters were incredible. I had the feeling of being inside a luxury hotel, with three levels of rooms lining the circular arena and dozens of staircases connecting each floor. Potted magnolia trees stood in the middle, surrounded by black, forged iron benches with wooden backs. Witches and warlocks buzzed around, while several men dressed in black uniforms guarded the ground floor.

"You guys have security here?" I asked, noticing the uniforms' resemblance to what I'd seen on O'Halloran.

"Not always," Wade replied. "There's been a string of, uh, peculiar incidents, and the coven decided to add some extra detail to the more vulnerable areas, just in case."

"Define 'peculiar.'"

"Out of the ordinary."

"Now you're just pulling my leg," I said. "Why is this area vulnerable, then?"

"We live here. These are our homes. We sleep here. If anyone were to ever try and attack the coven, this is where they would come first," Wade replied. "We're relaxed here. We put our feet up; we close our eyes."

I nodded slowly. It made sense. If I were a bloodthirsty warlord, I'd definitely go for the tents first—at night, when the soldiers slept. The thought of that level of vulnerability made me uneasy. To be honest, if I were to follow my instincts to the letter, I would've ended up in a hole in the ground somewhere, sleeping with my eyes open and a string connecting my toe to a booby trap outside, in case of intruders. I did appreciate the risk in living, sometimes. But the coven was different. There was an antithesis between a feeling of home and a hint of danger, and I couldn't really put my finger on the latter.

Across the circular hall were floor-to-ceiling windows, three giants made of thick glass and framed in gilded wood. I held my breath as I walked over and realized that I was looking out into the real world. Right before me was Balboa Park, sprawling with its short grass and anemic trees, crude green buds popping all over the branches. The sky above was bright and blue, and people were out there, walking their dogs, watching their kids play, and taking selfies by the fountain—all of them completely unaware that we existed. That we were watching them.

"It's time for you to meet the director," Wade said, startling me as he once again stood too close, his breath tickling my ear.

"The… who… what now?" I spun around with a stutter.

He made me nervous. I couldn't tell why, exactly, but there was something about Wade, that electric feeling I'd felt before. It was rippling through me, and my brain wasn't sure what it meant. I'd done my best to keep my distance from people, in general, with only a handful of exceptions. My social skills weren't the greatest, and neither were my reactions to new people stepping into my personal space. Whenever Wade got too close, a shot of adrenaline coursed through me.

I walked back toward the corridor, with him by my side. My gaze wandered around the hall. A young woman, probably my age, with curly black hair and chocolate-brown eyes, stood at the top of the stairs in front of Room 234—only then did I notice the brass numbers on each door.

There was a twinkle of curiosity in her eyes, and while she was a bit too far for me to feel her emotions with accuracy, I could definitely get a whiff of amusement. I had a feeling I was some kind of shiny new toy in this place, because she wasn't the only one looking at me like that.

Farther down from her was a warlock in his mid-twenties, with short platinum hair and sky-blue eyes, who offered the same facial expression. He leaned against the railing as he smiled at me—but it didn't feel like a welcoming smile. Just like with O'Halloran, I couldn't get a good read on his emotions. For the first time in my life, I didn't like not being able to sense someone's feelings. It was a first, and it was full of unknowns.

As weird as it had been for me growing up, I'd learned to use my Empath abilities to forge ahead. Knowing how people felt helped me keep my distance and steer clear of trouble. Most of the time, anyway. The platinum-haired guy was cold as ice. A blank wall I couldn't breach.

"You do want to meet the director of the coven, don't you?" Wade said, reminding me that he was still there, waiting for me to come along.

I realized that I'd stopped in the middle of the circular hall, staring at the platinum-haired guy. Wade followed my gaze, then raised an eyebrow at me.

"Making friends already?" he asked.

"Surely they're more fun than you," I shot back, regaining my composure.

Don't let them see that you're worried or scared. Keep your cool.

"Smartass," Wade said, then walked back into the corridor.

I followed, scowling at the back of his neck and wishing I had laser eyes, so I could burn right through and make him suffer a little.

The director of the coven.

My pulse spiked. I was going to meet the big boss. The big kahuna. The chief wizard in this place.

Would they agree to leave me alone, if that's what I wanted? I needed my freedom. The coven seemed nice, for the most part, but I didn't want to be forced into it. I deserved the right to choose.

Chapter Seven

At the end of another hallway was a set of black double doors with heavy brass lion heads for knockers. I felt eyes on me and, as I looked over my shoulder, noticed more witches and warlocks staring. They were all curious about the stranger with bright red hair, even brighter blue eyes, and a leather jacket. Some were wary of my presence, and, for the life of me, I couldn't figure out why. I wasn't there to hurt anyone.

Wade gave me a sideways glance, observing my uncharacteristic silence.

"Don't take it personally," he said, looking back at those watching us. "You're new here. They'll get used to you. Eventually."

He gripped one of the large brass rings mounted in the lions' mouths and knocked it against the black wood. The doors opened with a loud creak, revealing a spacious office. The bottom half of the walls was covered in lacquered dark walnut paneling, while the top half was dressed in an elegant black-and-beige wallpaper, its intricate design catching my eye. Red roses blossomed in crystal vases mounted on decorative wall shelves.

The furniture matched the wall paneling, the shelves loaded

with hundreds of voluminous leather-bound books, and the lights were partially dimmed—enough to cast a warm, amber glow over the room. There was a seating area in the middle, consisting of a sofa and two armchairs, and a massive desk at the far end, where a man stood up.

I followed Wade as we walked through the study, my gaze wandering and catching snippets of book titles along the way: *The Aberdeen Bestiary, Slavic Folklore and Sorcery, The Chronicles of Salem.*

"Harley Smith," the man standing behind the massive desk said, and smiled.

He was tall and classically handsome. Maybe in his late thirties, at most, he'd stopped trying to control the waves of his short, chocolate-brown hair. His eyes were sharp and emerald green, framed by curved eyebrows against the slim blade of his nose. His masculine features were brought out by the navy-blue suit he'd opted for, matched with a white shirt and dark red tie. The dragon-head cufflinks were impossible to ignore, as was the way he seemed to stare straight into my soul.

In many ways, he reminded me of Wade, though I knew they weren't related, since Wade would have gladly bragged about it otherwise.

"I take it you're the big boss?" I raised an eyebrow, preparing for more snark and arrogance. Two Wades were worse than one. And yet, the vibe I got off the guy was noticeably different. He was curious, like most of the witches and warlocks I'd seen earlier, but he was also genuinely excited and downright fascinated by my presence. It was a nice change from the wariness I'd sensed up to that point, not to mention Wade's heartfelt frustration, which was still echoing through me.

The man smiled and held out his hand. I stepped forward, and, after half a minute of debating whether I should or shouldn't, I shook his hand—instantly reading his emotions. Direct physical contact had an impressive impact on my Empathic abilities, as I felt what the other person felt at high intensity.

"I'm Alton Waterhouse," he said, a gentle Southern twang sweetening his speech.

"Well, you know my name already," I replied bluntly.

He chuckled, then motioned for me to sit in one of the leather chairs facing his desk. I took my seat, then looked up at Wade, who preferred to stand. *All the better to look down at me, I guess…*

"Thank you for coming, Harley," Alton said, then sat behind his desk. "I'm sure you have a lot of questions, so I'll try to cover as much ground in this introduction as possible."

"I'm all ears," I muttered, crossing my arms.

He gave me another smile, as if my thorny attitude was somehow adorable. I didn't like it, but I did have a lot of questions that needed answers.

"I'm the director of the coven, and I'm also in charge of the Fleet Science Center," Alton explained. "Given our complicated nature, witches and warlocks have reached a certain balance while having to share this world with non-magicals. We live and work like everyone else, but we also carry out our duties as members of this coven. In my case, taking over the board of directors at Fleet Science Center seemed like the perfect way to seamlessly integrate both aspects of my life. A significant number of witches and warlocks work at the Center with me, for that matter."

"So, what, you herd kids through the museum during the day, and fight evil at night?"

"Not really, no." Alton chuckled. "We're not heroes, Harley. We are simply gifted people, and we play our part in this world. I'm sure Wade has already explained the number issue, with regards to why we keep our magical existence a secret from the human world."

"Yeah, he mentioned something," I replied, giving Wade a quick glance. The look he gave me chilled me to the bone, so I shifted my focus back to Alton. It was better to focus on the polite adult in the room, not the arrogant thorn in my side.

"Okay," Alton continued, and took out a massive old registry from a bottom drawer. He flipped it open, then used a quill and ink to add my name onto one of the pages. "This is the assessment log. Your name needs to be in here in order for the coven to let you in and out. You have restricted access at this point, but once you progress and make your pledge, more doors will open for you."

I frowned. "Wait, what pledge? That pledge of allegiance you make your people recite?"

Alton looked at me for a couple of seconds, then took a deep breath and finished writing my name. "Harley, this is a safe haven. All the coven does is protect its people. There aren't too many of us out there and, as you know, people don't take kindly to those who are different. Man has a natural tendency to destroy what he doesn't understand, and, unfortunately, it stands true even in the 21st century. For now, I'm not asking you to pledge yourself to the coven. The decision will be yours. All I did was add your name to the assessment log, so the coven's magic can allow you to move freely, within certain limits. Highly sensitive areas of our little pocket in the universe are still restricted, though."

"All you need to do is learn the phrase I used to get us in from Kid City," Wade explained. "*Aperi Portam*. It's Latin. Open the door. Simple."

"Fine." I nodded, narrowing my eyes at Alton. "Now, spill the beans. What's going on here? What am I? Why am I this way? What do you *want* from me?"

"From what Wade has told me, I think it's safe to assume that we are the first *magicals* you've met, despite your age," Alton said with a patient smile. "So, I'll have to start from the very beginning. Like I said, I'll try to give you as much as I can during this first conversation, but you will have more to learn and understand farther down the road."

"Magicals?" I prompted.

"Witches. Warlocks. Monsters," Alton replied. "You've met one of those, too."

"The gargoyle. Ugh, yes."

"To best understand what you are, you must know about Chaos.

It is the force behind the universe, the energy that flows in countless forms. It gives life. It fuels the stars. Chaos is everything and nothing, all at once. Matter, antimatter, it's all Chaos. It's present in humans, in animals, in everything that grows and breathes, too. Witches and warlocks are simply creatures through which Chaos flows with greater power. We're special because we have this connection to the universe on a subatomic level. Our powers, our abilities, stem from Chaos."

Alton put his hands out, and his dragon-head cufflinks glimmered golden. They were beautifully crafted in gold, with green enamel scales and two red garnet eyes that lit up white. Wade's rings came to mind as I watched threads of concentrated energy pour out of the dragons' open mouths, swirling into a sphere the size of my head. It hovered above the desk, and an image formed inside.

I understood then that I was being shown a vivid illustration of what Alton was telling me. The universe glimmered at the center of it, shifting to closeups of distant planets and constellations.

"Chaos is exactly that. Unruly, wild, and intense. If we let it do as it pleases, it will consume and destroy us," Alton explained. "At the same time, Chaos is a ruthless negotiator. What it gives, it takes. For every action, there is a reaction. As magicals, we have developed a strict set of rules meant to guide us and keep us on the right track. If we slip up, if we expose ourselves to the humans, we'll risk not only our lives, but the safety and wellbeing of our entire species. We respect the unwritten laws of Chaos, and we obey the written laws of our covens. It took us a long time, but over the past two thousand years, we have successfully organized into these secret societies."

"So, there's more than one coven," I replied.

"There is a coven in every major city in this world, each in charge of its surrounding areas. In the US, each state is ruled by a Mage Council. Our society is commonly referred to as the United Covens of America, and we function much like the American government—minus the corporate interests and corruption, of course. Everywhere else in the world, every country has its own Mage Council to oversee the covens. We've had to close ranks and organize accordingly, especially after the seventeenth century," Alton explained.

"The Salem witch trials," I murmured.

"Thousands of innocent people, as well as magicals, were killed around that horrific period." He sighed. "Which is why we are strict, why we monitor our kind, and why we adhere to these rules. Normally, once a magical is discovered, the regional coven assesses and registers the individual. That way, the magical is raised in the system, educated and taught to use his or her abilities for good, for balance... for peace."

"Don't you get the occasional rotten apple?" I asked.

"More than occasional, unfortunately," Alton replied, shaking his head. It wasn't a pleasant subject for him, filling him—and me—with angst and grief. "Some think they can take on the whole world. Some consider themselves superior to humans and have utter disregard for innocent lives. Some even believe they can navigate both worlds while indulging in criminal behavior. Unfortunately, all three categories hurt us, because they put us at risk of discovery. Which, again, is why we are strict in enforcing the coven rules."

As I looked into the holographic sphere, I was shown snippets of different witches and warlocks committing horrible crimes—burning entire villages down, killing people, and wreaking havoc over different cities. The coven laws made sense. I'd lived my whole life fearing discovery, keeping my abilities to myself. Knowing that there were others like me out there who did the same felt strangely reassuring.

"How are you doing this?" I asked, pointing at the sphere.

Alton smiled, then gestured at his cufflinks.

"The power inside us is raw. It needs an object that we connect with, something special that we're particularly fond of, or that has great significance to us, to channel this energy, to give it structure and meaning," he explained.

"Kind of like wands, right?"

"Well, yes and no. Mostly no. You can still perform magic without an Esprit, but it's just not as strong, or as accurate."

"Esprit?" I frowned, my gaze darting between Alton's cufflinks and Wade's rings.

"An object of soul," Alton replied. "It's something that your being resonates with. Don't worry if you don't have one yet. You'll find it now that you know what you're looking for. Everything else is just technique, practice, and education. There are thousands of spells, devised over thousands of years. Words and thoughts that manipulate the energy of Chaos and translate into your abilities."

"What can *you* do? Other than put on fancy graphic shows?" I replied, prompting Alton to laugh.

"We're all different on the surface, but the same at our core," he said. "As byproducts of Chaos ourselves, we are deeply connected to its Children, in one way or another. The Children of Chaos are concentrated forces of the universe, agents of great power. The main ones are Erebus, also known as Darkness; Lux, or Light; Nyx, commonly referred to as Night; and Gaia—Earth, our home."

"What difference is there between Darkness and Night? They sound the same to me." I shrugged.

"They're not," Wade interjected with a scoff. "Darkness is permanent. It's the twin brother of Light, and all-powerful, all-consuming, and unforgiving. Night is like sleep. It's subject to a cycle, and its sisters are the stars and moons."

I looked up at Wade.

"Look at you, all poetic and stuff," I said, and he replied with an eye roll and another scoff. I had to admit, I enjoyed pushing his buttons. If they were going to force me to stay here, tormenting Wade had to be permitted.

"Gaia has her own children, the four elements. Water, Fire, Air, and Earth," Alton continued. "And they're the ones we're all connected to. One way or another, all magicals are able to manipulate one or more of the natural elements. In some rare instances, a magical can influence all four."

I stilled, realizing that I was one such rare instance. I had a history of causing natural disruptions. From freezing the bath water in a moment of bloodcurdling fear with an aggressive foster dad, to setting the Corbin family curtains on fire at Christmas when I was twelve. That was after their son tried to touch me in all the wrong places. And let's not forget accidentally splitting Ginger's backyard in two, shortly before my fourteenth birthday. Oh, and knocking pigeons off the electrical wires outside the Smiths' home last year with sudden wind gusts, after they'd pooped all over my Daisy—among other examples. Yeah, I had definitely handled all four elements, particularly where difficult foster families were involved...

Though I was nowhere near Wade's level of expertise with fire, I was comfortable saying that setting stuff ablaze came easily to me; this ability was closely followed by skill with water. Air and earth were still in their early stages, but, based on how I'd seen my powers evolve over the years, I'd already figured it was only a matter of time.

Alton noticed the change in my expression, and leaned forward, smiling as his holographic sphere puffed away.

"Any of that sound familiar to you, Harley?" he asked. Judging by the fluttering in my stomach, he was excited about my potential abilities. "What can you do, where the four elements are concerned?"

"Not much, to be honest." I shrugged, the term "rare instance" still blaring in the back of my head. Even in the world of magicals, I was a weirdo.

"She can use fire, though that's a very loose description," Wade interjected, keeping his hands in his pockets. The dude loved his suits, just like Alton. Two peas in a pod, yet the elder pea seemed to have more common sense and sympathy.

"Aha." Alton nodded, his eyes twinkling with interest. "And what else?"

"Water," I replied, then let out a long sigh and told him what he clearly yearned to hear. "Air and Earth."

A couple of moments went by in absolute silence, while I analyzed both Alton's and Wade's emotions. They were surprised—particularly Wade. Alton had seen it coming, from what I could tell.

"Let me get this straight." Wade blinked several times. "You can manipulate all four elements?"

"I listed all four, didn't I?" I murmured, keeping my gaze fixed on Alton. He seemed uncertain of what to do next, until a revelation filled him with relief and excitement.

"Harley, we should get you tested properly," Alton finally said.

"Tested? I'm not getting poked and prodded here. I didn't let the government get me, and there's no way you boys are sticking me with needles and whatever else!" I shot back, instantly closing up like an armadillo before its predators.

"It's not like that," Alton said, shaking his head. "You have to understand something, Harley. The San Diego Coven is relatively young and… not stellar. Not yet, anyway. It went through years of neglect, until I took over. We have talented magicals here, but most of them are mediocre, so to speak. Having someone who can manipulate all four elements in this city is rare. And Wade mentioned Telekinesis, too?"

I scowled at Wade, mentally branding him a snitch. He replied with a disinterested shrug, then took his hands out of his pockets and put them behind his back, in a solemn posture.

"Shall I escort her to Adley?" Wade asked.

"I'll come with you." Alton stood up and walked around his desk.

"Wait, what? Where are we going? What tests? Hold on!" I growled. I shot to my feet, wrestling with panic and fear as I tried to keep my composure.

Alton and Wade stopped just before they reached the double doors, and turned around to face me.

"It's okay, Harley," Alton said. "We're not going to hurt you. We just need to find out exactly what you can do. I'll make assessments based on that. It's part of the process, nothing to fear."

In his defense, Alton had been nothing but kind and courteous, explaining stuff I'd waited my whole life to hear. There were rules in this place, and, since he'd basically allowed me in, even if on a temporary basis, the least I could do was indulge the guy and let him assess my abilities.

"I can't believe it. I'm meeting real-life warlocks and witches, and you all sound like bureaucratic pencil pushers, with processes and assessments and whatever else makes you think you're in control of your lives," I complained, following them as they crossed the hallway.

"From Chaos comes Order," Alton replied with a wink.

Chapter Eight

Wade pushed open the doors to another chamber ahead, while Alton stayed by my side as we walked in. Judging by the pristine white walls and square neon light fixtures on the ceiling, this was a lab of sorts. My stomach churned in response to the various chemical smells, while my gaze darted from glass vials and jars to potted plants, ceramic dishes loaded with colorful powders, and a plethora of herbal and mineral paraphernalia.

A white plastic chair stood in the middle of the room—a sturdy-looking thing, with a stainless-steel podium base, two attached side tables, and brown leather straps on the armrests and front legs.

"Whoa," I breathed, then stilled, staring at the chair.

"Relax, the straps are not for you," a woman said. There was a hint of amusement in her voice as she emerged from behind a large potted hibiscus bush in the far-right corner of the room. The floor was smooth and white. I felt like a rat in a testing lab.

The woman was a head shorter than me, and in her mid-thirties, with fine expression lines bringing out her violet eyes. She wore her black hair in a short pixie cut, with purple tips, in deep contrast to her elegant gray pantsuit and white lab coat.

"Harley, this is Adley de la Barthe. She's our physician," Alton said, as Adley reached out and shook my trembling hand.

Only then did I realize how nervous I was.

"Pleasure to meet you, Harley," Adley replied, and I gave her a brief nod in return. Curiosity emanated from her, and it was aimed at me. There was also a tinge of excitement as she smiled. "Why don't you have a seat?"

I looked at her, then at Alton, Wade, and the white chair, before I crossed my arms and shook my head.

"That thing looks like what's at the end of a death sentence," I said, grappling with my anxiety. I'd spent my whole life staying out of labs and hospitals, so I was having a hard time associating this room with anything good.

"Like I said, the straps are not for you, Harley," Adley insisted, and motioned for me to sit.

"Then who are they for?" I replied.

"For Purges," Wade interjected, impatiently rolling his eyes. "Just sit in the damn chair."

"What are Purges?" I didn't budge. Like a kid about to get into the dentist's chair, I was stalling.

"Purges are a natural process for magicals," Alton replied, giving me a warm smile in an attempt to soothe me. "When we use magic, when we enlist the powers of Chaos, our bodies gather a type of toxic waste—negative energy, poisonous darkness that builds up as we exercise our abilities. It's directly proportional to the strength of the magic we use. The more powerful the spell, the more toxins that gather inside us."

"Purges are a healthy and necessary way for our bodies to expel this dark energy," Adley added. "In the beginning, they weren't monitored or conducted in contained environments, such as this room, but now we know better. We can even predict when a magical needs to Purge, as there are certain symptoms."

"Why do they need to be in a controlled environment?" I asked.

"Because the Purge can be extremely painful," Alton replied.

"Witches have described it as worse than childbirth. Personally, I can tell you it hurts. It burns and claws at your insides, as if you're being torn to shreds in slow motion."

"You've Purged?" I tried to visualize the process.

He nodded. "More than once, yes."

"What happens to the toxic... whatever?"

"Once it makes contact with the air, it materializes into a monster. Shapes and dimensions vary, but, usually, the beast's size echoes the magical's power. A powerful witch can generate a creature the size of a mountain, for example. I'll tell you more about this later, though. For now, Harley, we need to get you tested." Alton motioned toward the chair once more.

The gargoyle from the other night came to mind. Was that a Purge monster, too? Clearly, I had more follow-up questions at this point, but Alton didn't seem interested in answering until I complied with his request. After a few seconds' worth of back-and-forths in my head, I eventually conceded and sat in the white chair, my skin crawling as my fingers touched the armrests.

"How do you plan on testing me?" I asked, my gaze following Adley as she walked over to a nearby cabinet and pulled open a drawer. I couldn't see more from that angle, but I could hear various metallic instruments clanging, sending shivers down my spine.

I can still run, if need be. I'll just whack the three of them against the wall or something and shoot out of here.

"I'll need a little bit of your blood," Adley replied, turning around to face me.

Dread froze the blood in my veins at the sight of a metal syringe in her hand. It looked like something they used back at the turn of the century, with a needle thick enough to probably kill a small animal. *Oh, this is going to hurt like a mother—*

"Nope, I'm out of here. Okay. Thanks. Bye!" I sprang up, my brain instantly switching into survival mode. There was no way I'd let them stick that thing in me.

"Good grief, stop overreacting." Wade's voice pierced through me, and my muscles stiffened.

The connection to my brain cut off, somehow. Frost coated my veins, as I looked at him and saw his hand raised, his rings glowing blue. *Oh, crap.*

Wade had Telekinetic abilities, too, and they were much more powerful than mine. My limbs creaked, and the next thing I knew, I was back in the chair.

"You need to hold still," he said more calmly, relinquishing his Telekinesis. Alton put a hand on my shoulder, giving it a reassuring squeeze.

My heart pumped erratically and my breath hitched as Adley came closer, holding up the empty syringe for me to see.

"I'm sorry, Harley," she said. "But honestly, it will just pinch for a bit, and then we'll let you go. We need to assess your powers."

"Let me guess, your dumbass rules?" I spat, narrowing my eyes at Alton and Wade.

Alton nodded slowly, watching as Adley brought the needle closer to my arm. "Yes. We must all follow them. For your safety and ours."

"Relax, we've all done this," Wade replied.

"May I?" Adley asked, turning over my left forearm.

I gritted my teeth. "Just get it over with, then."

She stuck the needle into my vein. I cursed under my breath, heat spreading through my forearm, swiftly followed by a sharp sting as Adley's needle pierced my skin. She drew a few milliliters of blood. It was over quickly, at least, but I grumbled all the same.

"Ow."

Adley put a piece of sterilized cotton against the puncture wound and pushed my forearm up, for me to keep pressure until the bleeding stopped. This reminded me of my first vaccines—fortunately, my Telekinetic abilities manifested after the shots; otherwise, there would've been some pediatricians in San Diego with permanent psychological and physical scars.

"Again, truly sorry, Harley, but we had to—" Alton tried to apologize, but I gestured for him to shut up.

"Shush," I muttered. "It's done. Now what?"

"We see what you're made of." Adley smiled and brought out a wide copper bowl with strange markings engraved on the inner lip. I could've sworn they were runes. Or hieroglyphs. I should've paid more attention in "preppy" history class.

"You'll pay for that, by the way," I muttered, pointing a threatening finger at Wade, who replied with a light chuckle.

"Dream on," he said.

I didn't pursue it further, but he was going to get paid in kind for his surprise little trick. The irony didn't escape me, as far as my outrage was concerned. I'd used my Telekinesis on others, after all. I'd physically harmed them, too. *Ugh, do unto others and so on.*

"Okay, let's see what Harley Smith can do," Adley said, as she emptied the syringe into the copper bowl, with Wade and Alton moving closer, while I craned my neck to get a better look.

The blood trickled down into the center of the bowl, before purposefully spreading out in thin crimson streams, forming a variety of patterns against the copper surface, like some kind of mandala—swirls and lines repeating in a circular fashion.

"We call this Reading," Adley explained, analyzing the blood pattern. "It gives me a clear picture of your key traits and abilities."

"Okay," I murmured. "What does it say?"

"Oh, wow," she replied, her forehead smoothing. She seemed to recognize something in those lines and curves. "You have all four elements. That is truly impressive, and rare. Very rare, actually... Telekinesis. Oh, you're an Empath!"

She beamed at me, her excitement genuine and quickly replicated by Alton, whose eyes widened as he stared at me with pure, unadulterated joy. I'd referred to myself as an "empath" up to this point after some online searches for what I was experiencing. It had simply come across as the most relatable term I'd found in the dictionary. It was interesting to see how the magicals were using it as an actual label.

"You're an Empath, Harley? Why didn't you say so?" Alton beamed at me.

"It's not exactly something I just blurt out." I shrugged, my gaze shifting to Wade.

As exposed as I felt in that moment, I did feel partially avenged. Judging by the stunned look on his face and the flurry of raw panic pouring out of him, Wade was coming to terms with the fact that I could read him like an open book. And he freaking hated it. I stifled a grin, pressing my lips into a thin line, as I looked at Alton and Adley again.

They were both looking at me as if I were some rare specimen. A magical unicorn.

"Hm, this is strange," Adley said, frowning as she turned the bowl around. "I can't read further into you."

"What do you mean?" I asked, still wrapping my head around this new reality of mine, while Wade was boiling on the inside. His anger at his own vulnerabilities made it difficult for me to concentrate. It then hit me that I could enjoy this a little more, while he was still coping. "Wade, can you please get yourself under control? You're making it hard for me to focus."

"Why do you say that?" Alton replied, somewhat confused, while Wade cursed under his breath and scowled at me. My heart grew three sizes.

"He's worried because I can feel everything he feels," I shot back. "I mean, he's nervous because he feels vulnerable, now that he knows. Which is okay. I'm enjoying the look on his face."

As soon as he heard that, Wade seemed to find the last ounce of self-control he had left at the bottom of his consciousness, and crossed his arms over his chest, pretending to look inside the bowl. Alton didn't bother to reply, but he was definitely amused.

"I… No, I can't read you further. And that's not a regular occurrence," Adley concluded, her brow furrowed.

"Do you know why?" Alton asked.

"Nope." She shook her head. "But based on what I'm seeing here, Harley is a walking contradiction. She has all these abilities already, and yet her power levels are weak, at best. According to what her blood is telling me, she is a—"

"Mediocre. Harley Smith is a Mediocre," Wade interrupted her with a twitch of his lips. It was his turn to enjoy something I wasn't sure I understood yet.

"Does the term mean something else for a magical?" I asked.

"No. It means exactly that." Alton sighed, confused and disappointed at the same time. "You're what we call a Mediocre. Lackluster. Moderate abilities, with not much power. You'll probably experience a single Purge in this lifetime."

"Oh. Okay," I replied, somewhat disappointed myself.

For a brief second, the idea of being destined for greatness had appealed to me. With all my struggles to fit in somewhere, to find my purpose and place in the world, I'd thought I might be able to excel as a witch. A super special magical.

Unfortunately, it seemed as though the universe—or Chaos, for that matter—had decided that I was going to be a Mediocre. And I had no idea how much I hated that word, until it was used to label me. I let out a deep breath, my shoulders dropping slowly.

"Don't despair, though," Alton tried to encourage me, though I could tell from his tone and his emotions that he wasn't very hopeful either. "You can practice and get better. Being a Mediocre doesn't make you useless in any way. On the contrary!"

"What, now you're trying to boost her morale?" Wade said. "Let's not sugarcoat this. She's a Mediocre, and that's it. There's no point in making her think she'll ever amount to more. She'll get herself killed trying to do something that's out of her league."

"No, no, it's cool," I said. "I'm still a better person than you ever will be, so at least I've got that going for me."

"Now, now, no need to get spikey. Both of you, take it down a notch," Alton intervened, raising his hand in a pacifying gesture.

The red garnets on his dragon cufflinks glimmered in the white neon lights.

"I still don't get why I can't read deeper." Adley frowned, still staring at the bowl.

"I'm sure you'll get to the bottom of this. Reading is your expertise, Miss de la Barthe, not mine," Alton replied, trying to end the matter there.

I caught a whiff of something… different coming from him. It felt like suspicion, but it lingered quietly beneath layers of renewed curiosity. I had a feeling that Alton was going to research the subject further. He seemed guarded, almost closed off.

The way he looked at me made me feel like he wasn't done with studying me, with trying to understand what I was about. However, in the absence of more information, he had nothing else to go on. One thing was clear, though.

I was a Mediocre magical, and an orphan who had no idea what she wanted to do with her time on this earth. While I'd gotten answers to some of my most burning questions, I'd yet to resolve the one thing that bothered me the most:

Who is Harley Smith? What is she meant to become?

Chapter Nine

"Wade, I need you to meet us back in the Main Assembly Hall in an hour," Alton said. "I'll continue Harley's tour and introduce her to our trainers, then bring her over to the Hall for the announcement."

"Understood." Wade nodded and turned to leave the room, without bothering to even look at me. From what I could tell, he was too busy trying to keep a cool and calm demeanor now that he knew I was an Empath. I watched him disappear somewhere beyond the white room, wondering what had given him that arrogant sense of superiority he enjoyed flaunting before me.

"Wait, what announcement?" I asked.

"You'll find out soon enough. I need to bring you up to speed on a few more topics before anything else," Alton replied with a faint smile, then motioned for me to walk out first.

I let out an audible sigh, just to make sure I got my frustration across, then headed for the hallway, followed by Alton.

"Harley, should you decide that this is where you want to be, I'd like to see you again for another Reading," Adley said.

I gave her a quick glance and a nod over my shoulder, and waited for Alton to lead the way to wherever we were going.

"I didn't know I had a choice," I said in an undertone, my gaze wandering around as we proceeded toward the end of the hallway. The sculpted dragons were both beautiful and fearsome, and I couldn't help but wonder why they'd chosen such a controversial creature to adorn their public spaces. For people who advocated for balance and rules, it seemed ironic that they'd chosen a monster of Chaos to decorate their coven.

"It's a bit more complicated than that," Alton replied, walking by my side, "but this is how it stands right now. You're an unregistered and untrained magical, Harley. We cannot just let you wander around San Diego all by yourself. However, I also understand how new and difficult this must all seem to you. So, I'd like to put you on a one-month probation with the coven, just to get you started and see how you come along. We will provide you with training and education so you can catch up with the other magicals who've already pledged themselves to the coven."

"And after that?" I asked, not sure I was liking my post-trial-period prospects if they involved compulsory joining.

"Think of it this way. You'll learn to control and develop your abilities, you'll get a better understanding of the magical culture, and you'll get to meet other witches and warlocks while you're here," Alton explained. "All we need you to do is work with us and obey the rules. Consider this trial period a stepping stone to something better. We need to assess you in the long term and this is the best way. It'll teach you a few things about self-control, and you'll better understand why we need to stick together."

"That doesn't answer my question," I replied.

"No, it doesn't. I'll be honest—your options will be limited at the end of this trial. You either join the coven or leave town and go somewhere where other covens will accept you as unaffiliated, though your chances are slim on that one. We cannot have it any other way. This coven is young, and it has been through years of neglect. In order for us to turn it around, we have to be strict. The one thing we don't want to do is encourage rogues. There are a lot of eyes on us right now, and we can't afford any mistakes. Plus, I'm confident that, by the end of this trial period, you'll want to stay with us. The coven is like a big family. While we don't carry a blood connection, we're tied by something much deeper, and far more powerful."

"So, it's either join or get out, as long as it doesn't affect your public image, right?" I concluded, my stomach aching with the prospects. Their attitude toward rogues sounded pretty shallow from where I stood, particularly after they'd been so adamant in describing their desire to keep humans safe from harmful magic. It seemed as though they were more worried about their reputation than anything else.

I was an independent creature, and I'd been through a lot to get to this point. My freedom was my most precious asset, and I had no intention of handing it over to anyone, not even a coven. On the other hand, I didn't want to skip town, either. This city was everything I knew. I had roots here, no matter how skinny they were.

"As an unaffiliated rogue, you'll just end up going through the same hoops with different covens. Nobody wants a magical who can't be registered or controlled, not after what our people went through during the past four centuries. However, there is a third option, of you making a solid case for yourself as a Neutral and gaining permission to keep living in San Diego, as long as you don't use your magic on humans. And that will come with a lot of monitoring and potential imprisonment, if you break the rules of such an accord. But the decision will not be made by the coven. It will be made by California's Council of Mages," Alton said. "And if you want them on your side, you need to help them get to know you better. Which brings us back to—"

"The one-month trial period," I said, nodding slowly.

Okay, it wasn't too bad. At least there were options. I could spend the next month assessing the coven, in return. This was a serious, life-changing commitment, and I hadn't even decided what college I wanted to go to.

"That sounds reasonable," I added. "Though, I wouldn't hold my breath if I were you."

"That's fine, Harley." Alton chuckled. "I don't expect you to even consider a decision yet. But you should know that the trial period is the only way I can give you time to think things through. The Council… let's just say they're not easy to deal with."

We reached the end of the hallway, where a set of double doors awaited. He pushed them open and went in. I followed, gawking at the sheer size of the room, which was shaped like a dome. A massive chandelier poured down from the ceiling in swirls of brass and tear-shaped crystals. The walls were a slate gray, with gilded details, and four giant bronze dragons gazed at me from symmetrical points around the room.

Ten rows of individual desks were placed in a semicircular pattern, facing a floor-to-ceiling blackboard and a solid oak table loaded with books and various study objects, including a gorgeous, hand-painted globe with a map of the world.

Three large French windows covered the walls to my left and right, providing a healthy amount of natural light. Six magicals stood in front of the oak table, watching and smiling as we walked toward them.

"This is one of the six classrooms we provide for our young magicals," Alton said. "You'll be expected to attend lessons with the rest of the kids. You'll be the oldest, but I'm sure that won't be a problem. And these are our six preceptors."

"Preceptors?" I replied, quickly scanning the three men and three women patiently waiting for us at the end of the narrow corridor between study desks.

"Trainers. Instructors. Teachers." Alton offered synonyms, prompting me to purse my lips. I may have gone through two years of prep school, but it didn't mean that everything they'd taught me had actually stuck. "They are here to help magicals control and develop their abilities, to teach them history and spells, and to provide guidance whenever necessary. Most of them were already here when I joined, but I've established two more subjects for the kids, as part of the upgrade of the coven."

"Welcome to the San Diego Coven, Harley," one of the witches said, offering a broad smile, while the others quietly measured me from head to toe, already forming their own opinions about me. The common emotion between them was curiosity. They all wanted to find out more about me, and it was a weird feeling, given that I'd spent most of my life trying my best *not* to stand out.

"Harley Smith, this is Jacintha Parks," Alton said. "She's the preceptor of Alchemy and Occult Chemistry. Her title is somewhat self-explanatory; I trust you don't need me to explain anything at this point. She's also our resident… pharmacist."

I raised an eyebrow. "Why the pause, though?"

"Because they've yet to figure out another term for the health services that I provide." Jacintha grinned. "Thing is, aside from what I teach, I also procure medication and healing herbs for the magicals of this coven. I work closely with Adley de la Barthe on this, but neither of us is a medical professional, so our paperwork is a little vague."

I nodded slowly, taking in every detail of her appearance. Jacintha was slightly taller than me, and slender, poured into a dark green velvet suit complete with a snug waistcoat and white shirt. The gold cufflinks and buttons brought out her amber eyes, and she kept her long black hair in a tight bun. Her features offered hints of Spanish heritage.

"This is Hiro Nomura, preceptor of Physical Magic. Everything related to attack and defense spells belongs to Hiro. He's also a master swordsman, well-versed in human forms of combat," Alton continued, introducing one of the warlocks. This guy looked like he'd been in a war or two, with several slim scars crossing the left side of his face. He wore a black tunic, simple and elegant, with broad sleeves. His name and features betrayed his Japanese origins, his black hair cut short, and his cheekbones sharp enough to slice a mango in half. I was particularly fascinated by the color of his eyes, as one was blue, and the other an almost reddish orange. I'd never seen such a combination before.

"It is an honor," Hiro said, bowing curtly before me. I responded with a brief nod.

"Our athletics and combat instructors report to Hiro," Alton explained. "Including O'Halloran, whom I believe you've already met?"

"Yeah, sort of. He said he wants to see what I'm made of later, though I'm not sure I like the thought of that," I murmured.

Alton chuckled, while the others, including Hiro, smiled. I wasn't sure if they were laughing at me or O'Halloran.

"O'Halloran is quite a firecracker," Alton replied. "But he's a very good instructor, and a friend of Hiro's."

"I take it you're all tight here," I said, noticing the warmth exuding from all of them at once. There was a bond between them, something profound and far more powerful than that between siblings—a deep affection that probably had more to do with their abilities as magicals, rather than anything else.

"Like I said, we're a family here," Alton replied. "We stick together."

"How do you know how 'tight' we are?" another witch asked, narrowing her eyes at me.

She was just as fascinating as Hiro, mainly because she was atypical, and had nothing to point out her profession as a preceptor. Her pale blonde hair was short, a smooth buzzcut that brought out her big eyes—a peculiarly bright shade of amber with flakes of gold. She looked more like a goth band groupie, with a swath of tattoos covering the left side of her face and neck, and I assumed there were more beneath the layers of black leather she'd tucked herself into. Metal accents and piercings jingled whenever she moved.

"Harley, meet Sloane Bellmore, preceptor of Charms and Hexes. It's a new subject we're teaching in the coven, as there is a lot to cover beyond the boundaries of Occult Chemistry. Sloane will teach you how to cast them and, most importantly, how to break them, covering everything from charmed objects to curses. Not all magicals are good, and that's where we come in," Alton said, then smiled at Sloane. "You should all know that Harley here is an Empath. She tends to know things that we don't normally share with the world."

"Yeah, I know what an Empath is, Alton. I just didn't know she was one of them," Sloane replied, somewhat irritated as she glanced at me. I couldn't read her, though, just like I couldn't read O'Halloran or the platinum-haired guy back at the living quarters. I'd yet to figure out why, but that was only a matter of time. Chances were that she was putting on the tough-girl act, just to keep others from getting too friendly.

Sound like someone you know?

"Nice to meet you," I replied with a nod, which she briskly returned.

"And this is Oswald Redmont," Alton continued, introducing a short but spry middle-aged man with sprinkles of white in his light brown hair.

"It's a pleasure to meet you, Harley," Oswald replied. "I'm the preceptor of International Magic Cultures. I teach crafts from across the world, both binding and unbinding. And before you ask, yes, that includes voodoo, hoodoo, Santeria, and all the real, good stuff. Not what you find on the Internet these days."

"The key to this course is for our magicals to understand, recognize, and counteract magic from all over the world," Alton explained. "America is a melting pot, after all, of so many different cultures. It would be difficult to do our jobs without knowing what we're dealing with."

"And the stuff you find on the Internet?" I replied. "Any of it real?"

"Have you tried it?" Oswald asked, crossing his arms.

"Nope."

"Good. Don't. It's all a waste of time. None of it works. We just put a lot of bogus lore out there to keep the humans busy. Not that they'd be able to perform any of it, anyway, but we've been deceiving humanity with made-up magic rituals for millennia. That's something you'll better understand once you start attending Mr. Ickes's classes," replied Oswald. He nodded at the warlock standing next to him.

"Speaking of which, Harley, meet Lasher Ickes." Alton continued with the introductions. "The preceptor of Coven and Magical History. He's in charge of all our archives and historical documents and teaches our culture from its earliest days to the present, including our brushes with mankind."

"Like the Salem witch trials and so on?" I asked.

"Yes." Lasher nodded. He was slightly taller than me and wiry, with pale blond hair, watery blue eyes, and glasses, looking like the typical nerd you'd find in the Sunday newspaper cartoons.

"Not a man of many words, I see," I murmured, as he smiled and shook my hand.

"Lasher is shy by nature," Alton replied with amusement, "but he's also very strict and an accomplished historian. I think he'll have a lot of answers for you, Harley. And last, but certainly not least, meet Marianne Gracelyn, preceptor of Herbalism."

Marianne was a beautiful young witch with long red hair. Her bell-shaped jeans, loose cotton shirt, and plethora of colored beads and feathers reminded me of a hippie thrift store, in a good way. There was just something positive beaming out of her, though I couldn't put my finger on it.

"Hi, Harley." Marianne smiled, and we shook hands. The moment my skin touched hers, I was inundated with a sense of calm and serenity—like Ryann times a hundred. If there was one word I could use to describe Marianne, it was "good." Just good, and kind, and decent. Rarely did I form an opinion about someone so quickly, but when that happened, it was set in stone. I was never wrong.

"So, herbalism, huh?" I asked.

"Mm-hm," she said with a wink. "It's mostly stuff of Wiccan origin, healing potions, growth spells with herbs and crystals. The whole worship-Mother-Earth thing, basically. It might sound romantic, but we have a rich culture of herbalism, and everything I teach is bound to come in handy sooner or later. I'm directly connected to the earth."

We all looked at each other for a few moments, as if they were giving me some time to adjust to all the new faces and names. I got a positive vibe out of all of this. Alton was right—if I was looking for someone who could provide me with answers, these preceptors were the people to talk to.

"Now, to clarify, we need to bring your life in order," Alton said, while the preceptors listened with interest. "All our students take part-time or full-time jobs at the Science Center, as part of an adjustment period. We've recently filled all our reception positions, but we do have a couple of open spots in the Archives and Library. One is yours."

"I already have a job," I said, frowning slightly.

"Spotting cheaters in a casino?" Alton replied, raising an eyebrow. "Surely we can put your gifts to better use here, Harley."

"In the Archives and Library?" I shot back.

"No, that will be your cover. Working a human job in the beginning is an essential way of helping a magical fully integrate into human society. It's also a steady source of income, especially since I've gotten the Center to increase its salaries," Alton said. "You'll only be working for three to four hours, four days a week, and it will be enough to keep you financially satisfied."

"Dude, I've got rent to pay. On a good night at the casino I walk out with three grand," I replied, shaking my head. "I'm saving up for college. How well does your museum job pay, for me to give up on the casino?"

"It's only for a month, to begin with. Just to see how you would fare with a job at the Center," Alton explained. "Whatever you make in a month at the casino, on average, I will make sure to pay through the Archives and Library. You have my word on that. After the trial period is over, we can assess everything and see what the best options are, for you and for us. I doubt the casino would refuse to take you back in a month. I understand you're quite skilled."

His appreciative smile succeeded in tickling my little ego. I thrived on validation, anyway. Whenever Malcolm told me I did a good job, I was over the moon and eager to start the next shift. And, as much as I didn't want to admit it, Alton was right. The casino would have no problem with taking me back.

"I'd also like for you to move in here for the trial month," Alton continued, and I instantly shook my head.

That wasn't going to happen, for two reasons. First, I needed to give a three-month notice if I planned to move—I'd signed a crappy lease. And second, I didn't want the coven to have that much control over my life. It was enough that they were going to employ me and teach me, and basically feed me. I didn't feel comfortable with them putting a roof over my head. After all my foster experiences, that was just a big fat no.

"I can't just move out of my apartment that easily," I replied. "And besides, we need to get to know each other a little better before I give the coven *that* much control over my life."

Alton thought about it for a couple of seconds, then pursed his lips and nodded in agreement.

"Fair enough. I'll let you think about it some more, then," he said, scratching his chin. "I need to do an in-depth assessment in the meantime. There's something about you, a few inconsistencies I need to figure out."

"What inconsistencies?" I felt something tug at my stomach.

"Nothing to worry about," he replied. "I'm just curious about your abilities versus your magical strength. It's just never happened before, not with a full Elemental, anyway. We'll look into it later, not to worry."

"What are you talking about, Alton?" Jacintha asked.

"Harley here has control of all four elements, plus Telekinesis and Empathy." Alton beamed with pride, then frowned. "But the power inside her... it's stifled. Reduced. She's a Mediocre."

"How on earth did that happen?" Oswald exclaimed, surprised.

Alton shrugged. "No idea whatsoever."

"What about her parents?" Marianne asked.

"I don't have a family. I was in the foster system my whole life. The closest thing I had to a family were the Smiths, my last foster parents. I'm an orphan." I sighed. It wasn't something I could ever say with ease. My throat closed up whenever the word "orphan" rolled off my tongue. It still hurt, even after all those years.

A thought crossed my mind then—that I could maybe find a way to dig into the archives and find out who my parents were. I'd considered it before, but I never knew where to start, given that my parents' names were unknown. At least now I had the confirmation that they were magical. Surely, the coven must've kept records. It was an extra reason to at least stick around for that month and find a way to access those archives. Alton had said that I had limited access to this place, so I either had to convince him to help me, or find a way to sneak in.

The only problem was that I didn't even know where to start my search. All I had from my parents was the note, and even that didn't yield any useful information, just the same words that kept blaring in the back of my head.

Stay safe. Stay smart.

Chapter Ten

After we left the preceptors in the study hall, Alton took me to another part of the coven, at the opposite end of the hallway. I followed him through a series of narrow corridors. The deeper we went, the tighter the walls got around me, and the smaller I felt.

"You said earlier that there were a lot of eyes on the coven these days," I said. "What did you mean by that?"

"I'm just about to show you, actually," Alton replied softly, as we stopped in front of another door. The corridor seemed to warp around it, as the door itself was significantly taller. It was as if whatever lay beyond it had been added last, and the coven's structure had had to adjust like play dough, stretching beyond its predefined limits.

The walls were covered in dark-purple-and-black wallpaper, loyal to the neo-Gothic aesthetic, and the door was glazed in shiny black paint. A metal plaque was mounted at eye level: *The Bestiary*. Alton turned the doorknob, and we both went in. I stopped as soon as the door closed behind me, stunned by the colossal weirdness unfolding before my very eyes.

The Bestiary was an enormous egg-shaped hall with what seemed like a series of walls and stairs cutting through it on multiple levels, creating a complicated yet fascinating 3D maze made entirely from dark gray marble with brass railings and wall-mounted sconces. The light refracted through a series of randomly placed glass and mirror lenses—until I realized their positions weren't random at all. I could see every corner, every nook and cranny of that place in all the reflective surfaces.

"Whoa," I gasped, trying to wrap my head around the optics of it all. This was either an incredible feat of physics and geometry, or really cool magic. Given where I was, both were equally possible.

"This is the Bestiary," Alton said. He stopped several feet ahead, then turned to face me. "Remember we talked about Purges earlier?"

I nodded, my mouth wide open as I stared at the immense structure. From what I could see in various mirrors, this was almost like a shrine, with a multitude of thick glass boxes in a variety of sizes. I caught glimpses of movement here and there, but nothing clear, nothing I could identify.

There were also sounds—hissing, crinkling, and purring—bringing the term "bestiary" to a more literal description. They were keeping some kinds of creatures in here, but to what end?

"And I told you that all that toxic energy materializes into a monster as soon as it makes contact with the air, with the world outside the magical's body," Alton continued, and I nodded again. "Well, over the past thousand years or so, we've found a way to harness that dark energy and put it to good use. By that time, we were already conducting controlled Purges, so we could immediately capture the monsters that emerged. One of our previous preceptors, from a different coven in France, discovered a way to draw energy from these creatures and fuel large-scale spells, such as these interdimensional pockets where we've built our covens. The power that these beasts hold is endless, and, if drawn moderately, it allows the creatures to naturally replenish and keep fueling our spells. Everything you see in this place, every atom, every particle of electrical current, every solid surface, and every leaf… it's all materialized with the help of these monsters' energy. We've been collecting them inside the Bestiary for a long time."

I understood then that the sounds I'd been hearing didn't belong to animals, but to monsters. The memory of the gargoyle I'd dealt with outside the casino flooded back, turning my blood to ice, as the Mason jar that Wade had stuffed it into finally made a lot more sense.

"How… How does this work?" I asked, staring at Alton.

"Think of the Bestiary as a giant battery that fuels all the covens around the world," he said. "Some magicals are more powerful than others, and the monsters resulting from their Purges are proportionally bigger and deadlier. But they can all lose their material form once they're stuck inside these proprietary glass boxes. Come along, let me show you."

I followed him deeper into the Bestiary. He took a sharp left turn and stopped in front of a wall with about fifty glass boxes, each roughly the size of my head, with brass edges and small locks with symbols engraved around the keyholes. Each box was filled with puffs of black smoke, much like what the gargoyle had turned into the other night, prior to getting sucked into the Mason jar.

"These are small monsters, mostly the result of Purges from young witches and warlocks who've used a lot of magic over a short period of time," Alton explained. "The more magic you use, and the more powerful you are, the bigger the monster and the more painful the Purge. Looking at you, I imagine you've never had a Purge yourself. You won't need to worry about having one for another year or two. It's usually in our early twenties that we start to let the toxic stuff out."

"So, let me get this straight," I murmured, unable to take my eyes off the puffs of smoke. "These are all monsters. Like the gargoyle?"

He nodded. "More or less, yes. They're not as big or as dangerous as the creature you and Wade encountered, but they're the result of the same process. The moment they first touch the air, these clouds of black smoke manifest into beasts. Shapes vary depending on the magical's nature, but they all fall into a certain category—gargoyles, changelings, trolls, and goblins, mostly. Size-wise, it's the gargoyles and trolls you want to be careful with. Changelings and goblins are just pesky and troublesome little turds."

Alton gritted his teeth while referring to changelings and goblins, immediately pointing out a personal disdain for the creatures. I couldn't stifle my grin. "I take it you don't like them, huh?" I said.

"I'd burn them all to a crisp, if I could," Alton said with mild amusement, "but we need their energy. You see, once we put them in these glass boxes, they lose their physical manifestation and return to their original smoky form, and that's when their energy can be drawn into the central system of the Bestiary. It's the stem, the core of this structure, and it processes it all into the power that our covens need, worldwide. It is truly one of our greatest accomplishments."

"I can imagine," I said, slowly tapping the glass on one of the boxes. The smoke reacted to my touch, swirling closer to my finger. I could almost see a crooked lizard head shaping up, when Alton put his hand on my shoulder and startled me. "Son of a—" I croaked.

"Sorry." He chuckled, and the smoke lost its attempted shape, scattering around the box. "Let me show you the bigger ones."

"Oh, yay, bigger monsters," I replied sarcastically. "Because that's how you convince me to move into this place. Tell me it's filled with flesh-eating whatever."

"I'll be honest, 90 percent of what's in here definitely wants to kill you—us, for that matter," Alton replied. "But as magicals, we really try to avoid killing. Which is why the Bestiary was such a good idea. It gave us the opportunity to spare the lives of these creatures and help develop our societies at the same time."

"You can't go without them anymore, huh?"

"Not after a thousand years of progress, of building our covens and fueling them with this power. If the Bestiary were to fail, everything we've erected in these dimensional pockets will either cease to exist or, worse, it will burst out into the human world. Either way, it would be a disaster on a global scale. The loss of life would be cataclysmic."

"What if you let the monsters out?" I asked, the worst-case scenarios popping into my head with alarming speed. This place made me feel so uncomfortable.

"Well, the same, really. Plus, a horde of supernatural monsters roaming freely through the human world." Alton sighed. "Thing is, before we were able to capture them, some of these monsters were free. Some cultures clashed with them, and others worshipped them. These are strong beasts that, even in their glass boxes, retain their gruesome forms. Here."

We stopped in front of a large glass box, about as big as my apartment, filled with dirt, grass, and jagged rocks. Just like the other boxes, this one was kept shut with an engraved lock. It looked worryingly small, compared to the size of the box itself, prompting me to frown as I pointed at it.

"How does that tiny thing keep the monster inside?" I asked.

"It's a charmed lock." A low, gruff voice made me turn my head to the right. I froze on the spot, watching a massive creature walk toward us. It was twice my height, with a man's body—mostly, except for the talons and claws it had for feet, and the bright golden-and-white feathers covering its arms. Its head was that of a lion, with a thick mane and soft, amber eyes. The whiskers moved as it spoke. "It doesn't need to be big. What matters is the symbol, the magic used to contain the beast."

My heart started pumping fast, and I slowly moved backward, until Alton caught my arm and squeezed gently.

"Don't be afraid. He won't hurt you, Harley," Alton said. "This is Tobe, the Beast Master."

"Oh, the Beast Master," I blurted. "Because that's totally normal and makes all the sense in the world, that you would have a big-ass beast looking after a *bestiary*."

Both Alton and Tobe chuckled, while I tried to adjust to this new reality without screaming and kicking. Alton was surprisingly strong, though, easily keeping me in place with just one hand. Tobe bowed before me, and it was then that I noticed his feathered arms were purely extensions to a pair of wings.

"Tobe here is 1,058 years old," Alton explained, "and is the only monster with a conscience and cognitive abilities to ever come out of a Purge."

"Oh, wow," I breathed, unable to stop myself from staring at Tobe. His muscular mass was impressive, even beneath the layers of gray linen he'd fashioned into a toga. I was willing to bet he could crush a twenty-pound melon in one hand. Effortlessly.

"The witch that ejected me was one of the kindest, sweetest souls to ever roam this earth," Tobe replied, sadness drawing a frown between his feline eyes. Despite his animal head, he was surprisingly expressive, especially through the raw tone of his low, masculine voice. "She was also one of the most powerful magicals. She was known as Selma, though very little is known about her origins today. After so many years, I can barely remember her."

"Tobe here is a wonderful and welcome anomaly," Alton said, "mainly because he is the only one that these monsters fear and listen to, perhaps because he too was born from a Purge. He's not a magical per se, but he is the result of magical activity, and has some Chaos-related abilities. Tobe has been with us magicals since he was created, shortly after Selma died. She couldn't bring herself to kill him, as was the custom at the time, because he was kind and, well, harmless, despite his impressive size."

"Once Theodore Dumonde created the glass boxes and the idea of a Bestiary came to fruition, I found my calling," Tobe added. "I've been the Beast Master ever since. I look after this place. As of recently, I've been getting additional support from the coven's magicals."

He frowned, then gazed into the giant glass box. Alton didn't seem happy either, for some reason.

"What's wrong?" I asked.

"I'll explain later, in the Main Assembly Hall. But, in short, we've been having some issues with the Bestiary. Someone's been sneaking in and letting monsters out, which is why I've added some extra security here, to help Tobe manage. He half-sleeps like a dolphin anyway, but I'm hoping the magicals assisting him will play their part in preventing further leaks." Alton sighed.

"The gargoyle," I said, thinking back to that fateful night at the casino. "Did it escape?"

"Yes. We mark all our beasts," Tobe confirmed. "However, there are some still at large. Most are the result of unexpected Purges from magicals that have yet to be registered with a coven. A few I know personally to have been around for centuries, hiding from us, fearing capture. But we'll get them sooner or later. We cannot let them roam free in the human world. Too many lives at risk—"

A heavy, spine-chilling hiss made me turn my head, slowly, to look inside the glass box. I yelped, then quickly covered my mouth as I watched a massive snake slither out from beneath a large rock. It wasn't a regular serpent, though. Its body was unnaturally thick, at least three feet in diameter, and covered in bright golden-and-green scales, each the size of my palm. Its head was huge, with a rich collar made of white-and-fuchsia feathers, which extended along its spine, all the way to the tip of its tail.

This thing was a colorful killing machine, and I didn't know whether to scream or to marvel at its beautiful scales and plumes.

"Ah, there he is," Alton exclaimed, grinning with excitement.

"Normally, people scream when they see a giant snake," I retorted. "You, on the other hand, sound like you've just found your favorite toy!"

Alton chuckled. "I'll be honest, this guy here is definitely one of my favorites."

"Good to know you have… favorites," I mumbled, then shifted

my focus back to the giant serpent. Its big, turquoise eyes were fixed on me in a way that gave me goosebumps.

"His name is Quetzalcoatl, but we call him Quetzi, for short," Tobe explained. "He's one of the oldest monsters to ever be Purged and was once worshipped by the Aztecs. He has some abilities of his own, like all the large creatures in this Bestiary, but he's contained in this glass box."

"Abilities? Like a magical?" I asked, cocking my head to the side. Quetzi mirrored my gesture, and I wasn't sure whether that was cute or creepy.

"Well, yes. He's said to have been Purged by a powerful Aztec warlock, but we were never able to pinpoint his origins," Alton said. "Nevertheless, Quetzi here can influence the weather. Rain, sun, hail, winds, and everything in between. He's quite adept at creating natural disasters. And he is incredibly powerful. He was also known to use mist to confuse his prey."

"His prey," I repeated, waiting for someone to tell me what kind of prey they were referring to.

"Humans. He eats humans." Tobe nodded, confirming my worst nightmare.

I shuddered, then glanced around at the place. From that angle, I could see the stem that Alton had mentioned. It was a superb brass construction, much like a spine to which thousands of cables were attached, each connected to a glass box. A soft white light glimmered inside, bursting through every hole and joint. I counted over twenty levels of glass boxes, interconnected by various sets of stairs.

"The Bestiary is given to a coven to look after, over the course of a century," Alton said. "Tobe moves around with it and, as of January this year, the San Diego Coven was elected to take over. It came as a surprise to everyone, really, given how young and relatively Mediocre this place is, as far as its magicals are concerned. But the selection process was random, and, although we could have conceded, I wanted us to prove that we could keep it safe. Tobe looks after the monsters, and we look after Tobe, in a way."

Alton and Tobe walked farther down the aisle, and I followed, catching glimpses of scaly heads and beady eyes staring at me from large glass boxes on both sides. We reached a massive glass enclosure, where large, dark gray shapes fluttered frenetically, like overgrown bats. Chunks of limestone lined the back of the enclosure, while the creatures gathered around the small pond in the middle, sitting still long enough for me to realize that they were all gargoyles.

"The creature you and Wade encountered the other night is in here," Alton said, nodding toward the enclosure. The beasts with bat wings, horns, and ghoulish faces scowled at me before they all growled and exploded into puffs of black smoke that then scattered around aimlessly.

"They are restless," Tobe murmured, watching them with what came across as concern.

I couldn't feel him like the others, as an Empath, and that was probably because Tobe wasn't human, or fully magical. I could sense his emotions—but not mirrored through me. They came across more like distant thoughts, faded memories. Concern, affection, wariness... it was all there, and genuine.

It was a very different experience for me, one that I honestly appreciated. Feeling others' emotions the way I did could be exhausting, and I'd been surrounded by curious and suspicious magicals for the past couple of hours. Tobe's diluted emotions were a welcome respite.

"But they're locked away now. They shouldn't be able to get out anymore. Guards are on, twenty-four seven," Alton replied. "They may not succeed in killing or capturing the beasts right away, but they can at least alert Tobe and the coven, so we can take the necessary precautions. This is what I meant when I said there are a lot of eyes on us now, Harley. With the Bestiary in our hands, the Mage Council keeps us under a magnifying glass. We can't afford any mistakes, and we seem to have made a few already."

"We'll discuss this further in the Main Assembly Hall, with the others," Tobe added, then looked at me. "Is that your Esprit?"

He pointed a feathered finger at the small, golden medallion around my neck. It was the only piece of jewelry I wore on a regular basis, a gift from the Smiths. They gave it to me when I graduated high school, and I was extremely fond of it. Not only was it the first gift I'd ever gotten from a foster parent, it was also a beautifully crafted depiction of Saint Christopher. I wasn't the religious type, but I liked his story as a protector of travelers.

"This? No, I don't think so," I said, lifting the medallion up with two fingers. "It's Saint Christopher, patron saint of—"

"Travelers." Alton smiled gently, looking at it. "It's beautiful."

"Yeah, my last foster parents gave it to me," I replied. "I've always wanted to travel and see the world, at some point. They felt like Saint Christopher would be a good companion."

"They sound like nice people," Tobe said. "But it's not your Esprit..."

"She hasn't found her Esprit yet." Alton shook his head, giving me a reassuring smile. "She will, sooner or later. I'm sure of it."

Tobe stared at me for a while, narrowing his amber eyes, while I listened to the variety of noises coming out from the glass boxes around us. He then exhaled, and nodded, as if having made his assessment of me.

"You're an orphan," he concluded, prompting me to look at Alton, who shrugged in return.

"I didn't tell him anything about you," Alton replied.

"How did you know, then?" I asked Tobe, narrowing my eyes at him.

"I can read people. It's my gift. And it's written all over your face. The longing, the sadness, the desire to belong. That, and the fact that you said your foster parents gave you that medallion," Tobe replied with a smirk.

"Ah, dammit," I groaned. "Sorry, I just had one of those 'duh!' moments."

My brain wasn't operating at full capacity anymore. It was overloaded with new information, and more questions popped up with every step I took, making it more and more difficult to concentrate. Basic details were starting to escape me.

"But you are different." Tobe smiled. "I mean that in a good way."

"In a good way, eh?" I said.

"You remind me of someone I once knew," Tobe continued. "It's in the way your eyes glimmer when you look at these monsters. And in the amount of power soaring through you. It's rare."

"What power? I was just classified as a Mediocre," I replied.

Tobe frowned, then stared at Alton in disbelief. "How can that be?" he asked.

"Adley tested her. It was clear," Alton said. "Harley is Mediocre. But, as I've said, it doesn't make her useless."

"I find those results hard to believe," Tobe replied, shaking his head, then shifting his focus back to me. I was still as skeptical and confused as before, but I couldn't ignore the sliver of hope that Tobe's disbelief had given me—that maybe there was more to me than so-called magical mediocrity. After all, nobody wants to go through life labeled a Mediocre.

"Adley wants to do another Reading later on, anyway," Alton said. "We'll have to wait and see. In the meantime, however, Harley has been classified as a Mediocre and will be treated as such."

"What does that mean?" I asked, crossing my arms. I couldn't help but feel a little insulted.

"Limited access to magical knowledge. You'll learn about spells, but you won't be taught how to perform the powerful stuff. We don't want to risk getting you or others killed by mistake. Mediocrity doesn't mean literal weakness, but rather an inability to perform stronger spells without losing control over them," Alton replied, pressing his lips into a thin line.

I had to admit, there was a certain disharmony looming over their heads, as I looked at them. On one hand, the coven seemed nuts about its rules and regulations, and yet they couldn't keep their

Bestiary under control. One gargoyle alone could have killed a lot of people before getting captured again. I didn't even want to think what would happen if more of them got out.

At the same time, they were worried about me accidentally hurting or killing someone if I tried using a spell that was well above my Mediocre level. But it wasn't like I knew any spells, and I doubted I'd get to the big stuff within a month's time, anyway.

At first glance, the San Diego Coven came across as a bit of a bureaucratic nightmare, with very little of the mystical charm I'd expected to see in a place like this. Lots of rules and locks on glass boxes, sure—but not enough control over its most dangerous corners.

Despite the contradictions, I couldn't ignore my interest in this place. Even if it was just for a month, I was becoming more and more determined to make the most of my time here.

Soak it all up like the redheaded sponge that you are.

"Come, Tobe, it's time we go to the Main Assembly Hall," Alton said, and walked past me toward the exit at the far end of the aisle.

Tobe nodded and followed, and I stayed close behind him, once again marveling at his size and hybrid features. Any other person would've probably screamed and fainted by now, but there was something about Tobe that I found oddly comforting. It felt as though I was in the presence of an old friend.

"What do you want me to do, then?" I asked.

"You should attend as well," Alton replied, without turning to look at me. "You're a part of the coven, even if it's only for a trial period."

"For now," Tobe added with a half-smile, which looked kind of endearing and weird at the same time, on the face of a freaking lion.

"The matter of the Bestiary concerns you, too," Alton said. "Besides, it's time you meet some of the other magicals you'll be working with."

Ah, yes. Those magicals probably included the ones I'd seen in the living quarters. The way-too-cold platinum-haired guy, the girl with black curls and chocolate eyes… and Wade. Ugh, I was going to see Wade again. It had been so nice and calm and quiet since he'd left us.

I was curious, though. Particularly about the Bestiary issues. From what I'd understood and from what I could also feel from him, Alton was worried about the Mage Council, the big kahunas of the magicals, and their reaction to a gargoyle escaping from the Bestiary. I had a feeling that I'd get a lot more information from this meeting in the Main Assembly Hall.

A young coven trying to reform itself. A Bestiary that was simply too big and complicated to control. Alton had his hands full already. He certainly didn't need me to put up a fight and make things even more difficult for him.

Frankly, I didn't want that, either. The month trial was my best way forward—for now, at least.

Chapter Eleven

My brain was already overloaded with new information. As I set foot inside the Main Assembly Hall, however, I understood that a lot more was coming my way. Thankful that I'd yet to get the urge to turn around and just run away as fast as I could, I stayed close to Tobe and Alton as the gathering crowd parted before us.

The Hall was huge and rectangular, with more of the coven's signature dragon statues cast in bronze stretching between the marble floor and the high ceiling, flickering chandelier lights reflecting off their wings.

Flames burned bright in wall-mounted torches as a couple hundred witches and warlocks moved to the center, in front of a wide, circular podium. All eyes were on me, for some reason. I wasn't comfortable with all that attention, and it was becoming more and more difficult to shut out the flood of emotions chipping away at my self-control. All those people were looking at me, wondering what my presence there meant. I recognized the wariness, the suspicion, and, in some cases, the disdain. It was as if they didn't need another magical on the premises, an idea further cemented by an overall air of competition between them.

I recognized the looks they gave each other, the confident half-smiles and arrogant smirks. The athletes back in my high school did the same whenever a competition was about to begin.

Seven tall mirrors with frilly bronze frames were mounted on the floor at the back of the podium, their surfaces rippling as if liquid. Something told me those weren't regular mirrors.

Large paintings of various witches and warlocks—or so I thought, at first glance—were hung on the wall behind the podium. Judging by the clothing styles and brush strokes, they belonged to different periods, some going as far back as the 1100s and even earlier. Their eyes seemed to peer into my very soul, and I really didn't like that vibe, given what I was already experiencing as an Empath in a room full of people.

"Harley, I need you to stay by Wade's side for now, while I make some announcements," Alton told me, pointing at Wade, who was among the first people to reach the podium.

"We'll get to speak more afterward," Tobe said, giving me a soft smile. "I'm looking forward to getting to know you better."

There was something so sweet and heartwarming in the way he said that, it almost smothered my growing anxiety. That state of mind quickly dissipated, unfortunately, once I moved to stand next to Wade, whose forced wariness and struggled reserve were quick to get on my nerves.

I watched as Alton and Tobe went up the podium stairs, where a microphone mounted on a tall stand awaited, before looking at Wade, who gave me a rushed sideways glance and a brief nod. He was trying so hard not to pay attention to me, while his emotions screamed at me. I found it ironic, though—the more he tried to hide, the better I could read him, and the more noise it made in my head.

"You know, you can't really hide your emotions from me," I said, gritting my teeth, as I felt a migraine coming on. Wade's head snapped around, and he looked at me with raised eyebrows.

He's going to try and play it cool, just wait for it.

"I have no idea what you're talking about," he replied.

There it is.

"Are you serious?" I shot back. "Listen, the more you try to hide, the louder it gets in here," I explained, pointing at my head.

"How good is your… radar, anyway?" he murmured, his brow furrowed.

"Right now, it's off the charts because of all the people." I sighed. "I'm not good with crowds. They make me hypersensitive. And for some reason, the more you try to keep me out, the better I feel what you feel. And, Wade, it's okay to be wary of me. I totally get it. I'm still getting used to this ability, and I've never had to deal with people *knowing* that I can feel them. But you should just let it go. Whatever you're feeling, just feel it. I'm not going to pay attention, anyway. There are so many feelings going through me right now, I can barely focus."

He seemed to relax a little, and, as suspected, the avalanche of emotions coming from him seemed to fizzle down a bit. There were about two hundred souls left around me, each feeling something different, and not all of it was aimed at me. As I lost my spot at the center of their attention, other emotions came through.

They were all eager to find out what Alton had to say. Some were worried. At least forty of them were in love, half of their crushes currently in the room and just one third reciprocating. Ten were extremely tired, and two were confused and in desperate need of their families. I had a feeling the latter were new arrivals in the coven, too. The overall picture was exhausting, like hundreds of paint tubes simultaneously stepped on, the colors blobbing out in a tiresome mish-mash, spread across the canvas of my already-worn-out brain.

"They're exhausting, aren't they?" Wade said slowly, watching me as I took a few deep breaths.

"For lack of a better word, yeah," I said. "But it's a little better when they're not paying attention to me. They're like bullhorns, in a way. When they're pointed elsewhere, they're still loud, but tolerable. But when they're pointed at me, it's just… excruciating. Not sure that makes sense."

Wade shrugged. "It kind of does. I have to deal with them on a daily basis, so I can relate, sort of. Let's just say I understand what it's like when they *don't* pay attention to you."

I stifled a chuckle as Alton took center stage, tapping the microphone twice.

"Hi, hello, everyone!" He smiled, his voice echoing loud and clear throughout the assembly hall.

My gaze wandered around the place, and I was able to recognize some of the faces I'd already seen, including the chocolate-eyed girl and the platinum-haired guy, farther to my right. O'Halloran and other uniformed instructors were in the front row to my left, along with Adley de la Barthe and the preceptors, as well as a few other elder magicals I didn't recognize. Adley's gaze wandered across the room and settled on the platinum-haired guy for a second, enough for my heart to pound with something strong, akin to love. I'd felt it in others plenty of times; I could easily recognize the butterflies and the ache of longing. Whether the platinum-haired guy reciprocated those feelings or not was a mystery. Either way, not my business.

Tobe stood quietly behind Alton, his broad back reflected in three of the rippling mirrors.

The murmurs in the crowd died down as we all listened to what the director of the San Diego Coven had to say. I was still processing the fact that I was *inside a freaking coven*, surrounded by witches, warlocks, mythical monsters, and a ton of… well, a ton of magic.

"As mentioned in my message request to have you gather here at this hour, there have been some new and unexpected developments with the Bestiary," Alton said. "For the purpose of avoiding panic and unnecessary concern, however, we've held off on telling you all about what happened. Now that the problem is contained, it's time for you to know that seven days ago, one of the gargoyles in the Bestiary escaped."

He paused, allowing the collective gasp to rise from the crowd, and nodded at Wade, who straightened his back with beaming pride in response.

"Wade Crowley, one of our exceptional warlocks, was quick to go after the beast and return it safely to its glass box." Alton smiled, then looked at me, and I froze, almost hearing heads turn as people suddenly paid attention to me. "He had help from a new, yet unexpected member of our coven, whom you will all be introduced to shortly."

Oh, God.

In hindsight, I was thankful I didn't have any telepathic abilities —like hearing thoughts. Dealing with a tidal wave of emotions was one thing, but having my brain bombarded with a flurry of random words and thoughts? Ugh, I would've ended up hospitalized and heavily medicated for sure.

"I want you all to be more vigilant, going forward," Alton continued, drawing the audience's focus back to him.

Only as I let out the nervous breath I'd been holding did I realize that I'd gripped Wade's hand, squeezing tight for some kind of comfort. I looked down, getting visual confirmation of our unexpected physical contact, then up at him. Though his expression remained stoic, he was shocked. I could feel it.

When did I take his hand, though? Did I just black out when they all looked at me, or something?

"Sorry," I murmured, instantly letting go. My palms were clammy. I rubbed them against my jeans and focused on Alton once more.

"We've added a security detail to the Bestiary in order to assist Tobe," Alton said, "but we have yet to identify how the gargoyle got out in the first place. Tobe's magical abilities are raw, and, frankly, it is up to all of us to ensure that further incidents do not occur. If they do, I trust you all know what to do, as you've all been given your full Bestiary induction."

The magicals in the crowd nodded in response, prompting Alton to smile and bring his hands together in an enthusiastic clap.

"Now! I know we're all still getting used to the idea of a Bestiary in our coven, but it is for the greater good. Given the high percentage of Mediocrity in this place, we can at least excel at looking after the Bestiary that fuels our entire society," he added.

"Yeah, it's a bang-up job we're doing so far," a young warlock said, somewhere behind me.

I looked over my shoulder and identified him quickly, based on the smirk which accompanied his statement. He was about as tall as me, and quite handsome, too, with short black hair and piercing blue eyes. He had the cutest dimples, and that triggered a warning inside me—the good-looking ones were usually jerks. *Case in point: Wade Crowley.*

"That's Garrett Kyteler, pompous jerk extraordinaire," Wade muttered, following my gaze. "If ever you need a contrarian to paint the coven in an ugly light, he's the guy you want to talk to."

"I don't know, you seem to be doing a pretty good job yourself, if you ask me," I replied. He took it seriously, and I felt he was genuinely offended. For some reason, I didn't like making him feel that way, so I quickly brushed over it, shifting the focus back to cutie-pie Garrett. "If he hates this place so much, why doesn't he just leave, then?"

Wade shrugged. "He doesn't hate it. He just doesn't like it."

"Is there a difference?"

"There is when you're part of a coven," he replied. "He's been in two other covens before this. I don't know how he ended up here, but it wasn't because of his exemplary track record. He's an excellent warlock, highly skilled in his craft, but his demeanor can be difficult to handle. He messed up something at some point. You don't get sent to the San Diego Coven for high points."

"What points? And how come this coven is like detention to magicals?" I asked, getting more confused the more Wade talked.

"I'm guessing Alton hasn't told you about the point system. You'll find out soon enough, but, in short, your performance and actions create points, which go into the coven. At the end of the year, a line is drawn, and the top five performing covens in the States get substantial prizes, mostly in cash and artifacts. As for the 'detention' part… I don't know, it's always been like this. Alton is trying to change that, but with the characters we've got in-house right now, it doesn't look like he'll succeed."

Alton was still going on about their efforts to improve the coven when Garrett spoke up again.

"With all the Mediocres in this joint, I must say, you're quite the dreamer, Director Waterhouse."

Alton responded to Garrett's remark with a dry smile and a shrug. "Well, then, Mr. Kyteler, perhaps if you spent more time actively involved in actual coven work instead of bragging to your parents over Skype about how good a job you're doing here, we might get ahead a little faster." Alton's sting was deep and painful.

Chuckles erupted from the crowd. I got a quick look at Garrett —he was fuming, but there was nothing he could do, other than cross his arms and scowl at Alton. I had mixed feelings about Garrett at that point. On one hand, the more I looked at him, the more handsome he got. Given how little socializing I'd done in my lifetime, and now that I was suddenly faced with people with whom I could be myself, my hormones were starting to loosen up a little. On the other hand, he seemed obnoxiously arrogant, although the animosity that Wade displayed toward him made Garrett even more interesting. I was officially intrigued and abstaining from a final verdict—other than the fact that he was really cute—for the time being.

"Don't sulk, Mr. Kyteler," Alton continued. "I wouldn't pick on you if I didn't think you have what it takes to be a top performer in this coven. You just have to put in the effort, that's all. Anyway, moving on. Like I said, we're hoping to get a higher score by the end of this year. Last year was quite… dismal, to say the least."

"We only got 203 points," Wade whispered.

"How bad is that?" I replied.

"The San Francisco Coven took the fifth spot with 9,789 points."

"Oh. Okay."

Clearly, the San Diego Coven had its work cut out for it. But was it worth it? How much money were we talking about? What artifacts were handed out as prizes? I made more mental notes to ask Alton later. My skull was becoming a pile of index cards and sticky notes.

"The Bestiary has been checked from top to bottom, and there was nothing on the cameras," Alton said. "So, please, all of you, be careful. Unauthorized access to the Bestiary will be severely punished."

"I do apologize," Tobe said, staring at the marble floor beneath him, his head bowed in what felt like shame. "This has never happened before. The Bestiary has always been fully secured. I've never even needed additional security."

"Tobe, please," Alton said gently, placing a hand on his shoulder. "Do not blame yourself in any way. We don't know how the gargoyle made it out of its glass box, but we will find out, sooner or later. In the meantime, we just need to be more vigilant. We'll be deploying a few patrols through the city, as well, particularly where the gargoyle was captured. The creature is likely to have left energy residue in the area. Other monsters still running loose might be drawn to it, which would bode well for our Bestiary. The more creatures we capture, the more energy is provided to our covens, and, of course, the more points for us."

"I'll post a list of names for patrol rotations by midnight, tonight, outside the dining hall," O'Halloran interjected. "There will be short, three-hour shifts, in pairs, in allocated districts of the city. Nothing too difficult. Just make sure you stock up on glass jars."

"That being said, I will let you know of any future developments," Alton said, then smiled at me. "Now, I want you all to meet Harley Smith, who was quick-witted and brave enough to assist Wade in capturing the gargoyle."

Oh, crap, no!

As soon as he mentioned my name, my body was nearly crushed under the landslide of emotions pummeling me from all sides. I instinctively grabbed Wade's forearm and immediately chastised myself for it, but it was the only thing I could think of. The harder I squeezed, the less intense the emotions of two hundred magicals felt. This was all so new and... heavy.

"Ouch," Wade issued a low-voiced warning.

"Sorry," I murmured, but didn't let go. Instead, I squeezed harder, overwhelmed by so many feelings at once.

"Harley will be with us for the next month, and she'll be attending classes with the juniors," Alton added. "Given her late discovery, Harley is quite far behind, but I trust she will—"

The mirrors behind him and Tobe all started to hum, their surfaces rippling more visibly and their bronze frames squeaking at the joints. The crowd forgot about me as they all looked at the mirrors, along with Alton and Tobe, who moved farther to the side.

I gasped, finally able to properly breathe again.

"Oh, man, I need to tell Alton not to mention me to people anymore—or ever again—especially in a crowd," I muttered, then wiped the sweat off my forehead, letting go of Wade's arm. I got a peculiar whiff of disappointment from him, before the hum got louder, reminding me that something weird was going on with those mirrors.

"What's happening?" I asked.

"Someone is coming through," Wade replied.

"Is that normal?"

"Normal, yes. But it's usually expected. This wasn't scheduled."

"How do you know?" I asked.

"Because Alton clearly wasn't expecting it, as evidenced by the look on his face," Wade grumbled, prompting me to get a better look at Alton.

He was right. Alton was stunned, and not in a good way.

Chapter Twelve

"So, you people just… what, travel through mirrors? Like parallel dimensions or something?" I asked. I'd stopped wondering how weird things happened from the moment I accidentally tossed my first-grade nemesis across the road with just the power of my mind. I was more interested in the actual process.

"You're not too far from the truth, actually," Wade said. "The coven is in an interdimensional pocket, like a strip between blobs of space. But the strip is infinite, and you can sort of poke it in different places. Think of our world as a giant bag of… blobs, bundled and glued together with this interdimensional strip. The mirrors are like holes in different blobs. You step into one, and you pass through the strip, then make it out into another blob."

"Like teleporting."

"Except you don't get disintegrated and reintegrated upon arrival to your destination," Wade replied. "Mirror travel only works with a particular spell and if you know your destination. And any mirror will work. It's an old spell, conjured up by ancient Egyptian warlocks. They were the first to discover the magical properties of reflective surfaces."

I nodded slowly, watching in awe as three figures slowly emerged from the mirrors, like bodies coming up to the surface of a mercurial lake. Two warlocks and one witch came forward, all three in their late thirties or forties, and superbly dressed. Had this not been a magical gathering, I could've easily seen them sauntering down a runway for custom, tailor-made outfits—with a predominance of dark blues and gold, as they all seemed to adhere to a similar color palette.

"Are those uniforms?" I whispered, taking in every detail, every crease and hand-crafted button, every thread and shimmering lapel. The warlocks were in full suits, complete with waistcoats and ascots, while the witch had opted for an elegant skirt-and-jacket combo.

"You could call them uniforms," Wade replied, his voice filled with tension. "Navy blue and gold are the colors of the California Mage Council. They tend to wear them when they attend assemblies such as this."

"Oh, this is the Mage Council," I murmured.

"Part of it, yes. There are seven members, but, as you can see, only three came to visit this time around."

"So we weren't expecting them?"

"Nope. Which is why I'm a little concerned."

"Yeah, I can feel that," I replied.

"And that's creepy," he shot back.

"You'd better get used to it." I shrugged in response. "Who are these Mages, exactly?"

As Wade pointed them out to me, I couldn't ignore Alton's displeasure at seeing them here. They made him uncomfortable, for some reason. Putting two and two together, I figured this unannounced visit had something to do with the gargoyle getting out of the Bestiary.

"That's Leonidas Levi, the deciding vote in most Council-related conversations, and one of the most powerful warlocks I've ever met," Wade said, nodding toward the eldest of the group, a tall man with salt-and-pepper hair and dark brown, almost black eyes. My gaze wandered to his ring, a solid gold piece with a multitude of gemstones that glistened under the amber light. "The other is Nicholas Mephiles, revered alchemist and one of the very few to achieve transmutation of stone to gold," Wade continued, pointing at the short and stocky warlock, whose waistcoat looked a size too small and whose reddish beard covered a double chin.

"So, what, a genius?"

Wade nodded slowly. "You could say that, yes. Creating gold out of stone takes very precise formulation and time, and a lot of power. He singlehandedly funds the Sacramento Coven, and I think there are at least ten gargoyles in our Bestiary that came out of his Purges."

"Ah. The price paid for gold, right?" I concluded.

"Exactly. Everything costs with Chaos," Wade said. "And that's Imogene Whitehall."

Imogene had my full attention. She reminded me of a fairytale elf, with delicate, diaphanous skin, sky-blue eyes that felt eerily familiar, and a cascade of pale blonde, almost white hair that poured over her back and shoulders. She was tall and graceful, with soft features and the warmest smile I'd ever seen, directed at me. *Crap, she's looking at me.*

I'd quickly learned to dislike the attention in that assembly hall, but Imogene felt… quiet. The emotions coming off her were unclear, at best. I found that relieving and intriguing at the same time. She gave me a brief nod, then shifted her focus to Alton, who stepped forward to address the Council.

"What's the deal with Imogene?" I asked, looking at Wade. I was surprised to see and feel him like that—he was in sheer awe of her, as if gazing upon a star. His reaction seemed perfectly understandable, given that she was by far one of the most beautiful and surreal creatures I'd ever come across. Wade had every right to crush on her. She'd chosen a simple pencil skirt and smart jacket, with a gold-threaded vest and white shirt, diamonds dangling from her delicate earlobes and matching the tear-shaped pendant resting in the dip between her neck and collarbones. And it all looked perfect on her. Sculptors and painters of the Renaissance period would've killed to have her as a model.

"Isn't it obvious? She's perfect," he mumbled, blatantly fawning over her. It quickly got irritating for me to watch, so I saved additional questions for later. Preferably when Imogene was far away and out of his line of sight.

"Imogene, Nicholas, Leonidas," Alton said, nodding at the Council as they took center stage. "What brings you all here today?"

"I wish we didn't have to do this, Alton," Imogene replied, her voice as sweet and soft as the rest of her. A few more minutes of her and I would've wound up swooning like Wade.

"But we must," Leonidas added, in a sharp, dark contrast. "The gargoyle incident came to our attention, and we are here to deliver a stern warning."

"It's taken care of, though." Alton shook his head, frowning. "No one was injured. The beast was recovered and is now back in the Bestiary. There was no need for the Mage Council to come all the way here for that."

"That's where you're wrong," Leonidas replied. "This is completely unprecedented, and, frankly, it's unacceptable. No monster has ever escaped the Bestiary before, and it is cause for grave concern."

There was a certain gravitas in Leonidas's voice that didn't match the honey-like sweetness of his Persian accent. He'd probably been in the States for a long time, his English almost fully set in, but his roots still crept up, particularly in the weight he placed on certain consonants. One of my earlier foster parents was Iranian by birth, and I could recognize those inflections anywhere.

"Like I said, we have it under control," Alton insisted, and I could feel his discomfort stiffening my joints. He *really* didn't like Leonidas.

"We know, and we're pleased to see the Bestiary otherwise well managed here." Imogene smiled, then put on a pained expression. "But that doesn't change the fact that a monster escaped. We cannot let that slide without repercussions, I'm afraid."

"The San Diego Coven is thus stripped of fifty points," Leonidas announced, prompting the crowd to gasp and murmur in response. An overall air of discontentment filled me, by default. "Should further such incidents occur, the California Mage Council will submit an unfavorable review on the San Diego Coven, directly to the United Covens of America. You've already got slim chances of earning a decent score this year, Alton. Don't make it any worse."

"And the penalties will be much more severe if other monsters get out," Nicholas added, his double chin high and his brow furrowed. "The Bestiary is our most prized possession, and it is our most dangerous, too. We can't afford any more mistakes. The San Diego Coven may have been randomly selected to manage it, but, Alton, you had a chance to turn down the nomination. Instead, you assumed full responsibility. It's not a zoo, and Tobe here is not the caretaker. Death and destruction will swallow this earth if the Bestiary is ever let loose. We need you all to pay attention."

"That won't be the case, I can assure you!" Alton shot back, standing on the verge of fury at that point and doing his best to hold it all back. His hands balled into fists, his knuckles turning white. "Consider your stern warning received and registered. Is that all?"

"You've been here for, what, three years?" Leonidas replied snidely, raising an eyebrow. I had to admit, I wasn't fond of the guy, either.

Alton nodded. "That is correct."

"You don't have much to show for it, Waterhouse. Get your house in order, and don't become another Halifax," Leonidas said. "We're serious. Don't screw this up. We'll be paying extra attention to the San Diego Coven from now on."

I couldn't ignore the chill running down my spine. The California Mage Council made me feel… wary. Apart from Imogene, who seemed genuinely nice. The other two had their noses so high, they were probably frosted. I could only imagine what the other four were like. Elitism seemed like a defining feature for them, and after my brief stint in a California prep school, I just didn't want more of *that*.

We were all made of the same stuff. Blood ran through our veins. We ate, we breathed, and we all certainly pooped. One's riches should never be a standard for some kind of superiority, and I sincerely loathed anyone who tried to perpetrate that idea—particularly in the 21st century, in the age of smartphones and social media, the era of fights for equality and decency. History was meant to serve as a lesson, not a guideline. Errors were meant to be recorded and later avoided, not repeated. Elitism raised the masses once, to the point where the people got angry and toppled entire monarchies. Had we really learned nothing?

Alton was boiling. The mention of Halifax seemed to make a little vein pop in his temple. I could see it throbbing from where I stood.

"Who's Halifax?" I asked Wade, who was nervous and concerned. The Mage Council and the mention of the United Covens of America seemed to hit a nerve in him, too.

"The previous director of the San Diego Coven," Wade muttered. "A useless slob. Always took the easy way out and hammered us all into Mediocrity. He was more focused on setting a little fortune aside to buy a farm somewhere in the Midwest than on helping magicals strive to achieve more, and better."

"Did he get his farm, then?"

"He was penalized a fortune and fired for utter incompetence, then Alton was brought in," Wade said. "Last time I heard, Halifax was back on the East Coast, working three jobs to cover his mortgage. No coven wanted him after the San Diego debacle. They agreed to let him live as a rogue, but he's under constant monitoring."

"Will that be all, then?" Alton repeated, gritting his teeth.

Leonidas narrowed his eyes at him, and they glared at each other for what felt like an eternity. But then Leonidas chuckled and walked back through the mirror without another word. The others followed, and they all disappeared beyond the silvery ripples of the mirrors, leaving a very annoyed Alton behind.

"I'm pretty sure we closed it up nice and tight, this time," Alton said, mostly to himself.

"I promise I will be more vigilant." Tobe sighed, his massive shoulders dropping.

"There's only so much *you* can do, Tobe." Alton shook his head. "You're there all the time, and you do an exemplary job of keeping the monsters in their place. It's up to us to offer assistance. We'll just need to draw up a good plan to avoid another Council visit. Levi seems eager to see us burn."

This Bestiary issue sounded a lot worse now. After all, the California Mage Council had felt it necessary to step in and issue a warning. It wasn't just the danger that it posed to the outside world; judging by how concerned the San Diego Coven magicals felt, they were seriously worried about the financial and regulatory repercussions.

From what I'd learned so far, Halifax had already done a lot of damage, which Alton was trying hard to undo, while looking after the Bestiary with Tobe. They simply couldn't afford any more mistakes. The worst part was that they had yet to figure out how the gargoyle had escaped in the first place, and I didn't know enough about whatever magic and technologies were used in the Bestiary to form an opinion.

All I could do was feel the weight of their worry as the entire coven feared for their standing in the magical world, their funding, and their safety, as well as that of the billions of humans who stood to suffer and die if the Bestiary was ever set loose.

Chapter Thirteen

The crowd grew noisy around me, their restlessness bursting through me with knee-shattering vertigo and way too much anxiety for me to handle. Wade seemed to notice, and discreetly wrapped his fingers around my forearm, squeezing gently, while Alton raised his voice to calm everybody down.

"Take it easy," Wade said, his voice low and strangely soothing.

"Everybody, please be quiet," Alton shouted. "There is no reason to worry, or to panic! We'll simply have to take additional measures so we can keep everything under control, that's all."

"How do you propose we do that?" one of the magicals asked, her sultry tone echoing from the other end of the assembly hall.

"Focus on Alton," Wade whispered in my ear. My skin tickled, and instead of doing as he suggested, I instinctively focused on him. Right then, he was radiating calmness and reassurance. He was the closest thing I had to an anchor that could keep me from spiraling into panic.

"We'll put together two teams," Alton explained, then moved toward the edge of the podium. "One to further investigate the Bestiary, and one to do an extensive follow-up cleaning in the affected areas of the city, particularly where the gargoyle was active. Like I said, chances are there might be some monster activity wherever the creature left energy residue. The investigation team will work closely with Preceptor Nomura and Tobe to look into the Bestiary and check every single glass box, every charm, every spell, and every lock in that place. If needed, Preceptor Bellmore will be more than happy to assist."

Judging by the look on Sloane's face, she wasn't all *that* happy, probably because she didn't like people, in general. *My kindred spirit.* Wade sensed my gradual relaxation and let go of my arm. I was thankful that the crowd's emotions came in waves—or maybe my body had some kind of defense mechanism, automatically shutting them out, just to give me a few minutes' worth of breathing room. I wasn't sure how to control my Empath skills within big crowds just yet. Sweat trickled down my temples and neck as I inhaled deeply and regained my composure.

"If you're a good girl, I might even recommend you for the investigative team," Wade muttered, and I noticed a smirk stretching his lips. "Given your newbie status, Alton will want you on the cleanup team, to start you off easy. But that's lower-level stuff, for Mediocres and below."

I raised an eyebrow. "I *am* a Mediocre."

"And you're just going to be okay with that?" he asked.

He had a point. Being labeled a Mediocre didn't mean I couldn't try to do better.

"So, what, does that mean you get the lead in the investigative team, and I'm supposed to be nice to you if I want to get in, too?" I replied.

"That's the way the cookie crumbles, Harley," Wade said. "I'm the best at what I do. Of course I'll lead."

"Garrett Kyteler, I'll give you a shot at leading the investigative team," Alton said. I glanced behind me and saw Garrett beaming with satisfaction, then giving Wade one of the most arrogant smirks

I'd ever witnessed. *Cute, but damn, gives me the urge to punch him.* "It's time you make something of yourself in this place."

"Wait, what?" Wade blurted, his eyes wide as the shock settled on his face. "How... Why him? He's an arrogant idiot with no respect for authority and something bad to say about absolutely everything and everyone!"

"And does your offensive description of a fellow magical make you worthier of the position?" Alton replied, pursing his lips. "Besides, Garrett is an exceptional warlock, with great intuition and a set of skills that will most certainly come in handy in this endeavor. And it's time for him to shine. I believe he's already paid his dues for his bad mouth in previous covens, despite his earlier slip-ups. He deserves a chance."

Wade blinked several times, struggling to find the right words to express his outrage. I could barely stifle a chuckle at the sight of his dismay. "It's not fair! I'm far more equipped, and I'm an actual professional, unlike him! I don't care what his skills are. He's done nothing but piss you off since he first set foot in this coven!"

"And right now, *you're* the one pissing me off," Alton retorted. "I'm putting you in charge of cleanup, then."

Wade gasped, his mouth wide open. He would probably have an aneurysm if someone handed him a broom in that moment. I instinctively looked around for one, just to mess with him, until I realized that my chances of getting onto the investigative team had dropped below zero, without Wade's recommendation.

But do I really want that? Do I even want to be involved?

I kind of did. There was nothing good about monsters being let loose in the city. It put Ryann and her parents at risk, not to mention Father Thomas, from the orphanage, and Malcolm, and another handful of people I didn't completely dislike. Innocent lives were at risk, and, for the first time, I felt like I could actually do something about that.

"Hah, Crowley's got the Rag Team." Garrett chuckled, then

walked toward the podium, the crowd parting before him. He passed by us, and gave me a brief sideways glance and a wink—what was that about? It looked flirtatious, but I wasn't getting any emotions from him. I now counted five people I couldn't read: Garrett, O'Halloran, Bellmore, the platinum-haired guy, and Imogene Whitehall. As I scanned the crowd, I noticed there were others whom I couldn't feel. Not many, but still, enough to confirm that my Empathy didn't work with absolutely everyone. I saved the question of why for later.

"What can I say, Crowley? I really am *very* good at what I do, and, as much as it probably kills you to admit it, you know it, too, deep down. Despite my premature departure from my previous covens, I *was* the top scorer there," Garrett added, mocking Wade. "You should stick to what you're good at. You know, lighting up candles and being the rule-abiding goodie two-shoes nobody likes. It suits you better."

Based on the confidence exuding from his tone, and the frustration boiling through Wade, Garrett was telling the truth. His verbal stings were just a façade for his grand warlock skills. Several warlocks and witches chuckled, including the platinum-haired guy, whose eyes glimmered with blue, hateful fires. He definitely didn't like Wade. The brief glance he gave me announced that he wasn't too fond of me, either.

"I suggest you tone it down, Kyteler," Alton interjected, prompting Garrett to abandon that smug grin. "I'm giving you a chance here. Don't blow it. Focus on your talents, not your personal dislike of certain highly skilled magicals in this coven. Now, get your team in place. I trust you'll pick capable people to work with."

"Oh, yeah, absolutely. My apologies, Director Waterhouse." Garrett nodded, then pointed at the platinum-haired guy. "Finch Anker, you're with me."

I had a name for the guy, at last. He was pleased with the nomination, smiling as he advanced through the crowd and joined Garrett, Alton, and Tobe on the podium. Garrett then pointed at five more magicals behind us, inviting them onto his team. "Rowena

Sparks, Lincoln Mont-Noir, Poe Dexter, Ruby Presley, and Niklas Jones. Time to show whoever's messing with our Bestiary what we're made of," Garrett announced.

"I do appreciate the enthusiasm, but you're investigating the Bestiary, not leading an assault on the ancient Kingdom of Troy," Alton said, smiling. "However, you've done well with your choice of teammates. Thank you for not making me already regret this decision." He chuckled, then switched back to his more serious self. "You'll now be liaising with Nomura and Tobe on the next steps, and you'll be reporting to me on a daily basis. Are we clear?"

They all nodded while doing secret high fives. They were all young, in their twenties, with a shared taste for smart jackets and starchy cream pants—like snotty Ivy League undergrads with magical abilities. Briefly reminded of the obnoxious characters I'd dealt with back in prep school, I shifted my focus back to Wade, who was watching the whole scene unfold like a horror movie. He seemed seconds away from a heartfelt bellow of pure rage. A feeling of helplessness poisoned me—it was Wade's, as he watched what I assumed to be a coveted position get occupied by someone whom he considered unworthy.

It'll be a constant battle of the egos in this place.

"As for the cleanup team—"

"You mean the Rag Team," Garrett interrupted Alton, who rolled his eyes and snapped his fingers. Garrett's lips were forcibly pressed into a thin line, his eyes nearly popping out from shock. He tried to open his mouth, but couldn't. Alton had magically shut him up.

"As for the cleanup team, Wade, come up here and choose the people you want to work with," Alton continued, undisturbed, while Garrett boiled at his side.

Wade let out a sigh, and I couldn't help but chuckle. Alton quickly spotted my reaction and raised an eyebrow in response, as Wade joined him on the podium with a defeated look on his face.

"Congratulations, Wade, I just found you your first team

member," Alton announced, patting Wade on the shoulder. "Harley Smith, come up here. It's time to start your practical induction."

Ah, crap.

All eyes were on me, a flurry of emotions pummeling me again. After a couple of deep breaths, I slowly made my way up onto the podium, focusing on counting my steps, in a desperate attempt not to let myself be overrun by the feelings of two hundred magicals. Amusement flickered in most of them, as I was another example of how karma worked—you only get as good as you give. I shouldn't have taken such amusement in Wade's misery.

"Deep breaths," Wade whispered, then searched the crowd for certain faces.

Even after I'd laughed at him, he was still nice enough to try and comfort me, knowing how overwhelmed I was in that moment, as an Empath. I was confused. Wade seemed to have achieved the perfect balance between being a smug jerk and a kind, supportive friend. *So confused right now.*

"Santana Catemaco," Wade said, nodding at the girl with curly black hair and chocolate-brown eyes I'd seen earlier in the living quarters. He briefly explained his choice to me, while the crowd murmured, and Santana made her way to the podium. "Santana is a Santeria practitioner. She's quite antisocial because of how most magicals view the Santeria culture, but she's fierce and rather easy to work with."

"*You* find her easy to work with," Alton said under his breath. "Personally, I'm glad you chose her. It'll keep her busy enough to not bicker with the other magicals."

"Wait, Santeria… Like dead chickens and blood and all that creepy stuff?" I asked, trying to dig through the memories of what I'd read on the subject during my long hours of Internet research.

"That's not what Santeria is about," Santana replied as she joined us on the podium. "You're too green and gullible to understand the intricacies of Santeria. These magicals love using the humans' fictional lore to taunt me, but you'll soon learn what it's all about.

They laugh now, but they all grovel when they realize they need my help to free people from *brujeria* curses."

I caught her subtle Mexican accent, along with a subtle sense of irritation. She was frequently misjudged and sort of used to it, from what I could tell, but it didn't mean she liked it.

"It's true," Wade murmured. "She's one of the few Santeria practitioners in California, and most of them are—"

"Bad *hombres*," Santana said, taking her place next to Wade and me. She gave me a subtle nudge. "Don't worry, newbie. It might not look like it now, but you're better off on the Rag Team than with those mouth-breathers," she said, nodding at Garrett and his team, who were sneering at us. I was tempted to agree with her.

"Tatyana Vasilis!" Wade called out, squinting at the crowd as he looked for her. Soon enough, a tall and slender figure with long, pale blonde hair and icy blue eyes emerged, walking toward the podium. She was gorgeous, with all the cover-girl features, including the perfectly glossed lips and impeccable sense of fashion. Based on the style of her jeans and iridescent silk shirt, she was into the high-end brands.

"Her parents run the Moscow Coven together," Santana explained, slightly amused. "Don't let her fabulous looks scare you. She's a misfit like the rest of us. Terrible people skills, loves drilling holes into Alton's patience. She's new here, too, by the way."

"And you?" I asked, unable to take my eyes off Tatyana as she glided onto the podium with a slightly dissatisfied expression.

"Six months." Santana shrugged. "I bet Wade will use newbies for the Rag Team. We need to be given some magical stuff to do anyway, and the other departments aren't all that keen to work with us."

"Why not?" I replied, trying to understand what stigmas hung over their heads.

"Because we're very adept at telling people the uncomfortable truth, including what we think about them." Tatyana joined the conversation, her Slavic accent making her stand out even more.

"Californians are too politically correct for my taste, but I think we'll break them in by the end of the decade. Especially the ones who are so insecure and frustrated that they pick on witches they simply can't handle."

Both Tatyana and Santana chuckled as they glanced at Garrett and his team, who didn't look happy to see what the Rag Team was becoming. I couldn't feel Garrett or Finch, but the others were definitely uncomfortable. There was history between these seemingly opposite sides, but neither came across as part of a classic "good versus bad" formula, but rather "unsociable misfits versus smug, preppy jerks."

"Dylan Blight." Wade continued with his selections. "Get over here. You're new, too. You need some practice."

Dylan didn't look like he belonged there. He seemed like the typical all-American heartthrob, with plenty of muscles beneath his red-and-cream varsity football jacket, short brown hair, caramel eyes, and a cleft chin that further made the overall image of him *scream* "mundane." He belonged on a football field, not in a coven—or, at least, that was my first impression.

"He's been here a couple of months, like Tatyana," Santana told me, as we watched him make his way through the crowd to join us. "Comes across as a good guy. Too good, if you ask me. Garrett keeps trying to get him on his side, but the boy prefers football and his human friends. He'll take some time to assimilate."

Ah, another kindred spirit! At least I wasn't the only one trying to ease into this whole magical business.

Dylan gave us a broad smile, then stood next to Tatyana, whom he couldn't seem to take his eyes off, until she gave him a brief glance and he instantly looked away—he liked her. She made him nervous, I could feel it. Other than that, there was just a consistent conflict brewing inside him, something I'd experienced myself when trying to reconcile my abilities with the human world I'd been raised into.

"Raffe Levi! Get up here, brother!" Wade called out.

A tall, wiry dude with olive skin, short black hair, and the most peculiar dark, gray-blue eyes stepped forward. His last name sounded familiar, and his features echoed someone I'd seen before, too. "He looks familiar," I said.

"He's Leonidas Levi's son," Wade replied.

"Oh." Who could forget the overly pompous and mean Leonidas, the "deciding vote" in the California Mage Council?

"He's nothing like his father," Wade said, as if reading my mind. "He's different."

Raffe smiled and shook his hand, and I realized that Wade was absolutely right. Raffe *was* different, in more than one way. On the outside, he seemed peaceful, calm, and sweet. On the inside, however, I could feel the eye of a dark storm, a hundred varieties of rage and malice whirling through him, all of which he kept to himself, desperate not to affect anyone.

He didn't come across as… evil, but there was something unsettling beneath that kind expression. Even more interesting was the look on his face, particularly when our eyes met for the first time. He stared at me, and he knew. I could feel that he knew exactly what I was. He was aware that I could feel him.

"The Rag Team is better than no magical work at all. Thanks, Wade," Raffe said.

"Any time, man," Wade replied, patting him on the shoulder, visibly thrilled to have Raffe on board. I could feel the bond between them, too. They were close friends, a fact also confirmed by Santana.

"Raffe has a troubled history with his father," she explained, keeping her voice low. "He was sent here about three years ago as a form of punishment, but it doesn't look like the Levi clan will take him back anytime soon. Which is cool. We like him better here, surrounded by people who actually care about him."

There was something in the way she spoke that left room for follow-up questions, but I saved them for later, as Wade called out to one more team member. "Astrid Hepler!"

"Oh, this is going to be fun." Santana chuckled.

A young African-American girl came forward. Her brown eyes had specks of emerald green, and her hair was a medium curly Afro. She pushed her black-rimmed glasses up the blade of her nose with one finger, then stepped up on the podium, giving Wade a brief nod before she moved to our side.

"Hi, I'm Astrid." She beamed at me, and I couldn't help but smile back. She was full of light and warmth, just like Ryann, and I was relieved to be able to focus on her emotions, instead of the crowd before us. It dawned on me then that, as long as I had someone as an anchor, I could focus enough to get by without losing my mind between so many people in one room.

"Harley. Nice to meet you," I replied, and we shook hands.

"Astrid here is human," Santana said with a wink.

"I thought we're supposed to keep our magic away from them," I said, confused.

"Astrid is special," Santana replied. "She's been with the coven for a while, helping on the IT side, mostly. She also serves as a bridge between us and the human authorities."

"I'm the perfect witness in cases of unexplained phenomena." Astrid giggled.

"Keep her out of trouble, Wade," Alton said, a frown drawing a shadow between his eyebrows. "She had enough excitement during her last mission."

"We're doing cleanup. That'll be, what? Scrapping CCTV footage, wiping any memories that weren't cleaned after the gargoyle incidents, and clearing out whatever slipped through the cracks since." Wade shrugged. "It doesn't get more uneventful than that."

"You'll also be looking out for monster activity. I told you, keep an eye out for energy residue," Alton said, crossing his arms. He was concerned about Astrid. I figured she'd helped the coven a lot, for them to let her work here when they were all so fearful of human discovery.

"I'll pack the scanners, then, no biggie!" Astrid quipped. "I'm just happy to get out in the field again."

"I'm not comfortable with that," Alton grumbled. There was something endearing about him, reminding me of Mr. Smith after I got my driver's license. He wasn't comfortable with letting me drive on my own, either.

"Don't worry, Alton," Santana said. "We'll take good care of her."

"You're a terrible influence, in general, but I do appreciate your survival skills," Alton replied, jokingly. "Just bring her back alive."

Finch, Garrett, and the others on their team were standing next to him. They heard everything, while exchanging amused glances and the occasional mean joke.

"Bunch of bleeding hearts," Finch snapped at us. "No wonder you're stuck on the Rag Team. And no wonder we've had low ratings compared to other covens. Less *feelings*, more magic. Let's be professional about things, okay?"

Ugh, the platinum hair and piercing blue eyes didn't work too well with that sneer on Finch's face. He irked me to unexpectedly high levels. "How old are you, Finch?" I asked him, as innocently as possible.

"What business is that of yours?" he shot back, scowling at me. I had a feeling he just didn't like new people, in general.

Why the hate, though? What did I ever do to this boy?

"Because you sound like a whiny five-year-old who doesn't like his new kindergarten, and you're starting to get on my nerves," I spat. "I thought this was a coven, not the Kid City next door."

I heard chuckling around me and from the crowd below, but I couldn't tear my eyes off Finch. He looked as though he was about to do something stupid, and I never looked away from an aggressive fiend. He reminded me too much of the foster dad whose name I chose to forget—the root of many nightmares and the reason behind some of the scars on my back.

"Sounds like Finch just found another witch who won't put up with his nonsense." Garrett chuckled, putting his arm over Finch's shoulders.

"I suggest you and Wade take your teams elsewhere, and start planning your missions," Alton replied to Garrett. "Play nice and report back to me by the end of the day. You've got the rest of the afternoon to work out your roles and responsibilities. Preceptor Nomura and Tobe will answer any questions you might have. Magicals, dismissed!"

The crowd instantly scattered out of the Main Assembly Hall, while Garrett took Finch and the rest of his team off the podium. "Come on, let's go get our ducks in a row. Need to get those fifty points back, and more on top!" Garrett said, then glanced over his shoulder and gave me another wink.

Seriously, is he flirting or what?

One by one, the plethora of foreign emotions fizzled out of me, and my new team came into full focus. Wade was frustrated with the cleanup job but satisfied with his choice of team members—until his gaze found mine. He wasn't too sure about me yet, but hey, I had to give him the benefit of the doubt, since he didn't know me at all. Frankly, I wasn't sure how useful I'd be in this place, but I had to at least try and find out.

Santana and Tatyana seemed slightly amused. I had a feeling they'd been through similar gigs before, which made them interesting to follow, going forward. Dylan was stuck in limbo, somewhere between longing and excited, probably still adjusting to life as a magical. Raffe was thankful, mostly to have Wade by his side. And Astrid was psyched and eager to get started.

Alton was worried, on the other hand. The Council's visit had taken its toll on him, and I could literally feel how much was at stake—Alton was terrified of failure of any kind. It made his blood run cold, and, by the rules of Empathic proximity, mine too.

But what was I really feeling in that moment? If I peeled away at the layers of emotions from the magicals that I'd surrounded myself with, what did I think of all this?

Well, for starters, there was a little voice in the back of my head, telling me that things were about to get even weirder, though I wasn't exactly sure how or why. But my instincts never betrayed me, and I was never short on ominous feelings.

I was embarking on a new journey, with people I barely knew but with whom I shared a primordial bond of Chaos. It was strange and scary, but it also gave me some much-needed perspective on who I was and, most importantly, who I wanted to be.

Chapter Fourteen

"I can't believe they're making me quit my job," I complained, as I filled out an application form for a research assistant position in the Fleet Science Center's Library and Archives section.

Shortly after the Main Assembly Hall had been cleared, Wade and the rest of our newly formed Rag Team—a term which we all seemed to hate and love at the same time—had accompanied me to one of the common rooms of the coven.

Santana and Tatyana had raided the small cafeteria for a variety of hot drinks and snacks, while Raffe and Astrid were getting to know Dylan a little better. Wade was sitting next to me at the table, carefully checking the information I put into the employment form. There was still tension between us, mostly because of his strong dislike regarding my Empath ability, but there was nothing I could do about that. Sooner or later, he was going to get used to it. What did he have to hide, anyway? I already knew that I was getting on his nerves—it didn't take an Empath to see that.

"It pays better, and you don't have to hang around all those undesirables," Wade replied, pointing at a box that required my date of birth. I didn't have a real birthday, just an approximate, almost randomly chosen day and month of the year when I was dropped off at the orphanage. "Fill that in."

"Only if you people promise not to get me any sappy cards for that date," I grumbled. "It's not my real birthday, and I don't celebrate it, anyway."

"Why not?" Santana asked, sitting across the table and pushing a freshly brewed coffee my way.

"Thanks." I retrieved the paper cup, blowing over the hot black liquid before the first sip. I could almost feel the energy flowing through me. "I don't know my exact date of birth, just that I was about three years old when I was left at the orphanage."

I said it rather matter-of-factly, which didn't surprise me. I'd gotten used to the idea a long, long time ago. My Rag Team, however, was nonplussed, judging by the way they looked at me. Then came pity, and I instantly hated that feeling. I hated *feeling* pity, especially when I knew it was directed at me.

"You're an orphan," Dylan said. He was the only one who didn't feel sorry for me. Instead, I got a whiff of understanding from him. It was a rare reaction. Most people didn't like being aware of the hardships of others. They didn't even look at the homeless veterans they passed on the street, as if they couldn't handle someone else's misery. I didn't get that luxury. I felt everything. "So, you were in the foster system?" he asked.

"Yeah, why?"

Dylan smiled. "Me too." The idea of a kindred spirit came back, twice as loud. I couldn't help but beam at him. There were plenty of us foster kids in the San Diego area, but we had a tendency to avoid one another. Most of the kids in the system didn't turn out as well as I had. Most of them never got a family like the Smiths to guide them into adulthood, so they slipped through the cracks. Dylan looked like another fortunate exception, with his crew cut and crisp varsity jacket.

"Seriously? I want to say, 'That's so cool,' but we both know it isn't." I chuckled, and he laughed out loud. He was so bright and jovial, so genuine and just plain nice.

"It's okay, it kind of makes sense in this place," Dylan replied, while Wade watched our exchange with a slight frown. "It's why we're 'late bloomers,' as they call us here. We got lost in the foster system and we didn't have anyone to teach us about what we are."

"Most of us magicals join the coven at a very young age," Santana explained. "But people like you, Dylan, and others don't get that lucky. Nevertheless, better late than never, I say!"

"What about you?" I asked Astrid. "How'd you end up in the coven, as a human?"

"Oh, that's a bit of a long story," she said. "I'm useful, and I do a lot of work on the IT side. You know, the usual. Encryption, security, surveillance, and good ol' fashioned hacking, mostly. There's only so much that magic can do in a human world dominated by technology."

"Plus, she's our only zombie," Santana said, grinning.

"Seriously, as if this conversation wasn't complicated enough, we're bringing zombies in, too?" I said, confused.

"What she means is that I've been through a couple of rough patches on field missions," Astrid replied, a blush coloring her cheeks. "Hence Alton allowed me to go with you guys, on the Rag Team. He wants to avoid another… incident."

"Define 'incident,'" I replied.

"I died," Astrid said bluntly, and it took me a couple of seconds to fully register that little morsel of weird. "Three times, to be precise. Alton brought me back, but the price he paid was… awful."

"Huh?"

"Alton's a rare type of magical," Wade added. "He's a Necromancer. One of five in existence."

"He brings people back to life?" I said, utterly shocked.

"It's not as easy as it sounds," he replied. "It's not easy at all. Certain conditions have to be met for a resurrection to occur. The body needs to be in good condition. Any resurrection performed after twenty-four hours will result in a literal, mindless zombie, because the brain decays fast, and the neural pathways start glitching like crazy. On top of that, it takes a massive toll on Alton. After a single resurrection, he goes into an automatic Purge, the worst and most painful kind, that might even kill him. The monsters that came out of him are some of the scariest things I've ever seen in my life, and I've toured the entire Bestiary. Necromancy is never a solution to death, nor is it portrayed as such."

"It's kind of sad, actually." Astrid sighed. "Having that power and not being able to use it. I mean, he could, but the coven obviously has rules about that. The only reason he resurrected me is because I died while *helping* the coven."

"And you can't keep doing that. It's taking a toll on him, in the long term, too," Wade said.

I nodded slowly, before Wade gave me a blunt nudge, pointing at the form. "Come on, fill that out so we can work out your schedule next."

"Look at you, all stern and serious, like a mentor." Santana grinned. "I guess you're eyeing Alton's position and you've started early prep work, huh?"

Wade shook his head. "I found her, so she's kind of my responsibility. At least until she gets her induction. Then she's on her own."

"We both know that's not true, Wade," I replied. He was worried about me—it was an underlying feeling that I could've missed, had I not paid extra attention. He was an interesting bundle of emotions, from what I'd gathered so far. I frustrated the hell out of him, and yet, he couldn't stay away. And the fact that I could read him made him extra nervous. I was going to burn in hell for how much I was enjoying that state of mind.

"Whatever you think you're reading, you're wrong," he shot back. "You can barely hold it together in a crowd, so I doubt you're that good at this whole Empath nonsense."

"Holy crap, you're an Empath?" Tatyana gasped, and I could almost feel her closing off—or elegantly trying, anyway.

I was already exhausted, and knowing that the more they tried to hide from me the louder their emotions blared through me, I let out a heavy sigh and decided to address the problem. "Listen, yeah, I'm an Empath. I feel you all, and the more you try to keep stuff from me, the heavier I feel it. I strongly recommend that you all just relax when I'm around. I won't tell anyone what I'm experiencing, unless asked, and only if it's for a good cause. I'm not comfortable with it either, and I'm still learning to keep it under control, but today has been kind of crazy and my control buttons are all... glitchy. Just don't worry about me feeling you. I can. And that's cool. I won't judge, I promise. Chances are I won't even pay attention," I said in one long breath, then turned to look at Wade. "As for you, Mr. High and Mighty, my sensors are quite attuned after all these years, so yeah, I know exactly what you're going through whenever you're around me. We both know that I annoy you, and that I make you uncomfortable. And that's cool. I like making you uncomfortable."

I ended my statement with a grin. Raffe stifled a chuckle, then pretended to drink from his coffee mug when he noticed my gaze shifting to him. He was a peculiar creature indeed, and I had a hard time putting my finger on what was off, exactly.

"What's up with you? What's your story?" I asked him.

He blinked, as if taken by surprise without his pocket notes handy for quick answers. "What... Um, what do you mean?"

"Why are you here? I hear your dad's the big kahuna in the Council, and this is a coven of Mediocres and jaded rejects," I replied, giving Wade an intentional sideways glance—instantly feeling his wrath boiling through my veins. My inner devil giggled. "So, how'd you end up here?"

Raffe was a little worried, choosing his words carefully. Anxiety was creeping up, too, along with what sounded like maniacal laughter in the back of my head. This was all kinds of weird, and I was fascinated.

"Can we just call it 'difference of opinions' when referring to why I got transferred here?" he replied with an impish smile.

"That doesn't clear anything up," I said.

"What you need to do is fill out the damn form, so I can pass it to HR by the end of the day," Wade interjected.

I gave him a brief scowl, then continued writing my bogus birthday into one of the boxes, followed by my current address and social security number.

"My dad and I don't get along," Raffe conceded. "At all. He's a very powerful warlock, and everybody looks up to him. Some even fear him. I'm very different from the rest of my family. That's pretty much the whole gist. And they're all traditionalists, while I'm more of a… liberal."

"Yeah, I get the whole different-from-the-rest-of-the-family part," Dylan said. "My mom thought I was going to take up a football scholarship at Yale. Instead I'm here, and I'm signed up for community college so I can stay close to the coven."

"Why didn't you go to Yale?" I replied. "Surely there's a coven in New Haven."

"I thought about it. Thing is, my magical abilities have a lot to do with my athleticism," Dylan said, his shoulders dropping. "I'm what they call a Herculean. And the New Haven coven is currently under investigation. The last thing they needed was a raw, late-blooming magical who was bound to stand out on the Yale football team, and not in a good way."

"A raw magical is kind of like letting a wildfire loose," Tatyana explained. "Dylan needs constant monitoring in the first year as a coven magical, mainly because he's just found his Esprit and he has to learn to control it. Right now, he's like a nuclear warhead, without any safety measures. One wrong nudge, and boom, all of New Haven will witness one hell of a… football game."

I frowned. "I thought the Esprit was meant to control one's power, not make it worse."

"It does. Once you get used to it. And that takes time and practice," Dylan replied. "Trust me, I know!"

"What's your Esprit?" I asked.

Dylan showed me his high school graduation ring, cast in silver, with a football encrusted in mother of pearl against a black enamel backdrop, and smiled. "I love football, and I got this from my coach when I graduated high school. It means the world to me. It reminds me of what my life could've been, had I been born a human."

"You don't sound too excited to be a warlock," I said.

"Honestly, I'm not." He sighed. "But it's kind of growing on me. I'm in an adjustment period, I guess. They want me to spend less time with my college buddies, but that's not going to happen. Those are my boys."

I had a feeling he'd spent his whole life pushing his magical abilities back, fighting his nature with everything he had, until one day he went, like Tatyana had so eloquently put it, "boom," and was detected by the San Diego Coven. My mojo had come in gradually. I'd already had my adjustment period, and I'd never denied my true nature. I hadn't embraced it, but I'd learned to make good use of whatever I could, to navigate my existence in the "normal world."

"Have you found your Esprit yet?" Santana asked me, apparently uncomfortable with where the conversation was headed. No one seemed to like hearing Dylan's longing for his human life. Their magical existence was a reason for pride, and they loved it, while Dylan was still struggling with the whole concept.

"Nope," I said, shaking my head.

"Don't worry, you'll find it," Santana replied, and showed me hers. It was a keychain shaped like a guitar, with intricate and colorful detailing engraved around a Mexican sugar skull in the middle. "I found this in a small souvenir shop in Catemaco, my hometown back in Mexico, two years ago. We just clicked. The moment I touched it, I knew."

Tatyana then showed me hers, a beautiful sterling silver bracelet with a single, round sapphire. Its crystalline blue was almost hypnotizing. "My mother gave this to me when I turned fourteen. It's one of the few good things I ever got from the Vasilis clan."

There was sadness in her voice, uncharacteristic of her otherwise icy demeanor, and I could feel it deep in the pit of my stomach. Wade noticed my expression, but didn't bother to fill in any blanks, like before. Instead, he pointed at the form.

"Finish that."

"I hate you," I replied dryly.

"I'm not here to be liked."

"Then why are you here?" I retorted.

"He's one of the best warlocks in this city, and probably the whole state of California," Astrid said, beaming at me. "He's not the most likable character in this coven, but his heart's in the right place and he's less of a jerk than, say, Garrett and his evil sidekick, Finch."

They all chuckled, and even Wade allowed himself a half-smile in response to Astrid's attempt at a compliment. I liked her. She was sweet but blunt. Like a sugar-coated hammer.

"What's up with Garrett, by the way? I can't read him. I can't read Finch, either. And a few other people in this place. I don't usually get that," I said, then looked up at Wade.

He didn't have an answer, and neither did the others. All I got in return were heads slowly shaking and mild shrugs. Raffe seemed interested, though. "Have you tried *feeling* them? Like, reach out, instead of letting their emotions come to you?"

"That's not how Empathy works." I pursed my lips. "I don't have to try anything. I automatically feel them. The only thing I need to work on is blocking certain or all emotions. I'm like a cellphone tower. Whatever signal comes out, I catch it."

"I've never met an actual Empath. I've only read about them in books. You people are so rare," Raffe replied, fascinated. "I guess they don't have accurate info on your ability."

"Or maybe it varies from one Empath to another. Beats me!" I shrugged. "Point is, there are some magicals I can't read. Five I know of for sure. Garret, Finch, O'Halloran, Preceptor Bellmore, and Imogene Whitehall. There were others in the assembly hall, but I don't know who they are."

"I wouldn't worry too much about that, if I were you," Raffe said. "Some magicals might have natural barriers. I can look into it, if you'd like. I could also suggest some light reading for you, to brush up on your Empathy knowledge."

"That would be great, thanks!" I smiled. "Seriously, I appreciate it."

"Like I said, you're rare." Raffe nodded respectfully. "Empaths used to be regarded with great reverence in the Middle Ages. They helped witches avoid the angry villagers and the religious zealots. Today, there are maybe three hundred Empaths in the entire world."

"Oh, hell, that *is* rare," I said, suddenly feeling like a white tiger. Or a white rhino, depending on the amount of carbs I consumed throughout the week.

"She's a full Elemental, too," Wade added. "And a Telekinetic."

The whole team gawked at me, as if I were the single most extraordinary thing they'd ever seen. It was awkward and flattering at the same time, and my cheeks burned with delight. I'd never felt so revered in my entire life.

"Wow," Astrid breathed, her lips stretching into a bright smile. "You're freaking incredible, then! I think you could easily compete with Wade here. Scratch that, you're a full Elemental. I'll bet with a bit of practice and education, you'll be running circles around him *and* Garrett!"

"Dial down the enthusiasm," Wade said. "She just got a Reading from Adley and was classified as a Mediocre."

Their faces went blank, and I felt my heart sinking. The mediocrity reminder was efficient in its crushing of my wings—I'd just started soaring and soaking up all the admiration from our Rag Team, and Wade just stomped in and left me tattered. *The jerk.* Clearly, he was extremely competitive, and that just made me want to beat the odds and actually end up running circles around him, just so I could wipe that smirk off his face.

"I don't buy it," Santana said, shaking her head.

"What? That she's a Mediocre? Adley is never wrong, Santana," Wade said, crossing his arms.

"Nope. Not buying it. Something's off. Harley, you should get tested again in a few months," Santana replied. "There is no way that you're a full Elemental *and* an Empath, on a Mediocre level. That title stays with you your whole life, and it seriously limits your magical prospects. I can't believe it, sorry."

I shrugged hopefully. "Adley did say I should get tested again."

"You should!" Astrid nodded. "I've been with this coven since I was ten, and trust me, someone like you is once in a generation, at most. You being a Mediocre is like saying that Hiroshima was just a firecracker. I'm with Santana on this one. Not buying the verdict."

"I'm not surprised." Garrett's voice slithered in, prompting us all to look up. "You're all usually in denial, anyway. But once a Mediocre, always a Mediocre. I can't believe I'm saying this, but Wade's right. Miss Smith here is… bland. At best."

Garrett was smirking at me, hands in his pockets, his beige waistcoat unbuttoned and his navy-blue shirt sleeves rolled up. Standing next to him was Finch, along with the other magicals on his investigative team, and they made my stomach churn. I could feel the disdain toward me, and it brought back the nastier prep school memories—specifically the ones that got me sent to the principal's office one too many times. It wasn't a good idea to provoke me. I always retaliated.

"I take it you're the token handsome jackass in this place?" I retorted, putting on an Arctic smile.

"You think I'm handsome?" Garrett replied.

"Don't you have something better to do, Kyteler?" Wade stood, his irritation burning through my nerve endings.

"Garrett and Wade have been sort of competing with one another since they first got here," Astrid whispered to me. "They're both ridiculously good but end up acting like raucous teenagers whenever they're in the same room."

That little morsel of information suddenly put things in

perspective, where these two alpha males were concerned. Garrett was the harsh realist with a bad mouth and great magical skills, who seemed to love and hate the San Diego Coven, at the same time. Wade was the by-the-book kind of warlock, equally respected as far as his magical skills were concerned, but he still carried that stiff arrogance around like a badge of honor. Both of them were hot, and yet in need of a good slapping.

"We've got our action plan ready." Garrett shrugged. "I see you're still struggling with an employment form."

"Alton placed you in charge of the investigative team so you could put your time and resources to better use," Wade said. "And yet, here you are, proving exactly why you *shouldn't* be put in charge of anything other than drinks at the cafeteria."

"My team and I were just stopping by for some drinks, Crowley," Garrett replied. "I figured it would be nice to say hello and remind you of the inevitable outcome of whatever you try to do. By the end of the year, I'll be the top scorer in this place. Not you."

"I like how you say things out loud, sometimes, Kyteler. It's almost as if you're hoping that'll make them true," Wade shot back. "Why don't you focus on the investigative team, for now, and not squander this amazing opportunity you've been given? Though, we both know you don't deserve it."

"Jealousy is not a good color on you, Crowley," Garret sneered, while Finch's steely blue gaze attempted to drill holes into my very soul. *Seriously, what in the world did I do to him?*

"If you think *that's* what this is about, you're an even bigger idiot than I thought," Santana chimed in, leaning on her elbows on the table.

"Why don't you mind your own business, *chica*? Don't you have a genie to babysit?" Finch shot back, narrowing his eyes at her.

"Are you so insecure that you feel the need to degrade those who don't put up with your crap, Finch? You should know better than to actively try and piss off magicals who are more powerful than you," Santana replied through gritted teeth as she shot to her feet.

Raffe gently caught her arm in an attempt to hold her back, and I could feel her softening up a little. She seemed to respond to his touch, her anger subsiding, while Raffe's dark, gray-blue gaze settled on Finch.

"I could take you on anytime, anywhere," Finch said, grinning. "You're delusional to think otherwise."

"Oh, yeah? How about we try that right now? You clearly haven't learned your lesson since last week," Santana said, once again riled up.

"Don't fall for these cheap tricks." Raffe intervened, standing up next to her. "You already have two warnings. They're just trying to get you to lash out."

"Oh, yeah, that's right," Santana said, watching Finch's expression turn from bright to sour. "Since it's forbidden to strike a coven member unless it's in self-defense, you boys are such cowards that you need us to hit first, so you can have an excuse to behave like the monsters we keep in the Bestiary."

"I don't need an excuse to make you choke on humble pie," Finch retorted.

"Now, now." Garrett stepped in, visibly amused. "No need to get all aggressive here. If you Rag kids can't take the truth, you should stick to more human jobs. Surely there are still openings in the center. I heard they were looking for tour guides."

He seemed to enjoy pushing people's buttons, avoiding direct aggression just so he could claim moral superiority. Garrett had the makings of an accomplished sociopath.

"Frankly, I'm perpetually fascinated by your species," I mused, looking up at him.

"I'm not surprised," Garrett replied. "You're a late bloomer. Magicals are obviously a thing of wonder for you."

"No, I didn't mean magicals when I used the term 'species.' I meant mouth-breathers," I said. "You're all so insecure and frustrated by your own shortcomings that you need to distract yourselves by picking on others. Anything to get your minds off your own inadequacies. It's kind of sad to watch."

The amount of hatred pouring out of the investigative team—except for the two stooges I couldn't read, of course—was almost suffocating. I'd hit a nerve. Finch opened his mouth to say something, but Garrett squeezed his shoulder and stopped him.

"If I were you, I'd be more worried about *your* inadequacies," Garrett replied. "The magical world isn't all glitter and unicorns, Harley. You either get tough or you get trampled. It's what the rest of your Rag Team doesn't get, and, apparently, neither do you. We're not here to spare your feelings. You kids need to toughen up."

"I don't need my feelings spared," I replied. "I just don't want a bunch of tools poking me because they don't have better things to do with their time."

"Someone should teach you to respect your elders," Finch burst out, and took a few steps toward me.

"*You* want to teach me about respect? Are you hearing yourself, mouth-breather?"

I didn't cave in. Years of bullying had already taught me not to put up with this kind of nonsense, even if I had to get physical. All it took was one hit to teach any bully not to try that again—not with me. Finch was clearly asking for it, and judging by the grin on his face, he didn't think I had it in me.

Before either Garrett or Wade could step in, Finch moved in closer, his hand reaching for my throat. He probably wanted to intimidate me, given that our glaring contest didn't seem to have an end in sight. My instincts kicked in, and I got him first with a Telekinetic thrust. The mental lasso gripped his throat, and I waved him away like a pesky fly. The hand gesture coincided with Finch being thrown across the hall like a rag doll.

He landed on top of another table. The legs gave out, and Finch ended up on the floor with another thud and a painful groan, as he held his side with both hands. I'd probably cracked a rib.

Gasps erupted from nearby magicals, while Wade and Garrett kept the rest of our teams away from each other.

"That's enough!" Wade growled. "Garrett, don't push this any further. You'll get us all in unnecessary trouble!"

"Get your girl under control, then!" Garrett hissed, then gave me an appreciative sideways glance, the corner of his mouth twitching. "Though, I have to admit, she's got spunk!"

"I'm confused," I murmured, before Wade grabbed my arm and pulled me back a couple of feet.

Poe Dexter rushed over to Finch and helped him up, followed by Lincoln Mont-Noir. Both held back Finch, who'd come to his senses and was eager to retaliate. Poe even snatched Finch's custom-made copper-colored lighter, which had started to glow white between his fingers—that was Finch Anker's Esprit, I realized. One could take the Esprit away from a magical, if they wanted to prevent them from inflicting too much damage. *Good to know.*

"Let's go," Garrett called out to Finch and the others. "We've got prep work to do for tomorrow. Leave these snowflakes be."

With one final smirk, Garrett and his team walked out. Finch threw me a deadly glare over the shoulder, and chills ran down my spine. I needed to keep my guard up going forward. He'd either learned his lesson, or he was going to come back for seconds. In any case, I was ready. Hopefully, others watching had also understood not to try and pick on me.

"What the hell, Harley?" Wade turned to face me. He was livid, and I took advantage of his emotions coursing through me to hold my ground and stand by my actions.

"What the hell *what*? I defended myself!"

"You provoked him! You're lucky we were all here!" Wade replied. "Don't do that again! Don't let them get to you. They're jerks who know every loophole in the coven regulations, and you're new here. There's only so much Alton will be willing to overlook before he starts handing out the penalties. This isn't just a school, it's a *coven,* and Alton's not a headmaster here to tackle the bullies.

We fend for ourselves before it gets to the point where it needs to be reported."

"So, this doesn't need to be reported? Really?" I asked, incredulously.

"No, because Alton's too busy to deal with this crap, and Garrett's too gifted and well connected to suffer any consequences over a minor brawl. The same goes for Finch, since he's Garrett's friend," he said, heavily displeased.

"So, what, was I supposed to just let him hit me?"

"His arm would've come off if he did," Santana said from the side.

"You're not helping," Wade reprimanded her, then shifted his focus back to me. "You're part of a team now. If you take a hit, we take a hit. But we stick together. So, measure your thoughts and your actions carefully from now on. Everything you do has an impact on all of us."

"That's not fair," I mumbled, feeling his anger subside.

"Tough luck, Harley. Life isn't fair." Wade sighed.

"Oh, gee, thanks, Wade. I had no idea. I've been living it up in my elite ivory tower for so long, it's good to finally come across a bundle of wisdom such as yourself to enlighten me on how *tough* life can be."

A few moments went by in absolute silence, and I caught glimpses of my surroundings. Two magicals from the cafeteria were hauling the broken table out, giving me annoyed glances. Their frustration made me feel terrible. I should've at least thrown Finch into a clear space, and not ruined the furniture.

Santana, Tatyana, and Astrid seemed mildly amused. Dylan was impressed, and Raffe… well, Raffe was still confusing, half of him laughing on the inside with almost childlike delight, while the other worried about the repercussions.

"Now, fill out the damn form and let's get this out of the way," Wade said, resuming his seat at the table.

I sat next to him and put in the last of my details, ending with a signature, while the others watched in silence. Despite what I'd just endured with Garrett and Finch, I still kind of liked this place. It was definitely better on the Rag Team. At least they treated me with respect, my banter with Wade aside. I couldn't bring myself to trust anyone easily, but I was fascinated by the people I'd been teamed up with. They were all misfits, in one way or another.

Flaring tempers, sharp tongues, and difficult personalities seemed to be defining features in this group. In that sense, I was a perfect fit.

Chapter Fifteen

After I filled out the employment form, we spent about an hour putting together an action plan for the following day. Well, technically speaking, I listened and nodded while Wade told everyone else what they needed to do, in his signature slightly condescending tone.

Before I left the coven, Wade also had me stand in front of the emergency door in Kid City for another half hour, until I got the *Aperi Portam* spell right. Not that it was all that complicated. Once I pronounced it correctly, the door opened back into the coven. It took ten fails till I got it right, given how Americanized my Latin pronunciation was, after which he made me get it right another ten times in a row, between short bouts of bickering.

I'd also learned that this was one of three access points into the coven—the most inconspicuous one, for that matter, since no one thought to look in Kid City for a way in. It was an interesting risk to take, but it seemed to work.

I was quite pleased with myself, as I'd never uttered a spell before in my life. Wade, on the other hand, insisted on toning down my enthusiasm.

"It is literally the easiest spell you could perform. A parrot would be able to do it, if it were gifted with Chaos energy like a magical," he'd said.

Oh, Wade, the nail clipper to my wings.

By the time I got home, the evening was slowly setting in, strips of dark pink and orange splashing across the sky. I was tired, but strangely at peace. There was leftover Chinese in my fridge, but, for some reason, I wasn't hungry. My brain was so pumped with everything I'd learned about myself, the coven, and the magicals, that my appetite didn't make it back home with me, and food was literally the last thing on my mind.

The coffee beans were still scattered on my bedroom floor. I chuckled, then took out the broom and dust pan and proceeded to clean that up, while I quietly went over the events and discoveries of the day. The Main Assembly Hall had really messed with my Empath senses, and I was finally in a state of mind that was relaxed enough to allow some proper mulling.

I started to wonder whether I already had my Esprit, but just didn't know what it was. After tossing the beans away, I touched my little medallion of St. Christopher, hoping I'd feel something that wasn't there before. However, nothing came through, other than the soft coolness of gold against my fingertips.

"Could it be something else I own?" I said thoughtfully, glancing around the living room.

What were the objects that I was most attached to? What items made me feel intensely about something, anything, or everything at once? What was I emotionally invested in?

I looked out the window, my gaze settling on my Daisy, parked outside by the main entrance. She was my most beloved belonging, but I doubted she'd make a good Esprit. She was way too big, and I couldn't see myself wielding her with the dexterity that Wade displayed, for example, with his ten rings.

Then, there was the note from my father. I pulled it out of my wallet, running my fingers over its yellowed paper. It was losing its battle with time already. In another ten or twenty years, it would start to disintegrate. *My connection with the Esprit is eternal.* This was just a piece of paper, with loving and apologetic words from my dad.

Besides, it didn't feel… different.

It still offered me comfort, along with the notion that I wasn't really alone in this world, but it didn't feel like an Esprit—at least not based on how I'd heard others describe its link to the magical. Both Tobe and Alton had said that I would instantly feel my connection to the Esprit. Santana had taken it a step further, describing the sensation like something akin to liquid happiness.

I moved around the house, touching random objects—from keys to rings and bracelets and even the cutlery I'd bought the other week—but nothing came through. It dawned on me then that I didn't really know what real happiness felt like.

Letting a sigh roll out of my chest, I sat on the floor with my legs crossed. I stared at my father's note for a while, until tears burned their way up and clouded my vision. I'd never experienced happiness, not in the way Santana and the others had described it.

I'd felt relief and joy, especially when I realized that the Smiths were a decent foster family, and not the dysfunctional maniacs I'd been forced to put up with before. But real happiness… that was out of my reach, somehow.

Tears fell from my eyes, droplets spreading on the wooden floor, as I finally let go and just cried. I'd been apparently holding that in for a long time, given how relieved I felt at being able to let it all out. There were so many emotions I'd bottled up inside, since I'd always been busy holding it together as an Empath, feeling others more than myself.

I longed for my real family, the parents that left me at an orphanage. My mother, my father. I couldn't understand why they'd abandoned me, and that note was barely a Band-Aid on a much bigger wound.

And the thing that hurt me the most was the fact that the coven sounded like a real family, but I was so terrified of being abandoned again, that I couldn't bring myself to trust them. I was afraid they might kick me to the curb the moment I did something wrong, and, for someone used to being on her own, that would've been devastating.

Opening myself up and allowing myself to trust others was a huge step. This underlying fear of abandonment was actively sabotaging my thought process. I worried that the coven might reject me, in the end. With all my tough talk about being an independent girl, I secretly longed for someone to throw their arms wide open and say, "Welcome home, Harley."

The closest I'd ever gotten to the idea of a real family had been the Smiths, but by then, the emotional damage had been done, thanks to the foster system. I'd been unable to really open up to them, to accept them as a permanent part of my life. There was something awfully wrong with me. I was, by all definitions, damaged goods.

My heart stopped as a large shadow loomed over me.

Ice trickled through my veins, goosebumps racing across my skin as I recognized the low growl coming from behind me. I'd heard it before, behind the casino parking lot.

Claws scratched the floor, and I caught movement at the corner of my eye. There were three of them, I realized, as dread clutched my throat and cut my air off.

I slowly turned my head, just in time to stare into the horrific face of one of three gargoyles in my apartment. The ashen, leathery skin. The crooked stump of a nose. The sharp, bony limbs, and the skinny wings. I'd learned already that not all gargoyles looked alike, but, from what I could see, they were all the epitome of grotesque.

Why me?!

There was no time to figure out an answer to that question, not when a monster was literally crouched behind me, its bat ears flicking, as it bared its humongous fangs with a spine-chilling hiss.

Strings of drool stretched from its jaws to the floor. It was hungry, as were the other two beasts circling around me.

Big, black marble eyes watched me as I moved slowly, ever so slowly, so as not to set the gargoyles off before I could at least put a couple more feet between us. The main one was big and burly. The other two were slightly smaller in size, but just as vicious.

I managed to switch into a position facing the beast, just as it lowered its head and opened its mouth, a guttural rumble pouring out of its throat. It came at me. I waved it away, using my Telekinetic force to knock it back a couple of feet.

The others growled and scampered across the floor, their jaws snapping as I pushed them away, then ran into the kitchen. The big one lunged after me, its jaws crashing through one of the kitchen counters as it missed me by inches. The marble tops crumbled and the wood panels splintered, but I managed to turn the water faucets on. The gargoyle tried to bite into me once more, but I had enough water coming through to pull a thick sheet of ice over its head. Apparently, my fear and survival instinct were great at bringing out my Elemental abilities.

I pushed the frozen gargoyle away with a Telekinetic pulse, then jumped over the remaining counters into the living room area. The big one was busy shaking its head and clawing away at the ice covering its gnarly face, while the other two gargoyles rushed toward me, their wings fanned out as they knocked over everything in their path. Lamps, magazines, and trinket boxes fell to the floor with heartbreaking clanks and screeches as the creatures damaged everything in their path.

My phone was still on my bed, where I'd dropped it prior to cleaning up the coffee beans, and my father's note was on the floor. I knew I couldn't handle all three gargoyles at once. In less than a minute, the big boy was going to get free and come at me again.

Out of options and desperate to call for help, as well as retrieve the single, precious object my parents had left me, I pushed out another Telekinetic wave, surprisingly stronger than my previous attempts. The gargoyles were slapped to the side like overgrown flies, and I dashed across the living room, jumping over an armchair and grabbing the fire extinguisher I kept in the hallway.

I grabbed the note and quickly tucked it in my back pocket, but there was no time to get the phone, too, as the two smaller gargoyles attacked again. I flipped the safety loose and shot out a thick white cloud. The foam blinded them, giving me the two seconds I needed to slip past them and run to the door.

The big one, free of its icy mask, cut in, preventing a clean escape.

"Dammit," I cursed under my breath and glided backward, as the gargoyle thumped through the living room toward me, its claws breaking the wooden flooring.

I froze, my back against the window, my whole body shivering as the beast in front of me shuddered with delight.

Another second and I would become its dinner.

Something inside me roared like thunder, unwilling to give in yet. The air around me thickened—I could feel it tickling my fingertips, beckoning me to wield it. I'd done it before, though not with the strength I would've needed to disable a fiend as savage as this.

But I had to try. There was no other choice.

I summoned all the energy I could muster, and, for the first time ever, I sensed the particles of Chaos flowing through me. My mind went into overdrive, and I thrust my hands out. The winds outside listened, rumbling and whistling as they crashed through the window.

I ducked as broken glass exploded everywhere. Shards cut through the beast's face and eyes, and it hissed from the pain.

With no other route to safety, I braced the winds and leapt onto the windowsill. My breath hitched as I looked down at the sheer drop, and then I closed my eyes, abandoning myself to the air.

The winds circled around me, and I could feel the cool flow of air brushing against my body as I hovered closer to ground level. I couldn't hold the current for much longer, and I ended up dropping for another ten feet.

The gargoyles roared inside my apartment, just as I landed in the middle of the street. People screamed around me. Of course. I was in the city. People were everywhere.

My shoulder throbbed, as it had absorbed most of the shock of the fall.

I managed to look up, counting six innocent people about to get introduced to gargoyles, plus more coming in from both ends of the street, along with the ones poking their heads out through the windows of my apartment building. They were all drawn to the noises and the sight of me crashing in the middle of the street.

"All of you, stay back!" I shouted, waving them all away. "Run!"

Some of them listened, and immediately darted away, while dialing 911. Others weren't as fast, but at least they couldn't actually see the gargoyles, from what I could tell. Otherwise, they all would've screamed at the sight of three monstrous fiends snarling at me from the fifth-floor window.

"Oh, no," I gasped, my eyes wide as I caught sight of the gargoyles jumping out.

The small ones landed on the pavement, crushing the slabs of concrete beneath. I heard people gasping. Then a scream—that was me, watching the big gargoyle land on my car, and mauling it in the process.

"My Daisy!" I cried out at the sight of the Mustang's hood mangled under the weight of that beast. My heart was instantly torn. Rage became my primary fuel as I sprang to my feet. "You son of a—"

I stilled, noticing the smaller gargoyles set their sights on a couple of humans, who were gawking at my car, unable to understand what invisible force had crashed into it. The big one sneered at me, its hind wiggling as it prepared to pounce and come at me again.

I was still overwhelmed, but with more space to move. At the same time, there were humans that needed protection. *Dammit.*

A flash of fire shot across my field of vision, hitting one of the smaller gargoyles. Wade came through the gathering crowd on my left, whispering a spell. His rings lit up blue and a pulse shot out of his hands, spreading outward into an iridescent globe that swallowed us and the gargoyles, keeping everybody else out.

Time seemed to stand still on the outside, people wide eyed and frozen as they stared at us.

Relief washed over me at the sight of Wade, but my troubles weren't over yet.

"Keep the big one busy for a minute!" Wade instructed me, then shot fire beams from his fingers at the other two, who were trying to claw their way out of the globe-shaped shield that was keeping us in.

The flames licked at the two gargoyles, while I temporarily shifted my focus back to the big one. It moved fast, zigzagging across the street as it raced toward me. I managed to latch onto it with a mental lasso, then dragged it to the left with a swing powerful enough to slam it into the energy barrier of the protective shield.

It shook its head, momentarily dazed, then sprang to its feet and came at me again.

Wade lashed fire whips at the gargoyles, killing them both with one devastating blow, as the thick rope of fire cut through their chests. They crumbled to the ground, wheezing and hissing as they disintegrated in two puffs of charcoal smoke and dust.

I pushed out a Telekinetic barrier in an attempt to shove the remaining gargoyle back, but all it did was nudge it. It growled and continued its advance, as I scampered backward and tried to latch onto it with another mental lasso. It was moving too fast, having already learned my move.

Wade slipped between us, muttering a spell as he put his hands out, rings glowing red. Crimson beams shot out from his fingertips, then softened into fluorescent strings that wrapped themselves around the gargoyle. One by one, the energy ropes tightened around the beast until it could no longer move and fell flat on its face.

"Open this!" Wade said, then handed me a Mason jar.

I took it and removed its lid, while Wade rushed around the beast, dropping green entrapment stones along the way. The gargoyle struggled against its magical restraints, which started to pop and vanish, one at a time. Wade spoke the entrapment spell, the sturdier green beams I'd witnessed during our previous gargoyle encounter stretching out and trapping the beast beneath.

Only then was I able to breathe, the last of the red strings fizzling out. The gargoyle was well secured, this time.

"What is going on?" I managed, my voice trembling.

The adrenaline was storming through me, my limbs shaking and my breathing broken and ragged. My heart struggled against its ribcage, as the reality of what had just happened started to sink in.

"I had to use the red ropes first, just to keep it busy while I laid out the entrapment stones," Wade replied, then motioned for me to step forward. "Come closer, I need to jar this bastard. It's bad enough I had to kill the other two."

I glanced around, noticing the world was still and quiet beyond the bluish bubble.

"What's this?" I asked, my voice trembling.

"We call it a time lapse. It only holds for about seven, maybe ten minutes, at most," Wade explained. "It isolates a specific patch of time and space, enough for me to do my job, basically."

He then spoke the spell that forced the gargoyle into its smoky form. It got sucked into the jar, and I quickly put the lid on, twisting it tightly as the formless creature tumbled around in its glass receptacle.

I then remembered Daisy. My car was utterly destroyed, as if a fifty-ton cement ball had been dropped on top of it. I could barely distinguish its original design. My Daisy was a pile of mangled metal and rubber.

Tears rolled down my cheeks, while I came to terms with the fact that I no longer had a car. It hurt like hell, and Wade didn't seem to understand.

"Why are you crying?" he asked.

There was a pang in my heart that I didn't recognize. It was his. He didn't like to see me cry.

Tough luck, bro. I'm bawling like a little girl right now.

"That's... That's my car!" I cried out, pointing at my Daisy.

He casually glanced at it, then shrugged and took the jar from my hands. "It's just a car. Inanimate object. You can buy another one. A better one, for that matter. You should switch to electric, anyway."

"Oh, please." I scowled, rubbing my eyes. "You wouldn't understand."

"It's just a car, Harley. You're alive, that's what matters."

"It's not just a car. It's *my* car! This was the first thing I bought when I became independent. Daisy meant the world to me. She was my symbol of freedom. Not just a car!"

Wade stared at me for a few moments, while I tried to regain my composure. My body was reacting to adrenaline withdrawal, my muscles and joints shaking like crazy. He moved closer and put a hand on my shoulder, squeezing gently.

"It'll be okay," he said. "You're good. You made it. And you held your own against three gargoyles. Not something that a Mediocre can easily pull off, believe me."

Was that a compliment?

I nodded, sniffing as I looked around again. "What do we do now?" I asked, worried about the people outside the protective bubble.

"They didn't see or have any direct contact with the gargoyles. I bet they just saw a crazy girl falling out the window," he replied, reaching for his phone. He dialed a number, then waited for someone to pick up. "Yeah, it's Crowley. There was an incident at Harley Smith's apartment. Park West. Yes. Requesting permission to flash witnesses, until we do a thorough cleanup tomorrow. Yes, thank you."

He hung up and gave me a brief smile.

"What?" I frowned, too bummed out to enjoy the sliver of satisfaction coming out of him.

"Let me show you something cool," he replied, then gave me the jar again. "Actually, you can hold on to this."

He put his hands out, the rings on his fingers lighting up blue.

"What are you doing?" I asked.

"The upside to using a time lapse in the form of a sphere is that we can add another spell to its surface," Wade explained. "What happens is that the sphere usually explodes outward in a puff of energy once the time lapse expires, so we can use the force of that explosion to push out another spell—in this case, a memory wiper."

He muttered another spell, and the sphere turned from blue to white, then burst outward in a blinding flash. I had to close my eyes for a second. Once I opened them, I saw the people around us blink several times, then walk away, absentmindedly. Time resumed its normal flow, and nobody seemed too bothered about the mangled car or the broken windows on the fifth floor.

"You made them forget," I murmured.

"Not exactly. It's short-term hypnosis. I'm not capable of performing mass hypnosis, yet. But this will keep them in a haze for about twenty-four hours, which gives us enough time to come back tomorrow and wipe their memories, one by one."

"How will we find them tomorrow?" I asked, watching as the crowd dissipated on the left side of the street, as well.

"The spell leaves traces of my energy behind," he replied. "I'll be able to detect it tomorrow."

"Like a tracking device," I concluded, and he nodded. The biggest question finally made its way past my lips. "What the hell were three gargoyles doing in my apartment? Why'd they come after me? Where did they come from?"

Okay, three questions. Compared to how many I had for follow-up, I figured I'd ease him into it.

"I honestly have no idea," Wade replied, and I could feel his befuddlement. "The one you're holding came from the Bestiary, that I'm sure of. I recognized its tracking number."

"Huh?"

"Remember, we track our monsters. They're all tagged, right behind the ear." He instinctively pointed at his ear. "You won't like this, though… It's the same gargoyle you and I captured the other night at the casino."

"Wait, what?" My jaw dropped, and I stared at the smoky jar for a couple of seconds. "What about the other two? Also from the Bestiary?"

"No," he said, shaking his head. "They're wildlings, and judging by how they behaved, they were freshly made, too. Which means there are more undiscovered magicals in San Diego, and they've recently Purged."

"I don't get it, Wade. Why did they come after me? Why me, of all people?" I asked, unable to wrap my head around the concept that I had been the deliberate target of a gargoyle attack.

"I wish I had an answer, Harley, but I don't. My first thought was that this bad boy here came looking for revenge, but I can't explain how he got hold of the other two, or how they found you here. I'll go over this with Alton later, though. He might have some insights."

Another question slipped to the front of the line in my head. "What were you doing here, anyway?" I asked him.

Wade stilled, then scratched the back of his head awkwardly.

"There's a good Chinese place just up the road from here," he replied. "I heard the growls."

He wasn't very convincing, but he was definitely hungry. I could feel the knot in his stomach echoing in mine, the psychological pressure to eat something, soon. Or was that me? Chances were that, after what had just happened, my Empathy was a little glitchy or inaccurate. I was still shaking in my boots, after all.

But I was thankful to see Wade. Had it not been for him, I probably would've gotten killed, and who knew how many innocent people would've died in the process.

"Can I buy you some Chinese dinner, then?" I asked, putting on a faint smile. "It's the least I can do for the fact that you just saved my life."

He looked at me for what felt like a minute, then offered a brief nod.

"I never say no to free food," he replied. "And you're welcome."

Chapter Sixteen

"You're obviously not going back to your apartment tonight," Wade said.

He'd already notified the coven of what had happened at my place, and we were waiting for our food order at Wong's, a local Chinese restaurant with red-and-gold wallpaper and one too many paper lanterns hanging overhead. It wasn't too busy at this hour, but there was always a bit of time to burn while waiting for the freshly made spring rolls and fried rice. This place was a hidden gem.

"Yeah, I figured that much." I sighed, fiddling with a pair of chopsticks. "But my rent's paid up. I will go back at some point. I guess I'll be staying at the coven for a few days, after all."

"You should put in your notice, still," Wade offered. "You're much safer in the coven. You might even end up liking it better than that apartment. Plus, it's rent-free."

"I'm not letting a bunch of gargoyles drive me out of my first real home," I replied, then chuckled softly. "Wow, I never thought I'd say something like that."

"Welcome to the real world," Wade said.

I was seeing a slightly different side of him. Brave, noble, and protective Wade Crowley. He'd swooped in and saved me—but only because I had felt overwhelmed. I'd barely known how to handle one gargoyle, not to mention three. It seemed those preceptors were going to help me fill in a lot of gaps, with knowledge that made the difference between a living Harley and a dead-as-a-doornail Harley.

Wade's phone beeped, a text message showing up on the screen. I couldn't see who it was from at that angle, so I raised my eyebrows at him.

"It's Santana," he said, quickly glancing over the text. "She wants to know if you're okay."

"That's... sweet," I replied. Santana was one of the few magicals who didn't look at me with wariness, just curiosity.

"She wants you to know there's a room ready for you at the coven," Wade added, re-reading the text with a slight frown. "She made sure it's right next to hers."

"She strong-armed Alton?" I chuckled.

"No." He sighed. "Knowing Santana, she probably messed with the architecture, and forcibly relocated one of her neighboring magicals. She's very determined by nature. The laws of physics don't have much of an impact on her decisions."

"I've noticed there's a competitive spirit in the San Diego Coven," I said slowly. "Especially where you and Garrett are concerned. What's up with that?"

Wade was caught off guard by the question. I felt his anxiousness and disdain coming through, all of it aimed at Garrett.

"It's nothing personal." He shrugged. "Garrett's not a Mediocre, but he sure likes to act like one, unless it involves making me look bad. He's lazy, and rarely have I seen him perform at full capacity—which can border on jaw-dropping, once he lets loose. He's truly spectacular. But he's got a bad mouth on him, and he's not particularly adept at the thinking part. You know, prior to speaking. And that just enables brats like Finch and Poe to think it's okay to be absolute jerks. The difference is that Garrett gets away with a lot of crap because of his parents. His mom runs the San Francisco Coven, and his dad is on the Texas Mage Council. They're divorced and spoil Garrett as a result."

"Why is he in San Diego, then? Why isn't he with his mom, or his dad?" I replied, a clearer picture of Garrett forming in my head.

"I know for a fact that Garrett got on the wrong side of the San Francisco Coven, and his mom had to transfer him here, but nobody knows the details. Except for Alton, and he won't tell," Wade said. "Alton hates gossip. Which is funny, because it's been a defining trait of this coven for years. He's hoping to fix that. Well, he's hoping to fix a lot of things, but I'm not sure how much he'll get done in *this* lifetime."

"What about you? What brought *you* to the San Diego Coven?" I asked, realizing I wasn't all that interested in Garrett's backstory. He came across as the rich, arrogant bully who never got in too much trouble, despite his blatant misdemeanors. He was also an enabler of Finch's toxic behavior, and that had almost gotten *me* in hot water. It was better if I just kept my distance from that group. Wade, on the other hand, had captured my interest, in more than one way, and reading his emotions didn't feel like enough.

"I came here five years ago, around the same time as Garrett, but of my own volition," Wade replied.

"Why? I mean, from what you're all telling me, the San Diego Coven isn't exactly illustrious."

"It isn't, but it has potential," he explained. "Halifax was running the show when I got here, and we didn't get along very well. I raised flags with the Mage Council, and eventually had him removed. I believe that the magical society is only as good as its lowest-rated coven, and San Diego is very close to the bottom line. I took it as a challenge, and I've been working to improve it ever since."

I grinned. "So, you *are* eyeing a leadership position in the future."

"It would be foolish not to." Wade cocked his head to the side, a smile flickering across his face. "Alton won't live forever, and I am of noble descent, after all. My name means something in this world, and I'm expected to achieve great things—which, of course, I intend to do."

"Oh, noble descent!" I said, feigning a British accent. "Shall I call you Sire?"

He didn't immediately respond. Instead, his deep green eyes drilled through me, while I sensed amusement and pride emanating from him. "Have you ever heard of Aleister Crowley, Harley?"

"The name rings a bell."

Given my murky state of mind after the gargoyle attack, my synapses weren't functioning as smoothly as I would've wanted. The name did sound familiar, but, for the life of me, I couldn't find its origins.

"He was a famed English occultist in the first half of the twentieth century," Wade said, as I started remembering what I'd read on the subject. "His public life, the one known to humans, that is, was mostly a hoax. He founded a religion, experimented with drugs, and fathered three children. He's known mostly for his writings."

"But the magical world remembers him differently?"

Wade nodded. "Beyond the façade of the ceremonial magician, 'the wickedest man in the world' was, in fact, one of the most accomplished warlocks in modern history. He dedicated his life to portraying that whimsical, dysfunctional man, while his surviving children continued his work. He lived during a time when wars were tearing through our world, and magicals were risking exposure, particularly in times of such disputes between nations."

"Why were war times extra risky?" I asked, struggling to make a connection to the history I knew.

"There were magicals who sought to profit from their presence on the battlefield." He shook his head in disdain. "The World Wars weren't just a matter of humans versus humans. We had to get involved, too, trying to protect our society from discovery, because of those terrible few. Crowley's persona did the job and managed to discredit many who tried to come forward as magicals."

"I take it you're related to Aleister Crowley, then?" *And happy to brag about it...*

"Lola, one of his daughters, was my great-grandmother. I never met her, though," Wade replied. "You'll learn all about the Crowleys in your Coven History class, but just to finish my point here: yes, I am related to him. And yes, I plan to continue honoring the name as best as I can. Though, I'm not a fan of such theatrical deceit as Aleister Crowley's."

"Yeah, you don't strike me as charismatic enough to pull off such a persona." I giggled. For a second, I worried he might've gotten offended, judging by his straight face. But all I was getting from him was a gentle chuckle on the inside. "What about your parents?"

"My mother is the director of the Houston Coven, and my father is on the Texas Mage Council," he replied, a tinge of pride in his tone.

"Ah, that's why you know about Garrett's troubled past."

"My father is friends with Garrett's dad, although he avoids telling me any interesting secrets," Wade said, and I could sense he felt sorry for Garrett, in a way. There was probably more to this story, but I was too tired and shaken to pursue it further. *Dinner first, then hot shower, then sleep*. Maybe five more minutes and our food would be ready. I could already smell the fried rice from the kitchen.

"So, about the points system," I said, trying to sort the various questions in my mind by order of importance.

"If we manage to increase our score by the end of this year, it'll pave the way for next year's efforts. Once we start getting the bonuses, the other covens won't look down on us anymore," Wade said. "The bottom line is that this coven deserves better funding. Our magicals are good people, just jaded and undervalued."

"How does the scoring work, though?" I asked. "What's the criteria? Save a cat from a tree, get ten points? Park illegally, lose five?"

"Something like that," he said. "The greater the deed, the higher the number of points awarded to the coven. We run a number of missions, mostly focused on discovering and registering new magicals, educating the ones we get in, maintaining the secrecy of our society, and helping humans when rogue magicals attempt to hurt or influence their world."

"How would a magical influence the human world? I mean, other than standing on top of the Empire State Building and announcing a new world order?"

"Some sneak into government and military positions. Out of all the spells and potions we've gathered over eons, the one thing we don't have is a 'magical detector' of sorts. We rely on investigation and observation. We cannot feel other magicals. If you put a magical in a room full of people, he won't be able to point out other magicals unless he pays attention and catches them while performing spells. I hold hope that someday we *will* come up with such a spell, but until then, it's good ol' fashioned detective work for the covens to identify new magicals. To be honest, most of the time it's easy. As children, we have little to no control over our abilities. Accidents happen."

"What about Adley de la Barthe? She did that Reading on me. Can't you work on mainstreaming that particular process?"

"She is working on something, but the Reading requires the subject's consent. You were reluctant, for example, but eventually allowed her to Read your blood. If you were to adamantly say no, she wouldn't have been able to see a thing. She's researching ways to bypass that, but it takes time and plenty of tests. With sufficient funding, Adley might find a detection method within the next decade."

The bell above the main entrance door jingled, prompting both Wade and me to turn our heads. To my surprise and, based on what I was feeling, Wade's, too, Garrett walked in. He was absently swiping through his phone as he headed toward the counter. He looked up, his lips stretching into a grin as he saw us.

"Crap." Wade watched as Garrett made his way between several tables to stop by ours, first. Only then did I notice sadness, somewhere deep inside him. Using logic and the information I'd gathered so far, I understood why. Their dads were friends; it stood to reason that Wade and Garrett had once been friends, too. Something had clearly changed, to put them at such opposite poles now. Something Wade felt sorry about.

"Funny running into you two here," Garrett said, though he didn't sound amused. I really disliked not being able to feel him. He narrowed his eyes at Wade. "I see you didn't waste any time trying to get into the new girl's pants."

"Watch your mouth, Garrett. This is human territory, and you don't want to set her off," Wade warned him, and I wasn't sure whether I should feel flattered or offended. For the first time ever—and much to my surprise—I decided to keep my mouth shut and watch their dynamic unfold.

"So, what, I'm not interrupting a date?" Garrett raised an eyebrow at me.

I simply shook my head in response, ignoring the flames in my cheeks. My stomach tightened, but that wasn't me. That was Wade.

"No, we're just waiting for food," Wade replied. "I'm guessing you haven't heard yet."

"Heard what?" Garrett frowned, his gaze darting between Wade and me.

"There was another gargoyle attack," Wade said. "Three of them came after Harley in her apartment."

I showed him the smoky jar on the table, next to the condiments basket. His jaw nearly dropped, his eyes wide with shock.

"Only one made it," I added. "We had to kill the other two before they hurt people."

"Are you okay?" Garrett looked at me, sounding concerned. I didn't see that coming, so all I managed to think of in response was a shrug. He then scowled at Wade. "Why wasn't I notified?"

"I don't know," Wade replied, slightly amused. "I texted Alton about it. He decides who is privy to this information."

"And you didn't think to call me, too? You know, since I'm

leading the investigative team? Or are you that jealous that you're willing to sabotage the actual investigation just to spite me?" Garrett spat.

"Tone it down, Sherlock. I'm sure Alton will call you soon enough," Wade said. His fingers tapped the wooden surface of the table in no particular rhythm, but his rings were giving off a faint, warm white glow. I wasn't sure what that meant, given how little I knew about an Esprit, but I had trouble looking away—the delicate light cast elegant shadows over his long, piano-player fingers. "It happened less than half an hour ago."

As if summoned, Garrett's phone rang, and I caught a glimpse of Alton's name on the screen before he picked up. "Yes, sir?"

"Sir?" I mouthed, looking at Wade with slight confusion. Garrett had been quite disrespectful earlier during the assembly, so "sir" sounded alien coming out of his mouth. Wade stifled a grin, as he patiently waited for Garrett to finish his phone call. I found myself fascinated by the fine line forming at the corner of Wade's mouth whenever he smiled. He didn't have Garrett's dimpled cuteness. There was something more mature and… masculine about his expression.

I shook the thought out of my head, then shifted my focus back to Garrett, who was still listening to Alton's instructions.

"Yes, sir. I'll do that, then," he replied, then hung up and gave us both a sheepish smile, dimples and all. "So, yeah, I've just been informed there was a gargoyle attack at Park West. I trust you'll have the full report ready tonight, Crowley."

"It might come as a shock to you, but some of us actually do our jobs in this coven. So, yes, Garrett, you'll get your report in a couple of hours, tops. I just need to debrief Harley," Wade replied bluntly.

"No need. I can debrief her," Garrett retorted, then gave me another one of those winks that I didn't quite get. "Over drinks, later? There's a great bar just around the corner from the science center. Ditch this loser first, though," he added, nodding at Wade.

"You're just a bundle of messed-up, dysfunctional crazy, aren't you?" I said in response, befuddled by his contradictory remarks. Did he hate me, or was he asking me out? Not being able to feel his emotions made it very difficult for me to ascertain his true intentions.

"Probably, but you're gorgeous, and I'd like to take you out for a drink. Hopefully, you'll give me a chance to apologize for being a jerk earlier," Garrett replied, putting on a charming smile. And it was working. Why was it working?!

I looked at Wade, and anger poured through my veins. A couple minutes more of this and I feared I'd end up breaking up a fight between these two.

"That's very… nice, and unexpected, of you," I mumbled. "But I think we should—"

"You either debrief us both or I debrief her and give you my notes, along with my account of the event," Wade replied, his voice low and cold enough to send chills down my spine. "Either works, provided you wish to prove to Alton that you're a professional and not busy chasing skirts."

"Whoa," I gasped, my face flushed.

Tension crackled between them, and somehow, I was caught in the middle of it. However, I didn't take kindly to being called a "skirt," especially not in that bubbling sea of testosterone. And I had a bad habit of making rash decisions on impulse when annoyed—which didn't even begin to cover my state at that point.

Given that we were in a public space and I'd already drawn enough attention to myself earlier, while jumping out the window of my apartment, a more discreet solution to end this ridiculous standoff was needed.

"You know what?" I said, suddenly enlightened. "No one's getting into my pants, and no one's chasing this *skirt*, either. Garrett, sure, I'll go out for a drink with you, but not tonight. It's been a long freaking day and I just need to sleep, after I eat. Wade, you need to debrief me tonight, and I need to stuff my face with spring rolls and fried rice. So let's get moving." I stood, pointing at the restaurant counter, where our order had just been bagged. "Food's ready."

I then walked over to the clerk, who smiled at us as he handed over the food. Wade followed, without saying anything, but I could feel the shame and anger boiling inside him. He knew he'd messed up, his mouth talking without him, but he couldn't concede in front of Garrett. He was probably saving the apology for later.

We left Garrett, who was staring at me with a mixture of shock and amusement, behind. If I didn't know any better, I would've said he was impressed, somehow. Maybe other girls just swooned over him and tolerated his snappy retorts, but I had no intention of giving him the satisfaction.

The main reason I'd accepted his invitation for drinks was to try and gather some intel from the investigative team. I had a personal interest in the gargoyles now. I also wanted to annoy Wade a little for referring to me as a "skirt." And that had worked like a charm. At the same time, I requested that Wade debrief me because I wanted to hit Garrett where it hurt most—in the investigative team. If my assumptions about him were correct, he'd yet to realize that sure, he got to go out with me, but missed out on the opportunity to debrief me in an official capacity.

Hm, guess Mrs. Smith was right. Men can only think with one brain at a time.

"You have the makings of a deviant," Wade said in a low tone as we stepped outside, and I passed him the food bags in return for the jar.

He knew exactly what I'd done, and I didn't know whether I should fear future retaliation or take it as a compliment. Wade could be very confusing.

"I don't know what you're talking about," I said, keeping my eyes on the road ahead.

The sound of cars driving by hurt my very soul, as I remembered the state of my Daisy, back at Park West. I'd worked hard to get her in driving shape. I'd bought her from a secondhand dealership, and she was barely running at the time, choking whenever I switched gears. All it took was one big-ass, vengeful gargoyle to render her useless.

Wade's Jeep was parked just another block ahead, between two bland sedans. There was no sign of its scuffle with the gargoyle back at the casino. *Good mechanic...* It stood out like a black metal giant, which seemed emblematic of Wade's personality somehow. I stole a glance at him, just as he turned his head to steal one at me, and our eyes met for an awkward second.

"Come on, get in," Wade said, looking away, suddenly cold and distant. He clicked his key fob and the Jeep let out a double beep, its doors unlocking. "We still have a lot to do before tomorrow."

"Can I eat in the car?" I asked, my stomach pulling my sleeve.

He scowled at me as we got in. "Would you let anyone eat in *your* car?"

I thought about it, and he was right. I would've blown a fuse if someone wanted to eat hot Chinese food in my Daisy. "Sorry, never mind," I said, looking down. "But you'll have to put up with my stomach growling louder than a gargoyle."

"That's cool," Wade replied, then turned the radio on, and the volume up.

A heavy metal song blared through the speakers. Yeah, my stomach didn't stand a chance with that noise. I gave Wade another sideways glance and noticed the muscle twitching in his jaw as he twisted his key in the ignition.

He was definitely annoyed, maybe even upset.

I understood then that the "deviant" part wasn't meant as a compliment. I'd upset him by choosing to go out with Garrett, but he was conflicted because I'd also given him the task of my debriefing.

And he really didn't like being conflicted.

"Can you try and turn the Empathy off when I'm around?"

From the sound of his voice, he was also still irritated by my ability. He couldn't hide from me. I almost felt sorry for him, while stifling a grin as I pressed my lips tight.

"I usually do, but I can't shut it off entirely. I still get whiffs of emotions here and there. But my system's all upside down after the assembly today. I need to sleep it off."

"I kindly ask that you try, nonetheless. It's extremely uncomfortable to be around you, otherwise."

Oh, ouch.

Yeah, I'd pushed the wrong buttons on the guy. Did I feel sorry, though? Or did I find his anguish amusing?

Food for thought, right after the spring rolls and fried rice.

Chapter Seventeen

After I scarfed down my Chinese dinner while Wade debriefed me, Santana took me to my room. She'd kicked another magical out of there to get me in. The guy hadn't even had a chance to take down all his movie posters, and he'd also left his toothbrush and shaving cream behind.

After a hot shower, I sank into the memory foam bed, expecting to quickly drift into deep sleep. I didn't. Instead, I tossed and turned, my eyes popping open every five minutes. My brain was too busy processing everything that had happened, from the moment I'd first seen Wade, down to Garrett's flirtatious wink as he asked me out earlier.

In between, snippets of preceptors, Readings, Finch's "flight" across the cafeteria hall, and the gargoyles kept bothering me, each carrying question marks and warning signs. If the Bestiary was so secure, how come monsters kept slipping out? How did the same gargoyle manage to escape twice?

If the boxes were so amazing and super charmed, how did that creature outsmart them? Or did it? What if it was an inside job? Was someone from the San Diego Coven trying to stir it all up? What was their endgame?

Ugh. I am not prepared for any of this!

I sat up with a frustrated huff, disliking the darkness that had settled around me. The windows showed me the outside world, as they overlooked the park. The circular fountain was somewhere farther to the left, and there was no moon out tonight, just stars and strips of clouds.

Clearly, I wasn't going to get any sleep, not after everything that had happened. My heart was still aching over Daisy, and over the fact that I couldn't enjoy my own place anymore. If one gargoyle had made it out twice, and brought two more with him to hunt me down, chances were that there could be a third attack, if the Bestiary was still vulnerable.

Remembering the Mage Council's warning, I couldn't help but worry about Alton, Wade, and all the other magicals, especially my Rag Team. Not that I was emotionally attached or anything, but still, I felt bad for them. If they lost points on this, chances were that Adley's research was going to suffer.

Like it or not, for the next month, the coven is your concern, too.

I slipped into my jeans and T-shirt, then went for a walk through the coven, looking for the Bestiary. It was a little after midnight, and barely a handful of witches and warlocks were still out at this time. I couldn't remember the exact route that Alton had taken to get to the Bestiary—not that there would be signs pointing to the most dangerous place on Earth, anyway.

So, I wandered through the hallways for a while, gawking at bronze dragons along the way. I caught a glimpse of a familiar corridor to my left, so I went through, remembering how the walls closed in on me as we got closer to the Bestiary.

Fifteen minutes later, I was standing at the end of the distorted hallway, fitted around the tall, oval door. I didn't see any of the extra security yet and figured they'd yet to start their shift. I turned the knob, but the door was locked. It made sense, though. *I wouldn't keep a terrarium full of poisonous spiders and deadly snakes without a lid.*

"I wonder... *Aperi Portam*," I whispered. It was a shot in the dark, but a shot nonetheless. And a good one, it seemed, as I heard the locking mechanism click.

I turned the knob again, and the door opened with a subtle creak.

The lights were mostly off, except for the wall sconces that still flickered quietly, casting a warm glow over the crystal boxes filled with formless, smoky monsters. I wasn't sure what I was doing here, but I figured I could at least take a better look at those rune locks and glass casings. Maybe I'd see something the others had missed.

Thinking a little too highly of yourself there.

I walked through the narrow corridors with walls made of monster boxes in different sizes. My skin crawled as I felt countless pairs of eyes watching me. I heard voices somewhere to my right, so I slowly and quietly made my way to the source.

Two figures stood beyond a massive glass box with tropical greenery and a plethora of dark limestone rocks. It looked familiar, but I didn't give it a second thought, crouching by its side so I could get a better look at the two figures—one particularly massive, which I identified as Tobe, and one whose soft, honey-like voice instantly reminded me of Alton.

I leaned forward, my face against the glass, until I could see both clearly.

"I don't think we should keep the Mage Council out of this, Alton. It's too risky."

As suspected, Tobe and Alton were engaged in what sounded like a heavy conversation. I listened quietly, ignoring the goosebumps I was getting from the monsters' attention. They couldn't do anything while stuck in those glass boxes, anyway.

"Right now, only you, me, and Garrett's and Wade's teams know about this," Alton replied. "You heard Leonidas today. One more slip-up and they'll start handing out the penalties."

"And you'll lose what, money bonuses? Is that worth putting this coven's magicals at risk?" Tobe said, crossing his feathered arms.

"We can handle this on our own, Tobe. All the Council can do is look down at us and deprive us of future funding. And Adley's getting so close to a fully functional detector. We can't risk it. No one got hurt, and we can clean this up before any rumor makes it back to the Council. You know they'll put some blame on you, too. Leonidas will stop at nothing to make us look like idiots."

My Daisy got hurt.

"Leonidas will one day die of old age, and I will still be here. I have seen plenty of his kind, and I am not intimidated," Tobe declared, and pride flowed through me like liquid fire.

"Nor do I expect you to be intimidated, Tobe, but you must understand that the times are changing. They all expected us to turn down the nomination, and the covens have been laughing at us for too long," Alton insisted. "One more push with Adley, and we'll prove our worth. Whatever problems we're having with the Bestiary, we can handle them on our own. We don't need the Council holding our hands and humiliating us further."

"What do you suggest we do, then?"

"Let's start by doing another sweep of the Bestiary tomorrow. I'll have Garrett and his magicals do a thorough search of every box, every lock, and every mechanism," Alton proposed. "Wade and the Rag Team will handle the cleanup, and I'll send out more magicals to search for rogues. Those two wild gargoyles came from the San Diego area, for sure."

"What if others escape from the Bestiary? What then? What if someone gets killed?" Tobe frowned. "I've been around for over a thousand years, Alton, and this has never happened before. It's completely unprecedented, and I am worried for the safety of this coven."

"So, what? Do we tremble in our boots and expect the Mage

Council to solve something we can handle ourselves?" Alton replied. "Listen, if it gets worse, I will notify the Council. In the meantime, let's reinforce security and investigate this properly. I'll give you some of Nomura's instructors to help around the Bestiary, particularly when you're resting. I'd advise you not to leave here for a while. O'Halloran can do live monster training with the new recruits. He's fought most of the creatures in here, already."

Tobe shook his head slowly, his thick mane rippling in soft, golden waves. "The monsters only listen to me, and me alone. The only thing that added security can do is alert me and try to catch them in Mason jars."

"The more, the better, I say. At least we'll know we've tried everything. And I'll ask Sloane to devise more charms for the boxes, too, just to be on the safe side. I'll restrict access to the Bestiary, as well. Whatever I can do to ease your mind that doesn't involve calling the Council, I'll do it, Tobe. Just bear with me, and I know we'll get to the bottom of it."

"I've locked Murray in a separate box," Tobe said, scratching the back of his head.

"You named that gargoyle Murray?" Alton chuckled.

"Letters and numbers don't do these creatures justice. Besides, getting out of the Bestiary twice and going after Harley just for revenge has made him stand out." Tobe shrugged. "So, I called him Murray. He sounds like a Murray."

That ugly, winged bastard responsible for the destruction of my Daisy did sound like a Murray, indeed. I knew a bully in kindergarten named Murray. He used to eat glue, blame me for it, then put chewing gum in my hair. My first foster mom had to cut my hair short because of bird-brained Murray. *Yeah, Murray sounds about right.*

"I'd advise you to keep an eye on the 'kids' tonight," Alton concluded. "I'll come by in the morning, and we can discuss this further then. Trust me, Tobe, once we figure out what the problem is, we'll be able to resolve it without any Council involvement. I simply can't flush two years' worth of Adley's research down the drain because of this. You know full well that if we nail one of the bonuses, I'll be sure to upgrade central parts of the Bestiary, too."

"Agreed," Tobe replied. "We do need special replacement parts for the stem, to amplify the energy output to African and South-East Asian covens."

"All the more reason for you to stick with me on this one, Tobe." Alton smiled, then gently patted his shoulder. "I'll see you in the morning, friend."

Tobe gave him a brief nod, and we both watched him leave. As I turned my head to follow him from the other side of the glass box, I froze at the sight of two huge turquoise eyes with black slits in the middle that took center stage in front of me. I quickly recognized the white-and-fuchsia plumage of its collar. Quetzalcoatl, the massive snake, stared at me from inside its glass box—the same box I'd chosen to hide behind.

Its jaws snapped open, and it hissed violently, its feathers trembling aggressively.

Chills ran through me as I jumped back on pure instinct, catching Tobe's attention. He didn't seem mad, but rather amused. "I think Quetzi likes you," he quipped, as I stood up straight, ignoring the waves of adrenaline surging through me. It was a natural response to having just two inches of glass stand between me and a giant, monstrous snake that could gobble me up in seconds.

I looked down at the creature, just as it lifted, then cocked its head to one side, its haws flicking black over its gem-like eyes. Again, I wasn't sure whether that was cute or creepy.

"Sorry, Tobe," I murmured, putting on my most innocent expression. "I didn't mean to eavesdrop on you and Alton."

"What are you doing here? You should be resting, after such an eventful day."

"I couldn't sleep." I shrugged. "I just wanted to look around. Maybe see if I could find something to help with the investigation.

As of tonight, this whole Bestiary issue got really personal, really fast."

"Don't worry about it, Harley," he replied gently. "We'll take care of it, but, as I assume you heard what Alton said, keep the incident to yourself and your team. No one else can know. At least for now."

I nodded, putting my hands in my pockets. I was still very restless. "I won't tell, of course. But how do you think the gargoyle escaped the second time around? I thought you guys checked and secured the boxes already."

"We did, and that's what bothers me the most. There are approximately two thousand gargoyles in the Bestiary. They're the most frequent Purge manifestations, and they tend to team up in packs. Murray came out and rallied two wild ones to join him, for example. I fear that if another comes out, it will do the same, or worse." Tobe sighed, then gazed across to his left, through several walls of glass boxes, where black smoke swirled around, as if responding to his attention. "I'm afraid we might be dealing with an inside job, and I don't like how it's making *me* look incompetent. I have never had such issues with my monsters before. They all fear and obey me, without exception. And yet, Murray keeps getting out, and I fear others might follow his example."

That confirmed one of my suspicions. At least I knew my reasoning wasn't faulty on this one. But the follow-up question still bothered me. "Why would anyone try to sabotage the Bestiary? What would their purpose be?" I asked.

"I'm not sure, but I do know Alton drew the ire of many covens when he didn't reject the nomination for the Bestiary. The Los Angeles and San Francisco Covens, in particular, are still fuming, as they consider San Diego to be woefully inferior and unprepared for such a task."

"And what do you think, Tobe? You've been the Beast Master since its inception. Surely, you've seen worse covens than this?" I replied, the corner of my mouth twitching.

Tobe needed a couple of seconds to answer that. It didn't work in San Diego's favor...

"I don't know, honestly," he replied. "On one hand, there is so much potential in the magicals here, but, at the same time, due to poor funding and low morale prior to Alton's arrival, they have so much to catch up on, compared with other covens."

"Potential?" I asked. "You see potential here? I'm told a substantial amount of magicals in the San Diego Coven are Mediocre, like me."

"But that's not necessarily a bad thing." Tobe smiled. "Personally, I find the label to be quite elitist, and I don't think it cancels out the tremendous potential of every magical in this place. They simply need more confidence in their own abilities. They lack motivation. Alton is doing a fine job, and he'll probably make more progress in the years to come, but even he is too deeply attached to the rules and regulations. This whole Mediocre concept is completely unnecessary, if you ask me. And yet, magicals in positions of power often use it to deny other magicals the possibility of advancement in the coven ranks."

"That's cruel. And foolish," I said, my dislike for the magical society swelling in my throat, like a painful lump. Would I pledge my life and services to a coven that was so quick to slap me with the Mediocre label? Would I ever be given the chance to evolve beyond that?

"Tell me, Harley, do you agree with *your* Mediocrity?" Tobe replied, as if reading my mind—something Wade seemed good at, too. For a split second, I wondered what Wade was up to right now.

Probably snoring his butt off.

But Tobe asked a good question. Was I okay with being classified as a Mediocre?

My ego screamed, *"Hell, no!"* and my instincts also disagreed. I shook my head in response. "Not really, no. It's not just because of the Reading, though. I mean, sure, it does sound ridiculous to be a full Elemental *and* an Empath *and* a Telekinetic and be deemed a

Mediocre. And I'm just using common reasoning here, no magical knowledge whatsoever. But there's also something deep down, like this little voice in the back of my head, and it's telling me I'm not Mediocre, at all. It's almost laughing at the prospect. I *feel* like I can be more, and better."

Tobe nodded slowly, carefully considering my answer, then took a couple of steps forward. He was so tall that I had to tilt my head back a little. "You see, in circumstances such as yours, having some information about your birthparents would have been very useful. Parental heritage often determines a magical's prospects, including the chances of being labeled a Mediocre. Do you know anything about your biological family?"

"Nothing whatsoever." I sighed, then remembered the note from my father, still stuck in the back pocket of my jeans. I took it out, then handed it over to him. "All I have is this note from my father. I was three years old when I was left at the orphanage. Nobody knows how I ended up there. Father Thomas was kind enough to check hospital records in the city at the time, but nothing came up. No babies missing, nothing that could be traced back to me."

Tobe listened, while studying the note. I tried to get a sense of what he was feeling, but all I got was curiosity, with a faint whiff of concern. "What are you thinking?" I asked. "I feel you, but I can't exactly read you."

"You will, some day." He winked at me. "Your Empath ability is still very green. Once you develop it properly, and once you get a better understanding of emotions, in general, you'll be able to identify and interpret everything with incredible accuracy. Tell me, Harley, do you remember anything from before the orphanage?"

"Nothing… I don't think so, anyway," I mumbled, flashes of previous dreams rushing before my eyes. Tobe was quick to notice.

"What is it?" he asked.

"Um. I think I've had dreams about my parents… but they're too hazy," I confessed. "When I dream, it's all clear, and it's like I know exactly what's going on, who I am, who they are. But the moment I open my eyes, I forget everything. I'm left with bright spots and the warmth of a smile."

"Wait here," Tobe said, then disappeared behind a glass box wall hosting ten formless monsters. They rippled across the crystalline surface, then scattered at the bottom, and I could see Tobe on the other side, bent over a wooden chest. I glanced over to my left, to find Quetzi still watching me curiously, the tip of its tail twitching.

"I can't believe I'm saying this, but you are creepy and gorgeous at the same time," I said, staring at the mythical serpent.

"Thank you, I get that a lot," Tobe quipped, coming back with what looked like a Native American dreamcatcher.

"No, I meant Quetzi," I replied, then worried he might feel offended, somehow, which threw me into a most awkward stammer. "Not that you're not gorgeous… Well, not *gorgeous,* but… Um, I mean, good-looking. You are. Despite the lion head. Not 'despite,' sorry, it's not like there's something wrong with your head. It's perfect just the way it is, and you're not creepy at all. I… I mean… Stop me, please, I'm digging myself into a hole I won't be able to get out of."

Tobe stared at me for a couple of seconds, then laughed. His laughter was strange, like a soft purr, his jaws open and his white fangs glistening. At least he had a sense of humor and wasn't easily offended. *Thank heavens.*

"It's all right, Harley, do not worry," he replied. "I am well aware that my appearance doesn't exactly match my nature or my vocabulary—or my ability to *use* a vocabulary. Here, take this."

He handed me the dreamcatcher, and I spent a good minute looking at it from all angles. It was really old, judging by the yellowed sinews used for the net. The edges were wrapped in worn, red leather, and the feathers were simply stunning, each the size of my palm and bright red. They were quite peculiar, too, mainly because they looked a lot like peacock feathers, with big white-and-black eyes in the middle, but the coloring simply didn't feel natural.

The beads were shiny and black, with tiny reddish striations. It was truly a beautiful piece.

"What does this do?" I asked.

"It's a dreamcatcher."

"Of course it is," I said. He was stating the obvious, but I had a feeling our concepts of "obvious" were quite different. In human culture, dreamcatchers had lost their mystical origin, and were simply regarded as beautiful Native American decorative objects. Something told me this wasn't just for decoration. "I'm guessing it's magical?"

"Yes. It's a very old charm. Only a handful of these still exist. They were woven by Navajo warlocks before the first European settlers came to America," Tobe explained. "All you need to do is hang it above your head, before you go to sleep, and say, *'na'iidzeel.'* That's Navajo for 'dream.' It will capture your dreams in vivid detail."

"Oh. Wow."

I was floored by his gesture, and by what this meant for me, on a very personal level. This was a rare artifact, and Tobe was simply handing it over to help me remember my dreams. Who does that?

Wonderful creatures do, Harley. Wonderful creatures.

"How… How can I ever repay you for this?" I breathed, my eyes glassy with tears, and my throat closing up.

"Just look after it, Harley. Like I said, it is extremely rare, and highly valuable. So, be careful whom you tell about it." Tobe smiled, and I nodded in response.

"Thank you, Tobe. Thank you so much… Wait, quick question. How do I see my dreams, afterward? You said it captures them."

"Ah, yes. Good question. It's a very intense experience, much like taking peyote," he replied, slightly amused.

"I've never—"

"Of course you haven't, and I don't think you should." He shook his head vehemently. "It's a powerful hallucinogenic to humans, but to magicals it is far, far more powerful, much more intense. It is a literal separation of consciousness and body. Some magicals even fail to return to their physical forms. But, anyway, you'll learn that from Preceptor Bellmore; she uses peyote in some of her charms and hexes. To see your dreams, you need only to hold the dreamcatcher with both hands and say, '*yáshti*'. That means 'speak,' and it allows the dreamcatcher to speak to you with the images from your dream. You'll see what I mean."

I nodded again, my gaze shifting repeatedly between Tobe and the dreamcatcher. I rarely got gifts, and never one of such importance. It felt humbling, and, at the same time, it filled me with an unfamiliar but warm light, as if I'd finally found my place in the world.

The pragmatic side of me quickly kicked in, reminding me not to get too attached. Tobe was clearly an extraordinary creature, but I'd yet to find the same appreciation for the rest of the coven. I had to take my time before giving the coven an answer—no matter what that answer may be.

"Thank you, Tobe." I offered a warm smile, which he returned with a gentle expression.

"Now go to sleep, Harley," he replied. "You shouldn't be out at this hour, anyway. You have a long day ahead tomorrow, don't you?"

"Ah, yes. Totally." I sighed. "I'll see you tomorrow, then."

I left Tobe in the Bestiary and eventually found my way back to the dorms. It was going to take some time to get used to all the passageways and corridors in this place—not to mention all the floors! I'd only seen one today. From what I understood, there were five, and if they were as huge as this one, I would need a couple of days just to visit them all.

By the time I reached my room, my eyes were already droopy, and my brain had slowed down, to the point where I had a hard time remembering the Navajo words Tobe had told me to use for my dreamcatcher.

"Crap," I muttered, then tucked the dreamcatcher into the

bottom drawer of my nightstand. I'd find a better hiding place tomorrow. I couldn't even stand anymore, my arms and legs weighing a ton.

I was far too tired to struggle to remember the words. "I'll ask Tobe again tomorrow," I murmured, resting my head on the pillow.

My mind went back into overdrive as I remembered the gargoyle attacks. Maybe a minute later, however, I let the darkness embrace me, closing my eyes and finally drifting away.

Stay safe, stay smart, baby girl...

That voice. I knew it. I was slipping into a dream and, with my last sliver of semi-consciousness, I made a mental note to ask Tobe to write down those Navajo incantations tomorrow.

I needed to see the face of the man that voice belonged to.

Chapter Eighteen

A knock on the door made my eyes snap open.

Sunshine poured through the windows. I'd left the thick, dark green curtains open. Only then, after a heavy sleep, did I take in the colors of my room—dark green on the windows and carpeted floor, and walnut paneling on the walls, with matching furniture. I was so tired yesterday, so overwhelmed, I didn't even notice the mid-century vibe.

It didn't match the rest of the coven, and I had a feeling it was decorated by the previous magical, as the furnishings sort of matched the 1950s movie posters. A second knock made me sit up.

"Yeah?" I called out, readjusting to consciousness.

"It's Astrid! Can I come in?"

I blinked several times, the memory of yesterday coming back in full color. *Man, I was knocked out last night*. I couldn't remember a single dream. Come to think of it, I could barely remember how I got back from the Bestiary.

"Yeah, sure," I replied, pushing the blanket aside.

My jeans and T-shirt were still on. It was a miracle I'd made it out of my boots last night.

The door opened, and in came Astrid, dragging a solid metal clothes rack with her, the wheels squeaking a little too loudly. It was loaded with a plethora of clothes, with a bottom rack on which several boxes wobbled as she stopped in the middle of the room.

"What in the world?" I murmured, getting out of bed and rubbing my eyes.

Astrid put on a presentation pose, beaming as she pointed at the rack.

"These are all for you, compliments of the San Diego Coven!" she said.

Upon closer inspection, I realized that all the clothes were in my size—all my favorite brands and styles, in a variety of whites, blues, and reds, mostly, along with a couple of leather jackets. She opened the boxes one by one. Boots, biker style, ankle height, and not too heavy on the soles, just the way I liked my footwear, as well as a pair of sneakers.

"Astrid. What's all this?" I managed, while she opened one last box, which was filled with lingerie, and a bag of essential girly stuff —shampoo, conditioner, personal hygiene, and makeup, all my regular brands. How did they know? *Wait. My apartment.*

"Well, after the gargoyle attack last night, there wasn't much left that we could salvage from your apartment," Astrid explained, taking one of the leather jackets and turning it over to get a better look at the metallic accents. Judging by the look on her face, she liked it.

"I don't... What?" I was still quite confused.

"The gargoyles trashed the place, and I don't mean just the broken water pipe and windows—"

"No, that was me," I replied, replaying the entire scene in my mind.

"Ah, okay. Cool." She nodded, slightly amused. "You really need an Esprit, girl." She chuckled, then switched back to serious-looking Astrid. "Thing is, one of the gargoyles flipped over the TV, then pulled out and tore some of the live wires in the wall. I'm quite fuzzy on the details right now. Bottom line, your place burned down. A little."

"What?!"

My jaw dropped. My heart sank. I could almost cry, but after what I'd seen happen to Daisy, the apartment didn't seem like the worst part of my encounter with the beasts.

"There was a fire. The sprinkler system was set off, eventually, but most of your stuff was scorched, and everything else was soaked. Your place is a mess. Sorry, but I think you'll be staying here for more than a day or two." Astrid offered me a sympathetic smile.

A couple of seconds went by as I did a quick assessment in the back of my head.

"The place is insured," I remembered. "The lease covers accidents and stuff. Pretty sure it covers fires. I think it'll be okay. I won't lose my lease. I got a three-month deposit on that place."

"Don't worry about that. We're the cleanup crew; we'll take care of that, too." She winked, then pointed at the wardrobe. "Do you like it?"

"I… Yeah, I do. A lot, actually. How did you know my size and stuff?"

She hesitated, offering me the jacket. I took it, briefly looked at it, then left it on my bed. I didn't like the silence coming off her. She was hiding something. I could feel it—there was a lot of awkwardness coming from her, too much for me to handle pre-coffee.

"Astrid, how did you know?" I asked again, adding a bit more gravitas to my voice.

"I didn't. Wade did."

"Huh?"

"Wade bought all this," Astrid said, her voice barely audible.

I looked at the wardrobe again, then moved closer to get a better view of the lingerie box and—*oh, my God, there is so... much... black lace…*

"Everything?" I managed, staring at the bundle of bras and panties with various lace designs, all worthy of artistic praise. They were all high-end creations, the kind of stuff I couldn't afford but would've loved to wear, especially if I ever met a special someone… at some point.

This was so private, so intimate. I was stunned, flustered, and a little creeped out. It was as if someone had peeked into my mind, plucking out my most hidden sartorial desires and turning them into reality.

"Um, yeah." I heard Astrid's reply as I bent down and noticed my favorite shampoo and conditioner set. Freesia and jasmine.

"You're telling me that Wade went out this morning and bought all this for me?" I turned to face her, still having trouble processing the information.

She sighed, then nodded, her lips pressed into a thin line. "I didn't even know until they were delivered to Kid City. Some of the parents who had kids playing there looked a little confused, but… Anyway, yeah. I mean, he used the coven card, though. He didn't pay out of his own pocket or anything."

"How did he know to buy all this? I mean, these are all my size, my style. Even my favorite brands. This is weird… or creepy. I'm not sure which," I blurted, and Astrid chuckled, which further befuddled me. "How come *you* aren't creeped out?"

"Oh, honey, I've been here for too long to be creeped out by something as innocent and, frankly, as cute as this," she replied. "Wade is a very special kind of guy. He pays a lot of attention to details, even when you think he's not. Christmas has been amazing since he came into the coven. He's in charge of the gifts, every year, because he just… knows everybody's tastes. He won't tell us how he does it, though. It's his secret, he says."

"Okay, so I'm not the only one he's creeped out like this!" I said.

"Come on, don't be so hard on the guy. That's just Wade. It doesn't mean anything, if you ask me. Though, I've never seen him buy lingerie for anyone—that's a first." Astrid giggled, then checked her watch. "Shoot! Breakfast is ready! Hurry up, get dressed, and I'll meet you in the banquet hall!"

She didn't wait for a reply as she rushed out, leaving me with my wonderful wardrobe. Handpicked and purchased by Wade freaking Crowley.

After twenty minutes spent gawking at the rack and then a quick shower, I slipped into some of the new clothes, opting for jeans, a smart cotton shirt, and the leather jacket I'd left on the bed. My face was on fire when I put on the lingerie, and I struggled to ignore the thrills when I saw how perfectly it fit me, how every black band hugged my form and brought out my curves.

I put on a pair of boots, then slapped on some BB cream and brushed my bright red mane. After a week of absolute weirdness and two near-death experiences, I had to admit—I looked great. I had always felt comfortable in my own skin, though I often tried to stay invisible, unnoticeable, but I'd already gotten used to the fact that there was only so much I could do to hide my natural features.

My hair was long, soft, and straight, reaching just beneath my shoulder blades. The tips curled up when the humidity was higher than usual. My eyes were sky blue, and I often wondered whether I'd gotten them from my mom or my dad. The same question applied to the sprinkle of freckles on my nose. I was taller than the average girls in my age bracket, which was why I often chose flat soles—so as to not stand out even more.

After about ten minutes of getting lost in those humongous hallways, I finally found the banquet hall, with its pristine white tables and silverware. There was a huge breakfast buffet at the end, loaded with a variety of pastries, fresh fruit, coffee and tea, pancakes—basically breakfast heaven, complete with three types of maple syrup.

I scanned the room, looking for my Rag Team. My eyes met Finch's, and the hairs on the back of my neck stood up at attention. I offered a brief scowl, then found Garrett at the same table, along with Poe and the rest of the investigative team.

After another minute, I eventually found Astrid, Santana,

Tatyana, Dylan, Raffe, and Wade at the opposite end of the same long table, with one spare seat. My heart warmed up a little, thinking they'd actually saved it for me.

Aw.

I glided through the hall, taking deep breaths as all the magicals' emotions started licking at my senses, like silent but nagging flames. I made it to the buffet, making sure to ignore everyone around me and in my path. My hope was that if I avoided eye contact, somehow my Empathy wouldn't be so intense.

With slightly shaking hands, I managed to pour myself a cup of coffee with three sugars, then loaded a plate with a pastry and some red berries. I wasn't too hungry, but I figured I had a long day ahead. Carbs were welcome. I counted to a hundred in my head as I made my way to my team's side of the table.

Anxiousness, anger, jealousy, curiosity, frantic heartbeats, and affection, fear, and concern—these were the overall vibe of the coven that morning. Every magical had something to worry or be thrilled about, and it was all piling up on top of my already-frayed nerves. I needed to eat really quickly and get out of there.

"You made it!" Santana greeted me with a smile, then nodded at the empty chair. "Sit, eat, take it easy."

"Take it easy." I chuckled softly. "Easier said than done."

Wade watched me quietly, measuring me from head to toe, most likely assessing his shopping skills on me, the live model. His gaze darkened as it wandered up and down, before he looked right into my eyes for a second. My heart skipped a beat. Without so much as a hello, he shifted his focus back to Astrid.

"Alton said he'll bring over the assignments this morning," he told her, while I sat down and chose to focus on his emotions, since everybody else was so freaking loud and everywhere in my soul.

He was tense. His self-control was spectacular, since there was something akin to a storm brewing inside—a raw state that I didn't recognize. There was a pang in my stomach, which I attributed to hunger, so I mowed through my breakfast and washed it down with coffee.

"Do we know what we'll be doing first?" Astrid replied, while Santana watched me, amusement twinkling in her brown eyes.

"Probably Park West cleanup. That's a priority," Wade replied.

My heart was beating a little faster than usual, but, given the number of people surrounding me, it was becoming difficult to ascertain whether it was my feeling or someone else's. I'd never been so out of control as an Empath. Nights spent in the casino had taught me to master the self-control part, and yet the coven made it extremely difficult to hold it all together.

Or maybe I was still tired, even overwhelmed by the previous day's events.

My Daisy…

"So, sleep well?" Santana asked, ignoring the cleanup conversation.

"Like a log," I replied, then took another sip of coffee. The food was settling nicely in my stomach, but something was still tugging at me on the inside.

That's not me, for sure.

I looked at Wade, persistently even, but he refused to acknowledge me. Santana was quick to catch on. "Did something happen?" she asked, somewhat amused.

"Nope, all good. Weird good. But good. For the most part, anyway. You know, after we set aside the fact that my car and my place were trashed by—"

"Not another word!" Wade cut in, gritting his teeth and giving me a deadly glare.

Whoa.

"Oh, yeah, right. Sorry." I remembered the secrecy part about the triple gargoyle incident, as per Tobe's request.

I didn't show any remorse, though, not while Wade's eyes were still on me. There was something a little too sharp, too rough about Wade this morning, something that contradicted the kind (though slightly creepy) gesture of buying me a whole new wardrobe. He clearly had no intention of making a habit of being nice. So, I considered it a slip, and switched back to treating him with the same abrasiveness that he showed toward me.

"Thank you for the lingerie, Wade," I said, barely recognizing myself.

The man had an ego, and I was ready to take a stab at it. The coffee was kicking in.

Wade's forehead smoothed, a muscle flexing nervously in his jaw as he continued to glare at me, this time for a much different reason. It was hard to keep a grin from slitting my face in that moment, but I managed nonetheless.

My remark was enough to draw the attention of the entire Rag Team. Astrid chuckled and, for a moment, was the target of Wade's deadly scowl. She hid her face in her coffee mug in an attempt to stifle her amusement.

"Is that what you meant by 'weird good'?" Santana grinned. "Wade Crowley buying you intimates? Did he get the bra size right?"

"Santana." Wade's tone was flat and filled with warning, but she was anything but bothered. I was in for a treat.

"Wade," she shot back, mimicking his tone. "Is there something you wish to share with the class?"

"Nope," he said. It was his turn to hide his face in his coffee mug, but there was no amusement coming from him. Just burning embarrassment. I'd struck a nerve, as he'd probably expected me to stay quiet about the whole lingerie thing. *In your dreams, Crowley.*

"So, Harley," Santana said, smiling at me. "Did he get the size right?"

"Santana," Wade tried again, trying so hard to be polite.

"He did. Perfect fit," I replied, trying so hard to keep a straight face. Wade's turmoil was delicious, and it seemed like fair pay for my flustered morning. The intention may have been noble, but, seriously, you don't just buy a girl that kind of lingerie right after you call her Mediocre. Magical pun intended.

"Don't be alarmed," Dylan chimed in, grinning. "Wade's gift-buying skill is out of this world."

"Yeah, I told her the same thing," Astrid added, and Wade seemed to relax a little, while Tatyana and Raffe watched with straight faces. "Nothing to be… you know, creeped out about. Wade just knows us a little too well, without actually knowing us."

"Has he bought you any black lace lingerie?" I asked Astrid, not ready to let Wade off the hook just yet. I made her blush, as she shook her head. I then looked at Dylan. "Did he get you a perfectly fitted jockstrap, by any chance?"

"Oh, hell, no—" Dylan burst out, then stilled when a heavy hand landed on his shoulder. Attached to said hand was Alton Waterhouse, freshly shaved and fitted into an elegant, dark gray suit, complete with his dragonhead cufflinks—his Esprit.

Fun's over.

And just like that, Wade could finally breathe again. I caught a glimpse of Tatyana smiling, and that was a first, given her otherwise icy demeanor. Only then did I realize how hard she was laughing on the inside, as was Raffe.

Good, at least they get some early entertainment before the workday begins.

"Good morning, team," Alton said, then dropped a file on the table before Wade. "I have your assignments for the day. I kindly ask that you and the investigative team play well together, going forward. You're all grownups in a magical coven, not raucous children in a schoolyard."

He looked at me, specifically, as he added weight into that last sentence. My face burned with shame, remembering yesterday's incident with Finch. But that quickly went away when I caught a glimpse of Finch's satisfied sneer from where he sat, farther down and across the long table.

"Yes, sir," Wade replied.

I could feel the glimmer of hope that this was where the conversation ended, as he flipped open the file. Then Garrett decided to rub it in.

"Don't worry, sir, my team is made up of professional adults. As long as we're not provoked, it will all work out to the coven's advantage," he said.

"Then keep Finch on a leash," Alton shot back. "I have a low-tolerance policy for bullies."

Oh, snap!

"She threw me on top of a table," Finch interjected, narrowing his steely blues at me.

"I'm a late bloomer with no Esprit, so what does that say about you, then?" I replied with a grin.

Alton let out a frustrated sigh. "That's enough. We have enough on our plates as it is. Petty feuds will not help us redeem this coven's honor."

"What honor?" Garrett scoffed.

"Like it or not, Kyteler, you *are* associated with this coven. Its honor is *your* honor, too. I suggest you start acting accordingly," Alton replied, then gave me a brief, encouraging smile. "Good luck today. I'll be expecting a full report in the evening."

He then left the table and met with the preceptors, who were waiting for him on the other side of the banquet hall, by the main exit. I turned my attention back to our table, where Wade was busy reading through the folder, while Astrid craned her neck to get a better look at the pages.

"You had better bring that smart mouth with you to our date night, Harley," Garrett said, then stood up, followed by Finch and the others on his team. "I absolutely love it."

He gave me another one of those charming winks, complete with a dimpled half-smile. It made Wade boil with anger. Nevertheless, while I understood the animosity between Wade and Garrett, I needed the scoop on the investigative team, and what better source than the leader of said team?

"You're dating Garrett?" Santana asked, her mouth twisted with disapproval. She didn't like him much. Actually, she kind of hated him. There was some history between them, I could feel it.

I shrugged, stealing a glance at Wade, whose green eyes were fixed on me. "I never say no to free food."

A hammer dropped heavy in my stomach. That was Wade. For some reason, I'd hit deep with that one.

"You should be careful with him," Santana said. There was a hint of sadness in there, tucked away between layers of stifled anger. "He's charming as hell, but he's an absolute prick and a sociopath. He will not hesitate to throw you under the bus if it works in his favor."

"Thanks, but I'll be okay. I've dealt with his kind before. I see it as a good opportunity to play nice with him, and hopefully get some insights into their investigation," I replied. "You never know, he might let some juicy stuff slip, if he gets comfortable enough."

"That's why you agreed to go out with him?" Wade asked, surprised.

"That was the main reason, and it still is. Though, I have to admit, I did enjoy pissing you off a little while I was at it." I smiled.

He exhaled sharply, once again irritated, but, at the same time, somewhat relieved. What was there to be relieved about, though?

"Look at Harley, all conniving and devious," Tatyana said appreciatively, grinning like the Cheshire cat. "Watch out, guys, I think we've got a champion on our hands. She just needs some good old-fashioned nurturing and guidance."

"Oh, teach me, master," I replied, offering an overly reverent nod.

The Rag Team chuckled—with the exception of Wade. All he did was let the corner of his mouth twist a little, enough to show me he was slightly amused. Deep inside, however, there was concern and… something else, an emotion I had a hard time identifying, a feeling that gnawed at my stomach uncomfortably.

Chapter Nineteen

"I'm supposed to walk into my own workplace with a fake ID and tell them I'm there to inspect the premises?" I asked, staring at the plastic card in my hand that said I was a Homeland Security agent, while standing in front of the casino where I'd been working for the past six months.

Wade, Tatyana, Santana, Raffe, Astrid, and Dylan were next to me, all suited up in shades of gray and black. I was the only one in jeans and a leather jacket, which made me stand out—and not in a good way, especially when waving around a phony Homeland Security badge.

"You're an agent in training," Wade replied, straightening his navy-blue tie, which he'd matched to a dark gray suit and white shirt. His Esprit rings didn't exactly match the outfit, but then again, looking at the rest of the team, they all had something that didn't quite click. Nevertheless, they looked serious enough in those suits to pass as government employees. "And this is a good opportunity to let the casino know you're starting a new job."

Wade looked around, his hands on his hips. His suit jacket was open, revealing his narrow waistline in sharp contrast with his broad shoulders. I couldn't stop myself from staring. In my defense, only then did I notice how good he looked in a suit. The pants were tailored to gently hug his muscular thighs and calves.

"See something you like?" Wade asked, breaking me out of my… analysis.

"Nothing whatsoever," I replied, my face blazing, thankful he wasn't an Empath. A sliver of disappointment trickled through me —was that mine or his? "Why are we here, exactly? You haven't told me anything about the mission file. Is it a secret?"

"No, I just don't want you to get overwhelmed on your first day," Wade said. "But, to ease your mind, we're simply doing a second sweep of the casino, checking security footage again and questioning other potential witnesses in the area. The investigative team is handling your apartment this morning, so we're not needed there till the afternoon."

Given that it was well before ten a.m., the only people in the casino at that hour would be Malcolm and the bar staff. Wade was right, it was a good opportunity to tell Malcolm I was trying on this new job. Although, I planned to leave room for a return, in case I decided not to stick with the coven.

"Okay," I said, nodding slowly. "How do we do this, then?"

"Santana and Raffe will take the parking lot and 55th Street, where the attack took place, then check the records of the City Heights Family Health Center, in case someone checked in during or after that night with gargoyle-related injuries. Like Alton said, just in case someone slipped through the cracks, since we have no account of the gargoyle's whereabouts from the time it escaped until the moment I saw it lurking around the casino," Wade replied. "Tatyana and Dylan will cover the block between 56th Street and El Cerrito Drive. Astrid will cover everything between El Cerrito Drive, Madison Avenue, and El Cajon, all the way up to the Golden Stiletto Bar. There's no point in going beyond that point. Astrid can tap into street cameras, if needed."

"What do I do?" I asked.

"You're coming inside with me. I'll check their CCTV again, and you'll submit your resignation."

"Okay, see you all back here in, what, two hours?" Santana replied, looking at Wade with raised eyebrows. He responded with a brief nod, and the team scattered in their designated directions.

I followed Wade to the main door, which, of course, was locked, since the casino was scheduled to open much later in the day. He knocked on the glass, then waited until Malcolm opened the door.

"Harley! What brings you here? Your shift is tomorrow," Malcolm said, surprised to see me.

"Yeah, we need to talk about that," I replied with a sad smile, hands in my jacket pockets.

"Are you okay? You were pretty much out of it the other night. I left you some voicemails, too," he said, looking concerned. The last time he'd seen me, he, along with the rest of the casino, had been under Wade's business card spell, reciting his details and freaking the daylights out of me. I'd stormed out and hadn't said anything since.

"I'm so sorry about my outburst, Malcolm. I think I had some bad Chinese. It totally messed with my nerves. I don't know what I was thinking. But, anyway, back to my shift tomorrow," I said, then pointed at Wade. "This is—"

"I'm Wade Crowley, Homeland Security," Wade cut in, flashing his fake badge. "We're investigating an incident that occurred across the street from your establishment eight nights ago. Mind if we come in?"

"You're investigating, as in the two of you?" Malcolm replied, a confused frown settling across his face. He moved aside, allowing us both to go inside.

"Yes," Wade said, keeping a stone-cold expression on his face. In all fairness, we were both quite young, but in our defense, Homeland Security had hired five thousand new operatives in the state of California last year, most of them new recruits. Our fake identities weren't too far-fetched. "Miss Smith is in a probationary period, so we figured it was a good idea to start her off with some familiar places on her first field mission."

Malcolm was astounded, his eyes wide as he stared at me. "It's what I wanted to talk to you about," I added softly. "I'm going to have to resign from the casino—"

"Effective immediately," Wade interrupted me again. He was starting to get on my nerves, so I gave him a discreet, but hopefully uncomfortable, nudge. I heard him grunt, then his irritation flared through me. *Yup. He got the message.*

"I couldn't pass up the opportunity. I hope you understand, Malcolm," I said.

He nodded in response, then offered a heartwarming and sympathetic smile. "Of course. I'm very proud of you, Harley. Well done. I knew you wouldn't be with us for too long."

"Save the spot for me, though." I chuckled. "They might end up sacking me in a month, and I don't do unemployment."

Wade shot me a brief but sharp sideways glance, as if I'd said something out of line. *You can suck on that bitter pill, then, Crowley. I was only telling the truth.* It was bad enough I was impersonating a Homeland Security agent; there was only so much I could bring myself to lie about in front of Malcolm.

"I'm surprised, though," Malcolm replied, scratching his stubbled chin. "You don't have a college degree. Why'd they let you in? I thought they were quite rigorous over at Homeland."

"We've had to lower our standards substantially over the past couple of years," Wade said, and I could feel his satisfaction at that gratuitous jab. *Oh, it is on, Crowley. I will make you cry by the end of this month, I promise.* "It's not college education that is crucial in our assessments, but rather the skillset that each candidate brings to the table. I think we can both agree that Miss Smith's… talents make her a special case. Homeland decided she was worth a try, which is why she's in a probationary period for the time being."

"Well then, again, congratulations, Harley!" Malcolm beamed at me. Even though most of that was a blatant lie, I couldn't help but relish the pride glowing through me, courtesy of Malcolm. He was fond of me and, in many ways, a father figure, as important to me as Mr. Smith. Needless to say, I welcomed his validation. "Now, how can I help you?"

"Like I said, there was an incident eight nights ago, on 55th Street, just past the casino parking lot," Wade explained. "There were no police involved, just two of our agents. Unfortunately, I cannot disclose more information at this time, but we require access to your CCTV cameras, particularly the ones covering the parking lot."

Malcolm was happy to oblige, and escorted us to the security room, where a multitude of TV screens were mounted on a wall. Most of them were focused on the interior parts of the casino, but there were twelve cameras installed outside, with three in the parking lot. I knew each very well, remembering their coverage areas and blind spots.

We watched the footage from that fateful night, and I saw myself at the poker table… the dealer incident, where the image got slightly blurry, as if the cameras were suddenly out of focus. Wade frowned as he saw the entire scene, then gave me a concerned look. I responded with a shrug, then pointed at the screens covering the parking lot.

"There I am," I said.

"What were you doing on the other side of the parking lot?" Malcolm asked, squinting as he looked at the footage. I was just a black stick from that angle, but we could still see my car shake a little from the gargoyle impact. Wade and I could see the creature, but, judging by Malcolm's expression, he couldn't.

That's interesting. I get to see these monsters on camera, too, but the humans are spared the nightmare.

"I heard noises, but I didn't see anything," I replied, then looked at Wade with an innocent look on my face. "Was this when the incident happened?"

"Yes."

Wade wasn't a man of many words at that point, his gaze fixed on the screens.

"I didn't even see the footage until now," Malcolm said. "Had the police been involved, I would've had to pull it up sooner. This is strange. Why's your car moving like that, Harley?"

"I… I have no idea," I replied, unsure how to gloss past that particular anomaly. He couldn't see the monster sliding into my car to produce that nudge.

"Probably a gust of wind," Wade said. "So, you're saying no other Homeland Security agent came in to check the footage the night after the incident?"

Malcolm shrugged. "No one. I had no idea something had even happened so close to our establishment."

Wade straightened his back, and I could sense he was upset. From what I'd learned so far about him and the coven, the protocols did involve scrubbing any CCTV footage related to a monster incident. And yet, there we were, a loose end of the gargoyle affair slapping our faces. *Ugh, someone's going to get reprimanded for this.*

"Harley, can you please go outside for a minute?" Wade asked. "I need a word in private with Malcolm."

I nodded, then gave Malcolm a warm smile and left, closing the door behind me.

Two minutes later, Wade emerged from the room, his rings still glowing blue as he adjusted his tie. "I've wiped the CCTV footage for the entire night, just to be sure no one catches on to your little card tricks, either. I've also adjusted Malcolm's memory regarding the footage. As far as he knows, the cameras glitched that night, and all the footage was lost."

"You tampered with Malcolm's memory?"

I didn't like the sound of that. The technique itself was manipulative and invasive. But in the end, it was in Malcolm's best interest if he didn't remember anything. Something else bothered me, though—it wasn't my issue, but Wade's. "The magicals in charge of the first round of cleanup did a very poor, sloppy job.

That camera footage should've been scrubbed the morning after," Wade said, glaring ahead as I followed him out of the casino. "The fact that no one checked the casino left us with a dangerous opening."

"Do you know who was in charge of cleanup?" I asked.

We reached El Cajon Boulevard, and Wade looked both ways before crossing the street, his gaze fixed on the shops facing the casino. The wide building held a number of businesses, including a Vietnamese grocery store and a printing shop.

"Poe Dexter and a couple of other magicals from his clique. I knew he was a Mediocre, but this borders on incompetence," Wade replied, gritting his teeth. "This means we have to go around this side of the block, too, and ask around, in case that imbecile didn't think to check the neighboring area at all."

"Shouldn't there be a report?" I offered with a shrug.

He stared at me for a couple of seconds, before a smile stretched his lips. "You're not that useless after all."

"Wow, you sure know how to make a girl like you," I said, crossing my arms.

He checked his phone, then quickly typed a text message. "Astrid has access to the reports. I'll have her send it over. Now, let's go in. There's more to check out in the meantime."

Wade walked into the Vietnamese store first, stopping by the main counter. "Hi, Homeland Security," he said, flashing his badge again. "I need to see your CCTV footage."

The store clerk, a middle-aged Vietnamese lady who was half his size, looked up at him. I could feel she was afraid—either wary of government employees or simply wary of strangers in suits with badges. Whatever it was, it worked as a defense mechanism, as she started speaking in Vietnamese.

Wade was confused. *Obviously, does not compute.*

I picked a random magazine from a rack and walked up to the counter next to him, with a warm smile on my face. "Hi, can I get this, and two packs of gum, please?"

She nodded, her brow furrowed, as she scanned my stuff and pressed various keys on her electronic cash register.

"Ma'am, I need to check your CCTV footage," Wade said again, slightly irritated. The woman deliberately ignored him, flashing me a crooked smile.

"Do you want mint or fruity gum?" she asked. Wade's patience was wearing thin, fast.

"Mint, please," I replied softly. "Do you remember me?"

She looked at me, narrowing her brown eyes as she sifted through her memory, then offered a brief nod. "You work at casino, don't you? Pretty girl, always in black dress, right?"

I chuckled, pleased to have made an impression on her. As much as I enjoyed my anonymity, it served no purpose in this case. "Yes, ma'am, that's me. Listen, I wanted to ask you for a favor."

"Anything for you, sweetie. Eight dollars and twenty cents, please," she replied, drawing my total. The one thing that made it out of the apartment with me, besides my father's note, was my wallet, which I'd stuffed into the inside chest pocket of my leather jacket. I handed her my credit card, which she swiped through the card reader. "What do you want, pretty girl?"

"Well, first of all, I need you to ignore this stooge here," I said, nodding in Wade's direction. "He doesn't have any people skills. The only thing he's good at is flashing that stupid badge around. But I do need to check your CCTV if possible. Someone stole my car eight nights ago, and I need to see if your cameras caught anything. It's really important. My insurance company is busting my ass."

The woman listened quietly, a twinkle of amusement in her eyes whenever she glanced at Wade, who was fuming by my side, but kept his mouth shut. He wasn't getting anywhere with her, anyway. It didn't hurt to try a classic con, instead. Besides, I knew this area well. Most of the people here didn't take kindly to badges and uniforms. Even casino security made them jittery.

"If I show you, will he go away?" she replied, her gaze fixed on Wade.

"Absolutely."

"Is he really Homeland Security, though? He's too young!" She frowned at him.

"What, him?" I laughed wholeheartedly. "No, no, he's in drama school, first year in acting. Badge is a fake. He's just trying to help, but like I said, zero social skills."

I purposely avoided looking at him during the exchange, but I could feel my blood boiling on his behalf. The woman chuckled, then motioned for us to follow her behind the counter. "He's a lousy actor, then," she quipped, and guided us through a small side door, leading into her back office, which was cluttered with cardboard boxes and accounting folders.

CCTV footage didn't show too much to the human eye, but both Wade and I could clearly see ourselves—two small black sticks in the distance, wrestling the gargoyle. Wade worked his magic on the Vietnamese lady, wiping her memory and the DVR's hard drive, and leaving her with a similar story about a CCTV system glitch.

"We were never here," he said to her, and she offered an absent nod in response, a faint yellow glimmer in her eyes as she watched us leave.

I ran back to the counter and took the chewing gum packets.

"You forgot your magazine," Wade said as soon as we reached the boulevard again.

"I only needed it as an excuse to get to the counter and stop that disaster you'd probably call an 'undercover sting,'" I replied. "You are absolutely terrible at dealing with these people."

"What do you mean?" he asked, slightly offended. I kind of felt sorry for him. He was a typical elitist drone who followed rules and didn't seem to understand that people in these parts of San Diego were... different.

"Waving a badge around won't get you anywhere in El Cerrito, my friend," I said. "Nobody likes a cop asking for camera footage, not with the gangs working in the area. You know what happens to snitches."

"You seem to have a very good understanding of gangsters and interlopers, I see," Wade replied.

I gave him a brief shrug. "I've worked in that place for long enough. I've met all kinds of people in there. I know this area like the back of my hand, and I'm telling you, next time you want to do a cleanup mission like this, ditch the suits and badges. Simple lies work better. Hell, breaking and entering works better!"

We moved farther down the boulevard, repeating the pattern—checking CCTV, asking people if they remembered anything from that night. Some had had their memories wiped by the previous investigators, based on Wade's assessment, but plenty had slipped through the cracks.

Two hours later, we were back on El Cajon, the casino just eighty yards away to our left. Wade was thoroughly displeased with the amount of memory wiping he'd had to do. "Poe barely did anything," he grumbled, then checked his phone. "And based on what I'm reading from Santana's and Tatyana's texts, the rest of the block is just as bad."

"Did Astrid send over Poe's report?"

"Yes, I'm looking through it now," he replied, swiping through the pages on his phone and shaking his head with disgust. "It's full of vague notes and several lies. I know for a fact he didn't check certain places he says he did."

"You should definitely tell Alton about this," I said, gazing around.

Astrid came into view, as she turned the corner and walked toward us from the north side of the block.

"You bet I'll tell Alton about this," Wade muttered.

"Guys, this whole block was a mess!" Astrid exclaimed as she reached us, holding up a computer tablet. From what I could see on the screen, she was operating some kind of CCTV software with several windows open. "I had to tap into the main network and do manual overrides to wipe out multiple recordings. What the heck did the cleanup team do here last week?"

"Apparently, nothing," Wade said, putting his phone away.

"What's that?" I asked, looking at her tablet.

"This is Smartie!" Astrid beamed at me, holding the device up and pointing at various parts of the screen. "It's a proprietary software I put together. State-of-the-art AI, to be specific. Named him Smartie because he's brilliant."

"Him? It's a he?" I chuckled.

"Absolutely. My soulmate." Astrid giggled, then flipped over several screens. I could see footage from all over the neighborhood through a live feed, and I was officially impressed. "Smartie taps into any system, basically. I've fitted him with several encryption and decryption algorithms, to the point where all I need to do is tell him where to go and what to do, and he does it. Flawlessly, I might add!"

"That's pretty cool," I said, unable to take my eyes off the screen. Even the software design looked good, warm white graphics against a charcoal background—elegant and discreet. She tapped a couple of controls, then pulled out a list of cameras in a separate file.

"These are the systems I've cleared, all the way up to the Golden Stiletto Bar, on a half-mile radius," she said. "Where are the others?"

"They're on their way back," Wade replied. "We should get back to the casino, too. We're done with this side."

My blood chilled as I looked up and noticed movement on top of the Catholic church across the street from us. We were five minutes away from the casino—two minutes if we ran. That's how long it was going to take the rest of our team to reach us.

I tapped Wade's shoulder and pointed at the church roof, where several black figures slithered across the red tiles. Their bat wings and long, spiky tails confirmed what I already knew, deep in the pit of my stomach. "Gargoyles," I whispered.

Wade stilled, then followed my gaze. Astrid couldn't see them, given her human nature, but she was quick to tap a few icons on her Smartie tablet. "I may not have eyes for these suckers, but Smartie can read energy levels in the atmosphere. Monsters have exceptionally high body temperatures. They stand out like bright red spots once I get Smartie to look for them, and... there they are. I see them. Oh, crap."

"Ten of them," Wade finished her sentence, examining the rooftop. "Astrid, call the team back. We need to catch these suckers before they wreak havoc."

Astrid nodded and quickly texted the others, shaking her head in confusion. "I don't get it, though. What are they doing out in the middle of the day? It's completely unprecedented."

"It is?" I asked, gathering enough sense and strength to make myself ready and available to intervene if needed. I had a bone to pick with these ugly bastards, anyway.

"Gargoyles only hunt at night, and never on a full moon," Wade explained. "They thoroughly dislike daylight. Let's move in closer; we need a better angle. Astrid, stay back and keep the line open. Put your earpiece on."

Astrid took out a small Bluetooth device from her pocket, activated it, and put it in her ear. Wade handed me one, out of the two he had with him. "Put this on and press the main button. It'll take you directly into our communications channel. Each team has a different frequency. Yours is already tuned in."

I pressed the button as instructed, and the rest of the Rag Team's voices came through, crystal clear. "We're one minute away!" Santana said, breathing heavily as she ran.

Turning my head toward the casino, I could see her and Raffe darting across the pavement. Soon enough, they were joined by Tatyana and Dylan, who came in from a side street.

We moved closer, getting a clearer view of the gargoyles. They were all perched on the edge of the roof, but they didn't seem like they were going to attack anyone—and there were plenty of people out in the middle of the day. My heart shrank to the size of a pea as I watched mothers pushing baby strollers and churchgoers emerging from the building.

"Why aren't the gargoyles moving?" I asked.

"I wish I knew," Wade replied. "I'm more worried about why they're all looking at *you*, Harley."

"Huh?" I managed, then realized he was right. All ten gruesomely fierce gargoyles had their big, black, beady eyes focused on me. My blood curdled, but my anger was stronger. One of their pals had destroyed my car, after all.

The others reached us, just in time to watch the gargoyles stretching their necks and baring their fangs, thick drool pouring out of their gaping mouths. The spikes on the backs of their heads rattled—a trait I hadn't seen on the other gargoyles I'd dealt with. The sound sent shivers down my spine.

Tatyana cursed under her breath in Russian, from what I could tell, and rolled up her smart jacket sleeves. "I'll go set a ground-floor net trap," she said. "You guys keep them on the roof."

Without waiting for a reply, she rushed into the building, disappearing in the emerging crowd of people leaving the religious service.

"Dylan, Raffe, take the other side, behind the parish school," Wade commanded. "Santana, you've got El Cerrito Drive. I'll put out the ball. Astrid, make some noise somewhere farther down the road. Make it loud enough to get everybody off this block."

"Got it," I heard Astrid through the earpiece. "Would a fire alarm do?"

"It had better get people running as far away from the boulevard as possible," Wade replied.

"Air-raid siren it is, then!" she said.

"Wait, no—"

Wade didn't get to finish, as a fire siren started blaring out of several stores farther down the road. The noise was loud and stringent enough to draw people's attention. Like moths drawn to a flame, several people walked toward the source of the alarm, while most hurried down the boulevard in the opposite direction.

"I was kidding!" I heard Astrid chuckle through my earpiece. "Air-raid sirens would've brought fighter jets scrambling around on full after-burner. Imagine the joy of the gargoyles to have something with *wings* to hunt."

"Thanks, Astrid," Wade replied flatly, then moved toward the church with his hands out. His rings lit up blue as he pushed out a much bigger time-lapse bubble. The energy ball spread out, gradually encompassing the entire area around the church.

Santana started waving at the rest of the people left in the affected area, motioning for them to leave. I figured I could start making myself useful, so I used my Telekinesis to send out a couple of nudges, and push humans farther away and out of the time lapse. They couldn't see it, but it did slow time on the inside. We just couldn't afford any weirdness, not when fire alarms were blaring and people were beginning to panic.

The gargoyles looked up and around, confused by the loud noises and our movements.

"I don't get it," I said. "They're gawking at me, but they're not attacking."

"Let's focus on catching them first," Wade replied. "Take the left side, and don't let them get off the roof!"

I nodded, then rushed over to the doctor's office on the left side of the church. Wade stayed at the front, his gaze fixed on the gargoyles, who were starting to get restless, scampering across the roof.

Lights flickered inside the ground floor, followed by a number of popping sounds. Whatever Tatyana was doing inside, it was loud and flashy, and it was making the gargoyles even more nervous.

One of them tried to take flight, but a bright wisp of light smacked right into it, bursting into a myriad of fireworks. The creature fell backward, squealing as its eyes burned. The others spread their wings and hissed, then attempted to fly out, but Wade shot fire projectiles at them, targeting their heads.

Tiny balls of green energy shot out from behind the building, whirling around until they hit the gargoyles again. No matter where they went, there was a magical using some kind of spell to keep them on the roof.

As soon as the monsters came over to my side of the building, I knew what I had to do. Even without an Esprit, I could still do my part. I latched onto the billboard advertising some random life insurance company, pulled it off the doctor's office it was displayed on, then tossed it at the gargoyles.

It flew in fast, knocking three of them back, while the others tried to escape on the other sides again. They didn't stand a chance, though. Whenever they came back to my side, I focused my mental lasso on their heads, and waved them back like loose coconuts.

One final bang rumbled through the ground floor, followed by a bright white flash that spread outward and upward, swallowing the entire building. Just as Tatyana ran out, the light reached the roof, covering all the walls before it formed a super-fine net.

The gargoyles roared as they made one last-ditch effort to get off the roof, but the glowing net covered the entire surface and came down with such strength that it crushed the creatures hard into the terracotta tiles. They growled and shrieked as they struggled against their restraints.

"Santana, Tatyana, you've got Mason jars in your bags, I hope," I heard Wade say through my earpiece.

"Yeah, more than enough," Santana replied.

"Okay, grab Raffe and Dylan," Wade said. "Five minutes. You know what you have to do."

"Roger that," Tatyana's voice came through.

I went back to the boulevard, where Astrid joined us from across the street. Wade had made sure to keep her in the enormous time lapse. "Not bad, rookie," Wade said, giving me a subtle wink as I reached him.

My heart skipped a beat. This was Wade's first sort-of compliment.

"Thanks," I murmured, my cheeks lighting up like the 4th of July.

"Well done, Harley!" Astrid cheered, while tapping various

controls on her computer tablet. "I wonder if all these bad boys came out of the Bestiary."

"We'll check for serial numbers when we bring them in," Wade replied, crossing his arms as he looked up at the roof. I followed his gaze, and watched Santana, Tatyana, Dylan, and Raffe perch on the sloped edges, summoning the gargoyles one by one into Mason jars.

Once they were done, they snuck back through the windows and met us outside with two backpacks full of gargoyles. Pieces of the roof were missing, as terracotta slates lay crushed on the ground around the church. The gargoyles may have been invisible to the human eye, but the damage they left behind was clear as day.

"Does cleanup involve fixing the roof?" I asked.

"That's the humans' responsibility," Wade said, shaking his head. "The building is insured, anyway."

"Technically speaking, we're actually creating jobs right now. Construction jobs." Astrid chuckled, eyes on her screen. "Okay, I've planted a couple of phone calls to notify the authorities about the damaged roof. They'll send surveyors soon enough."

"I've never seen ten gargoyles in one place before," Santana said, her brow furrowed. "Outside the Bestiary, I mean. What could this mean?"

"And why were they all staring at me? Why didn't they attack?" I sighed, my shoulders dropping.

After a lifetime spent under the radar, being stalked by gargoyles wasn't exactly my idea of getting attention. If anything, it scared the life out of me. *Whatever happened to me trying to stay out of trouble?*

And how did I see the coven now? A cluster of pencil-pushing elitists and frustrated Mediocre magicals who were in charge of guarding a cesspool of humanity's worst nightmares—and doing a crappy job of that, too.

Why would I ever pledge my life and loyalty to a coven? Wasn't I better on my own?

Who was I kidding? I had no Esprit, no knowledge of who my real parents were, and a string of gargoyles following me around, eager to eat me alive. For the time being, I was stuck with these people. At least they had my back, and in all fairness, my Rag Team peeps were pretty cool, despite their antisocial dysfunctionalities.

"All the more reason for you to stay with us." Santana smirked, trying to get over the concerns brewing inside her. She was worried about me.

For good reason. I'm worried about me, too.

Chapter Twenty

We loaded the jars into the back of Wade's Jeep. My apartment was next on our to-do list. We left the fire trucks responding to the fire alarms behind, along with the church staff gawking at the damaged roof, as Wade shoved us in his Jeep and drove us up to Park West.

My stomach churned as we reached the scene of yesterday's attack—and my home.

The police had already been there and cordoned off my poor mangled Daisy with their yellow caution tape. They'd also taped the windows to my apartment, and I could see the blackened ceiling from below. The place had definitely burned up a little before the sprinkler system went on.

The team repeated the cleanup operation from the casino, going into and around the apartment building to check with potential witnesses and flash them, altering their memories where needed. Santana and Raffe took the inside of the building, while Tatyana and Dylan handled the surrounding area, and Astrid got to work on modifying CCTV footage, as well as checking police and fire department records.

Wade had me wait outside, not wanting me to get a closer look at my wrecked apartment. He quickly regretted bringing me over at all, once he saw me tear up as I walked over to my Daisy. I ran my fingers along the edges of her bent hood. My car looked as though a giant cement ball had been dropped on her, pulling everything down in the middle. Glass crumbled beneath my boots as I moved closer and retrieved a little hand-painted world globe from the passenger seat.

It was my rearview mirror ornament, the only thing left intact after Murray the gargoyle's crash landing. I used to look at it and dream of the places I'd visit in the near future. *No car, no apartment... Clearly, travel plans will have to wait.*

Wade's hand settled on my shoulder. "Are you okay?" he asked, his voice low. I looked up to find his face surprisingly close to mine—enough to make me hold my breath for a second. He was worried.

"How can I be?" I sobbed, no longer able to hold it in. "My apartment was trashed. My car is done for. I've got gargoyles following me around like I'm prime beef walking. Of course I'm not okay."

Not sure what to say, he kept his mouth shut. For about two seconds. "Material belongings of the human world aren't all that valuable, Harley. They can all be easily replaced."

"Easy for *you* to say, maybe," I said, wiping my tears. "Daisy was my soul. Raucous and loud, sturdy and feisty. And now look at her. Not going to bother explaining that to you. *Again*."

"Move on, Harley. There's no point in dwelling on these things. The sooner you do that, the better you'll feel," Wade replied. He clearly didn't understand where I was coming from, and I had to admit, it hurt a little. "With the money you'll be making with the coven in the future, you'll be able to afford a newer, better model, anyway."

"What, as a research assistant in a library?" I said. "Are you kidding me?"

"That job is just to get you started in the coven and the magical society. I trust you'll be able to work as a coven operative on a full-time basis once you take the pledge. But you'll get nowhere if you cling to sentimental nonsense like this heap of trash," he said, pointing at my Daisy.

"Don't call her that!"

My hands balled into fists, and I could feel the anger coursing through me like a violent waterfall. Wade didn't seem to care.

"It is what it is, Harley. This thing is going right into a junkyard. Get over it and worry more about why there are gargoyles following you around in the first place."

"Thanks for the reminder," I replied, rolling my eyes and crossing my arms.

As much as I hated admitting it, Wade did have a point. A car was replaceable, no matter how much I loved my Daisy. My life, however, was one of a kind. And yes, there were gargoyles coming after me now, and I had no clue why.

"I can't help but wonder, Harley, if there's something from your past that you're not telling me. Something that ties the gargoyles into this whole mess."

"Huh? Like what? I thought you knew everything about me. Including my bra size," I retorted, and instantly felt my throat burn —that was Wade's utter embarrassment.

"I don't know. You tell me," he shot back. "Maybe you *do* know something about your parents, for example?"

"Oh, so now I'm a suspect or something?" I raised my voice, my hands trembling with anger.

The ground beneath us started to shake, like a mild earthquake. Wade stilled, his forehead smoothing as we both came to the same conclusion. I heard people gasping as they came to a halt on the street. Tires screeched close by, as the entire neighborhood felt the shudder of my Elemental burst.

"Maybe I should try and calm down."

"You should calm down," he said at the same time.

Deep breaths. Deep breaths.

A minute later, the earth stopped shaking. Wade and I stared at each other—he was in awe of me, I could feel it. "I went overboard, I'm sorry," he said. "It's just that we've never had these Bestiary issues before, and it's eerie enough to coincide with the discovery of you. I can't help but think that there might be a connection."

"I honestly don't know anything about my parents," I replied. "I wish I did. I mean, even I'm thinking that the gargoyles might know something I don't. Maybe they're drawn to me for a specific reason that actually has to do with me, with who I really am. Then again, maybe I'm just tastier than the rest of you. I have zero input on this right now."

"And without an Esprit, you clearly have little control over your abilities," Wade concluded. "Your emotions are powerful enough to trigger them, though."

"Which makes me say, once more, that this whole Mediocre thing is absolute BS!" Astrid called out from the stairs. She'd been listening this whole time. I'd completely forgotten about her. *Wade's fault.*

Once the team reunited outside my apartment block, the cleanup job was complete. Santana, Raffe, Tatyana, and Dylan covered all the witnesses, and Astrid successfully altered everything we needed to make the story stick—a gas leak had resulted in an explosion, then a fire, followed by the sprinklers soaking everything. No one got hurt, other than Harley Smith. I was carried off to the hospital and discharged shortly after that. End of story.

It was more believable and easier to manage than a home invasion route. That would've brought more cops into the fold, and we wanted none. "I'll give Alton a report tonight," Wade said.

"Make sure you mention Poe's sloppy work," Santana said. "That boy could easily be classified as a liability to the coven. I don't get why Alton let Garrett put him on the investigative team in the first place."

"Either Alton is an idealist who thinks those schmucks will make something of themselves and actually help the coven, or he just let them play to appease their ultra-rich parents, and to then watch them crash and burn," Raffe mused.

"I'm rooting for the latter," Wade replied. "I refuse to believe Alton is gullible enough to think the likes of Poe, Garrett, and Finch might actually be good for the coven. He's been here three years and broken up too many fights started by those idiots."

"Meh, it's not like we've been stellar performers, either." Santana chuckled, hands in her pant pockets. Her curly hair gave her a very hip look, when paired with a dark gray pantsuit. She could've easily graced the cover of a fashion magazine, if she wanted. Judging by the warmth coming from Raffe, I wasn't the only one appreciating her look.

"Speak for yourself," Wade shot back. "My record is spotless."

"Ugh, let's grab some drinks at Waterfront Park," Santana said, rolling her eyes as she walked over to Wade's Jeep. "Another minute of Mr. Perfect here and I'll unload my breakfast."

"That would be a shame. Those scones were delicious," Tatyana chimed in, amusement twinkling in her icy blue eyes.

"Unless you want to walk there, I'd suggest you jump off the 'Insult Wade' train," Wade said, wiggling the keys.

After we left the Jeep in the Maritime Museum's parking lot, we went back around to West Ash Street, on the south side of Waterfront Park. It didn't look different. I was expecting something more magical.

"Out of all the places in the world, this is where you people like to hang out? This is basically Toddler Central," I said, pointing at the groups of parents herding their children across the park. "What is it with magicals and kids' playgrounds?"

We stopped in front of a glass refuge by the bus stop, a bland and nearly unnoticeable structure. There was a staircase leading downstairs to a public restroom. "You've got to be kidding," I said.

"*Aperi Portam*," Wade said, then pushed through the door.

One by one, we joined him, and, just like my first incursion into the coven through the emergency door of Kid City, I realized that there was a whole other world hiding in Waterfront Park. I heard myself gasp at the sight unraveling before me. Elegant steel-and-glass cubes rose on both sides of the single wide alley ahead. This both was and wasn't Waterfront Park, another interdimensional pocket. The human world was something akin to a lens flare, occasionally visible in the form of two-legged wisps—people walking through the park.

"Welcome to *our* Waterfront Park, home of some of our best nightclubs and craft-related stores," Wade said.

This version looked a million times better. It offered views of the city and the ocean, beyond the tall crystal walls surrounding the interdimensional pocket. "There's another exit on that side, leading to the Maritime Museum," Wade added, pointing across the park. "I just wanted to show you this entrance first, for future reference."

My mouth was wide open as I tried to take it all in—a plethora of stores, bookshops, cafés, and bars sprawled all over this alternate Waterfront Park, encased in a giant, glistening glass box. The sky was gloriously blue above, the sun smiling down at us as we moved forward. There were plenty of magicals out here, migrating from one venue to another.

An amalgam of words and giggles poured through from various terraces and cocktail bars, and I couldn't stop my heart from fluttering. I'd never seen anything so different, so intriguing, and so damn stylish. It reminded me of the photos I'd seen of London's Oxford Street and New York's Soho areas, with flashy signs and beautifully decorated store windows.

"What is this place, exactly?" I managed, utterly bedazzled.

"Well, it's not Toddler Central, for sure." Santana chuckled. "It's where we go to supply all of our magical needs. Books, recipes, spell ingredients. Drinks, food. More drinks. It's a place where magicals can be themselves without worrying about humans seeing them. Hell, you can even buy an Esprit here, if you have a hard time finding your own."

"Wait, what?" I asked, slightly confused. "I thought the Esprit was a personal object, something you connect with."

"It is," Wade replied. "However, sometimes it's hard for a magical to find such an item. Cabot's Esprit Reliquary over there stocks up on a variety of pre-owned objects, former Esprits of deceased magicals. They cost a fortune, though."

He pointed at a storefront not too far ahead. I could make out the Cabot name in shiny steel letters mounted above the main entrance.

"Okay, let's grab a drink and a bite at Moll Dyer's, first," Astrid suggested, "I'm starving. Then we'll show you Cabot's place, though I sincerely doubt you'll need it."

I managed a nod before all three girls flanked me and escorted me to a gorgeous little café and bar, with Moll Dyer's name lovingly written in swirly cursive gold letters above the terrace. The interior was decorated in charcoal gray and soft beiges, with a French feel—complete with classy smoked glass wall sconces and elegant silverware. The terrace was a tad more casual, with tables covered in white linen, each with a red-and-yellow flowerpot.

We gathered around a larger table, and a waitress brought over the lunch and specials menus. I let Santana order for me, given that she swore by their minty lemonade and quiche. Wade, as usual, requested sparkling water in a glassful of limes—his almost-limeade. It brought flashbacks of the night we'd met, and the glimpses I'd caught of a gargoyle's tail.

The team engaged in a conversation about today's mission, while I found myself gawking at a detail I'd somehow missed before. The night I met Wade, there was already a gargoyle inside the casino, long before the actual incident out in the parking lot. What was the creature doing there in the first place?

Oh, my God. Was it because of me, from the very beginning?

If so, I was probably, though indirectly, responsible for its attack on Jamie the drunk dude.

"Wade, I just remembered something," I murmured, feeling my

blood chill as I went deeper into my memories of that night. He looked at me, waiting for me to continue. "The night you were at the casino… When I was still at the poker table, and you were sitting in one of the booths… There was a gargoyle in the room, right? I thought I saw a tail up on the ceiling, by one of the vents."

"That's correct," Wade said.

"Why were you at the casino that night?" I asked.

"I saw the gargoyle outside, first. I was driving by, on my way back from another mission, when I saw the creature slither inside."

"And then it went back out and attacked the guy," I continued.

He frowned slightly. "Yeah. What are you trying to say, Harley?"

"I'm not sure. But, if the gargoyles are somehow following me, what are the odds that the one double escapee was deliberately after me from the very first night?" I asked. "What if it got out of the Bestiary once, came after me, then got out again, came after me again, and trashed my place and my car in the process, along with its buddies? Then more of its minions followed today… Does that make sense? By the way, Tobe calls that gargoyle Murray. Says it's a 'he,'" I added.

He thought about it for a while, as did the rest of the team, before Santana shook her head. "If *Murray* was after you since last week, why didn't he attack you directly? Why did he go after some random dude, then?"

"Also, we don't yet know if the gargoyles from today had anything to do with Murray," Wade replied. "Let's check with Tobe before we jump to any conclusions."

"Well, one thing's for sure. They all seem to want a bite out of me," I concluded, then breathed out a tremendous weight from my lungs. I was already tired, worn out by how quickly my life had turned upside down.

"Ah, crap." Santana's dismay broke my train of thought.

We all followed her gaze to the end of the alley, where a group of magicals emerged from the crowd. Garrett, Finch, and the rest of the investigation team. I couldn't help but scoff. Their snobbish arrogance was the last thing I needed.

"Bunch of stalkers," I muttered. "Maybe if we ignore them, they'll go away."

"Slim chance," Tatyana replied. "They're like wasps. The more you swat them away, the more vicious they get."

I braced myself for what I knew would be a tense exchange. Even from that distance, I could see the look on Finch's face. He was dying for seconds, and we were in a public place. "Whatever you do, Harley, don't let them get to you," Astrid said, squeezing my arm gently. I gave her a weak smile and a nod in return.

"What's up, losers?" Garrett said as soon as they reached Moll Dyer's terrace, then winked at me. "Except you, beautiful. I'll have a chat with Alton, see if we can bump you up to the investigative team."

"Who says I want to be clumped together with your rejects?" I said. "I tolerate you enough to let you buy me a drink, but let's not get ahead of ourselves here."

One point to Harley. I couldn't feel Garrett or Finch, but the rest of his team was already fuming.

"Is there something you want, or are you just trying to stir something up again?" Wade replied, giving Garrett a tired roll of his green eyes.

"We're just out for some drinks, Chief Loser. We already handed our report to Alton. It seems to me that the Rag Team's behind already," Garrett said, his lips stretching into a grin. Once again, I got distracted by those dimples. Garrett was the hot guy you loved to hate—like the sexy villain in a spy movie.

"I hope you didn't let Poe write the report," Wade shot back, going straight for the kill. I felt a grin slit my face as I studied the sour faces of the investigative team—Poe's, in particular. He was ready to boil over.

Garrett didn't seem too offended, just confused. "What are you implying?"

"I'm not implying anything. Just stating the fact. We spent the first part of the morning cleaning up after Poe's cleanup team. His incompetence left a ton of loose ends behind, and judging by the report he handed to Alton, he lied through his teeth about how good a job he did. Which really doesn't look good on *your* team," Wade replied.

I was impressed to see him in attack mode. Once he had something on someone, Wade didn't let go until his prey was utterly, irrevocably terminated.

"That's downright slanderous!" Poe blurted, though my cheeks burned for him. Shame and guilt weighed heavy on the guy. It was my turn to consolidate Wade's hits.

"Is that why you reek of guilt and embarrassment?" I chimed in, wiggling my eyebrows at him. "We all read your fairytale of a report. We had to flash people you said you'd already flashed, and Astrid here had to go into the city's CCTV mainframe and adjust the footage, because there was plenty there for a non-magical to consider suspicious, to say the least. Not to mention weird."

"Butt out, Mediocre!" Poe growled, taking a couple of steps forward.

"Pot, kettle, anyone?" I chuckled, leaning back into my chair and linking my hands behind my head, to show him exactly how little he intimidated me.

"You've got quite a lip on you today, Smith," Finch said, his glare burning through me. "Someone should really teach you about your place in this coven, before you get yourself or, worse, someone else killed."

"Is that a threat?"

I shot to my feet, finding it hard to control my murderous instincts. Finch did have a way of bringing the worst out in me. Wade caught my wrist, his grip tightening to the point where it was beginning to make my body temperature spike. "Harley."

"It's not a threat. It's a fact. It's bad enough you've got the loudmouth Santeria witch, Tatyana the snow queen, Raffe the freak, the dumb jock, and Crowley, the king of stooges, here already," Finch replied, nodding at each member of my team, including Astrid. "Not to mention the suicidal human. The last thing this group needs is an unhinged late bloomer who can't keep her mouth shut or her abilities under control. I'm just saying, someone needs to teach you some discipline."

"Or I could just show you the true meaning of 'unhinged.' Clearly, you haven't had enough since yesterday, and you'd like me to break some of your bones," I said, gritting my teeth.

"Okay, break it up, you two." Garrett intervened, placing his arm across Finch's chest and pulling him back. "Finch, you're ruining my vibe here, man."

"Then stop offering her a position on this team!" Finch hissed. "Don't try to shove her down our throats just because you want to get in her pants!"

"I doubt he'll get anywhere near her pants," Wade said, crossing his arms over his chest. I then remembered why it was important I stayed on Garrett's good side, and gave him a brief smile.

"No need to offer me a spot on the team. I wouldn't be caught dead working with the imbeciles you've surrounded yourself with," I replied. "Let's not mix business with pleasure."

I felt Wade seethe at that. I had an urge to trash the entire terrace and break it apart—and that wasn't me, that was all him. Pushing it aside, I waved Finch and the others away with a flick of my wrist, then resumed my seat. "Now, run along, little pups," I added. "Don't spoil my afternoon."

"I'll come get you later, then! How does Little Italy sound for tonight?" Garrett smiled, dimples in full effect.

"Nah, I'm into swankier stuff," I replied. "There's a secret little hip spot in Northblock Lofts I'd like better."

"Noble Experiment?"

"That's the place."

"Perfect. I'll come pick you up at nine, then," Garrett said, then sent me another wink and motioned for the rest of his team to follow him to another venue, farther down the alley. "Come on, there's better food at the Black Crow."

We all watched them leave, but Wade's fury wasn't ready to subside. If anything, it was getting stronger, throbbing through my temples. I gave him a brief sideways glance. "Tone it down, I'm not marrying the guy. Remember? Keep your friends close, yadda-yadda-yadda?"

The Rag Team shifted their focus back to me, eyes wide and sparkling with curiosity. I let out a frustrated sigh. "Intel, guys! Intel! This may not be a competition, given how different our activity scopes are, but I'll be damned if I let the investigation team screw us over in any way. If anything, I'm now even more determined to shove that humble pie down their throats," I explained, prompting Santana and the others to put on their most evil grins.

Funny enough, Astrid failed miserably at looking "evil." Dylan wasn't too good at it either, but Santana, Tatyana, and Raffe gave me the chills. I wouldn't have wanted to be on their bad sides. Wade, on the other hand, was still angry and awfully quiet, a muscle twitching in his jaw as he stabbed the wedges of lime in his glass with a straw.

I decided it was time to change the subject, just to give Wade some space to process what had just happened. His feud with Garrett seemed petty when compared to my objective of gathering intel from Mr. Dimples. At least I didn't have to fake that I was attracted to the guy—my hormones be damned.

"I've been thinking," I said, "and it's something I've briefly discussed with Tobe. I thought I should run it by you guys, too. What if this whole Bestiary issue is an inside job?" The dropped jaws I received in response were a sign for me to elaborate a little. In all fairness, with everything I'd seen today on the church roof, I had every right to question the coven's integrity. "Murray got out once, even though the Bestiary is secured. They added more magicals to guard it, they swept the place and found no trace of foul play, then Murray got out again. Something tells me that at least one of the church gargoyles we've got in the back of the Jeep is also from the Bestiary. So, my question is, what if the Bestiary's being sabotaged?"

"What would be the purpose? Why would anyone want to drown the ship while they're still on it?" Wade replied with a frown, and then it hit me. *Of course.*

"I don't know about the purpose, but you make a fair point there," I said. "If anyone would be trying to sabotage the Bestiary while it's still with the San Diego Coven, it would be someone who's not part of the coven or is looking to leave the coven. I'm using my logic here, guys, help me out."

"I see what you're trying to get at, but still, what's the endgame?" Santana asked, fiddling with a paper napkin.

"Well, think of it as something to mull over," I replied with a shrug. "Off the top of my head, my first guess would be that someone's really pissed off with the fact that the San Diego Coven didn't refuse the nomination in the first place and chose to go ahead with the Bestiary's management. Or maybe someone has a grudge against Alton?"

"We might as well widen the suspect net, then," Wade said. "It could be Alton, or even Tobe. The preceptors, the instructors… Adley… any magical in the coven. The Rag Team. Then there's Garrett, Finch, Poe, or the rest of that joke of an investigative team."

A couple of minutes went by in absolute silence, as they all processed the information. I could tell I'd rattled them a little—which was good. I certainly wasn't the only one on the team actively suspecting an inside job, but I was the first one to say it out loud. We'd all thought about it from the very beginning, but they didn't strike me as the type of people who would be comfortable suspecting each other of sabotaging the Bestiary. They seemed to be part of a tightly knit community inside the coven.

"Well, enough with the conspiracy theories for today," Wade finally said, apparently not yet ready to officially accept the possibility. "Let's get back to the coven. I've got a report to file."

He was thinking about the idea of an inside job, and, given the unsettled feeling in my gut, I knew he was taking it seriously. There was no way that these gargoyle escapes were just accidents or unfortunate coincidences. Once, maybe. Twice? Less likely. Three times?

Nope, something stinks for sure.

Chapter Twenty-One

"Let's check the reliquary first." Santana beamed at me as we left the terrace.

"It's too soon to resort to that," Wade said. "And way too expensive."

"It's cool, I just want to see what stuff they're selling in there," I replied with a shrug, then followed Santana inside Cabot's Esprit Reliquary.

The outside of the store looked like a contemporary steampunk dream, with a plethora of trinkets displayed in the dimly lit windows, and brass gears decorating the steel frames. A sterling silver replica of the solar system floated in the middle of the store—no wires, no hidden mechanism. They were just… hovering.

"Magnetism?" I asked, frowning at it. The planets orbited a large sun, which had been fitted with an internal light, glowing warm white through thousands of tiny holes.

"Nope," Wade replied, without bothering to explain.

"Magic," Santana said, winking.

We scattered throughout the reliquary. I let my gaze wander over several glass displays. Jewels of all shapes and sizes twinkled at me, loaded with mother-of-pearl inlays and precious stones. There were also looking glasses, pocket watches, walking sticks, pens, cufflinks, a dazzling array of sterling silver bracelets and rings, and various other objects. They'd all belonged to a magical at some point.

"Looking for an Esprit?" A familiar voice made me turn around.

I stilled, suddenly feeling tiny and insignificant in front of Imogene Whitehall of the California Mage Council. She was even more beautiful up close. Her eyes reminded me of a midsummer sky at noon, a pure blue that filled me with the urge to just… smile. Her pale blonde hair was caught up in a loose bun that covered the back of her slender neck. Her simple, white maxi dress flowed carelessly over her body, and dozens of slim, silver bracelets jingled on her thin wrists. I couldn't read her as an Empath, but everything about her gave me a peculiar, overall good feeling, as if she was kindness poured into the shape of a woman.

She was slightly taller than me, so I had to tilt my head back a little in order to look her in the eyes. "Ms. Whitehall," I managed. "Um, yes. Sort of. Not really. Honestly, I'm not sure. I guess I'm browsing?"

She laughed lightly.

"Surprised to run into you here," I added, wondering what she was doing in a shop like this.

"Oh, I have a friend who collects these antique objects. I buy her one every year on her birthday." Imogene smiled. "It's what all this stuff is, anyway. One in a thousand magicals might find an Esprit in here. For everyone else it's just expensive junk. And I just picked up a gorgeous silver-plated pocket watch for my friend."

My gaze dropped to the small gift bag in her hand. "So, you think it would be a waste of time for me to look for an Esprit here, huh?"

Imogene lifted her hand to show me a large pearl ring, elegantly connected to a silver bracelet, on which more pearls had been mounted in a delicate pattern. It was beautiful and quite unique, especially since the chain connecting it was made of tiny pearls. It glistened pale yellow in the dim store lights. "Do you know how long it took me to find this piece?" she asked.

"I have no idea. It looks custom made," I replied.

"It is. You have a good eye," Imogene said, making sure her appreciative tone came through.

I gave her a modest shrug in return. "I studied a bit of design in high school. But wait, if you had it custom made, you didn't find it. You had it made."

"Your logic is sound." Imogene chuckled softly. "But *I* didn't have it made. I spent five years without an Esprit, from the moment my powers came to light. Fortunately for me, I had magical parents to guide me, so I passed those five years looking, touching every object I came across, in the hope that I would feel that instant connection."

"How… What does it *feel* like?" I asked, unable to hide my sorrow. I'd only just found out about an Esprit, and yet, I was already moping over it.

"Trust me, you'll know it the moment you touch it. The feeling itself… Well, it's indescribable. But it's okay, Harley. From what Alton has told me, you've only recently learned about the Esprit. If you're just getting started with the search, I'm sure you'll find it much sooner than I did. When you're an adult magical, you're much more attuned to the Chaos. As a child, everything is… softer." She smiled.

"So, you found yours."

"Yes. But not in a reliquary, mind you. I found it in the human world, in a flea market outside New Orleans," she replied. "The seller was human. He didn't even know what he had. It turns out, *this* belonged to Agatha Southeil, one of the most renowned witches of her time!"

I blinked several times, trying to process the name. "Why does that sound familiar?"

"Her daughter was legendary! She predicted the Great Fire of London, among other things," Imogene replied. "Well, technically speaking, the spirits advised her, and she just passed the message on. She wasn't really a clairvoyant, but she did have the touch of the Necromancer, so she was able to speak to the spirits of those stuck between the planes of existence. They often see everything with greater clarity than the living. They can tell if a candle is at risk of causing a fire, or if a driver will hit the brakes in time before a boy crosses the road, and so on. Agatha, like her daughter, just communicated their conclusions."

"Oh, wow," I mumbled.

"I know, right?" Imogene giggled. "Who would've thought? Point is, don't struggle too much to search for it, and don't stress over it, either. No magical is ever without an Esprit. We all find it sooner or later. To be honest, the reliquary should be your last resort. You're still so young, with plenty of time to find your Esprit."

"Until yesterday, I didn't even know I needed one," I replied. "It's not like my life is over without it. But, you know, now I am looking forward to finding it."

"Are you fearful about not having control over your abilities?" she asked with a gentle frown, then placed her hands on my shoulders. I could almost hear her holding her breath for a few seconds, before she exhaled sharply and gave me another warm smile.

"I would like to have better control over my abilities, sure," I said.

"I'll tell you a secret, but you must promise you won't tell anyone, Harley."

I nodded. "Cross my heart."

"You want to make friends with Preceptor Nomura," she whispered. "It took him twenty years to find *his* Esprit, but he was an expert in his field long before that."

"Whoa. How did he do that?"

"Self-control," Imogene replied. "It's all about self-control, and I can't think of anyone who is better equipped to teach you about that. Take your time with him, though. Don't go straight to him with the request. Let him see you need help. He has many tricks up his sleeve, but he rarely shares them with other magicals. In our world, when we want to limit the powers of a delinquent magical, we take away their Esprit. You see, once you're connected to yours, you'll depend on it. Your raw abilities will shrink significantly, as the energy of Chaos settles inside the Esprit."

"Ah, so Nomura doesn't want other magicals to learn his techniques, because if they go dark-side and have their Esprits taken away from them, they can still do damage, right?" I concluded, and Imogene smiled brightly.

"Exactly. You're smart as a whip, Harley. Should you ever choose to move to another city, do let me know. I'd be more than happy to put in a good word for you in the Los Angeles Coven, for example."

"Apparently, I'm a Mediocre. Not sure LA would want me," I said.

"Nonsense. Your greatness is not defined by such a label," Imogene replied, shaking her head. "It's one of the things I truly despise about our society. Labels on everything!"

I liked Imogene. She was ridiculously cool—and nothing like the rest of the Mage Council. No wonder everybody swooned over her. I couldn't help but wonder what my life would've been like if I'd grown up with someone like her around. *I wouldn't be feeling so scared and insecure now, that's for sure.*

"Ms. Whitehall," Wade greeted her, almost gliding across the store and bumping into me, as if I was in the way. My heart fluttered and—*oh, God, he's crushing on her*. My ticker then sank, overriding his emotions. Why did I feel so… down, all of a sudden? Was my Empathy glitching? "What a surprise to see you here."

"Mr. Crowley, it's a pleasure to see you," Imogene replied with a neutral but still incredibly charming smile.

If angels were real, there would be a choir behind her, singing odes to her beauty and serenity. Wade's puppy-dog eyes were starting to get on my nerves.

"I see you've met our new recruit," Wade said, giving me a brief sideways glance. Somehow, it felt as though he was looking right through me. *Like I'm a prop.*

"I hope you're all treating her well, Mr. Crowley. I understand Harley is extremely gifted, and she's already having a hard time being what you call a 'late bloomer.' She requires patience and understanding, most of all."

My heart came back to the surface and grew three sizes.

"She's a Mediocre, Ms. Whitehall. There's only so much she can do, unfortunately."

And in came Wade with a sledgehammer, ready to make me want to gouge his eyes out.

"See, Harley?" Imogene said, once again smiling like I was the single most precious thing she'd laid her eyes upon. I could almost hear those angels singing. "Like I said, our magical society has fallen so low, tangled in all these foolish labels. Don't listen to a word they tell you, darling. You do *you*."

"Oh, I'm doing just that, believe me," I replied, then threw an acid smirk at Wade.

My stomach churned—that was him. He fell out of favor with her, and it burned. *Hah!*

"I'd love to stick around, but I've got a couple more meetings in the area before I head back to LA. Take care of yourself, Harley, and remember: labels are useless."

She squeezed my shoulder gently, then waved both Wade and me goodbye as she walked out of the reliquary. *I swear, if this was an animated movie, there would be birds, squirrels, and other cute forest critters following her around.*

Wade felt sorry to see her leave, and I enjoyed every drop of that mild misery. *That's what you get for being so eager to call me Mediocre.* I slapped him on the back, hard enough to make him grunt and loud enough for the rest of our team to turn their heads around, but kept a huge grin on my face to make it look friendly.

"Come on, Wade! Nothing more for me to see here, so let's get back to the coven," I said. "You've got a report to file, and I need to get ready for a hot date!"

I was laughing so hard on the inside, as my stomach twisted itself into an incredibly painful knot—all Wade. Imogene had left him behind with a sour look on his face, and I'd gone ahead and made it even worse.

Whatever issue he had with Garrett, it clearly bothered him that I was involved, even if it was in the honeypot role. I planned to have as much fun as I possibly could in this deranged triangle.

Chapter Twenty-Two

It was around six p.m. when I found myself back in my room at the coven, feverishly reexamining the events of the day. The gargoyles' obsession with me aside, there was something off about the way in which they kept getting out of the Bestiary.

Wade sent me a text after he returned the Mason jars to Tobe. "Confirmed, seven out of ten came from the Bestiary," the text said. It was highly unlikely that seven gargoyles had simply escaped from what was supposed to be a super secure facility, with added magical security, a massive Beast Master, and countless charms and witchy tech on top. It didn't make sense.

It reeked of an inside job. I mean, I might have understood one excessively stubborn Murray bypassing security, but seven? No way.

I wondered what Alton thought of all this, and who had made it onto his suspect list. I didn't know anyone well enough in this place to exclude them—except for my Rag Team, whom I'd been actively reading on an emotional level, looking for guilt, or fear, or anything that could point to such a betrayal. In hindsight, neither fear nor guilt was an undeniable marker. One could be vicious enough to feel nothing while putting the lives of magicals and humans alike at risk.

No matter how I looked at it, the place with the most answers was the Bestiary, for the time being. Tobe must've been gutted to recognize the seven gargoyles as "local residents." The other three were most likely wildlings, drawn to the city by the others.

I had three hours to spare till my so-called date with Garrett, so I decided to at least try and make myself useful. It just didn't feel right to sit there while all of this was going on. Sneaking into the Bestiary wasn't easy—not after more gargoyles had escaped. There were two security magicals stationed just by the door, turning everyone away. "The Bestiary is off limits for the time being, except for Director Waterhouse and the investigation team," they kept saying.

I had to wait until their shift was over. There was a small window of opportunity when their replacements came in, and they stepped to the side to briefly discuss updates.

I slipped through the Bestiary door just as a displeased Preceptor Nomura left, giving the security magicals a brief nod—perfect timing for me. *No wonder we're having security issues, given how I still managed to get in. Me, the magical noob.*

The gargoyle boxes were somewhere on the northern side of the Bestiary, from what I could remember about the layout. I snuck through, light on my feet, until I reached a massive glass case, with dozens of smoky, shapeless gargoyles swishing around, clearly discontent with their enclosure. *Tough luck, you ugly bastards.*

The box itself looked sturdy, as did the many others around it, all different heights and widths, all edges poured in brass, with various symbols etched into the metallic surface. The locks seemed intact, too. I held one between two fingers, turning it over to double check, though I wasn't exactly sure what I was looking for. *Signs of tampering, I guess. Magical or not, clearly someone can still mess with these things.*

"What the hell are you doing here?"

Wade's low voice startled me, and I sprang to my feet with a yelp. His hand immediately covered my mouth, and he shushed me. We stared at each other, wide-eyed, for a few seconds, his skin on my lips making my cheeks flush.

"What am *I* doing here? What are *you* doing here?" I shot back, pushing his hands away. The mild tingle in my lips was quickly upstaged by the knot in my stomach. I wasn't sure whether it was mine or Wade's.

"Investigating the boxes. Your turn," Wade said, frowning.

It took me a moment to process that. "You're on the cleanup team with us, in case you forgot. You don't investigate."

"I don't *have to* investigate. It doesn't mean I can't. Especially not when I think Garrett's doing a crappy job," Wade replied. "Why are you here, Harley? Shouldn't you be getting ready for your 'hot date?'"

How did I end up the culprit in this picture?

"We're just going out for drinks. It's not the Academy Awards. No red carpet to get ready for," I retorted. "I wanted to see if I could help. I just don't know what I'm looking for, exactly."

"Of course you don't. You don't belong here," Wade replied.

"Tough luck. I'm not going anywhere."

"Shh—" He covered my mouth again and pushed me against a tall, empty glass box. My first instinct was to kick him in the nuts, but that stilled when I heard voices not too far away. Garrett and Finch's voices, to be precise.

Crap.

Wade muttered something under his breath, then opened the glass box and pushed me inside. "What are you—" I managed, then froze when he joined me and closed the glass door behind him. There was very little room in there for the both of us. Our bodies were almost glued to each other, and it was seriously messing with my senses.

"Shut up, or we're both in trouble," Wade whispered, then uttered another spell.

A charcoal haze emerged from beneath, and I caught a glimpse of his rings glowing warm red, his hands resting on my hips. My heart fluttered, while the box filled with what looked like black smoke—similar to that of a formless monster. I had to tilt my head to one side to see beyond the glass box.

Garrett, Finch, Poe, and the rest of the investigative team came around, checking each glass box along the way. "Alton said to check it again, so we're checking it again," Garrett said, rolling his eyes. One of his teammates had most likely asked what they were doing there. I was going to ask the same thing…

Blood was rushing through my veins, while I struggled to breathe. Not because of the black haze, but because of how close I was to Wade. Every inch of him, all hard muscles stretching over his tall frame, pushed against my body. I felt all soft and gooey by comparison. Tender and vulnerable. Tiny and… with lips still tingling from his touch. *Get it together, Harley.*

I focused on what Garrett and the others were doing, trying my best to ignore the fact that I was stuck in a box with Wade, surrounded by smoke meant to conceal us.

"Tobe said seven of the ten gargoyles that Crowley and his deadbeats captured were from the Bestiary," Garrett said, turning an engraved lock over. "It means someone must be tampering with the locks, for sure."

"So, what, inside job?" Finch replied incredulously. "Who would be dumb enough to do that?"

"I don't know, man, but the stakes just went up on this one," Garrett said. "This is worth at least six hundred points, I bet."

"End-of-year bonus, here we come!" Poe chuckled, and Garrett instantly smacked him over the shoulder.

"You don't get to drool over that bonus, you idiot. Not after the crappy cleanup job you did at the casino! Having Alton breathe down my neck is exhausting enough as it is. I really didn't need Crowley snickering at me over your incompetence," Garrett spat, then pointed farther down the corridor. "Now, go check that side.

Look for any broken etchings on the seals. If either symbol is even partially scratched or destroyed, the locking spell no longer works."

Poe nodded, filled with guilt and shame, then turned and went ahead, as instructed.

Wade's heart thudded against mine, reminding me of how close we were to one another. His fingers were digging into my waist, most likely a reaction to Garrett's words.

"Come on, let's see what's on the other side," Finch said, pointing to the south, beyond our box. He got dangerously close, and I instinctively hid my face in Wade's chest, the drumbeat of his heart amplified and pouring into my ears. He didn't move a single muscle as Finch glided past the box, followed closely by Garrett and the others.

Once the coast was clear, he opened the door, and the black smoke dissipated.

Wade was the first to get out, while I needed a moment to breathe again. His gaze was dark and a little too intense for my frayed nerves, but I couldn't look away, either. My heart was literally pounding.

"Would you like to stay in there?" Wade raised an eyebrow.

"Why were we hiding in the first place?" I asked. "Since when are *you* afraid of Garrett?"

"Who said I was afraid? This isn't about fear, Harley. I just don't want him or anyone else to see us here," he replied, angrier than before. He really hated it when I brought up Garrett, it seemed. "Just so you understand, tasks given are clear. As per the regulations, we don't interfere in the work of other teams. Not unless instructed by the coven director, or if lives are put in immediate danger. Neither is the case right now, so, technically—"

"You're breaking the rules," I said.

His shoulders dropped, followed by an audible exhalation. "Yes."

"Okay, cool. Got it. Now what?" I replied, secretly pleased to see he *was* able to stray off the path, at least once in his lifetime.

"We keep looking. Check every corner, every nook and cranny, twice. I don't trust Garrett and *his* deadbeats to find the damn moon in the sky, not to mention evidence of magical tampering. Everything that feels off, strange, or simply irks you, tell me. Okay?"

I gave him a brief nod and started looking at all the boxes around us, ignoring the agitated, shapeless billows of smoke contained within. Less than five minutes later, I looked over my shoulder to steal a brief glance at Wade and found him on all fours in front of a gargoyle box. His face was glued to the floor, his gaze fixed on something underneath.

The smoke inside rippled into the form of Murray, my hellish gargoyle stalker. He imitated Wade's pose, while sneering at me. His body wasn't consistent, though, each movement giving off wisps of black fumes. I narrowed my eyes at it, tired of being afraid. He'd ruined my Daisy, and seeing him stuck in there didn't feel like it was enough to soothe my broken heart.

I drew my face closer to the glass as Murray lifted his to my eye level, his fangs extra long, sharp, and eager to cut through me. My anger and grief were most likely beaming through my eyes, because Murray seemed to enjoy it. "Yeah, but you're in there, and I'm out here," I whispered, then tapped the glass with one finger.

The gesture seemed to startle Murray, as he dissipated into black smoke, and it took him a while to regain his gargoyle form. I tapped the glass again, and he disintegrated once more. The slightest vibration on the glass surface seemed to have that effect on the monster's attempts at a form. I wondered if Tobe walked around the Bestiary, rattling a baton against the glass boxes, just to mess with the prisoners like a mean warden.

"The bottom of this box feels a little uneven in the far corner," Wade muttered from below, then muttered something else—a spell, based on how his rings lit up red—and reached under Murray's box.

"This isn't from here," he said, then stood up, holding something between his index and thumb. "And apparently everyone else missed it. I guess I'm better at finding secrets around here than the entire investigative team. Of course, the investigative team doesn't have my knowledge of revelation spells."

"Because you're a diehard nerd?"

"Precisely," he replied proudly.

I leaned in to get a better look at what he was holding. It looked like a two-inch copper coin, with beads, twine, shards of bone, and dried herbs glued on one side, into neatly organized little clusters.

"What's that?" I asked.

Wade's gaze found mine, and it didn't say anything good. "It's a spell disruptor. A very complicated charm," he said, then slowly brought the object up between us, pointing at various parts. "See this? This is dried amaranth, for invisibility. It makes the disruptor untraceable, if used in the right amount and with the appropriate spell. These are hoodoo beads, called 'chain breakers.' They're used to counteract spells. This... This is a custom-made charm, designed specifically to disrupt the Bestiary's protections. It's very complex and... impossible to decipher."

"What does that tell us?" I asked.

"It tells us that we're dealing with an extremely capable magical who's past the stage of learning existing spells, and is creating new ones," Wade replied. "This here is unique. All disruptors are built on a round, copper base, but the elements on top are the ones that dictate its purpose. Thing is, I think it fully bypasses any alarms that Tobe might have set for the boxes. Otherwise, I can't explain how he doesn't realize that monsters are getting out. This is grade A sabotage."

"Do you have any idea who made it?"

He shook his head, and I could feel his concern weighing on my shoulders. "Whoever it is, this is evil. This is deliberate. It's meant to get us all in trouble. And they're doing it covertly, so it's obvious sabotage. You were right, Harley, this *is* an inside job, the worst of its kind."

I stared at the disruptor, trying to wrap my head around its apparently complex build. Something told me my classes with

Preceptor Bellmore would be most useful, if I wanted to understand what this thing was made of. I was curious about the process for manufacturing such an object.

"What are you two doing here?" Tobe's voice thundered straight through me, and, judging by the stunned look on Wade's face, him too. "You're not supposed to be here."

Tobe reached us in just a couple of steps, his amber eyes narrowed and his mane slightly tousled. He was tired and frustrated —not that I could blame him. "I didn't know *we* were forbidden to enter the Bestiary, too, especially after I delivered ten captured gargoyles less than an hour ago," Wade replied, slightly offended.

"New rule." Tobe sighed. "All magicals are forbidden from coming into the Bestiary, with the exception of Alton and the investigation team. Not even preceptors are allowed anymore."

"I saw Nomura coming out of here, about fifteen minutes ago," I said, crossing my arms.

"I know, I had to politely ask him to leave," Tobe replied. "He wasn't too happy about that, but eventually complied."

"That explains the sour look on his face," I said. "Why the new rule?"

"Isn't it obvious? With ten gargoyles out, we're on high alert. Magicals are on constant patrol throughout the Bestiary. Garrett and his team are investigating. And I'm keeping watch and disciplining the monsters, as usual."

"It's funny that you say that," Wade said, "because I just watched Garrett and his team search an entire section of the Bestiary, and not one of them was able to find this."

He lifted the spell disruptor for Tobe to see. A growl escaped from the Beast Master's throat, as he realized what the object was. "Where was this, Wade?"

"Underneath Murray's box," he replied, handing the object over to Tobe.

"This is how they're getting out, then." Tobe reached the same conclusion, carefully holding the disruptor with two feathered fingers.

"It's definitely an inside job, Tobe," I said.

Tobe nodded slowly, then looked at Wade and me. "I'll take this to Alton, but you two really need to get out of here. You cannot be seen here right now."

Wade took me by the forearm and walked us both out of there, leaving Tobe and the spell disruptor behind. We sneaked out of the Bestiary, just as a couple of magicals turned a corner into the main corridor, missing us by a fraction of a second.

The tall, oval door closed behind us with a clang.

Wade and I stood there for a while, as he absently gazed ahead. "Don't tell Garrett about this," he said. "Now, go. I've got something to take care of."

"What's that?" I asked.

"None of your business, Harley. You've got a hot date, remember?"

Oh, wow, he can really hold a grudge.

I rolled my eyes and walked away, feeling somewhat helpless and rejected. Wade was going to keep investigating this behind Garrett's back—it was my only certainty in this situation, knowing how competitive those two were.

There was no way I was letting him do this alone. It had already gotten personal with the gargoyles, so if anyone in this coven was messing with the Bestiary and setting those fiends loose so they could chew me up, they were in for some serious ass-kicking.

Chapter Twenty-Three

Garrett picked me up from outside my room at nine p.m. sharp. I'd slipped into a short and tight denim dress, along with one of my new leather jackets and a pair of black ankle boots. My hair was pulled up in a loose and messy red bun, and I'd even added a touch of lipstick, just to make sure I had Garrett's full attention.

Which I totally did.

The Noble Experiment wasn't insanely busy, but it was crowded enough to put some noise in the background—laughter, glasses clinking, and plenty of flirtatious remarks. I focused on Garrett's emotional silence, since I was surrounded by… randy people, basically. I could feel desire flowing through me, pure physical attraction. It was date night for most of the patrons.

"I have to say, I'm very pleased to see you," Garrett said, breaking my train of thought, "but I'm feeling a little neglected. Where's your mind, Red?"

I gave him a shy smile, my fingers fiddling with the straw in my fruity iced tea. "I'm here, just a little tired. And everybody's got the hots for someone in here. It makes it difficult for me to focus at times."

"Oh, yeah, you're an Empath." Garrett grinned, biting his lower lip. It made him look like a mischievous teenager ready to show me his parents' bedroom at a house party. "At least you're aware of how hot I find you."

"No need to use my Empathy for that—you do a good job of making that clear with words and… gestures," I replied, my voice weak. I didn't want him to know that I couldn't feel him, but I didn't want to make stuff up. Lying about his feelings could land me in some very uncomfortable circumstances that would, eventually, lead to me telling him that I *couldn't* feel him. Either way, discretion and deflection were advised.

"Yeah, I'm not going to apologize for that," Garrett said. "I see something I like, I take it."

"You're not taking me. I'm the one nice enough to let you buy me a drink. Let's not get ahead of ourselves here, Garrett."

"Ah, red *and* feisty." He chuckled softly, his dimples doing a number on my head. "I like that. So! How are you liking the coven so far?"

"Frankly, I'm a bit worried about this whole gargoyle incident. Today's events show that it's gone from bad to worse," I replied. "How's your investigation going?"

"We searched the Bestiary again after you guys brought in those gargoyles," he said, then gave me a playful wink and an appreciative half-smile. "Well done, by the way. It couldn't have been easy for you and the Rags to successfully capture ten freaking monsters. Not that I was worried about you—you show promise. It's the others I have my doubts about."

"You're grossly underestimating my team, Garrett."

"No, you're grossly overestimating your team, beautiful. Wade's a pompous prick who can't think for himself unless there are coven regulations to follow, including how to tie his damn shoes. And that alone disqualifies the Rag Team from ever being taken seriously. I have little faith in Alton's lackey, and neither should you."

There was a tinge of anger in his voice, the emotional kind that came from someone who'd definitely once considered Wade to be his friend. I leaned in, noticing how his pupils dilated whenever I got closer. "You don't like Wade at all, do you?" I asked. It was an obvious question, but I was hoping I'd get him to ride that wave of contempt and spill the beans about their broken friendship.

"You *are* sharp," he said quietly, his fingers gently brushing mine across the table, before they moved to tuck a loose lock of hair behind my ear. His touch was soft and gentle, the complete opposite of his sharp, almost painfully blunt nature. "Nobody really likes Wade, Harley. Even you don't seem too crazy about him."

I would've liked to agree with him, based on my back-and-forths with Wade. But I couldn't. I had a feeling it was because Wade was kind of growing on me.

It was time to steer the conversation back to a more useful topic. We'd already exchanged the evening's allocated number of decent pleasantries and basic date-night questions.

"You know, I've been thinking," I said, eyeing him carefully. There was a playful flicker in his eyes, while his lips lazily stretched into a smile. "Have you considered the possibility of an inside job, regarding the Bestiary?"

That charming smile dropped at lightspeed. His gaze darkened, and a muscle twitched in his jaw. *Well, too late to take it back now. Ride it out.*

"We're out here, in one of the city's swankiest places, and you want to talk work?" Garrett replied, pursing his lips.

"You can't really blame me. Not after what happened to my apartment, my car."

My voice trembled a little, enough to touch a soft spot for him, it seemed. "I'm not rejecting the idea of an inside job," he conceded. "I just wouldn't know where to start looking for suspects. The entire coven is so… lame, I find it hard to believe anyone would be smart enough to pull this off."

"So, no one springs to mind?" I asked, then took a sip from my iced tea.

His gaze dropped to my lips, before settling on my eyes. "I wouldn't be surprised if someone on your Rag Team was responsible."

I chuckled softly. "What makes you say that?"

"They're all weird. Santana's a powder keg with a grudge, because everybody taunts her over her practice of Santeria. No one knows anything about Tatyana, though we all suspect she terrorizes puppies and babies in her spare time. And don't even get me started on Raffe. That guy's as weird as they come."

I couldn't help but laugh. The way he depicted my teammates clearly stemmed from a personal dislike. If I were to seriously consider any one of them as a potential suspect, I couldn't go on Garrett's impression of them. It was hilariously skewed. "What about your own team? Don't you think the likes of Finch, or Poe, or anyone else, for that matter, would be capable of such foul play?"

"I doubt it. Poe is incompetent, but loyal to a fault. Rowena's more interested in makeup trends," he replied, then paused for a couple of seconds. "Finch is an exceptional magical. His head is screwed on right, despite his short fuse. He can be a jerk, but hey, that applies to all of us. But anyway, back to you, Red. You're not dating anyone, are you?"

Though not the smoothest of transitions, I had to give him credit for trying. I figured that was as much as I was going to get out of him tonight, so I didn't pursue it further. He was definitely going to punch a wall or two once Alton showed him the spell disruptor—especially since Garrett had been trying quite hard to prove his investigative superiority to Wade.

One thing was clear, though. It was easy to suspect everyone in the coven for this. But it was damn near impossible to take anyone's suspicions seriously, as they were all based on personal feuds. It was all very subjective, so playing the guessing game wasn't an option.

"I'm here with you tonight, am I not?" I replied, offering a smile.

"Yes, you are." Garrett seemed satisfied with my response, and he leaned forward, leaving just a few inches between our lips. "Tell me something about yourself, Harley. Something you haven't told anyone in this coven. I want to feel special."

"I have a shellfish allergy," I said absently, still thinking about the Bestiary. I had a feeling we'd uncover more if they allowed the Rag Team to get involved and help, instead of turning this into a stupid competition.

Garrett chuckled, gently tapping my nose. "You're a funny girl. I like that."

"I'm serious, though. No shellfish for me. I'd swell up like the Michelin Man," I replied.

Something dark and heavy invaded my stomach. It felt deeply uncomfortable, like the indigestion of a lifetime. Not my emotions, but definitely aimed at me… and Garrett. I glanced around and stilled.

Wade had just come through the door, accompanied by a bubblegum blonde in a pale blue cocktail dress with a pearlescent scarf hanging loosely over her bony shoulders. She annexed Wade's arm in a possessive manner, as she gazed around the place. The satisfaction on her face irked me. It was as if she was proudly displaying her man-trophy, while said man-trophy was busy glaring at Garrett and me.

"Seriously?" I said.

Garrett followed my gaze and let out a sharp exhalation. "What's that stooge doing here? And with Clara Fairmont, of all people?"

"Do you know her?" I asked.

"I think 70 percent of the guys in the coven know her. If you know what I mean." He grinned. "Which is why I didn't expect to see Crowley with her. He's the noble and righteous type. And a pretentious one, too. He doesn't date anyone with the IQ of a bumblebee."

I stifled a chuckle, somewhat relieved to hear that Garrett didn't like her. *But why don't I like her? Is it because she's Wade's date tonight? Wait, why do I care who he dates?*

"Maybe he decided to change things up a bit," I replied.

"You mean change things down?" Garrett laughed.

"Funny running into you here." Clara Fairmont giggled, prompting both Garrett and me to put on straight faces. I hadn't thought they'd stop by our table—or, at least, I had been hoping they wouldn't. I hadn't even seen them coming. Then again, I'd been busy snickering with Garrett just now.

I gave Clara a polite smile, before I looked at Wade. "What's up?"

"What are you doing here, Crowley?" Garrett asked, sounding particularly bored.

"What does it look like I'm doing?" Wade replied.

"Do you want the unedited version or the politically correct one?"

"What… Um, what's going on?" Clara giggled nervously, her gaze darting between Garrett and Wade. The air had gotten thick and difficult to breathe all of a sudden, tension brewing between these two fine alpha males.

Someone needed to put an end to it before they fanned their tails out like freaking peacocks.

Garrett grinned. "I'm just out on a date with the most beautiful girl in the coven. What are you two rejects doing here?"

Ugh, and just like that I remembered the parts about Garrett that I thoroughly disliked. He threw insults around like a Pez dispenser, and, based on the hurt look on Clara's face and the stab of shame she felt, they were quite painful.

"Who are you calling a reject?" Clara asked, her soft, blonde brow furrowed.

"Don't let him get to you," Wade interjected. "Garrett tends to get aggressive when he feels threatened."

"What could I possibly be threatened about?" Garrett chuckled. "I'm having a drink with Red here, I'm leading the investigative team, and you're stuck doing cleanup and dating a very used model. There's nothing threatening me. But you two are butting into my date, so why don't you grab a table and pretend you like each other?"

Wade's rings lit up. I shot to my feet and instantly slipped between them. Wade was a little too close to me, making it difficult for my brain to function properly, for some reason, but I knew I had to diffuse the situation before they kicked off a brawl.

This was my first time at the Noble Experiment. I didn't want to get kicked out because of Wade and Garrett's measuring contest. "I was having a nice time until you showed up," I hissed at Wade.

He shrugged in response, his gaze darting between me and Garrett. "Clara wanted to say hi."

"Hi, Clara," I said to her, and she gave me a weak and confused smile. I then shifted my focus back to Wade. "There, I said hi. Now, do us all a favor and put some distance between us."

"Not until Garrett here apologizes to Clara," Wade fired back.

"Apologize for what?" Garrett said.

"You know what?" I replied, taking a few deep breaths. "I'm not doing this. You can blow yourselves up, for all I care. I just wanted a drink and casual conversation, but clearly I can't have that!"

I walked away, prompting Garrett to jump out of his seat. "Red, wait!"

"Nope! You should've known better than to act like a jerk!" I barked, and headed toward the main exit. To my surprise, Clara joined me.

"Hope you don't mind," she said. "I don't want to be left alone with those two. Garrett's an absolute jerk, and Wade... well, Wade didn't really want to go on a date with *me*, obviously."

"What makes you say that?" I asked, then pushed open the door, welcoming the mild evening breeze blowing against my face. I glanced over my shoulder. Wade and Garrett were both staring at us—gaping, to be precise, their jaws nearly hitting the floor. Neither had seen that one coming. *Good.*

"Because he's more interested in picking a fight with Garrett. Duh!"

She rolled her eyes as I made my way to the edge of the sidewalk and signaled a cab. "Well, then, they can fight all they want now. I'm not sticking around for their crap."

"Can I share a ride with you?"

She was a little hurt. Based on what I'd just heard about her, what I knew about Wade, and what I could feel from Clara, directly, she'd put her hopes into this date. She'd probably had bad luck dating others in the coven, making Garrett's remarks crass and downright disappointing. Wade asking her out had probably made her feel like she still had a shot at a decent guy. Or at least, that's how I was feeling, sitting next to her in the cab.

What was Wade thinking?

I'd made it perfectly clear that I was going to try and get some intel out of Garrett. Why the hell was he throwing pebbles at my wheels, then?

Chapter Twenty-Four

One good thing did come out of that botched evening. It was over sooner rather than later, so I could get back to the coven and start digging through my dreams for clues about my past.

After a long, hot shower, I mounted the dreamcatcher on the wall above my headboard. I finally remembered the Navajo words that Tobe had taught me and murmured the first one, then proceeded to sink into the mattress. My lights were out in less than a minute. With everything that had been going on, my brain had been working overtime.

I had some disturbingly weird dreams. Most of them involved Wade repeatedly asking if I liked him. As if fully aware of the ludicrousness of the situation, I repeatedly shook my head until my subconscious took me elsewhere. I didn't want to answer that question.

As if navigating through a lucid dream, I pushed deeper into the darkness beneath my feet. My view warped outward, all matter distorted into irregular swirls of color, until an image tried to come into focus. No matter how hard I focused, however, I couldn't see clearly.

My body didn't respond. I looked down and noticed my hands, my arms were small. I was little, maybe a toddler.

"Good morning, sweet little angel," a voice said.

It felt oddly familiar. I'd missed it, though I didn't know whose it was.

A blurry face came closer. Two dark spots served as eyes, and a thick, curved white line offered the hint of a smile. It filled me with joy and relief. Everything was right in the world, somehow. I belonged there, in that pair of strong arms.

"Hiram, you have to let her go," another voice came through. I didn't recognize this one. A woman.

"Hi baby girl," the first, familiar voice continued, ignoring the woman's warning. I was in the arms of a man named Hiram. It was all I could understand, other than the softness and warmth enveloping me. "Did you have good dreams? You did? Of course you did. Daddy made you a special charm."

"Hiram, they're getting closer," the woman said. "You have no choice. Let her go, so she can at least have a chance to live."

"Don't you think I know that?" he said. It hurt us both to hear him speak like that. *Why? Who is he?*

"My car is outside. Here, take it," the woman said, and tossed keys across the room.

"I love you, my sweet little Harley," Hiram said, his lips gently pressed against my forehead. I was safe and loved. And it felt so good. I could barely see, but I knew everything was going to be okay.

Who are you?

My eyes popped open.

Welcome back to consciousness.

Wisps of my last dream were quickly slipping through my fingers. I sat up, rubbing my face. I was covered in sweat, burning a little hotter than usual. A name was lingering in the back of my head. A very distant memory had popped up in my dreams, but I couldn't remember it anymore.

I took the dreamcatcher down, grasping its frame with both trembling hands.

"*Yáshti*," I breathed.

A sudden draft blew right through me. Frigid air burned cold, setting my skin alight. My eyes rolled into my head, and I suddenly felt weightless. The material world around me disintegrated, and the unbearable chill was replaced by… emptiness. It was difficult to understand what was going on, but I had no choice other than to follow through, and let the spell take me where it needed to.

Darkness swallowed me whole, and I lingered in the abyss for a few seconds, before I opened my eyes—*when did I even close them?*

I was in the dream I'd forgotten, but everything was crystal clear. Every color, every shape, every corner and shadow. I could see everything and… everyone.

"Hiram, you have to let her go."

That was the woman I'd heard. She was beautiful, in her mid-forties, with long, curly black hair and blue eyes. She looked a lot like the man holding me in his arms, the man she called Hiram… the man who looked at me with so much love, my heart was close to bursting.

He seemed tall, towering over me. *This is a memory*.

I was a toddler, indeed. I could see my little arms and legs, pale skin and chubby fingers, wrapped in a warm, furry blanket. He kept me close to his heart and dropped a gentle kiss on my forehead, making me smile.

"Hi, baby girl," he said, smiling. "Did you have good dreams? You did? Of course you did. Daddy made you a special charm."

I was reliving the dream I'd just lost, in full clarity. Hiram held up a small pendant made of sterling silver. It was shaped like a tear, with different roughly cut gemstones mounted on the surface. Red, white, blue, black, and pink. *I'd recognize them anywhere if I saw them again. I know I would. I have to.*

"Hiram, they're getting closer," the woman said. "You have no choice. Let her go, so she can at least have a chance to live."

"Don't you think I know that?"

Hiram was a handsome man. His hair was black, rich, and flowing in big, heavy curls over his forehead. I didn't get my red hair from him, for sure. *My mom…* His eyes were the color of the sky, like mine, though, and he had a sprinkle of freckles on the blade of his nose. He beamed at me, but I could see the grief in his heart.

"My car is outside. Here, take it."

The woman was related to him, somehow. They had similar features—sharp jawlines, blue eyes, and black curls. Brother and sister, maybe.

"I love you, my sweet little Harley," Hiram said to me.

It was definitely a dream. A memory playing out like a dream. I had no input, no choice but to watch this man. My father. It only just hit me.

This is my dad. Oh, my God. This is my father.

I did my best to memorize every line of his face. He was young, in his late twenties. The pain in his soul expressed itself through his faint, permanent frown. He'd lost enough already and didn't want to leave me.

But he had no choice.

I knew that, from the note he left me. *Stay safe. Stay smart.*

The image faded away. I cried out, clawing at the fabric of my memories, desperate to hold on.

I opened my eyes—*again, when did I close them?*

I was in my room in the coven. The dreamcatcher in my hands, the knotted threads glowing softly.

I shuddered, tears bursting from my eyes. I cried so hard, my stomach muscles hurt. For the first time in my nineteen years in this world, I knew what my father looked like. What he sounded like.

He loved me so much. It killed him to leave me behind. I knew it, deep in my heart.

He adored his little Harley.

His name was Hiram.

Chapter Twenty-Five

The shock took a while to subside. I'd been carrying that memory around with me for so long, missing it by milliseconds in my dreams. *Now what?*

First, I made a mental note to buy Tobe the biggest drink on the planet. I owed him big time, as I'd just gotten a sliver of my life back. Second, I rushed into a pair of jeans and a shirt, and called Wade until he picked up. It was well after midnight, and he didn't sound too happy to have actually heard the phone ring.

"Ugh, what do you want?" he grumbled.

"I have something to talk to you about. It's urgent," I said, with very little sympathy. He was probably exhausted, but I'd just remembered something about my past. He could sleep later. I briefly wondered why I'd thought of him first, before anyone else, but I refused to let my brain go down that particular rabbit hole.

"It took me forever to fall asleep," he protested.

"I remembered something," I replied. "About my father."

There was silence on the line, followed by a shuffle and a zipper being pulled.

"Meet me by the magnolia trees downstairs," he said, then hung up.

Less than five minutes later, he found me underneath the pink blossoms of magnolia trees, rooted firmly in the middle of the dome-shaped living quarters. His dark hair was tousled, his green eyes reduced to slits—he was struggling to stay awake. I felt sorry for about two seconds, until I decided to trust him with the knowledge of the dreamcatcher and my dream. By the time I was done, he was wide awake, two green gems cutting through the fabric of my soul.

"His name was Hiram," I said. "That's all I remember for now. I bet I'll capture more with the dreamcatcher going forward."

"Hiram," he repeated absently.

"Where can I find him? Are there archives, records we could look into? I can't wait till tomorrow, Wade. I can't wait another second. Frankly, I would've let you sleep, but I don't even know where to break in and start looking for answers."

His forehead smoothed as he gave me a stern look. "You will do no such thing. I'm here, I'm up, I've got this. And stop telling me about your intentions to break rules, or I'll have to report you."

"Really, Mr. I-Snuck-Into-The-Bestiary?"

He blinked a couple of times, then exhaled. "Fair enough," he replied, slightly amused. "Follow me."

"Where?"

"I know where to look for Hiram," Wade said, then dashed ahead through the main hallway leading toward the common areas.

My heart thudded nervously, and I could barely stay focused for more than a minute, before a million questions trickled through and loosened my grip on reality.

"Harley." Wade's voice pulled me back.

Only then did I realize we'd stopped in front of a set of double doors. There was a brass plate mounted at eye level: *Lewis Rathbone Wing*.

"What's this?" I asked.

"It's one of the coven's archives," Wade replied, then uttered a spell to open the doors. It wasn't the *Aperi Portam* incantation, though. It sounded longer, more complicated, and it made the doorknobs light up red right before they turned on their own.

I followed him inside, trying my best not to gasp at what seemed like endless walls loaded with leather-bound books. The ceiling was dark, and it seemed as though the shelf-covered walls went on forever, disappearing into the shadows far above. Wade snapped his fingers, and his ten rings took on a soft, golden glow, creating a source of light in the enormous archive hall.

There were reading tables scattered along the sides, with the occasional ladder mounted here and there—for access to what looked like seven stories' worth of books. *So... many... books...* If ever I needed to curl up with a book and a hot chocolate, this could easily be the perfect spot. A reading nook the size of freaking Grand Central Station.

Right in the middle of the hall was a small desk, with a very old computer on top—the '90s kind, with a blocky monitor and a processing unit that was literally the size of a large box. I'd only seen one in movies. They'd already become exhibits in science museums.

"We don't keep electronic copies in this coven," Wade continued. "There was a hacking incident a few years back, so we decided to hold on to the hard copies until a safer alternative is found."

"How does this work, then?" I asked. "Wouldn't you need electronic copies to search for anything? Like with keywords?"

"We do use keyword search. However, this old boy has a little magical upgrade." Wade playfully tapped the top of the computer monitor. "Here, let me show you. Let's try a search term. Hiram."

He typed my father's name, and I watched the letters appear in green on the black screen. Wade then hit the enter key, and the text vanished. The cables coming out from the back glowed white, going right into the wooden floor. The light spread across the entire surface, bathing the entire hall in a phosphorescent warm white.

I held my breath, watching every single shelf and book gleaming, before it all died down and a single object remained bright—a large registry on a top shelf in front of us. "Wow," I breathed.

"The computer is connected to the physical archives through a spell. Anything you need, just type the search terms in here," Wade said, nodding at the computer, "and it will find references of it everywhere in this hall. Every note, every page, every mention of that word will light up. Can you get that?"

He pointed at the glowing object with mentions of Hiram. I climbed up one of the ladders and retrieved the book. Its shimmer faded once I opened it on top of one of the reading tables nearby. Its title made my stomach churn: *Undesirables of the 20th Century*.

As I flipped through the pages, I caught glimpses of various headlines. Newspaper clippings dating as far back as the early 1900s had been glued onto the old, yellowed paper, each showing magicals who had been accused and convicted of various crimes against other magicals and, in many cases, humanity.

Most of the names didn't ring a bell. Others were known as serial killers and convicted war criminals. My throat closed up tighter with every page. My father was mentioned here, according to the search system.

Wade joined me, watching quietly as I flipped through, my gaze scanning the clippings for Hiram. "Undesirables," he said thoughtfully, and his furrowed brow didn't ease my worry one bit.

"Oh, man," I managed, my fingers trembling over a heart-wrenching headline, which I read out loud, my voice raw. "'Hiram Merlin, 28, Killer of Own Wife in NYC Murder Spree Was Executed'... Oh, God."

I leaned onto the table, my knees turning to sand. My insides burned, threatening to send back the little I'd managed to eat during the day. I broke into a cold sweat as I read through the article. Wade said nothing, his gaze following the text, as well.

The article was dated sixteen years ago, and it had been published in the *New York Coven Journal*, a local newspaper. Hiram

Merlin, aged twenty-eight at the time, had murdered his wife, Hester Merlin, née Shipton. I recognized the man in the black-and-white photo—his hair was shorter, but his devilish smile, his handsome features, his sharp cheeks... they were all there.

According to the report, he'd burned her alive, while she was presumably still pregnant with their first child. *Me? Had to be me, and she was no longer pregnant with me when he killed her.*

"He then went on a murderous spree and vanished for three years, despite consistent efforts to track him down," Wade murmured. "Hiram Merlin was the former director of the New York Coven, and a descendant of the great Merlin himself. Hester Merlin's sister, Katherine Shipton, is also missing, and a suspect in five other murders on top of the above. According to a slew of rumors, Hiram and Katherine were having an affair and conspired to kill Hester, in order to cash out on her life insurance and hefty inheritance. The lesser able of two sisters, Katherine was cut from the Shiptons' will at an early age, after she was caught embezzling Boston Coven funds, where she'd been assigned a couple of years back. Nobody knows when and how Hiram and Katherine planned this horror, but one thing is certain—"

"While Katherine Shipton is still missing, Hiram Merlin has been given his just desserts yesterday at 16:01 hours..." I kept reading, despite the tears glazing my eyes and the tremor in my voice. "Hiram willingly surrendered early last week, but denied all charges brought against him, claiming that it was all Katherine Shipton's doing. Persistent in declaring his undying love for Hester Shipton, Hiram refused to acknowledge his involvement in her murder, along with the gruesome deaths of six other magicals and humans. Among his victims were Telford Brown and Sharon Oxford, members of the New York Mage Council, and beloved magicals best known for their extensive research into the preservation of Esprits and magical powers upon the magical's death. However, the evidence against Hiram Merlin was undeniable, leaving the jury no other choice but to sentence him to death."

My legs abandoned me completely. I simply collapsed, but Wade was quick to catch me, his arms pulling me back up. He sat me on top of the table, and I could sense he felt my pain, his gaze soft and full of pity. I could barely breathe at that point, sobbing between hiccups.

My father was Hiram Merlin. And he was a murderer. *My father... killed my mother. He had an affair with her sister and... Good grief... Weren't couples supposed to love and protect each other? What the hell happened?!*

"I never should've looked into this," I cried out.

Wade placed a hand on my shoulder, his deep green eyes almost soothing me. "Don't be silly. You deserve to know the truth, no matter how bad it is," he said gently. "I'm sorry, Harley. I really am."

"He... He killed my mom," I said, shuddering. "My father... It's him. I recognize him in the photo. He's the man holding me in his arms... telling me how much he loves me. He... He killed his *wife,* my *mom*... He abandoned me at an orphanage... Left me that damn note and... What do I do, Wade? How... What can I make of this?"

I was at a loss. I'd gotten my hopes up. It hadn't occurred to me that my father might not be the hero I'd daydreamed him to be over the years. I'd put him in the boots of a knight in shining armor, lost somewhere in a daring quest, hoping that one day, maybe, he'd find me. I'd thought about it so many times, imagining where he was, what he was doing...

The truth was a horror show. Blood, murder, and betrayal. I'd lost my mother because of him and Katherine Shipton. I'd lost my chance at a magical upbringing because of them. I'd lost my family. My life.

Threads of red-hot anger intertwined with my gut-wrenching sorrow. His note was what, then? His way of making himself look good to his daughter? A façade? A lie? He had no other choice, he'd said. He could've *not* murdered my mother, for starters!

"Are you sure it's him?" Wade asked, as if hoping I'd gotten the wrong Hiram.

I couldn't blame him. I'd thought about that, too, for a split second. But the man smiling back at me from the newspaper clipping was definitely the man I'd seen kissing my forehead, calling me by my name, telling me how much he loved me.

"It's him. I just… I just don't get it," I replied between sniffles. "He had me for three years. This article says they couldn't find him. That he surrendered… Why would he surrender, if no one could find him? Why leave me behind at an orphanage?"

"My guess is he wanted to keep you away from the magical world," Wade said, then shrugged. "Though, that doesn't make much sense. You would've been much safer at least knowing what you were from an early age, not left to struggle the way you probably did."

I looked up at him, surprised by his sympathy. He was so kind, so gentle. I almost didn't recognize him. A part of me wanted the hard-ass Wade back—that guy didn't leave any room for me to wallow in self-pity. He nudged and kicked until I reacted, until I hit back. This Wade, however, as warm as he made me feel on the inside… also made me sad. He showered me with pity, and that just made everything feel worse, and real.

The doors opened, startling us both. Alton came in, carrying a large book under his arm. "What are you two doing here at this hour?" he asked, frowning.

Wade and I looked at each other for a moment. I swallowed another wave of tears, then pointed at the newspaper clipping. "I remembered something from my dreams. A lost memory. The name Hiram came up. My dad…"

Alton eyed me carefully, then joined us at the table and looked at the article. A couple of minutes later, he let out a flat, soft hum. "Yeah, the thought did cross my mind."

"*What?*" I blurted.

"Harley, I'll be honest," Alton said. "From the moment we shook hands, I felt there was something special, different about you.

Looking at this now, I'm not all that surprised. You do remind me of Hiram Merlin, in a way."

"You *knew* him?" Wade replied. He was as stunned as I was.

Alton shook his head. "Not personally. I mean, we never really met. I saw him, more than once. But we never spoke."

Silence settled, while my blood started to simmer. What else had he neglected to mention?

"By all means, keep going, I'm on the edge of my damn seat, here," I said, gritting my teeth.

Guilt poured through, in heavy, gut-twisting waves that made it hard for me to move. Luckily, I was still sitting on the table, and not at risk of collapsing again. Alton's pained expression felt like a hundred daggers poking at my heart.

"A jury was convened for your father's trial," Alton replied, his voice shaking slightly. "I was part of that jury. I did my duty as the New York Coven commanded at the time."

"You were on the jury that sentenced my father to death?"

I could barely hear myself at that point.

"I didn't know you were related, Harley," Alton said. "And even if I knew, that wouldn't change how I feel about you being here. My decision hasn't, and cannot, change. You belong here, with us, whether you see it yet or not."

"You… You sentenced my father to death," I repeated, feeling as though my consciousness had somehow left my body.

"I was on the jury, Harley. We submitted it to a vote. It was eight against three for the death penalty, but I am bound by law to keep my vote a secret. I am sorry for your loss."

My father was a convicted murderer. And Alton had sat on the jury that brought him to his death. It wasn't the latter that really hurt me. Alton had simply done his job. It would've been unfair to hold it against him.

"I'm sorry, too," I murmured.

"What happened, Alton? What made you think Harley was related to Hiram?" Wade asked, crossing his arms.

"Well, a number of things, actually. First, the eyes. Harley, you have your father's eyes, a perfect copy. I've got a photographic memory; I remember every single detail. It took me a while to connect the dots, though, until tonight."

He dropped the large book he'd brought in on top of the newspaper clipping album, and flipped through its pages. Various magicals were listed there as full Elementals, from what I could see at first glance. "What's this?" I asked.

"I've been looking through records of full Elementals," Alton replied. "This was the second thing that pointed me to Hiram Merlin as your father, and less of a long shot, compared to your physical similarities."

He pointed at a section dedicated entirely to my father. Hiram Merlin was a full Elemental. *And a murderer.*

"It was only a vague idea, to be fair, just my instinct tugging at my sleeve," Alton continued. "Until just now. What did you remember about Hiram?"

"Nothing much, really. Just his name. I was three, maybe… And there was a woman telling him that he had no other choice, that he had to give me up. I guess he was still on the run and I was holding him back. I don't know."

"What did the woman look like?" Alton asked, scratching his stubbled chin.

"A lot like him, actually. In her early forties. Maybe his sister?"

"Isadora Merlin. His elder sister, yes. She's off the grid. She vanished shortly after Hiram was executed," Alton confirmed.

"Good grief, I have so many questions."

"Me too, but I doubt you'd have answers," he replied, giving me a sad smile. "Nobody knew you were born. With what happened to Hester… We had no idea at the time."

"Yeah, I gathered that from the article," I said. "Who could possibly know what happened, besides my dad?"

"Katherine Shipton, but she vanished shortly after your mother's murder. The details surrounding that tragedy are still quite murky.

Your father maintained his innocence until he gave his last breath, despite the evidence pointing right at him. With no one to vouch for him or provide him with an alibi, he didn't stand a chance."

"You sound as though you think he was innocent," I replied, frowning.

Alton shrugged. "I never excluded the possibility. Everyone who knew him personally was shocked when the news of Hester's murder came out. Many didn't believe it. To this day, some continue to claim he's innocent. But he was tried and convicted, deemed irredeemable, and executed. We cannot change the past."

"At least now you know who your parents were," Wade said, trying to look for a bright side.

"Yeah. My dad allegedly killed my mom, lugged me around for three years, then dumped me at an orphanage. Oh, and apparently, he had an affair with my aunt. I think that about sums it up," I said.

Now there were two magicals in the hall who were feeling sorry for me. That just added to my inner broil, giving me the urge to just blow this joint and run off somewhere quiet, where I didn't have to deal with any of it.

But who was I kidding? I wanted to know more now. I needed to understand the relationship between my parents. I had to find out more about my mother. To understand why my father had done such a horrible thing.

"What about the other magicals he killed?" I asked.

"Their families never really recovered. Shortly after Hester's death, five others were killed, and all the signs pointed to him. The evidence was overwhelming, hence the verdict." Alton sighed. "Listen, I've kept something of his. I brought it here with me from New York. I actually had it stored here, in the archive. Come."

He motioned for Wade and me to follow as he took us deeper into the archive hall. At the very end, on a bottom shelf, stuffed behind a pile of old notebooks and journals, was a small, silver-plated box. *H.A. Shipton* was engraved on the lid, I noticed, as Alton took the box out and gave it to me.

I slowly leaned into Wade, once again feeling my legs turn to jelly. The box had belonged to my mother.

"Hester Anne Shipton," Alton said slowly. "Hiram had this box in his possession when he surrendered. It's still considered evidence, even after his execution, but we've never been able to look inside. I was entrusted with it, in hopes that I'd eventually find a way to open it. The lock is charmed with some kind of spell, but I've yet to identify what it is."

"Oh," I breathed. The image of a woman—my mother—burning to death was something I'd never get out of my head, even though I'd never seen her. "So, you don't know what's in here?"

"No. But I think it belongs to you. I've had no luck in getting it opened, and maybe you will. I hope," Alton replied. "The Shiptons passed away a long time ago, and Isadora was the last of the Merlins. I guess now *you're* the last of the Merlins."

We slowly walked back to the door leading back into the hallway, as I held the box close to my chest. Wade kept himself close, probably in case I collapsed again. I couldn't exclude the possibility—I felt weak, almost lifeless, as grief clawed at my insides and reopened old wounds.

Clearly, I'm not getting any sleep tonight.

"For what it's worth, Harley," Alton said after some time, "whatever happened with your parents and your aunt is in the past. They're all gone. At least you have some kind of closure, and you know where you come from."

"Yeah, my dad killed my mom and six other people, but hey, I have a fancy box now," I said, unable to keep my bitterness to myself. It hurt too much. I had to let some of it out.

We put the books away, then headed outside. I caught movement ahead, just by the door, and lifted my gaze. I could've sworn I saw Garrett just then, but by the time we reached the hallway, there was no one around. With the thought of Garrett and that botched date from earlier, it wasn't a surprise that he was, in some form, still on my mind. I could've just imagined it, anyway, especially since the main hallways and the adjacent ones were all empty.

"But you're you, Harley," Wade replied, his tone firm and strangely comforting. I had a feeling my hard-ass Wade was coming back. Great timing, too, because I was crumbling on the inside. "And Merlin sounds better than Smith as a last name."

"Your parents were nowhere near Mediocre, though," Alton mused. "They were both fearsome and extremely capable magicals. I'll put together some records for you regarding your parents' abilities, and send them over next week, for you to read."

"Thanks," I said, following up with a heavy sigh.

Alton's sympathetic expression was supposed to make me feel better, but I had a hard time looking at him and seeing the same magical I'd met the other day. This magical had known my father. He had been part of the jury that ended his life.

And I couldn't hate him. I couldn't even be angry with him.

According to the evidence, my father had killed a lot of people, including my mother.

And he ruined my life in the process.

Chapter Twenty-Six

As expected, I barely managed to get an hour's worth of sleep, as the rest of my night was spent tossing and turning between short sessions of crying and cursing at Chaos itself. I didn't have any energy left to even look at my mother's box, much less try to open it. I needed some space to breathe and put things in perspective, what with a killer dad and a dead mom, and more than my life thrown in the careless wind.

I dragged my ass down for a couple of liters of coffee in the banquet hall the next morning, carrying with me the idea that I had no other choice but to move forward. Alton and Wade were right. At least I knew where I came from. And who I was, by name and not by the actions of my father.

The entire coven had gathered for breakfast, and I was too tired to even try and control my Empathy. Their emotions hit me hard, like wrecking balls. Their looks, as they all turned their heads to look at me, were worse. *What happened?*

Something was off. There was too much pity gathering like lumps of lead in my feet, while contempt stabbed at me like an unsharpened knife. I took deep breaths as I walked across the hall, passing long tables loaded with magicals giving me the stink eye. Some were downright fearful.

What in the world?

I kept moving, focusing on the coffee machine reigning in the middle of the buffet table. The smell of freshly baked pastries and fresh fruit titillated my senses, but my stomach rejected the idea completely. *Coffee it is, then.*

"I didn't even know we had such *royalty* on the premises." Garrett's voice stopped me in my tracks, as it was followed by a round of snickering and malicious cackles.

I looked to my right, to find Garrett at the table, along with Finch, Poe, and the rest of the investigative team. They were all sneering at me, as if they all knew some dirty secret about me—like that time I'd told Ryann I was ten minutes away, when, in fact, I was just getting out of bed. *But much worse?*

Oh, crap.

"What?" I breathed.

"You're notorious, to say the least, and we had no idea," Garrett said. "You should've told us who your dad was, Red."

"That *was* you I saw last night by the archive hall, then," I said, my stomach moving somewhere down to spend time with my ankles.

"Hey, babe, you leave the doors open, people will hear you," he replied with a shrug. "But I don't mind. At least I know we're not going on a second date. No way in hell I'm going to hang out with the daughter of a serial killer."

The investigative team chuckled, along with a few others who'd overheard Garrett. My face burned, and my hands balled into fists. Rage burned through me like wildfire, and I welcomed it because it drowned out all the emotional signals that my Empathy was shoving down my throat in that moment.

Wade moved to intervene, but I motioned for him to stay back. I fought my own battles, and he seemed to get it. If I needed help, I would ask for it.

"Are you seriously going to sit there and say those things to me?" I asked, my voice cold enough to freeze the entire hall in less than ten seconds.

"I'm just telling it like it is, babe," Garrett replied, then stood up to face me.

Finch didn't seem amused anymore, watching Garrett like a hawk. That was new. I'd thought he'd be the head cheerleader in this particular crap-show. The others, however, grinned and giggled, watching with delight as he closed the distance between us.

"What are you going to do about it, Red? Slit my throat, like your daddy did to your mommy?" Garrett continued, and, for a split second, I contemplated walking away, my conscience telling me he wasn't worth it.

But my fist beat me to it, swinging into one hell of a left hook. Garrett's head jerked to the side. I heard something crack in his jaw as blood spurted out of his mouth.

Gasps erupted all around. Shock and awe—*how did they not see this coming, after what he just said?*

Wade decided to come between us, just as Garrett straightened his back, a grimace of pain distorting his pretty-boy face. He was so ugly on the inside, I was surprised I hadn't punched him sooner. Sure, he'd gotten on my bad side with his foul mouth from day one, but most of the bullies I'd dealt with were frustrated kids, so I'd given him *some* benefit of the doubt there. I may not have been able to read his emotions, but his words were poison. And my fists were itching for more. The first punch had felt so good.

Finch jumped across the table and pulled Garrett back, just as he took his first steps toward Wade and me. "That's right, your daddy didn't slit your mommy's throat, he burned her alive—" Garrett tried to rile me up some more, but Wade cut him off.

"I will finish what she started if you don't shut up, Kyteler," he said, his voice thundering across the hall.

A sea of wide eyes surrounded us. Our Rag Team slowly got up and moved closer. I could feel their anger; it wasn't directed at me, but at Garrett. They all wanted a piece of him.

"Garrett, don't—" Finch pulled him back, but Garrett pushed him away.

"Get off! This is a free country!" Garrett replied, then shifted his focus back to me. "I can say whatever the hell I want. Freedom of speech, remember? Besides, I'm only speaking on behalf of this entire coven, particularly the three magicals here who grew up without a parent because of your murderous father, Harley."

He pointed at two warlocks and a witch, all in their early twenties, and all glaring at me, like I'd been the one to orphan them… not Hiram Merlin. Their parents were among the six victims I'd read about.

Ah, man.

The emotional wrecking balls were tearing my walls down, chunk by chunk. The silent rage, the contempt, that sliver of fear. They were completely irrational because I was *not* Hiram Merlin, and yet, a part of me actually understood them.

I opened my mouth to speak, but my voice was gone. Pins pricked the inside of my throat, tears gathering in my eyes.

"She's not her father, you idiot," Wade hissed. "She lost both parents, and, until last night, she had no idea who they were. You should mention that, too, before you start pointing that self-serving, self-righteous finger at her."

"I take it Clara didn't want to talk to you after last night, so you decided to ingratiate yourself with the daughter of a serial killer?" Garrett spat.

Finch tried to intervene again, surprising me as a voice of reason, but Wade's anger was past the point of control. His rings lit up red as he put his hands out, shooting a myriad of fiery pellets at Garrett, who immediately lifted his wrist—his Esprit was a watch, and it glowed blue as it fanned out a thin sheet of water in the form of a round shield, protecting him from Wade's fire.

"You asshole!" Poe growled, and punched the air in front of him, sending out a pulse that knocked Wade back.

It went from bad to worse so fast I didn't even have time to react. All I managed to do was catch Wade before he fell, watching Santana, Tatyana, and Dylan jump in and start delivering fists left and right through the investigative team, with Finch, Garret, and Poe viciously retaliating.

Two seconds later, Wade jumped back in, while others joined, and I was left stunned and speechless on the sideline for a moment, watching one hell of a magical brawl evolving and swallowing more magicals in the process. I was ready to dive in and help, since I'd practically started it, but O'Halloran and the other instructors rushed in, swinging their batons around—which weren't regular, police-issued instruments. White flashes of magical electricity buzzed around the tips and sent shockwaves through the bodies that they touched.

One by one, the magicals involved in the brawl, including Wade, Garrett, and the others, fell flat on the floor, twitching with their eyes open and drooling like toddlers. The batons were obviously extremely effective, and I was suddenly glad I didn't follow my initial instinct to join the fight; otherwise, I would've been down there, too.

"Harley, Wade, Garrett, Finch." Alton's voice made my head snap toward the main entrance. He was extremely angry. My entire body shuddered in response. "My office. Now!"

I watched him leave, then looked down at Wade and Garrett, along with the others—still shaking from the electric shocks. O'Halloran smirked. "What's the matter, toots? Want to know what that feels like?"

"Nope, I'm good, thanks," I replied, shaking my head.

"Good. Let this be a lesson to you all," O'Halloran shouted, so the entire hall could hear him. "The San Diego Coven does *not* tolerate violence between its members, and we will not hesitate to use force if you decide to test us, like these brave warriors here."

The other instructors chuckled, while the electrocuted magicals struggled to get up. I helped Wade stand, somewhat relieved to feel so much fear coming in from everyone else. They'd all forgotten about me for the moment and were thoroughly spooked by those batons.

It gave me the window I needed to breathe a little and assist Wade in getting to the exit. I felt sorry for Santana, Tatyana, and Dylan. They'd jumped in to help too, but at least Raffe and Astrid were there, still standing and able to assist them.

I picked up the pace, as I glanced over my shoulder and saw Finch and Garrett not far behind. Damned if I was going to let them get to Alton's office first!

"Ouch," Wade grunted, as he struggled to walk, one arm over my shoulders.

"Ouch my ass," I said. "Come on, we're in enough trouble as it is!"

He gave me a slightly amused sideways glance. "I'm sure we are, but it was worth it."

Alton wasn't slightly angry, or irritated. He was *livid*. I could barely stand in his presence—though, to be fair, I had it easy. Wade, Garrett, and Finch were still spasming from O'Halloran's baton.

"Can we sit down?" Wade asked.

"No," Alton snapped, his back to us as he absently gazed at the bookshelf behind his desk. I heard Wade sigh before Alton turned around, his hands sunk in his pockets. "I must say, I'm disappointed. In all of you."

"If I may—" Wade tried to speak again, but Alton promptly shook his head.

"No, you may not," he said, then set his sights on Garrett first. "Effective immediately, your teams will be switching roles. Wade will handle the investigation of the Bestiary, and Garrett will be in charge of cleanup."

"Wait, what?" Garrett blurted.

I stifled a chuckle, catching a glimpse of a smile fluttering across Wade's face.

"I gave you a chance, Garrett, and you chose to insult and harass a magical," Alton replied. "You clearly aren't ready for a leadership position, since you seem to think it comes with a free pass at eaves-dropping on private conversations and verbally assaulting people. I don't take kindly to that kind of behavior. Besides, the Rag Team did another sweep of the Bestiary after you and found a spell disruptor—proof you didn't do your job right."

I didn't need my Empathy to see how angry and frustrated both Finch and Garrett were. I laughed on the inside.

"Wade, unless your team comes up with results over the next forty-eight hours, I'll have no other choice but to call in the Los Angeles Coven," Alton continued. "I can't keep this under wraps for much longer, especially after yesterday's incident. And we all know that if the LAC gets involved, the Council will also step in, and we'll suffer severe penalties. Your team has already proven itself more than worthy and capable to handle any challenge that comes your way, and you continue to have my and the preceptors' full support on the analysis of your investigation. We will help however we can, but you are the boots on the ground here, and I need you to pull through. You are this coven's next generation, and I've made it my mission *not* to keep you on the sidelines. Don't make me regret that decision."

"Understood," Wade replied with a nod.

"That being said, I don't approve of your aggressive behavior, either. Unless you make it up to me with some investigative break-through on this Bestiary issue, I'll reduce your pay for the next six months."

My stomach tightened—that was definitely Wade. "Yes, sir," he said.

"Harley, you're new, and you've had a rough couple of days, already." Alton sighed. "Frankly, I would've done a lot more damage to Garrett for what he said. I admire you for your restraint."

Really?

"Restraint? Seriously? I think she broke my tooth," Garrett said, holding his reddened jaw.

"Want me to break one on the other side, too, and make it even?" I replied flatly.

"Enough," Alton interjected. "You're all dismissed. If I get wind of you fighting again, I'll have you ejected from the coven altogether."

Whoa.

We all nodded and headed for the door, our heads down. Wade and I were particularly satisfied with the outcome, but we didn't show it. Every fiber in my body wanted to laugh in Garrett's face, but I was thankful that Alton was able to hand out such sweet justice. He was right, though: we weren't exactly role models.

"Harley, wait a minute." Alton's voice made me still.

As soon as Wade, Garrett, and Finch left, I turned around to face Alton again.

"Yes, sir?"

"You're not responsible for the sins of your father," he said. "I'll have a word with the children of Hiram's victims and make that clear, in case their grief gets the better of them. Don't let such words get to you in the future. You're not Hiram. You're Harley Merlin, and you're most likely the last of your bloodline. You have the power to make that name mean something again."

Tears stung my eyes as I gave him a nod and a weak smile. "Thank you, sir."

Chapter Twenty-Seven

The next day and a half went by in a haze. Alton decided to postpone my science center job induction until after the Bestiary investigation came to a conclusion, so I could focus my energy and resources on that. However, I couldn't skip the classes.

Even without an Esprit, I still needed to learn about my abilities and my heritage as a magical. Wade had also assigned me to do research on the spell disruptor. My best bet was with Preceptor Bellmore, since charms and hexes were right up her alley.

I joined one of her morning classes, and was rather flushed to discover that I was, by far, the eldest of her students. The other twenty magicals I shared the class with were all under twelve, and constantly making jokes at my expense. According to some of them, I was too old to be in school.

"You're never too old to be in school," I muttered, trying to pay attention to Preceptor Bellmore's talk on cursed objects. She was giving me a lot of useful information already, but the kids weren't making it easy to focus, their emotions raw and difficult to handle. Fifteen minutes into the class, I was already looking forward to the end.

"Next thing, you'll tell us books are your friends," a young warlock chuckled.

Great, I'm getting bullied by ten-year-olds.

"This isn't a school." Preceptor Bellmore intervened. "We teach magic in these halls, but the coven is much, much more, as you will all soon learn."

As soon as she finished the class, I held on to my desk, ravaged by the joy and relief of kids who were looking forward to playtime outside, and not another hour of school. While endearingly nostalgic, that wasn't the vibe I needed for my mission. I had every intention of finding something useful on that spell disruptor. From the moment I'd learned about my father, I'd made it my mission to prove—mostly to myself—that my last name didn't define me.

"Can I help you, Harley?" Preceptor Bellmore asked, after five minutes of quietly watching me squirm in my chair. The kids were all gone, and I could breathe again. My head snapped up from the doodles I'd viciously scrawled in my notebook throughout the lesson.

"Yes. Sorry! All the kids' feelings were… intense," I replied.

"I can imagine," she said. "They're bundles of energy and raw emotions. Though, I have no idea what it's like for you, as an Empath."

"It's… Imagine lots of water balloons hitting you in the face, over and over. Only it's not water. It's gasoline. And it's on fire."

The shadow of a smile passed over her face as she leaned against her desk. "Maybe you should consider private tutoring. I can make time, if you'd like," she said.

I stilled, a grin slitting my face. "That would be fantastic, thank you!" I replied, then remembered my mission regarding the spell disruptor. I fumbled through my jacket pockets, removing the disruptor, and held it out for her to see. "I wanted to ask if there was anything you could tell me about this."

Preceptor Bellmore came closer and picked the disruptor up

with two fingers, turning it over several times, her frown deepening with every move. "Where did you find this?"

"Can I count on your discretion?" I asked, remembering we'd been asked to keep the investigation on the down low, particularly since not even preceptors were allowed in the Bestiary anymore, and I still suspected basically almost everyone.

"You found it in the Bestiary," she replied, pursing her lips.

Well, that was awkward. I nodded slowly. "How did you—"

She cut me off. "The Rag Team got investigative dibs on the Bestiary. And you clearly didn't find this lying around in Kid City. I'm not stupid, Harley. I can put two and two together. Don't worry, I won't say a word. I want the culprit caught as much as you do. Anyway. I suppose you've already been told what this is?"

"A spell disruptor."

"That's correct. What is interesting about it is its complexity. It's quite rudimentary, but strong enough to bypass a charmed box. However, not just anyone can make it. It takes skill, and excellent knowledge of my field, as well as good contacts in the black market."

"The black market?" I asked.

"The dark web, to be specific."

"You're serious," I said. "I thought the dark web was for terrorists, pedophiles, and everything else that's wrong with our species."

"Including evil magicals, yes. You see this?" She pointed at the reddish bone shards. "These are Anirin beads, made with Irish troll blood. They are extremely rare, extremely expensive, and extremely dangerous, even deadly, if used properly. They're the elements on this disruptor that are actually capable of breaking the glass sigils. The others help but wouldn't get the job done without these little beauties. They're not sold anywhere, but I'm sure the resourceful evildoers can find them in a dark web chatroom, if they dig deep enough."

"I can't trace them back to an owner, can I?"

She shook her head. "It would be difficult to find such a spell."

The alarm on her phone rang with a gentle chime. She checked the screen and let out an exhausted sigh. "Unfortunately, I can't deal with this right now, but I'll think about it later," she replied, then handed me the disruptor. "I've got another class coming in. You might want to get out before they overwhelm you again. I'll talk to Alton about setting you up with private tutors."

"Thank you, Preceptor Bellmore," I said, getting up from my seat. I could hear children giggling and chatting outside, getting closer and louder.

"Call me Sloane, please—you're not one of the kids," she said, then waved me away just as all the kids poured into the room and I broke into a cold sweat.

I spent the rest of the morning muddling through a couple more classes with Preceptors Ickes and Redmont, both reaching the same conclusion: I could barely focus in a room full of kids. I needed private tutoring. Halfway through the physical magic class, Nomura called Finch into the room, to my surprise.

"I need you to take Miss Merlin here to one of the training halls, and teach her defensive Telekinesis," he said to Finch, who looked as befuddled as I was.

The change in my last name didn't escape me, either; I just didn't know what to make of it. Preceptor Nomura was quite good at keeping himself extremely cool. I got a hint of curiosity from him, but other than that, he was focused on teaching. The only thing that irritated him was when I wasn't paying attention, but he couldn't blame the developing Empath—for the time being, anyway. I was going to get it under control; it just took time and stronger nerves. Mine were temporarily tattered.

"Sir, I have to train with O'Halloran—" Finch tried to shirk the responsibility by pointing a thumb over his shoulder at the door, while attempting to come up with a good excuse, but Preceptor Nomura didn't give him the opportunity.

"One hour, Finch. That's all I ask, and you're the best one I know with Telekinesis who would be able to help her. She's distracted with all the children, and I refuse to let a class pass without all my students fully focused. I'll assign her a private tutor as of tomorrow but, until then, please."

Imogene had suggested that I cozy up to Nomura to get some training on using my abilities without an Esprit, but, judging by his decision to pass me over to Finch, that wasn't going to happen today.

Finch thought about it for a couple of seconds, then conceded with a heavy sigh and motioned for me to follow him. We went to one of the adjacent training halls, which was brightly lit and refreshingly quiet.

"Sucks being an Empath, huh?" Finch said.

"You can say that again," I replied with a shrug, then stopped in the middle of the hall, not sure what he wanted me to do.

He kept about twenty feet of distance between us, slowly turning around to face me. He was wearing a black outfit, with combat boots and a turtleneck sweater, bringing out his athletic build. He stared at me for a while, before the corner of his mouth twisted upward as he gazed out the window.

"Listen, Merlin—I hope it's not offensive or something if I call you Merlin?"

He didn't sound angry, just slightly irritated, though I still wasn't sure what his problem was, where I was concerned. He seemed to have disliked me from day one. *Maybe he's just a jerk by nature. Like Garrett. Birds of a feather and whatnot.*

"Apparently, it's my real last name, so… no, not offensive," I replied, my voice lower than usual.

I wasn't intimidated or anything. I just didn't know what to expect from him anymore. One day he was an absolute creep, basically begging for an ass-kicking, only to stop Garrett from throwing further verbal assaults at me the next day. Finch was the Russian roulette of insults.

"Okay. Listen, Merlin, I want you to know… I mean, I want to apologize on behalf of the investigative team… well, the team *formerly* in charge of the Bestiary investigation, for Garrett's behavior," he said, not too happy with having to say it. I didn't have to feel that; his flat tone said more than his words. "His behavior was way out of line, even by my standards."

He smirked, prompting me to chuckle. "I'm guessing murderous parents are off limits, huh?"

"You could say that," Finch replied. "Thing is, Garrett's a good guy, but he lets his mouth get ahead of him, especially when he's angry. Or, in this case, jealous."

"Huh?"

"You didn't notice? Okay. Wow." He laughed, crossing his arms. "Garrett has, or *had,* the hots for you. I think that went away the moment you punched him. Though, he can be a masochist, sometimes. He might still end up serenading you outside your bedroom door. Point is, he saw how you and Wade get along, and he didn't like it one bit."

"There's… There's nothing going on between Wade and me," I blurted out, my cheeks heating up.

"I know. Wade's got higher standards."

"Do you need me to warn you when you're being an ass?" I replied bluntly.

He sounded befuddled. "Why?"

"Or maybe you don't pick up on social cues." I decided to give up trying to explain why he'd been offensive. I figured if nobody taught you the basics past a certain age, there's no point in me trying. *Kind of like swimming upstream. In lava.*

"Wade likes his girls prissy, prep-school style," Finch replied.

I went to prep school. Briefly. It was as awkward as it could get, but that counts, right?

"Got it," I said, following up with a brief nod.

"Anyway, I digress. Point is: whether there's something going on between you and Crowley or not, Garrett thinks there is. And after you dumped him at the Noble Experiment the other night, well, he took it hard. Harder than I'd thought he'd take it, anyway. That whole thing about your dad and stuff, it was him acting out. The rest of us, we were just—"

"Protecting your own. I know," I murmured. "It's cool. He can apologize himself, though. I don't accept apologies via proxy."

He narrowed sky-blue eyes at me for a couple of seconds, then offered a half-smile. "Cool. So, Telekinetic, huh?"

"Pretty sure you've got first-hand experience with that," I retorted, slightly amused. "I'm not going to apologize, though. You had it coming."

"I'm not expecting an apology," he replied, shaking his head. "I'm expecting you to get better at it, within the next forty-five minutes."

His phone alarm rang. He rolled his eyes, then pulled out a small pill bottle from the side pocket of his black cargo pants, and popped two capsules in his mouth, chewing slowly. The sour look on his face told me exactly how awful they tasted. I couldn't help but squirm a little.

"Time for your vitamins?" I asked.

"You could say that. Show me your attack pose."

He didn't waste time, nor was he interested in telling me more about those pills. *Don't get your hopes high. For all you know, he'll flip back to asshole by dinnertime.*

"I thought you were teaching me defense."

"You thought wrong."

"But Preceptor Nomura said—"

Finch cut me off. "You don't want to give anyone the chance to attack you, in the first place. Defense is for kids. You're a grown woman, and you're clearly made for ass-kicking, so that's what I'm going to help you with today. Your private tutors will teach you about defense afterward."

"Okay," I replied with a shrug. "I don't have an attack pose, though."

"Which leg do you first use when you start running?"

I pointed at my right leg. He came around and showed me an attack position that involved transferring my weight to my right leg, to use as a pivot. He then lined up ten barrels at various distances in front of me and had me pick each one up with my mental lasso, then gently put them back down. "This will teach you control," he said. "If you can control your target, you're halfway there."

"I'm okay with static targets, though," I replied. "It's the moving ones I have trouble with."

He thought about it for a couple of seconds, then went over to one of the barrels, and threw it up in the air. "Catch it and put it down gently."

I missed the barrel by inches and cringed as I watched it crash onto the hard floor, wood splintering all over. Two barrels later, I managed to catch one midair, but my control was still quite weak. I could catch and fling a moving object, but I wasn't too steady with putting it back down in one piece.

Two more barrels later, I managed to smack one onto the floor. It didn't break, but it didn't land vertically, either. It wobbled, then fell over, but I was still pleased with myself. Finch, however, didn't look pleased. He was hard and unyielding as a teacher, but I found that I liked that—it wasn't the negative reinforcement, but rather the challenge that I responded to.

"What are you so giddy about?" he asked.

"I did it!" I grinned. "I put the barrel down without breaking it."

"You tossed it down."

"It didn't break," I said.

"It fell over."

"It's good enough," I retorted, getting slightly irritated, though secretly appreciative. I couldn't let him see I was enjoying myself. *He might flip.*

"Good enough is never good enough," he said, then walked over to the remaining barrels, and pushed them farther away, getting ready to throw them up from a bigger distance.

"Do you recite that in the mirror every morning?" I asked dryly.

"No, it's just something my mom—whatever. You're looking at a lifetime of Mediocrity, anyway," Finch replied.

That hurt a little, I had to admit it to myself. I exhaled and focused on the next barrel. I didn't get more progress done by the end of the training session. His words had cut deep, even though I'd been resilient to his jabs before. This time, it felt different.

Whether it had something to do with what I'd learned about my parents, or sheer exhaustion and stressing over gargoyles wanting to eat me up, it was clearly affecting my magical abilities—absence of an Esprit aside.

By the time evening fell over the coven, I was physically and emotionally drained. I definitely needed my private tutors if I wanted anything that they were teaching me to actually stick.

I skipped the banquet hall in favor of eating alone. After an entire day of magical kids messing with my senses, magical kids *plus* adults were literally the last thing I needed. I settled for a quick bite from the science center café, since they were closing up soon, and their last two customers were finishing their lattes.

My phone buzzed.

Meet at 10:15 p.m. outside Luis Paoletti Room. Don't be late. WC.

I couldn't help but chuckle, wondering if I should tell Wade that signing his messages with his initials didn't exactly make him sound cool. I felt a thrill of excitement at the thought of another late-night adventure—though I hoped this one would end on a happier note.

Chapter Twenty-Eight

I found the Luis Paoletti Room on the third level, thanks to the map in my so-called induction package. Wade was waiting outside, along with the rest of our Rag Team.

"You're late," Wade said, prompting me to check my watch. 10:16 p.m.

"And you sign your text messages WC. We're even," I retorted, relishing the heat in my throat caused by his embarrassment upon realizing what else WC stood for, then nodded at the double doors leading into the Luis Paoletti Room. "What's in here?"

"It's a generally restricted area for coven members," Wade replied, crossing his arms. "However, now that *we're* the investigative team, we've got clearance. It holds a collection of forbidden spells, too dangerous to put in just anyone's hands. I figured we could look through here for something to trace the spell disruptor back to its original maker."

"Sounds good. I'm guessing a now-forbidden tracing spell could easily be used to literally stalk innocent people, and that's why we need special clearance?" I asked.

Santana nodded. "Exactly. You catch on pretty quick."

"What can I say? I'm a fast learner," I replied.

Wade said the words of a spell, placing both hands on the doorknobs. His rings lit up white, and we all heard the click of the lock turning. He pushed through the double doors, and we followed him inside. The room was relatively small in size, its walls covered with shelves—all loaded with antique boxes with paper tags. There was no magical computer thingy in the middle, so I figured we'd have to do a manual search.

"Raffe, Santana, you two take the north side," Wade said. "Tatyana and Dylan can handle the west wall, and Astrid can check the south." He pointed over his shoulder. I glanced over my head and saw more shelves covering the walls around the double doors. "Harley and I will take the left."

We spread out as instructed. "What are we looking for, exactly? Just any tracking spell?" Tatyana asked, pulling out a box and browsing through its contents. I couldn't see from that angle, but I could hear sheets of paper shuffling.

"Pretty much. We need to find something, and fast. Our deadline expires tomorrow, and Alton is right. If the Mage Council gets involved, our coven is pretty much done, not just for the rest of the year, but probably for the next decade or so," Wade replied.

"Yeah, I get it." Dylan sighed. "We'll just pull out whatever's in the ballpark and see which one works best."

We all nodded and resumed our search through each shelf. I glanced around the room, while Wade checked an antique copper box with intricate gem details mounted on the rectangular lid. A section on the northern wall caught my eye, mainly because it was encased in thick glass with brass edges, and familiar symbols had been engraved on each side. It covered one fourth of the wall, and I could see it was filled with very old, leather-bound books.

"What are those?" I asked, pointing at the case, just six feet away from where Raffe and Santana were doing their search. Wade followed my gaze, stilled for a couple of seconds, then resumed his hunt for a tracking spell in another box.

"Grimoires. Those are strictly forbidden. We don't have clearance to look in there unless Preceptor Ickes is present to supervise," Wade replied, flipping through the brownish pages of an old pocket diary.

"What's a Grimoire?"

"A magical's own book of spells. Like a journal and a manual, all in one. Elder witches and warlocks have been keeping Grimoires since the beginning of time. Some of the spells are brand new, others are adaptations, customizations, and alterations of existing ones. You can change a single ingredient, for example, and a spell could go from healing a cut to inflicting horrible damage to one's nervous system," Wade explained. "The ones in the case were captured from evil magicals throughout the years."

"You're keeping them there because they're full of, well, evil magic?" I asked, then checked a small wooden box with various runes carved on all sides. There were small jars inside filled with what looked like charcoal powder, colored sand, small animal bones, and dried up seeds and fruit.

"That, and the fact that they're loaded with toxic, dangerous energy," Santana said. "Thing is, Grimoires are very personal items. There is a ritual through which we, as witches and warlocks, can start a Grimoire in the first place. We literally pour our thoughts, our memories, and our ideas into that book. The majority of Grimoires are beautiful, inspiring, and insightful, because they're collections of spells and notions of kindness, common sense, and rational thinking. Grimoires left behind by evil magicals are just as dark as their owners. Their pages are drenched in poison similar to that which we Purge… memories of horrible things they've done. Thoughts of hatred and rage. Difficult stuff to be around, in general. So, we keep them here."

"Every coven has a case with dark Grimoires, though ours is much smaller. You should see the New York one, it's freaking huge!" Astrid added.

"I wonder where my dad's is," I murmured, my fingers absently digging through small scrolls tied up with red string in another box. Exhaling, I gave up. "I don't know what the hell I'm looking for, exactly. I don't know what a tracking spell is supposed to look like."

I was frustrated on many levels, and the whole deadline pressure wasn't helping. Skewed dreams of my father killing my mother and other magicals had already screwed with my sleep—they weren't real memories, just my brain's interpretation of everything I'd learned over the past couple of days.

"Your dad's Grimoire is probably in New York," Wade replied, his gaze softening a little. There was warmth coming from him, the kind that soothed me—and it was most needed. "As for tracking spells, look for anything that lists items. The spells that *aren't* in that case with the dark Grimoires are excerpts from journals and manuals, mostly, along with samples of specific ingredients, and ready-made charms and hex boxes. It's a wide pool to look into, but we don't have much of a choice at this point."

"We should search for anything containing Anirin beads," I said, remembering what Preceptor Bellmore had told me. "It might help narrow down the search."

It didn't, though. There were many spells using Anirin beads, from what I quickly learned. We kept looking for about an hour, during which time I occasionally found myself staring at the Grimoire case. I could almost hear whispers tickling my ears, beckoning me to go over there and browse through their pages. There was an invisible string tugging at my stomach, pulling me toward them. *Maybe that's the dark energy they're talking about.*

"Am I supposed to get this urge to break through the glass and read those Grimoires?" I asked, my brow furrowed as I browsed through yet another box. I'd found all kinds of charms and hexes, most of them very powerful and intricately designed. They were right to keep them here—most could be used to do a lot of good, but, in the wrong hands, they could easily flip and kill thousands with a single incantation. Preceptor Ickes's curriculum did include a study of forbidden spells, but I had a feeling it wasn't as in-depth as an actual listing of ingredients and instructions. Nobody wanted a rebellious student to go out and try one of these on their own.

"It does happen, yes," Wade replied, carefully scanning my expression. "You can hear them, can't you?" I nodded slowly. "That's okay, just ignore them. You can't break through that glass anyway. Focus on your search, and you'll be fine."

"Harley's quite sensitive," Tatyana mused, staring at me. "Not everyone in this coven can feel or hear the dark Grimoires like that."

"Wait, is that a bad thing?" I asked, slightly concerned.

"Not necessarily," Tatyana replied. "It just means you're highly receptive to Chaos, in all its forms. Including the darkness. I wouldn't consider it something to worry about, especially not now, when you're still climbing that steep learning curve."

"Yeah, more like tumbling, falling, and breaking my neck," I said bitterly.

"Hey, we all had it hard in the beginning. Do you know how long it took me to get the Orishas under control?" Santana chuckled, then proceeded to explain her abilities better, once she noticed my befuddled expression. "Orishas are deities of Chaos. In the Santeria culture, they're considered minor deities, spirits of magicals that have passed on. They're wisps of energy, and a Santeria *bruja* or *brujo* has to form a relationship with them in order to get them to comply."

"And what do the Orishas do?" I asked, my mind going back to the church incident from the other day. The bright wisps of light I'd seen smacking the gargoyles before bursting into fireworks…

"Pretty much anything, though they're most adept at physical attacks and defense," Santana said. "They're concentrated energy, and they can mimic matter. They're also fully conscious, so they're able to discern what needs to be done. As a Santeria *bruja,* I summon them, I connect with them, and they're able to read my mind. They understand what I need in a split second, and they help. Of course, they have limits, and they require a lot of my own energy to break into this mortal plane. Orishas live in Chaos, and they need someone like me to pull them into the physical world."

I nodded slowly, then resumed my search through yet another box. I wasn't getting anywhere with this, but Dylan and Raffe had managed to find three potential tracking spells that we could use. By the time we finished searching each box, there were twelve options, scrawled on waxy scrolls and in the pages of two small pocket diaries.

"Now, the question is, which one do we use?" Santana said, her arms crossed as she studied the spells, which were carefully laid out on the reading table in the middle of the room. "Some of the items required here no longer exist or are incredibly rare and hard to find."

I followed her gaze across the texts, and one element jumped up at me. "Do we have all of these ingredients, by any chance?" I asked, pointing at an open scroll.

Wade leaned forward to get a better look and frowned slightly. "Diamond powder, mercury, wolfsbane root, dried cypress leaves, ground yellow jasper, feathered serpent's venom… I'm sure about all of them, except for the last one."

"Quetzi," I said, remembering one of the monsters in the Bestiary. "The former Aztec god!"

"What are you talking about?" Tatyana, like the others, seemed confused.

"The feathered serpent. Quetzi. I don't remember his full name. My tongue gets tied up when I try to pronounce it. The giant snake with bright pink-and-white feathers, big turquoise eyes, and jaws big enough to swallow a cow," I replied, trying my best to describe the slithering enormity that, according to Tobe, seemed to like me for some reason.

"Quetzalcoatl," Raffe said, his eyes widening with the same realization. "Holy hell, we have it. We have a full tracking spell!"

He grabbed the scroll in question and read it over and over, then handed it to Wade and put on a satisfied grin. Wade was both amused and relieved. "Raffe's right. We've got a tracking spell." He gave me a brief wink. "Well done, Harley."

Pride blossomed in my chest, while a voice inside my head cackled with joy. *See? Almost no knowledge of magic, and yet you still kick ass. Hah!*

"Okay, so let's get cracking then!" I declared, hands on my hips in a confident pose. I would've looked great on a motivational poster.

"Not so fast. Preceptor Gracelyn is out," Wade replied. "She'll be back in the morning, and she's the only one with access to the poison repository. That's where we keep the wolfsbane." He then went over the list again. "And, crap, where do we have yellow jasper?"

He looked at us, his eyebrows hopefully raised.

"Out of all the fancy schmancy jewels and decorative objects in this place, surely there's yellow jasper mounted around here somewhere," I mused, then crossed my arms, slightly deflated.

"It's not like we're jewelry experts," Wade replied.

"I might be able to help," Tatyana chimed in, then brought her hands together. The sapphire on her Esprit glowed blue as she muttered something in Russian, her voice low and chilling—toward the end of that incantation, I wasn't even sure if that was her speaking.

"What... Um, what is she doing?" I whispered, as darkness gathered around us like a thick cloud, drowning out the dim lights.

"That's right, you don't know," Astrid said, grinning. "Tatyana's a Slavic witch. Her people tend to specialize in seeking the dead to assist with various tasks. She summons the spirits of those who have died in her specific location—in this case, the coven—to enter her body and help her out."

"Whoa, she loans her body out to ghosts, basically?"

"Pretty much. Most of the time they're just spirits filled with energy, and she uses that to temporarily amplify her physical abilities and her spells. Sometimes, however, they're really powerful entities, and fully conscious, so they take over and bring their knowledge and memories with them," Astrid replied.

Tatyana's body glowed a cold, bluish white, as she took deep breaths and opened her eyes—two shimmering, pristine pearls. A gasp slipped from my throat. "Is... Is that—"

"A spirit, yes," Wade confirmed. "She just summoned a spirit from the coven, and, by the looks of her, it's a powerful one."

"She's going to collapse after this," Raffe added. "They always take a toll on her. Stand by, Dylan."

Dylan nodded and inched closer to her, just as Tatyana looked at me—but it wasn't Tatyana, per se. Someone else gazed at me through those blank, white eyes. "Ah. A Merlin still lives? I'm impressed!" She chuckled softly, the Slavic accent gone, replaced by a Southern drawl.

"Who are we speaking to?" Wade cut in, while I instinctively and quietly moved closer to him, taking comfort in the protection that his broad frame provided.

"Eleanor Hession-Doren, at your service, I suppose," Not-Tatyana replied. Her voice was different, rougher, like nails scratching the inside of a chimney. She didn't sound too happy to be here.

"It's definitely a strong one. It won't even let Tatyana speak," Astrid said worriedly, and I caught a whiff of her underlying concern.

"Relax, I'm not staying for long," Not-Tatyana drawled. "I've got better places to be, and, frankly, whatever this girl is eating, it's doing a number on my spirit! Now, tell me what you want to know!"

"We're looking for yellow jasper," Wade replied. "It's a big coven, with plenty of jewels. We were hoping you might be able to help us, Mrs. Hession-Doren."

"Oh. That's... That's actually very sweet." Not-Tatyana was pleasantly surprised, fluttering her eyelashes at him. "I'm guessing my reputation precedes me?"

"I don't know. Tatyana didn't tell us who she was summoning," Wade replied with a shrug.

Not-Tatyana pursed her lips, then shook her head. "I was the preceptor of Alchemy here before I got myself murdered by that Shipton shrew… Then Jacintha Parks took over and plunged the entire subject into mediocrity," she said. Had her eyes not been fully white and beaming, I would've seen her rolling them with dismay. "If anyone knows anything about gemstones in this wretched place, it's me."

"Wait, Shipton? As in Katherine Shipton?" I asked, unable to stop myself from deviating from the subject once my aunt's name came up.

"Yes. Horrible woman. I swear, if I ever get the chance—"

"Yellow jasper," Wade interrupted her, then gave me a stern sideways glance. "We need some. Now."

"Ugh, fine. Hold on," Not-Tatyana replied, frowning slightly. "What floor is this?"

"Third," Wade said.

"Ah, good. Follow me." She smiled and glided toward the door. Wade rushed past her and chanted the necessary spell for the locks to turn again.

We followed her into the hallway, then down the stairs to the second level, into one of the many open halls where various pieces of jewelry and fine art were put on display—dragons, shining suits of armor and elegant sculptures, necklaces and crowns, gold scepters, and a plethora of rings and bracelets bathed each room in a twinkling variety of metallic luster and colored gemstones.

"The thing with yellow jasper is that it can be easily confused with other types of cheaper, colored glass," Not-Tatyana said as she stopped in front of a glass case, where a beautiful regal crown was mounted, its band loaded with yellowish crystals and diamonds. Before either of us could react, she drove her fist through the case, shattering the glass.

We all gasped and froze, while Not-Tatyana shrugged and

picked the crown up. She bit her lower lip as she used her fingers to pry out the larger yellow jasper stones mounted on the front side of the crown.

"We're going to be in so much trouble for this," Astrid breathed, staring at the multitude of glass particles scattered across the floor.

Not-Tatyana chuckled, then handed over the yellow jasper stones to Wade. "Relax, it's not like anyone's ever wearing this piece of junk again. Here, do I look pretty?" She put the crown on her head and grinned. There was something slightly psychotic about her while under the possession of a spirit, and it felt wrong to find it funny, but I couldn't help myself.

"Okay, we're done here," Wade replied. "Thank you for your help, but we need Tatyana back."

"Typical man behavior," Not-Tatyana said, raising her chin. "I give you what you want, and you toss me aside."

"We have some pressing matters to attend to, that's all," Wade said, and I could feel the tension mounting as his rings started glowing red. He was ready to take action against the spirit if he had to.

Not-Tatyana shook her head slowly, her lips twisted with contempt. "That being said, you need to watch your back," she said, shifting her focus to me. "None of your father's victims stuck around to tell the tale, but someone knows you're alive, little Merlin, and they're not happy."

"Wait, what? What are you talking about?" I asked, chills running down my spine.

The glow in her body faded, and Tatyana sighed, returning to us for a couple of seconds, her blue eyes visible again. "Did it work?" she asked, and Wade nodded. "Good."

She blinked several times, then passed out. Dylan was quick to catch her, scooping her up in his arms.

"No, wait. What did she mean? Who knows I'm alive? Tatyana!" I called out, frightened and confused.

"She's not going to answer now, sorry," Dylan replied. "She's out cold and will sleep through the rest of the night. I've seen her do this before. It's exhausting."

"Dammit," I cursed under my breath. "Who was she talking about?"

"We don't know, Harley, but it will have to wait until the morning, along with the wolfsbane," Wade said. "Though I wouldn't hold my breath, if I were you. Tatyana doesn't remember the details of her possessions, not when she's taken over like that. And she'll need to replenish her energy to summon a spirit like Hession-Doren again. I doubt it'll happen soon."

I let out a frustrated sigh and ran my fingers through my hair. "Am I in danger?"

"When are you *not* in danger?" Santana chuckled softly, her dark humor infecting me. I felt a smile tugging at the corner of my mouth. "Listen, let's get some rest for now. We all need our strength for tomorrow, because once the tracking spell is complete and we find out who's been letting the gargoyles out, chances are we'll have a bit of a fight on our hands. I doubt they'll willingly surrender."

"Santana is right," Wade replied, then handed me the scroll. "Take this to Tobe first thing in the morning. Given that you're a part of the investigative team now, you don't have to *sneak* into the Bestiary anymore."

"Pot, kettle, sure," I retorted, then hid the scroll in the inside pocket of my leather jacket. "I'll get the venom from Quetzi, and meet you all downstairs for breakfast, I guess?"

"No, it's always going to be a mess for you until you learn to get the Empathy under control," Wade replied. "Let's meet in my office, right before breakfast. I'll have the wolfsbane and the other ingredients by then, too."

"*Your* office?" I said.

"I've been an illustrious member of this coven for a few years now. I've earned my own office," Wade said, a tinge of pride adding gravitas to his tone.

Astrid then cut in, taking the crown off Tatyana's head. "You guys go ahead. I'll clean this up and prepare an apology for Alton. He won't have an aneurism if I'm the one to tell him what we did here."

"Oh, yeah, that's right. Alton is easy on you." Santana giggled. "I mean, considering the number of times you've died for the coven, the man is in your debt for life."

We left Astrid behind with a murmured thank you, then headed downstairs to our rooms.

I spent some time looking at my mother's box, wondering if there was any way for me to open it. I was dying of curiosity as to what I'd find inside. I turned it over several times, hearing a faint jingle. Holding my breath, I peeped through its keyhole, but all I saw was darkness. Exhaling, I realized I was too tired for this. I hid it back under the bed and tried to get some rest.

Come morning, we were going to unmask the traitor in our midst, and that was supposed to be enough to remove the dark clouds hanging over my head. However, as I settled under the bedcovers, I couldn't stop myself from shaking.

Somebody knew that I, Harley Merlin, daughter of Hiram and Hester Merlin, was alive… Someone knew and didn't like the idea of me walking and breathing. Could the gargoyles have something to do with all that? It didn't make sense. It didn't fit with the timeline. The coven found out about my origins *after* we captured the last batch.

But still… *Who, and why would anyone want me dead?*

Chapter Twenty-Nine

I didn't hear my six a.m. alarm. My eyes shot open, and a sudden feeling of panic took over when I realized that I'd overslept. I checked my phone and yelped. It was 7:46 a.m. and the breakfast hall was opening in fourteen minutes.

"Crap, crap, crap!" I jumped out of bed and put on the first shirt and pair of jeans I could get my hands on, along with my leather jacket, then rushed straight to the Bestiary.

Oversleeping was not in my nature, but with everything that had been going on, it didn't exactly come as a surprise. I didn't even realize how disheveled I looked, until I came face-to-face with two of the security magicals stationed by the Bestiary door. There were also messages from Wade that needed a reply from me, all of them ending in "???", a written testament of his impatience and my being horribly late.

"Hey, guys," I said, putting on a friendly smile. "Harley Smith—sorry, Merlin. Harley Merlin. Still getting used to that." I laughed nervously. "Investigative team member. I need to get in."

"We know who you are," one of the magicals replied, as he

stepped aside. I offered a brief nod in return and pushed past the door, while checking my phone.

Where the hell are you???

I quickly typed a reply, telling Wade I'd be in his office in ten minutes. "Tops," I murmured while tapping the on-screen keyboard and navigating the Bestiary's glass corridors.

The air felt thicker than usual in there, formless smoke rippling and swirling around in the boxes as I headed toward Quetzi's enclosure. I hit send, then slipped the phone in my back pocket and glanced around, looking for Tobe.

"Tobe!" I called out, stopping in front of Quetzi's giant glass box.

The thick, tall grass trembled in the glass enclosure, notifying me of the monster's presence. Quetzi's huge, feathered head popped out, his turquoise eyes wide and fixed on me. The creature slithered closer to the glass pane standing between us, with jaws opening to reveal those gorgeous but deadly pearly fangs.

"Tobe! I need your help!" I shouted.

Hissing and growling erupted from nearby boxes. Various monsters were shaping up, clawing at the glass and snapping their monstrous teeth at me, ferociously hungry. "Yeah, yeah, yeah, eat me!" I muttered, then checked my surroundings again.

Gargoyles were gathering in full view inside one of the larger enclosures. But they were quiet, watching me intently with black, beady little eyes. "Oh, you're not into eating me, then? I'm not part of the gargoyle diet, after all, huh?"

"Actually, it's the quiet ones you should be most afraid of," Tobe replied, emerging from a nearby corridor. "The loud ones are just… well, just loud. Territorial, mostly. The quiet ones are the stalkers. It's like in an African savannah. It's not the roaring lions you need to be afraid of, but the quiet lionesses rushing toward you through the tall grass."

I dry-swallowed a sudden clump of fear, then gave him a weak smile. "Thanks for the insight. I'll keep that in mind and just refrain from taunting anything that came out of a Purge," I said.

"That's a good approach." He chuckled. "Now, what brings you here so early in the morning?"

"I need your help," I replied, handing over the tracking spell scroll. "We found something that can help us trace the disruptor charm we found under Murray's box to its original maker. We have all the ingredients, except for the last one."

Tobe read through the scroll and offered a single, soft nod. "And you're certain this will work?"

"It's worth a shot, don't you think?" I said, then shrugged. His big amber eyes settled on my face, and I felt his concern seeping through me like cold air through a window that wasn't closed properly. He was worried about something, but I couldn't say what, exactly.

Is he wary of the tracking spell?

"I do. It's just that this is a very old, forbidden spell. They're forbidden for a reason, Harley."

"Alton gave us access to look for something that could help us. This was the only one to which we have all the ingredients," I said, trying to analyze his emotions.

If it's an inside job, Tobe shouldn't be excluded from the suspect list. But what would be his endgame?

"Do you know why these spells are forbidden?" he asked, frowning slightly.

"Wade said it's because they could be devastating and deadly in the wrong or inexperienced hands," I replied, tucking my hands in the back pockets of my jeans.

"It's also because they're highly volatile and downright unstable. Some are so precise in the ingredient quantities that, if you put just one milligram over the specified limit, you could blow yourself and those around you to pieces," Tobe replied, then gave me the scroll back. "Which is why I'm asking again. Are you sure this is the only way?"

"If we don't come up with something by tonight, Alton will take the matter to the Mage Council, and I understand that will be *really* bad for the coven. Terrible. Sucky. Pick your favorite doomsday term."

He sighed, then moved his massive lion head around, stretching his neck muscles. I heard his bones crack as he waved his arms back and forth a couple of times, then took several deep breaths.

"What are you doing?" I asked.

"I'm about to go in and get you some of Quetzi's venom, Harley. It's not like he'll just open his mouth and drip it into a jar for me."

He fumbled through a nearby drawer—one of many mounted beneath the glass boxes—and retrieved a jar with a polished copper lid. He produced a huge set of golden keys from his right wing, hundreds of them jingling on a solid ring. I was surprised to see he carried those with him, since I hadn't once heard them clinking as he walked.

"What else do you keep between those feathers?" I chuckled. "Swords? A Boeing 747?"

He laughed, then selected the right key to insert into the lock mounted on Quetzi's enclosure. "Just a couple of useful knick-knacks. Now, watch this door, and keep it closed, no matter what happens, okay?"

My stomach tightened with the prospect of watching something horrific unfold right in front of me. "No, how about you just watch your back in there and get out in one piece, instead?" I replied.

"I'll do my best, but Quetzi is a worthy opponent," Tobe replied, then twisted the key in the golden lock. Its rune etchings lit up white as it clicked open. A flash of light traveled across all sides of the glass enclosure, temporarily revealing the magical sigils hidden in each crystal wall. The box was now open.

Tobe stepped inside, prompting Quetzi to raise his feathered head and look at him.

I moved closer, keeping my hands against the glass door, in case the monster decided to make a run for it. The one thing I knew for sure was that a monster was debilitated by its magical enclosure, despite its ability to maintain a form within.

Quetzi's tail rattled beneath the grass in a threatening manner that made my spine tingle. With careful and considered steps, Tobe inched closer. Quetzi raised his head to stay at his eye level. His jaws popped open, his pink, forked tongue rolling back—a sign that he was about to bite, not kiss.

"Hello, old friend," Tobe said slowly. "I need some of your venom, that's all."

He wiggled the small jar, for Quetzi to see, but the serpent didn't seem to care much. He lunged forward and went straight for the kill. I held my breath as Tobe dodged the attack, and Quetzi immediately came back and tackled him.

They became an agitated, entangled mass of giant feathered snake and Beast Master. Tobe growled and held his own, trying to catch Quetzi in a chokehold. They tossed and turned in the tall grass for about five minutes, until I saw Quetzi's fangs sink deep into Tobe's wing.

"No!" I cried out, and slapped the glass. To my utter shock, Quetzi stopped, then pulled his enormous head up to look at me, somewhat confused. *Worth a shot.* "I just need some of your venom, that's all! Please."

Quetzi seemed to ponder the issue for a while, before he let Tobe go.

"Okay. Wow. I can't believe that actually worked," I breathed.

Tobe was equally befuddled, his gaze darting between Quetzi and me. He recovered the jar he'd dropped in the grass, then removed the lid and slowly brought it up to Quetzi's head. The serpent stared at it for a few seconds, then opened its mouth and pushed one fang into the inner lip of the jar. A clear, slightly shimmering liquid poured out—the venom we needed for our spell.

"Thank you, old friend," Tobe said, and Quetzi instantly replied with a menacing, irritated hiss.

"Maybe you should get out of there," I said, anxious to the point where I felt my heart struggling against my ribcage.

Tobe nodded, then carefully moved back and out of the enclosure. He quickly handed me the jar of poison and put the lock back on, another flash of light announcing that the protection spell was back on. I gawked at Quetzi for a while, as he quietly watched me for about a minute, then slithered back into the tall grass.

"What was *that* about?" I asked.

"Guess I was right. Quetzi seems to like you."

"And not in an I-want-to-gobble-you-up-for-breakfast way," I murmured, then gave Tobe a concerned look. "Are you okay? He bit you."

"It's fine," Tobe replied, shaking his feathers with a pained expression. "I'm immune to his poison after all these years. It's the bite that hurts, but I'll be okay, don't worry—" He stilled as his eyes settled on the gargoyle enclosure to my right.

I followed his gaze and froze, clutching the jar to my chest. There were dozens of gargoyles inside the massive glass box, and they were all lined up on the sharp edge of a large rock, staring at me. "This is many kinds of weird," I murmured. "Why are they all looking at me like that?"

Tobe hummed, scratching his furry chin. "I think I know now. It makes more sense, now that we know more about your bloodline…"

A few seconds went by as I waited for him to continue. "Are you deliberately building up suspense here, Tobe? Help me out, man, what is going on?"

"Do me a favor, Harley. Walk over to them, slowly. And raise your hands to your sides. I want to see how they react to your movements," he replied, further baffling me.

"Shall I do a 360-degree turn and flaunt it like a supermodel, too?"

It was Tobe's turn to give me a frustrated scoff. I sighed, then did as he suggested, raising my hands as I walked toward the gargoyle enclosure. They all blinked, some cocking their heads to one side. None of them seemed on edge or aggressive, not until I reached the glass wall, and they got a better look at me. One gargoyle came closer, sniffing the glass in front of me. Our eyes met, and it startled me with a savage shriek. The rest joined in, flapping their bat wings and rushing in circles, some smacking their open jaws against the glass, desperate once more to eat me alive.

"That's enough, move back," Tobe said.

He didn't need to say that again. I hurried back to his side, my heart jumping like a sloppy track athlete running too fast to be able to handle the hurdles. "They changed their minds, or what?" I asked, utterly confused.

"You see, it didn't make sense at first. Gargoyles are very primal beasts. They live to hunt, to eat. They cannot be trained. They do not harbor any feelings. They're monsters, in the purest of forms," Tobe explained. "But with you, they seem conflicted, at least from a distance. Once you get close enough for them to… smell you better, basically, they go back into hunter mode. In all my years looking after these creatures, few magicals have ever had such an impact on gargoyles. Even fewer were able to actually herd them, command them. One of those magicals was Katherine Shipton."

I nodded. "Ah. Auntie dearest."

"Yes. Ever since she was a little girl, she used to sneak into the Bestiary without her parents, back in New York. She formed a bond with the gargoyles. A most peculiar thing. And she did the same with the ones out in the wild. In fact, she had this way with them that made it easy for her to use them as weapons."

"Okay, but that's Katherine Shipton. I'm not her. Why are the gargoyles being so sketchy about me, then?"

"I'm guessing they can smell the bloodline." Tobe sighed. "They probably recognize something that's somewhat familiar to them, something belonging to someone they're attached to, despite all their natural instincts. It's interesting."

"More like creepy," I said.

"That, too." He smiled. "But it's a skill you could use to your advantage in the future. Think about it this way: if you ever come across wild gargoyles out there, if you manage to distract them like this, even for a few seconds, it'll give you a window of opportunity. A chance to capture them, to protect others, or to flee."

"Oh, damn, you're right!" I replied, realizing the brilliance behind this grim coincidence. There was nothing of Katherine Shipton in me, but the blood relation could totally work to my advantage going forward. "Duly noted. Thank you, Tobe!"

He gave me a soft smile, which quickly faded at the sound of footsteps. I turned around to see Alton coming in, accompanied by O'Halloran and Preceptor Nomura, along with four more security magicals right behind them.

They all looked grim, downright sad, but determined, judging by the muscles twitching in their jaws. Sadness and anger poured out of them in hot waves, tying my stomach up in painful knots. Something was horribly wrong, and I was suddenly overwhelmed by a feeling of… helplessness.

"What's going on?" I asked, my voice barely audible.

"Step aside, Harley," Alton replied bluntly. Only then did I notice the computer tablet in his hand. He brought it up and opened a video file, showing it to Tobe. "Can you explain this, Tobe?"

I craned my neck to get a better look and found myself breaking into a cold sweat. Whether that was me or Tobe, I wasn't sure. What was certain, beyond any doubt, was the video's content. It showed Tobe, in full view, captured from multiple camera angles, holding spell disruptors up and mumbling something before he shoved them under several glass boxes.

Oh, no.

"How… How is this possible?" Tobe gasped, his eyes wide with shock. His heart broke, and I could feel each painful reverberation.

"This is you, Tobe. On the coven's CCTV system. We've managed to recover some files we'd first thought were damaged. What are you doing in this video? Because, from where we're standing now, it looks like you're activating highly complex spell disruptors and sabotaging your own Bestiary," Alton said. Anguish clutched at my throat.

"That can't be... That's not me, Alton! I would never do such a thing. Why? Why would I let monsters go?" Tobe replied, shaking his head. He was genuinely stunned.

"Maybe you're tired of seeing your brethren in cages," Nomura said with a shrug. "Maybe you've been harboring feelings against the covens for a long time. We don't know, Tobe. But you do. And you can tell us why you've been doing this in the interrogation room."

"No. This isn't me. I swear," Tobe insisted.

I believed him. I could feel him, and it hurt me deeply. "Alton, he's telling the truth," I said.

"Stay out of this, Harley. Your Empathy is still raw compared to other Empaths your age. And Tobe is over a thousand years old. He could easily have learned to mimic different emotions, just to play his part," Alton replied.

"That hurts," Tobe murmured.

"It does," I added.

"It hurts us the most," Alton said. "Until this matter is fully investigated, I've agreed with Preceptor Nomura that the best solution is for you to occupy one of the prison cells in the basement and submit yourself to a full review."

"This isn't right. I'm innocent!" Tobe said.

"Then you will have no problem cooperating with our investigation, right?" Nomura said, his dark brow furrowed, his lips pressed into a thin line.

"You don't need to lock me up for this. I will happily cooperate!"

"I'm sorry, Tobe, but the video evidence is compelling, and it clearly points to you as the main suspect. I can't let you walk freely around the coven," Alton said. "Preceptor Nomura will take you to your cell and proceed with the interrogation, and O'Halloran here will do another sweep of the Bestiary with his officers. Clearly, there is more than one spell disruptor on these premises, and they've all been nearly impossible to detect so far. If O'Halloran can't find them this time either, Preceptor Nomura will take whatever action is needed to compel you to tell the truth."

"Whoa, Alton. Come on, that's... This is Tobe!" I said frantically. "And don't undervalue my Empathy. I can tell he's being genuine, just like I can tell that you're all brokenhearted and moping like little girls on the inside, because you're all finding this hard to believe!"

Tobe sighed, then gently squeezed my shoulder. "It's okay, Harley. I will cooperate in full and go with Preceptor Nomura. You have everything you need to do your job. I trust you will come through for justice and truth."

A lightbulb went on in my head. *Hell, he's absolutely right*. I had Quetzi's poison in my hand. Wade and the others were already waiting for me in his office. And almost all of the coven was gathered in the banquet hall for breakfast. If there was ever a good time to unmask a traitor, this was it.

I gave him a brief nod, then scowled at Alton and left the Bestiary in a rush, my boots barely touching the ground. I heard the shackles clinking behind me, cursing under my breath as I ran faster through the hallways.

My pulse was racing. Deep down, I knew Tobe was innocent. Everything he felt pointed me to that truth. And Alton was wrong. If there was one thing I was absolutely, unequivocally sure of, it was the fact that Tobe was being framed. And with the Beast Master gone, the Bestiary was at even greater risk.

Chapter Thirty

I stormed into Wade's hilariously small office, startling the entire team. Dylan even let out an unnaturally high-pitched yelp, then immediately cleared his throat. Wade was the first to notice the sheet of sweat on my face.

"Whoa. What happened?" he asked.

"There's video footage of Tobe sabotaging the glass boxes in the Bestiary. Alton and Preceptor Nomura basically just arrested him. The images are genuine, and clear, apparently, but Tobe is innocent. He says he's innocent, and I believe him. I could feel him, raw and honest. He was as shocked as the rest of us. He didn't do this. He's taking the fall for something he didn't do," I said in a single breath.

"Hold on. What?" Santana was baffled. The entire Rag Team displayed a variety of gaping mouths before me.

"When did this happen?" Wade asked.

"Just now! In the Bestiary!" I replied.

"How do you know the footage is genuine?" he said, frowning. He couldn't believe it, either.

"I doubt Alton would've showed up with Preceptor Nomura, O'Halloran, and security magicals to arrest the freaking Beast

Master without verifying the videos first. And that's the thing! I *know* he didn't do it. I can feel it in my bones—"

"I trust you, Harley." Wade cut me off, and I stilled, surprised by his candor and, most importantly, his trust. "If you felt Tobe that way, then surely he wasn't deliberately involved. He could have been manipulated into—what, exactly? What does the footage show him doing?"

"Placing spell disruptors under the boxes," I said.

"And he has no recollection of doing that, at all?"

"None whatsoever. He's adamant about this. It's not him," I replied.

He thought about it for a couple of seconds, his gaze wandering from Tatyana to Santana, Raffe, Dylan, and Astrid, before settling back on me. "Maybe he was hexed. Some charms can be incredibly powerful. He needs to be screened, tested for every possible spell. I presume they've taken him to the basement, into one of the cells."

I nodded, then put the jar of poison on the table. "You know what we have to do next."

"Hah! You got it!" Santana cackled, a brilliant grin stretching her lips as she picked it up and admired the shimmering liquid within.

"Which is good, because we got the rest," Wade said, and pointed at the other ingredients for the tracking spell, carefully laid out on his desk: a handful of diamonds, yellow jasper stones, wolfsbane roots, fresh cypress leaves, and a small vial of mercury.

I took a deep breath and checked the spell scroll. "Okay. Not exactly, but we're almost there. The diamonds and the yellow jasper stones need to be in powder form. Actually, according to Tobe, we have to be *really* specific in preparation, because one mistake could blow this whole place up. He says some of these spells are extremely finnicky about quantities and stuff, so let's do this right. Also, the cypress leaves need to be dried, and, last but not least, *this* is your office?"

Wade put on an adorable pout. "What's your beef with my office? At least I have one," he grumbled.

"It's a shoebox, Wade. I'm getting claustrophobic in here," I replied, prompting the rest of our team to chuckle.

"It's a process. I'll get a bigger space next year. *Provided* we ace this investigation and find the culprit before Tobe gets wrongfully convicted," he said, then looked at Santana. "Any chance one of your Orishas can deal with the diamonds? We need this done fast. Like now. Every second that Tobe is out of that Bestiary, the real saboteur is getting closer to doing a lot more damage than a bunch of gargoyles."

"Sure thing. Hold on," she replied, then gathered the diamonds and jasper in two separate groups on the desk.

She covered each group with one hand and whispered something in Spanish. Despite the closed door and window, a powerful wind blew through the room, prompting Wade to cover the other ingredients with his hands, so they wouldn't scatter away.

Santana opened her eyes, which glowed an ethereal light blue. She smiled, her voice sounding like multiple people talking in unison. "The Orishas are here," she said, then went into a deep hum as her hands started to shimmer blue, as well.

I could hear the diamonds and jasper crumbling as the azure light beneath her palms intensified, and the wind died down. "*Gracias,* Orishas. I am once again in your debt," she added, in different voices.

She exhaled sharply, returning to her normal state, and lifted her hands. The diamonds were turned into white, glimmering powder, and the jasper was crushed into particles the size of ground sea salt. "Perfect," Wade replied, and took a small wooden bowl and a kitchen scale from a bottom drawer.

Placing it on the desk between us, he scooped up the diamond powder and glanced at me. "How much diamond powder, exactly?"

"Twenty grams," I said, checking the scroll. "And thirteen grams of jasper."

He nodded, then weighed the diamond and the jasper, respectively, and transferred them into the wooden bowl with the help of a silver spoon. "Fun fact, Harley. Only use silver spoons when mixing ingredients for a spell. They're like binding agents. Otherwise you'll get potentially catastrophic glitches. They'll teach you that in magical classes soon," he said. "Now, you said the cypress leaves need to be dried. How many leaves do we need?"

I nodded and read through the scroll. "Three."

He put one hand over the leaves, his rings glowing red as heat emanated over them. Within minutes, they were neatly dried up, his fire not too weak or too strong, but rather perfect for creating a natural, localized drought. He then slipped the leaves into the bowl and removed the cap from the mercury vial, waiting for me to give him the precise quantity.

"Five drops," I said, and watched as he produced a small pipette from another drawer and added five drops of mercury into the mix. The silvery droplets rushed around through the bowl, slipping over and through the powdered gemstones and dried leaves. "And nine drops of venom."

"And after that?"

"Okay, let's see," I replied, then handed the scroll over to Santana. "I think you're better at explaining the rest, plus the incantation. It's above my level at this point."

And I hated that. I couldn't wait to learn more, and eventually find my Esprit so I could be a full-blown magical. It thrilled me to be able to do such weird things, like Santana's Santeria deities lending a hand, or Tatyana's spirit possession, or Wade's fire power. I had some great skills of my own, and I could put them to better use. It hit me right then and there that Alton had been spot-on.

I didn't belong in a casino, spotting cheaters. Something inside me burned to hand out justice and to protect people who couldn't protect themselves. The urgency of a master-less Bestiary made my heart pump blood twice as fast through my body.

Others would've split by now, running as fast as they could in the opposite direction. I, on the other hand, was drawn to the flame like a warrior moth. I'd found my real name in this place. The least I could do, in return, was to keep it safe from a monstrous rampage.

"Okay, so! Once you add the venom, you stir it counter-clockwise three times with the silver spoon, and then five times clockwise," Santana said, reading from the scroll. "Then, you place the spell disruptor on top, cover it with three spoonfuls of the mixture, specifically from the left, and chant the Latin spell… Here."

She placed the scroll before him, so he could perform it all in one go. Following the instructions, Wade added the venom with a pipette, mixed accordingly, then placed the spell disruptor on top and covered it with the concoction. "*O, filia luna, cum venenum sanguinem, da mihi oculos, sic ego can reperio dominus hoc obiectum*," he chanted in Latin, his rings lighting up red.

"What does that mean? All I got was 'moon,'" I murmured.

"He asked the 'daughter of the moon with venom for blood' to find the owner of that object," Santana whispered.

Nothing happened, though. We all stared at the bowl for a while, until I finally gathered the courage to ask the uncomfortable question. "Why isn't it working?"

"Shush," Wade snapped, narrowing his eyes at the mixture.

I followed his gaze and stifled a squeal when I noticed the shimmer of diamond powder and Quetzi's venom increasing its intensity, until it enveloped the spell disruptor, taking on a green hue. Gradually, all the ingredients dissolved into the glimmering green mass, leaving the disruptor itself untouched.

"You guys have never done this particular spell before, have you?" I asked.

"Nope," Santana replied, shaking her head, curiously watching the green mass burn up into an emerald fire, until a single constant spark jumped up. "Oh, crap, I've seen something like this before. Get ready to run."

Wade frowned, slightly confused as he stared at the hovering green spark. "Why?"

"It's about to go fast," Santana replied.

As soon as she said that, the spark shot right through the door, and we scrambled out into the hallway, running after it.

"Keep your eyes on it! Don't let it out of your sight!" Wade shouted.

We stayed hot on its tail, running as fast as our legs could take us. The green spark had us dashing across multiple hallways and down the stairs to the ground level, before it turned a tight corner and whizzed into the banquet hall.

This is it…

"Let's hope this works, because if it fizzles out—oh look, the whole coven's here," Tatyana breathed as we all came to a sudden halt in the massive doorway.

The green spark flickered aimlessly for a couple of seconds, while a sea of emotions crashed into me. Tatyana was right. Most of the coven was gathered for breakfast, including Alton, O'Halloran, and Preceptor Nomura. *They probably dropped Tobe off in a cell and came back up for a freakin' latte and a scone.*

Many didn't immediately notice the spark until they saw us stumble in, then followed our collective gaze upward. It flickered restlessly, then shot down and smacked Finch right in the forehead, exploding into a myriad of tiny fireworks.

Pop! Pop! Pop!

Finch was stunned, covering his face to avoid any burns, and fell backward with his chair. Gasps erupted from the table. The air got knocked out of my lungs as the realization kicked in. Garrett had been sitting next to him and was still holding his coffee mug as he looked down and saw Finch hit the ground.

It was Finch all along.

Chapter Thirty-One

"*What* is going on here?" O'Halloran barked, shooting up from his chair. The stern frown on his face promised a lot of electric shocks unless someone came up with an explanation, fast.

The spark was gone, but the sight of Finch—his face covered in soot and mild burns as Poe helped him back up—was enough for us. I'd trained with Finch. I'd been conflicted about him, but, in the end, I hadn't thought he'd do something like this. Sure, he'd come across as one of the biggest jerks I'd ever met, but, still, I'd had foster dads who were way worse than him.

Then again, how bad do you have to be in order to release gargoyles and potentially kill dozens, if not hundreds, of innocent people?

Downright despicable. But did Finch fit the bill? I didn't really think so.

"It's him," Wade said, pointing a finger at Finch.

Alton stood up slowly, and I could tell from the shadows drawing up on his face that he knew exactly what Wade meant.

"What are you talking about?" Finch growled, wiping some of

the soot from his face with a white napkin, while Garrett still gawked at him, slowly putting his coffee mug down.

"Finch!" Santana chimed in. "It was Finch. He's the one who made the spell disruptor we found in the Bestiary."

"Disruptors, actually," O'Halloran said. "We found three more just now. Sneaky little things, too, since they didn't show up in previous sweeps."

"You people are crazy! Have you lost your minds?" Finch replied, seemingly shocked and extremely offended. I couldn't feel him as an Empath, and it pissed me off. That would've been the smoking gun.

"That was a trace spell we just used, with ground yellow jasper and feathered serpent venom. Ancient Latin, to be precise," Wade said, advancing through the banquet hall.

We moved as well, staying close to our team leader. Anger boiled inside me, and it was all mine. The gargoyles had nearly killed me, and Finch had been the one to set them loose, bypassing Bestiary protections. My Daisy was done for because of him. My apartment.

"The magic doesn't lie. Chaos does not lie!" Santana added.

All around us were expressions of awe, confusion, and increasing discontentment, as the attention gradually shifted from us—the Rag Team, the magical underdogs—to Finch Anker. The saboteur. The traitor. The looks on their faces confirmed what Santana had just said. *Chaos does not lie*.

"Tobe is innocent!" I said, drawing more befuddlement from the magicals around me. They hadn't been told yet. Tobe was stuck in a cell downstairs, and the coven didn't even know that he'd been wrongfully accused. *Oh well, leave that to Alton to explain*. "And you!" I pointed an angry finger at Finch, gritting my teeth. "You almost killed me. Twice! You've been bypassing security and Bestiary charms, letting those things loose! Why?"

"Guys, seriously. You've gone off the rails!" Finch said, slowly taking a couple of steps back. "I didn't do anything!"

Garrett seemed to be in shock, his movements slow. The rest of their group was baffled. They couldn't deny the tracer spell, but they were having trouble coping with the facts. Garrett finally spoke, getting up to face Finch. "What the hell did you do, man?"

"I didn't do anything! Didn't you just hear me? I'm innocent!" Finch replied.

"You can stop pretending, Finch," Alton said, his expression sour, his heart bleeding. He was disappointed, and it made my stomach churn, painfully. "I know the type of spell they used to point you out. I've heard about it before—a long time ago, before I got to this coven. I didn't even know we kept one here. It may be forbidden, but, if done right, it's infallible, and it cannot be contested. It only shows the truth."

"I—No," Finch tried again, but gave up when he saw the looks on everyone's faces, particularly Garrett's. I couldn't feel Garrett either, but that was the expression of a boy with a broken heart—the worst kind, too. The one caused by a best friend letting you down in an irreparable way.

Finch's shoulders dropped, as he exhaled and shook his head, his bearing morphing from outraged to bitterly amused. "I mean, I could only keep this up for so long, right?" He chuckled then, and Garrett, Poe, Rowena, and the others moved back, finally seeing him for who he truly was.

"You almost killed me, you son of a—" I lashed out and grabbed hold of his throat with my Telekinesis. He choked under my mental grip, and laughed at the same time, mocking me. I waved my hand and tossed him across the banquet hall. He landed on his side in the middle, between two rows of tables, as the rest of the magicals stood up.

Finch kept laughing as he stood once more, evil and defiant. "You're a quick learner, I've got to give credit where it's due," he replied. "But you'll never be as fast as me. You're a Mediocre, after all."

He didn't give me time to respond or prepare for what came next. His hand shot out, and his incredible mental strength closed around my throat and instantly cut off my air supply—his

Telekinesis was much more potent than mine. I frantically grabbed at my own neck, my brain switching to survival mode. I was being choked, and I needed to relieve the pressure. The only problem was that there was no physical pressure, nothing to pull back or break in order to set myself free.

He grinned, then waved his hand up, tossing me upward. I heard screams and gasps and boots thundering across the marble floor. The banquet hall got smaller, down to a bird's eye view, as I was slammed into the ceiling. Pain burned through my spine, my ribs, my shoulders, and my hips—the impact was one hell of a doozy.

Then, I fell. From that height, I was going to break plenty of bones. I held my breath and tried to do something, anything, but I was still limp from my ceiling slam. Wade shot back into view and caught me with a grunt. He fell backward, and I landed on top of him with a sloppy thump, but I survived. My whole body hurt like hell, but I was breathing again.

Security magicals flashed around Finch, their Esprits burning bright in a variety of colors—watches, rings, cufflinks, and bracelets, all loaded and ready to amplify the power of Chaos straight at Finch. He slowly raised his hands, constantly smirking. My palms itched to wipe that smug look from his face.

"Don't even think about trying something else," O'Halloran hissed, taking his position behind Finch, with the rest of the security detail. They were all fuming, and deep down, they were worried. Finch was far too relaxed for this situation. His life was practically over. He was looking at decades in a four-by-four cell, for sure.

"Why did you do it, Finch?" Alton asked, and moved in closer. "What possible reason could you have to do such a thing? This coven took you in, protected you—"

"Will you just shut up with all that motivational crap?" Finch cut him off, then rolled his eyes, his hands slowly raising and meeting behind the back of his head. His gaze followed Alton as he came around to face him. "You've been droning on like this for the two whole years I've been here. Aren't you tired, or do you really love the sound of your voice that much?"

"Why'd you do it, Finch?" I asked, trembling with rage, as Wade held me up. His hands gripped my shoulders, soothing me enough to keep me from going after Finch again, though every fiber in my body ached to hurt him.

Finch shifted his focus to me, his sneer stirring bile up to my throat. "I've had a bone to pick with the magicals since they drove my mother away," he hissed. "I just had to wait for the perfect opportunity to get the plan going. I needed the Bestiary in the hands of absolute incompetents, and... well, the rest is history."

"What do you mean? Who is your mother?" Alton asked. "I don't know of any Ankers who—"

"Anker isn't my last name," Finch spat. "It's Shipton."

My heart dropped, so hard and so fast that I nearly collapsed. "What... What did you just say?" I managed, a whirlwind of questions clobbering me as I looked right into his sky-blue eyes and saw everything that had been right under my nose this whole time.

"You know, by now, what happened between Hiram Merlin, Hester Merlin, and Katherine Shipton, right?" Finch replied. The shockwave was instant, as the rest of the people around me, including my team, came to the same conclusion. "Hiram had an affair with Katherine, before he married Hester. A son was born from that first union. *Me*. My mother had someone else raise me. She couldn't bear the shame of being a single mother, you see. Humiliated by her own sister. Rejected by Hiram and our grandparents. It was a travesty, really. The kind of blue-blooded elitism that has plunged the magical society into uselessness and weakness."

I nodded, ever so slowly, as his words filled in the gaps in my accounts of what had happened between my parents. "That makes you my—"

"Half-brother. Yes. Hello, Sis." Finch chuckled.

"You tried to kill me just now."

"I'll do a lot worse by the end of the day, I promise you," Finch continued. The man was an exquisite sociopath and psychopath, both rolled into a powerful magical whose emotions I couldn't read. "While I was being raised by a hateful, scrawny old woman named Agnes Anker—there you go, Alton, in case you were wondering,"—he winked at Alton, then went back to smirking at me—"Hiram was living it up with Hester. Both pillars of the community, so on and so forth. Everybody loved them. My mother wasn't done with Hiram, though. She reclaimed him the way she knew best, and boy, did Hiram come back with a bang! He ended up killing Hester, after which my mother dumped him. She'd gotten her revenge, after all."

I still couldn't wrap my head around my father killing my mother. I thought they were madly in love. They'd all said so, according to what I'd read so far. And what did he mean about Katherine reclaiming my father "the way she knew best"?

Finch wasn't going to tell me anything about that, but I figured Katherine might've had something concrete to do with my father's murderous rampage. *I'll find out, eventually...*

Nausea threatened to turn me inside out, but Wade's grip on me was firm. "Why do you hate me so much? What did I ever do to you?" I whispered, no longer able to stop tears from rolling down my burning cheeks.

"You wouldn't understand. Up until the other day, I didn't even know you existed, so take it down a notch with the melodrama, okay?" Finch replied. "You *have* made things harder here, I'll give you that. Nevertheless, I thought you were still in Hester's womb when Hiram killed her. Mom lost track of Hiram after the deed was done, and not much was left of Hester's body to identify... Oh, well. I've had to readjust my plans, too. Nothing that couldn't be fixed."

"Why did you do it?" I screamed, letting my anger take over just so I'd stop crying.

The others were surprised by my outburst. Wade's fingers were digging into my flesh. I could feel he wanted to tell me something, anything to soothe me, but no words felt right.

"Because I can, Harley. Because I want to. Because this world needs a drastic change, and it will come in the form of Katherine Shipton." Finch raised his voice, fear crippling the magicals around me. "This was just the first step to what will be the most memorable ascension of a magical to a godly status. You will all burn. The weaklings, the Mediocres." He gave me a brief smirk, just to twist the knife in. "They will not survive. My mother will become a true Child of Chaos, and only a select few will be honored to stand by her side. Should you resist, your skulls will be crushed under her feet."

"Katherine Shipton is alive," Alton concluded. There was dread inside him, and howling through me, as well. Clearly, I didn't know enough about her to fully understand the extent of that statement.

"Oh, yes." Finch grinned. "And she's coming for all of you."

"When?" Alton replied. "And how the hell does she plan to become a Child of Chaos?"

"That's for me to know, and for you to find out."

"We'll be ready," I said, as everything became all too clear.

"I very much doubt that," Finch sneered. "You're not even ready for what comes next."

"What are you talking about? You're about to get arrested. You're surrounded. You're not going anywhere," Wade said. He seemed calm, but his rings had a reddish glow about them. His instinct rattled mine and, somehow, I found myself prepared for something —though I didn't know what, exactly.

"It doesn't matter what happens to me," Finch replied. "Though, I doubt I'll still be here by the end of the day. You're too late."

We all fell silent.

Only then did I notice his sterling silver lighter, gleaming white between the fingers of his left hand. *Oh, no…*

"His Esprit!" I croaked, pointing at it.

O'Halloran was the first to make a move to grab it, but a blood-curdling shriek echoed through the coven and made him freeze—horror set in, as we all understood.

Finch burst into hysterical laughter, as that first shriek was followed by dozens more. Wings flapped. Objects fell and crashed against the hallway floors, the noises getting closer with every second. The banquet hall erupted into wave upon wave of shrills and screams as black shadows fluttered over us.

I looked up and felt my throat close up. Gargoyles, dozens of them, flew in. Their claws were out, their fangs glistening as they swooped down on the crowd of magicals. O'Halloran got over his moment of freezing panic and reached for the lighter.

Finch dodged him, his Esprit glowing white as it turned into a long knife. He swiftly turned around and stabbed O'Halloran in the stomach. I screamed, and Alton tried to tackle Finch, his dragonhead cufflinks beaming yellow. Finch evaded his attack, and I caught a glimpse of the knife headed straight for the side of his neck.

"No!" I cried out, and Telekinetically latched onto Finch's hand, then waved it away. The knife slid across the floor to the side.

Chaos ensued as magicals used a variety of spells and Telekinesis of their own to try and capture as many gargoyles as they could. My team spread out to help, while I kept my focus on Finch. The bastard was going down—I was going to make sure of that.

Tables were turned. Glasses crashed and crumbled against the marble floor. Blood sprayed across the pristine walls and linen tablecloths where gargoyles' claws went through magical flesh. The security magicals fanned out, as did the preceptors, using every ability and every spell handy to bring the monsters down.

Growls emerged from the hallway, and more gargoyles flew in. "Oh, my God," I breathed, watching the scene unfold for a couple of seconds, then glared at Finch. "You're not getting away with this!" I shouted.

Alton's hands glowed yellow as he said a spell under his breath, his eyes on Finch.

"Not gonna happen," Finch said, and his skin began to ripple. In a fraction of a second, before Alton could grab him, he turned into someone else—Clara Fairmont, Wade's failed date. The real Clara was fighting alongside the preceptors against ferocious gargoyles. *Holy crap, Finch can turn into other people.*

Alton seemed just as stunned as I was, and it didn't work in our favor, because Finch took advantage of that blank moment and, in the form of a blonde female, vanished into the crowd. "Crap!" I croaked, and chased after him—her.

I saw Finch pick up the knife-shaped Esprit, and I used it as a visual marker, in case I lost him again. Using my mental lasso, I managed to grip him—her—by the throat and pulled back with all my strength. A gargoyle flew overhead, and I ducked as it swooped down. It was yet another window of opportunity for Finch to escape my hold.

"Dammit!" I breathed, and went deeper into the crowd, my eyes fixed on the glowing knife. Finch sneaked through and made it to one of the enormous, floor-to-ceiling windows. Magicals screamed and grunted around me, as they struggled to contain as many gargoyles as they could. At first glance, several lives had already been lost, their bodies lying on the floor in puddles of blood. A couple of gargoyles had fallen, too, and were rapidly disintegrating into puffs of black smoke. They were gone, lost forever, but plenty were still roaming freely through the banquet hall. They were too fast and vicious, and there weren't enough Mason jars handy to actually capture them properly. Given the dire situation we were all in, the fastest and safest option was to kill as many of them as possible, before moving on to capture the rest.

"It's too late, Harley," Finch said, turning to face me. He rippled back to his original form, but he did seem irritated that I was still onto him. Whatever that ability was, I was far too determined to let him confuse me.

I didn't care whether it was too late or too soon. I summoned every ounce of energy inside me and focused it all on my Telekinetic abilities. They were the only thing I could control in an efficient manner and without an Esprit, at that point.

"It's never too late to set things right, Finch. You don't have to do this," I said.

"You see, that's where you're wrong," he replied bitterly, and raised his knife. He twisted the glowing white blade in his hand and muttered something in Latin, then shoved it into the glass behind him.

"No!" I shouted and launched a mental lasso at him. I caught hold of his throat and pulled him back. He didn't let go of the knife, though—in that pull, and as the blade was removed, the glass crackled all over, spreading out in an intricate spiderweb. The window then came down with a loud, thundering crash. Glass scattered all over, and the coven collectively held its breath.

This wasn't just a window breaking. This was the interdimensional pocket cut open right into the human world, the park behind Fleet Science Center now in full view. There were plenty of people out walking their dogs and doing their morning runs, and some children playing around the fountain, too.

My worst nightmare came true. Finch fell to his knees, and I didn't let go of my Telekinetic hold this time.

The gargoyles purred with delight, then let out deafening growls, leaving the magicals behind as they flew outside. Humans were first stunned, then horrified and screaming as they ran away from the sound, tripping over each other.

"Contain them!" Alton bellowed from behind.

"Too late." Finch grinned, looking up at me from the floor. *That's it.*

I punched him hard, my knuckles ramming into his jaw. "I've had enough of your crap!"

Finch's blade slashed at my leg and caught me by surprise. Pain burned through my calf, which I could no longer feel. I knew, right then and there, that it was no ordinary knife. He cut me again, just below the knee, and I screamed, while he sneered, his teeth smeared with blood.

I fell backward, and he instantly moved on top of me, his hands clutching my throat. His grip tightened as he sneered, looking all too happy to choke the life out of me. I slapped and punched as hard as I could, but I couldn't breathe anymore. *Focus, Harley, focus!*

People's lives were in danger. Gargoyles were out there, spreading out through San Diego, released from the Bestiary. And Finch was choking me to death.

Fire swallowed him whole, and he jumped back, grunting and flailing and desperately shrieking as the flames consumed him. I looked up and saw Wade running toward me, his rings glowing red. "Harley!" he breathed, then helped me up. I could stand, though only on one leg. The lower half of my right leg was still bleeding and paralyzed.

Finch was just five feet away, in the park. The fountain was twenty feet farther back. I limped toward him, watching as he struggled with the flames. I latched onto him again and swung him backward. He landed in the water, steam and smoke rising from the surface, and I rushed forward. Wade tried to get to him first, but I waved him away with a thought. He fell to the ground. Something had come undone inside me, and there was a surge of anger I needed to quell.

"Go help the others," I shouted, as Wade stumbled back to his feet, staring at me with befuddlement.

Something had definitely snapped. Even I didn't think I'd be able to wave someone away so easily, with one swift move of my hand. Wade nodded briefly, then ran over to Santana, Tatyana, and the others.

With the incredible amount of adrenaline flowing through me, it didn't even matter that I couldn't feel half a leg and that I had a constant sensation of nails scratching my throat. I jumped into the fountain and pulled Finch above the surface. He'd suffered substantial burns, his skin crackling red and black, but he was still awake and breathing.

His Esprit was at the bottom, the knife form rippling away until it returned to its original silver lighter state. It seemed to perfectly mimic his ability to change into someone else. "You're too late," he croaked, coughing and wheezing.

I punched him again. And again. The third time my knuckles gave out with the sound of a crack. But it didn't matter. Finch was out, fully unconscious. I dragged him out of the fountain, just in time for one of the security magicals to see us. He whistled to two others and ran over to take Finch back inside.

"Someone needs to let Tobe out," I said. "He has some control over these creatures."

"They're spreading out too fast," the magical said, looking up in sheer horror. "And our radios aren't working."

"I don't care! Make it happen!" I growled, and pushed him away.

All three nodded. One of the guards retrieved Finch's Esprit from the bottom of the fountain, and then they carried him inside.

Chapter Thirty-Two

I looked up and around, stunned by the semi-apocalyptic image before me. Choppers were flying in from the city—magicals spilling out into the real world had certainly drawn the attention of the authorities, even though they probably had no idea what was going on just yet. Gargoyles glided across the sky in larger and larger circles as they moved farther away. Alton shouted orders, and magicals fanned out and used different spells to fire at the gargoyles and keep them somewhat contained.

Many had died, and plenty were injured, including humans. I looked over to the coven, now burst open into the human world. The banquet hall was destroyed, with bodies lying on the floor. O'Halloran was still alive, though gravely wounded, and was being carried away by two other magicals. For a split second, I almost caved in, but my instincts refused to let me collapse. Instead, I seemed to jump back to full consciousness with renewed energy.

Just fifty feet away from me was Garrett, among others, fighting one gargoyle. They'd managed to get the beast in one spot, and Garrett was pulling water pellets out of the fountain and shooting them at the creature in frozen form. Each smacked the monster over the head and further irritated it, while two magicals below were tossing entrapment stones on the ground beneath.

The gargoyle managed to dodge several hits and swooped down, its jaws snapping open as it rammed Garrett into the ground. My heart stopped.

"No! Stop it!" I cried out, and, to my utter shock, the creature obeyed, its massive body still pinning Garret down. "Stop it!"

I made my way toward them. The other magicals took advantage of the creature's confusion and settled the rest of the entrapment stones on the grass, while Garrett was wide-eyed and pale as a sheet of paper. "Move away from him!" I shouted. *This had better work.*

The gargoyle shook its head, disoriented, its beady black eyes fixed on me. It didn't know what to do, sensing my blood relation to Katherine Shipton. If I got too close, it would quickly figure out that I wasn't her. I latched onto it with a mental lasso and threw it back, right in the middle of the entrapment stone circle. "I said move away from him!"

That was the break the magicals needed. One of them uttered the spell, and bright white strings lashed out and trapped the beast under the net, while another produced a Mason jar and captured the creature in its smoky form. I then helped Garrett, who stared at me in amazement, back up.

"I… Harley, I'm so sorry," he mumbled.

"Shut up, help the others," I said, then looked over my shoulder. "Keep the gargoyles as close as you can."

I left him behind and limped across the grass just in time to hear my Rag Team discussing potential solutions.

"We need a large-scale trap," Tatyana said.

"We need to draw them back," Santana replied, shaking her head. "They're fanning out, and we need to contain this fast. The coven will be spread thin. It will take a long time to clean up after this."

Wade cut in, his gaze scanning the sky. "We need to do both. Tatyana, what do you need to set a big trap? You're one of the most skilled on the matter."

"I need cover. Once the gargoyles get a sense of what I'm doing on the ground, they'll come at me," Tatyana replied.

"That's fine, Dylan and I have your back," Wade said, then looked at Santana. "How can we draw them back?"

"We could attract them with something. I don't know, lots of fresh meat or something. Loud screams, anything that'll stop them from flying ahead. Right now, they're scattered over the park, chasing humans and magicals, but they'll spill out into the city soon. Tatyana can use the edge of the park as a perimeter for her spell," Santana replied.

It hit me then. I could help, provided they had something to back me up with.

"Guys, they listen to me," I breathed. "The gargoyles! In the Bestiary, earlier. And at the church, too. Tobe said something about that… I'm related to Katherine Shipton, and, according to him, she nurtured a very weird bond with them. They obey her, and because of our blood connection, they get a little confused about me. Just now, one of them was about to munch on Garrett, and I made it stop. Once I get close and they sniff me properly, however, they decide I'm not really Katherine and they come after me, but—"

"We could get you to call out to them." Santana followed my train of thought, nodding. "Yes. I can do that. You just need your voice amplified."

"Do you have what you need?" Wade asked, and Santana tore one of the buttons from her shirt, showing it to us.

She grinned. "All I need is this and the Orishas."

"Good. Raffe, I need you circling the park, man. Let that critter out," Wade said. "You're our best tool to scare that many gargoyles back into the park area. Tatyana, I'll come with you and Dylan to set the trap. Astrid, take cover and start working Smartie. There will be a *lot* to fix, and we need to beat the humans to the punch. Harley…" His voice faded as his gaze found mine. I felt his concern tingling in the back of my throat. "You and Santana do what you have to, and stay safe."

I nodded, then watched him run off with Tatyana and Dylan across the park. Raffe gave Santana a brief wink, then darted away in the opposite direction. There was no time to ask about what 'critter' Wade was referring to, as Santana immediately ripped the hem of her shirt, producing a thin strip of fabric.

She wrapped the button in it, muttering a spell in Spanish until smoke started to fizzle out from beneath. "Harley, I need you to hold still. This is going to be very uncomfortable."

"Usually when you people say 'uncomfortable,' you mean 'painful,' don't you?" I replied.

She gave me an apologetic smile, then pushed the smoking button against my throat. It burned through, and I hissed from the pain. It did feel weird and uncomfortable, once the pain subsided. I ran my fingers over it and felt the thing literally embedded into my throat. "Holy crap," I murmured.

"Now, repeat this chant after me," Santana said. "Once you do it, it will amplify your voice to a ten-mile radius. Every creature within that circle will hear you, loud and clear, including the gargoyles. *Damen sus voces, Orishas del Catemaco*."

I looked out, watching some gargoyles come down in flames, while a couple were captured by well-organized magicals. Humans kept screaming and running, desperately trying to reach the city streets stretching around the park. They couldn't see the gargoyles, but they could hear their growls and screeches, and they could see the trees getting splintered as the creatures went after them.

Alton, Garrett, the preceptors, and everyone left standing were putting up one hell of a fight to capture or kill as many gargoyles as they possibly could.

Several gargoyles had flown deeper into the city. Helicopters had been deployed to find the invisible attackers and neutralize them. Obviously, the gargoyles had an advantage here, but the humans' preservation instincts were strong, especially when they had access to military-grade machine guns and, I figured, thermal scanners—since some of the choppers had begun firing in a few gargoyles' general direction.

Automatic Gatling guns popped relentlessly in the distance. Some gargoyles were brazen enough to try and chomp on the helicopters, ripping the tail off one in the process. The aircraft went into a frantic twist, then crashed into a nearby building. My blood froze, as I realized the extent of the gargoyle's damage—the innocent lives lost already.

A shadow rushed along the edge of the park, shapeless but incredibly fast, leaving behind a scattering trail of black smoke. It swished up and smacked the escaping gargoyles back, its spine-chilling roars making my heart jump. What in the world was that? Was that Raffe's doing?

"Damen sus voces, Orishas del Catemaco," I chanted, shifting my focus back to Santana, who offered me a reassuring smile.

"Good, now hold on to your senses, Harley. It's gonna get crazy. I just allowed the Orishas to work with you on this," she replied.

Before I got a chance to respond, pure energy filled me up, nearly cutting off my air supply. I burned from the inside, and I felt my feet leave the ground. I glanced down, then gasped, as I saw myself levitating about thirty feet in the air, the winds gathering and howling around me. That was all me, the Elemental part of me, summoning the wind to raise me higher, to a better vantage point. I needed a clear, full view of the gargoyles, and my body seemed to react with Chaos before my brain could send an order down to my limbs.

Whispers trickled into my ears, beckoning me in multiple languages to speak up. And I could understand each and every one of them, somehow. *Holy hell, that's what the Orishas sound like!*

"Stop!" I shouted, and nearly swallowed my own heart as it jumped back into my throat. I couldn't recognize my voice right away. It was weird because it was mine, but it was also unnaturally loud, as if I'd just been fitted with a bullhorn the size of the Fleet Science Center.

"Keep going!" I heard Santana below, encouraging me.

"All of you skinny, ugly-looking bastards, stop!" I called out, my voice thundering across the entire city. Humans and magicals alike stilled for a split second, as did my targets—the four dozen gargoyles trying to spread into the city.

Their ashen wings flapped frenetically as they snapped their heads to look at me from afar. "Yeah, you heard me right, I'm talking to you!"

The gargoyles were baffled, but obedient. They all stopped, and slowly moved back into the park's perimeter. "That's right. Get over here. You recognize me, don't you? Can you smell the Shipton blood? Come closer!" I bellowed.

The magicals quickly figured out what I was doing and proceeded to move toward the edges of the park, sending the remaining humans away. Of all the gargoyles slowly coming back to me, Murray was the only one I recognized. His crooked face was quite unforgettable, and so was his wrath when he realized that I wasn't Katherine Shipton at all, but the girl he'd already tried to kill before.

Just then, a loud bang traveled across the green field, while police sirens wailed in the distance. A bright flash followed, nearly blinding me for a couple of seconds. I opened my eyes, then held my breath as I watched enormous, white energy beams lash out and weave themselves into a net that stretched out like a dome over the entire park.

The gargoyles roared with fury, realizing what had just happened. They all tried to scatter again, but it was too late. The net came down hard and forced them all to crash into the ground. The net itself was pure Chaos energy. It didn't affect the material world, passing through trees and living creatures alike, but it had one hell of an impact on the gargoyles.

Almost fifty were recovered, trapped beneath the giant trap—courtesy of Tatyana's extraordinary efforts. The magicals did their thing right away, just as Tobe emerged from the coven with a sack filled with Mason jars. One by one, the gargoyles were returned to captivity, while Alton directed the preceptors and security magicals to organize a massive cleanup mission and to bring the wounded inside.

The winds beneath me faded, and I fell hard on the ground, suddenly drained. The button in my throat hurt to the point where tears flooded my eyes. Santana dropped to her knees beside me, her hands and her voice trembling.

"This is going to hurt a little more than before. I'm sorry, Harley," she said, then pushed the button deep inside.

It didn't hurt. It was freaking torture, as if someone had driven a red-hot knife right into my gullet. I choked and gurgled, then rolled on my side and retched, forfeiting the entire contents of my stomach along with the carbonized button. Fortunately, I hadn't eaten in sixteen hours, so there wasn't much for me to bring back up.

I coughed and wheezed, as Santana gently caressed the top of my head. "Is… Is it over?" I gasped, my eyes still hazy and glazed with tears.

"Almost, yeah," she replied softly. "Alton is sending out a major cleanup crew now. They've launched some temporary flashes to wipe memories on a three-mile radius, as per protocol. The humans who actually saw all this were all nearby, fortunately. Astrid's got Smartie hacking every single smartphone and social media network to wipe out everything about this event, and the preceptors are working on a mass spell to send out some kind of malware. It'll take a few days to wipe the memory of every single human in the city, but we'll be okay. Thanks to you, Harley. You were amazing."

I couldn't help but chuckle before another cough cut me off. I was curled up in a fetal position on the grass, hearing gargoyles squeal as they got sucked back into Mason jars, and magicals talking to one another.

For a while, I didn't move, my eyes half closed. Gasps and whimpers came through, as they all realized they'd lost some of their friends and colleagues in the disaster. A dark shadow covered me, blocking the sun's warm light, but I didn't have any strength left to look up. I still couldn't feel my leg, and bile was still searing through my throat.

But I could breathe, at least. It was over.

"Stay with me, Harley." I heard Wade and felt a pair of arms lift me off the ground.

A heart beating against me, thudding nervously. My Empathy was off. I was drifting away, and I couldn't do anything to stop it. My eyes closed.

"Harley, stay with me, please," he murmured.

He was just a whisper in the darkness that swallowed me.

Chapter Thirty-Three

I*'m drifting...*

It's so peaceful, so quiet.

Wade's soft voice came back for me in the darkness. "Harley, wake up."

Should I? Why? I'm so comfortable here—wherever "here" is.

I peeled my eyes open, welcoming the warm sunlight on my face. The ceiling above was white, with white neon strips. *The infirmary.* My gaze found Wade, sitting at my bedside, his brows drawing shadows over his green eyes. He looked tired. He felt worried.

My heart fluttered at the sight of him. Was that me, or him?

"Hey. Welcome back," he said, his lips stretching into a warm smile.

It felt so good, soothing my very soul—much like a drizzle of honey, sweet and soft. "Hey," I murmured, my voice scratchy and raw. "What happened?"

"What do you remember?" he replied, carefully analyzing my face. He reached out and brushed a lock of hair from my forehead, his fingers gently touching my skin. A myriad of tiny sparks spread out underneath, as if his touch was mildly electric.

I replayed the entire tragedy in my mind. The tracer spell. Finch. My relation to Finch and Katherine Shipton. The gargoyles and dead magicals. The broken window of the coven… Oh, God, the massacre in the park. The giant trap. My mangled body.

"Everything up to the point where the gargoyles came down," I said, quietly wiggling my toes. I breathed a sigh of relief when I realized I could feel my leg again. Wade nodded slowly, then straightened his back and swiftly went back into his stuck-up mode.

"You passed out after that. You've been here for two days now, which actually helped a lot with your healing. The new physician is really good at his job," Wade replied.

"New physician?" I asked, frowning. "What happened to Adley de la Barthe? Did she die—"

"She was arrested," Wade said. "A lot of things came to light while you were under, Harley. Things we didn't even think were possible."

"Why was she arrested?"

"Finch Anker—or Finch Shipton, actually—is a Shapeshifter," Wade explained. "It's a relatively rare ability, and virtually untraceable, unless a Reading is done. Adley did Finch's Reading when he first came into the coven, as standard procedure. She didn't declare him as a Shapeshifter, and Alton was quick to realize that as soon as we got a minute to breathe and go over everything. Once she was cornered, she confessed. She's been having an affair with him since before he joined the coven. She facilitated his entrance here and kept his ability a secret, at his request."

"But why?" I asked, trying to make sense of it all. Then a memory hit me hard over the head. "Oh, crap. I remember. Ugh, now it makes sense! Back at the general assembly, when I first got here, I saw Adley looking at Finch, and I could feel her… well, her love for him. I didn't think anything of it at the time. It wasn't my business. Did she know who he was from the very beginning?"

"She claims that she didn't, and that Finch just didn't want anyone knowing about his Shapeshifting skill. She identified his Telekinesis as well as his ability to work with metals, which is usually attributed to Earth Elementals," Wade continued. "Though, he's never shown his Esprit's shifting abilities. He's kept a lot of himself secret, in fact. That was all we knew about him, along with his uncanny ability to work charms and hexes—but that was relatively generic, since one third of the coven is good at that."

I remembered the training session then, wondering if anyone else knew about the pills I'd seen him take. "Finch took pills. Do you know anything about them? I asked if they were vitamins, but he wasn't straightforward."

"I don't know." Wade shook his head. "Nothing about him is straightforward. His ID was fake. His entire history was fake, and Adley didn't think to verify any of it when he asked her to keep his secret."

"Love makes you do stupid things, I guess," I said.

"Well, that 'love' facilitated the killing of fifteen magicals and five humans. O'Halloran barely made it out alive. One hundred and five magicals are currently receiving medical care, including him, not to mention the sixty-seven humans still in the hospital. She's going to Purgatory for a long time," Wade replied.

"Purgatory?"

That sounded ominous.

"It's what we call the central magical prison. Most—we call them 'misdemeanor magicals'—carry out their sentences in the covens' underground prisons," Wade explained. "However, the worst offenders go to Purgatory, which was given an interdimensional pocket of its own. It's an international facility hidden deep in the Antarctic. Magicals from all over the world are taken there, some for life sentences, others on death row."

"Was my father there?"

"I think so, yes," he replied with a brief nod.

"What about the coven, the cleanup? Tobe? The others?" I asked, overwhelmed by heart palpitations as the aftermath of the gargoyle massacre set in.

"We fixed the broken window; the coven is sealed again. Tobe was cleared of all charges, and he's been busy adding more protections to the Bestiary. You were right, Harley. That wasn't Tobe in the video footage. It was Finch, posing as Tobe," Wade said. "The rest of us have been doing ten-hour shifts on cleanup throughout the park and the city. Astrid is still modifying CCTV footage and police reports. Fortunately, Alton and the preceptors were quick to intervene, and we got the Los Angeles and San Francisco Covens to help, too. We'll be okay, for the most part."

"For the most part," I repeated, sadness filling my heart. Was I going to be okay, too, for the most part? I was never going to be the same again, for sure. My whole life I'd dreamed of one day finding my real family, my biological family. And what did I get?

A killer for a father, a dead mother, a psychopath of an aunt, and a murderous half-brother, who was also my cousin.

I shook my head in disbelief, then let out a long and heavy sigh. The pressure of eons was suddenly removed from my shoulders, as I understood the single, most important truth. Whoever and whatever my family was, they weren't me. Yes, I was Harley Merlin. Yes, my father murdered my mother, with the help of her sister, for reasons unknown—*again, jeez!* And I had a half-brother who was probably going to get executed or spend the rest of his life in Purgatory. But I was Harley Merlin, and I had a name to build, a history to write, better and nobler than other Merlins before me. I had my own path to clear.

For the time being, however, I had a lot of pain to get over. My entire body throbbed as I tried to sit up.

"For the most part," Wade reiterated. "We're burying our dead tomorrow. The human world is mostly taken care of. Mass memory fixes, plus a news story about someone hacking military drones and letting them loose in San Diego. They'll be chasing their tails on this one forever. The California Mage Council is downstairs, in the

Main Assembly Hall. They're holding a hearing on everything that happened here. It's why I had to wake you up, actually."

"They want to talk to me?" I asked, rubbing my face. My fingers brushed over the bandage wrapped around my neck. It still hurt.

"No, they don't know you're awake. But I need you to come down there with me," he said. "Alton, Tobe, and the rest of us have been making our case, but they need to hear you, too. You're the last of the Merlins, and now that we know Katherine Shipton is still alive and hell-bent on destroying our society, your input matters."

"Why? I'm just another victim," I said, suddenly wary, my earlier courage trembling before the idea of Katherine Shipton—the big, bad, scary witch who'd helped kill my mom and many other innocent magicals. She tore my family apart.

"No, you're Harley Merlin, and if it weren't for you, we would've suffered bigger, more horrific losses. You're an integral part of the Rag Team, too. I can't have you benched for this one. The fate of our coven depends on you."

"Oh, wow, no pressure or anything," I said, then inched closer to the edge of the bed. It got chilly once I pushed the blanket away. My hospital gown was crisp white and too thin to keep me warm, given the low temperature in the infirmary. "It's freezing in here."

"It's to slow down your metabolism and let the healing potions do their job," he replied.

Wade pulled a wheelchair over for me, then wrapped me in a blanket and put his arms around me, helping me to my feet. His strength had this quiet way of soothing me. I felt safe in his embrace. We stood like that for what felt like forever, looking into each other's eyes. There was that pleasant warmth again, the drizzled-honey sweetness and spine-tingling sensation that his grip caused beneath the surface.

He lowered his head slightly. "I'm glad you're okay, Harley. And I… I'm also glad that you're here," he breathed, and I started melting.

My cheeks flushed, and the chills I'd experienced earlier were gone. My heart fluttered like an obese butterfly, and I had no idea what to do with all these feelings. I wasn't even sure whether they were mine, or his. *Or both?*

A long moment passed, and I had absolutely no reply. My brain was glitching. Embarrassment took over—all Wade's, making my temperature spike and my stomach churn. "Anyway, let's go, no time to waste." He helped me sit in the wheelchair and pushed me through the double doors, into the hallway.

"Dude, I'm thirsty. I'm hungry. I'm sore," I said, crossing my arms and shaking away the feelings. Wade had yet to see the hangry side of me. "I've been out for two days. Has anyone thought to feed me, or anything?"

"Of course," he said, pushing me toward an elevator at the end of the corridor. *When did they get elevators in this place?* "You were intravenously fed and hydrated every six hours. Here."

He handed me a small bottle of water. I noticed the needle bruises on my hands, where the IVs had been, as I unscrewed the plastic cap. "Oh, God, this feels good," I groaned, after several mouthfuls of water. "So, what do you want me to do with the Council, again?"

"Just tell the truth," Wade said.

We slipped inside the elevator. The doors closed with a soft jingle. Several seconds later, they opened right into the Main Assembly Hall. There definitely wasn't an elevator there before. "This is a… special elevator, isn't it? Like, coven special."

"That is correct," he said, then pushed me forward.

The coven had gathered around the main podium, where a long, sturdy wooden table had been set, with two smaller ones perpendicular on each side. Behind the structure, the seven mirrors rippled quietly, as the California Mage Council emerged in their dark-blue-and-gold uniforms—all seven of them, this time.

Alton and Tobe were seated on the left side, at the smaller table. Finch and Adley were on the right, heavily chained to the floor with what looked like special cuffs. A series of runes and symbols were etched into the metallic bands.

All those directly involved in the investigation and cleanup operation had been seated in the front row, while the rest of the coven stood at the back. They cleared a path as soon as they saw us come through. My heart raced, once again being pummeled by so many emotions. There was so much grief and sorrow, my eyes instantly teared up. *Keep it together.*

As we reached the podium, the Mage Council took their seats at the long table, with Imogene and Leonidas sitting in the middle. Their expressions were a mixture of sadness and frustration, a lot of which I could feel directly—except for Imogene. She was very much immune to my Empathy.

I glanced around the hall, making brief eye contact with our Rag Team. Tatyana, Santana, Dylan, Raffe, and Astrid all gave me soft smiles and nods, which I was happy to return. The relief of seeing them all safe and in one piece was difficult to describe. I was just so thrilled to see them all there.

Garrett, Poe, Rowena, Lincoln, and Niklas were seated next to them. Shame and sadness oozed out of the group, since one of their own had been revealed as the evil mastermind behind all the gargoyle attacks. Garrett gave me a weak, sad smile, before shifting his focus back to Finch. He looked heartbroken and disappointed. Even though I couldn't feel him, his expression was indubitably genuine.

Alton and Tobe lit up when they saw me. Adley was pale, her lips trembling as grief and shame ate away at her. Finch, on the other hand, was annoyingly relaxed. His burns were healing slowly, but half of his face and his arms were still covered in bandages. His left eye and jaw were bruised and swollen, courtesy of my fists.

The moment our eyes met, a sharp, familiar pain shot through my right knee, where he'd cut me with his Esprit. I gripped it tightly, massaging until the ache subsided.

"Harley, I'm so happy to see you're okay!" Imogene exclaimed, beaming at me. It made me feel good.

"Harley Merlin," Leonidas cut in, raising an eyebrow. "Why are you here? We didn't summon you to this hearing."

Raffe's anger was clear and boiling in my chest. I stole a glance at him and noticed that he didn't make any efforts to hide his discontentment. Whatever was going on between him and his dad, it burned hot and full of rage. Frankly, I didn't like his tone, either. Not after everything I'd discovered about my family, and especially not after everything I'd been through.

And with an entire room of emotions constantly pummeling me, I had very little patience left. And literally nothing to lose if I went ahead and acted as my good ol' self.

"Wade thinks you all need to hear what I have to say," I replied. "I just so happened to wake up. We figured it was a good time to pop down here and say hello."

"And what is it you have to say that we don't already know?" Leonidas asked, the corner of his mouth twitching, despite his otherwise stern expression.

"I don't know, man," I replied with a shrug. "What have you got so far? I'll fill in the blanks for you."

"Try not to piss him off," Wade whispered above me.

"He's asking for it," I muttered.

"Well, what we have so far is a pretty clear picture. The San Diego Coven allowed an evil mass murderer's illegitimate and equally murderous son to infiltrate its ranks and sabotage the Bestiary, on which the entire magical world relies," Leonidas said. "As expected, Alton Waterhouse failed to notify the Mage Council of the coven's illicit activities and its attempts to cover up Finch Shipton's deeds, and is now looking at too many lives lost. We are currently about to reach a decision regarding the San Diego Coven's fate, as well as the Bestiary's new location. Clearly, it can no longer stay here."

A couple of seconds passed, as I thought over Leonidas's harsh assessment. "There's a lot to unpack there, hold on," I said. I went through my version of the events, from the very first night at the casino, every page of coven material that I'd read, every magical that I'd met and spoken to. I then remembered something from my induction package—at the very end of that folder was a list of the coven's senior magicals, including the preceptors, the physician, the security detail, and Alton himself. Naturally, that included files on each, including Adley de la Barthe. To my surprise, an interesting fact came up. "Director Waterhouse, can you tell me how Adley de la Barthe came to the San Diego Coven?" I asked.

At the sound of her name, Adley shot me a confused glance, still sniffing. I was angry at her, but I felt sorry for her, too. I could feel her grief, her remorse, and, most importantly, her broken heart. Judging by how detached Finch looked while sitting next to her, he didn't give a damn about her feelings, even though she didn't hold any of it back with her regretful sobs.

A faint smile tugged at Alton's lips. He'd figured out my angle. "Adley de la Barthe was referred to Halifax by the former director of the San Diego Coven, two years ago," he said. "The Los Angeles Coven agreed to her transfer and provided her with wonderful recommendations."

"And when did Finch come to the San Diego Coven?" I asked.

"Approximately around the same time," Alton replied.

Leonidas narrowed his eyes at me. "What exactly are you implying, Miss *Merlin*?"

Imogene didn't look too happy either, but given how quickly her shoulders dropped, she understood where I was going with this.

"I'm not implying anything, Mage Levi," I replied. "I'm merely stating a fact, which I believe both Adley and Finch will confirm, should they decide to cooperate with the coven. I assume the right to remain silent is a thing amongst magicals, too. Point is, the Los Angeles Coven sent over a supposedly cleared and trustworthy physician. They had no knowledge of Finch Anker's real name, or his ties to Katherine Shipton—not to mention his affair with Adley.

By your same harsh reasoning, if the San Diego Coven failed to identify the traitors, why didn't the Los Angeles Coven spot them either? Was nobody aware of the relationship?"

"I'm not following you," Imogene replied, frowning slightly.

"Whatever Finch has been planning, it's been going on for years. Long before he came to the San Diego Coven. That much he confirmed himself. Adley was a tool, one he used to conceal his Shapeshifter ability," I said. "Finch knew exactly what he was doing, and Adley played along, without asking too many questions because she was obviously head over heels for the guy. I don't see why the San Diego Coven should be held accountable for Adley's crooked ways. If you plan to punish us, you had better dish out the same for the LAC, who sent her here in the first place. Or, better yet, do the decent thing and simply admit that you were *all duped*. Instead of playing the blame game, we should be working together against the real threat."

"The real threat," Leonidas repeated, his bitterness turning my stomach inside out.

"Katherine Shipton," I declared. "She is alive and hiding somewhere, orchestrating all this from afar, through proxies. Judging by how chilled out Finch seems to be, I get the feeling he wasn't her only access port into a coven. More will come. The Bestiary was most likely a ruse. An attempt to destabilize magical society. The San Diego Coven was simply a great opportunity, because of the generally low morale and Mediocrity left behind by Halifax. Instead of bickering like old hags, you all should be thinking of ways to come together and work out a strategy, because what happened two days ago was only the beginning."

"How do *you* know? Was your entire orphan bit a charade? Are you in contact with Katherine Shipton? What else aren't you telling us?" Leonidas retorted, officially angry.

"Tone it the hell down!" I said, raising my voice. His anger was no match for mine at this point. "It's freaking logical! And Finch said so himself! Stop deflecting back to me, because I had absolutely nothing to do with this mess. I tried to stop it, like everyone else—"

"And stop it she did," Alton interjected. "She nearly got herself killed to capture Finch, and, had she not employed that painful Orishas trick, our gargoyle problem would've been far, far worse. So, please, Leonidas, show some respect."

My chest swelled with pride. "Finch knows more than he's telling us, too," I continued, recapturing Leonidas's attention. "I strongly recommend that you postpone any sentencing until we find and stop Katherine Shipton. If anything, he could be used as leverage for her surrender. Blood is thicker than water, after all."

"Yeah? How did that work out for you the other day, when I almost killed you, Little Sister?" Finch chuckled. "Don't kid yourselves. I have nothing to say to you all. *Nothing*. My mother will bring about a new world. The weak will perish. The strong will thrive."

"Good grief, you sound like a door-to-door preacher from the bowels of the Midwest," I groaned, rolling my eyes.

"What do you know about Katherine Shipton?" Imogene asked me, covering Leonidas's hand with hers to stop him from talking. I had a feeling Mage Levi had more snark to hand out, so I was thankful to see Imogene intervene.

"Not much, other than what I briefly heard from Alton, and what Finch told me the other day, right before the gargoyle massacre. She had an affair with my father, gave birth to his son. My father then married my mother. Katherine came back and convinced or manipulated my father to kill… my mother," I said, then choked up a little. I cleared my throat, unwilling to let Finch see how deeply it affected me. "Then she bailed on my father and went on to become a murderous bitch. Much to her surprise, however, I exist. She didn't think I was born in the first place, so… ta-dah."

Imogene stifled a smile. Finch was seething—I'd insulted his precious mother, after all. I could see it all over his face. Everyone else was slightly amused, including Leonidas. "So, in your opinion, and coming back to the main issue here, you don't think the San Diego Coven should be punished in any way for these Bestiary issues, Miss Merlin? You *were* warned, after all."

"It's because we were warned that we didn't tell you about the other incidents in the first place," I replied bluntly. "Had the Mage Council focused on providing support, instead of being all judgy and handing out harsh penalties, we would've gladly asked for more help—but the result would've been the same. *Nobody* would've guessed it was Finch. Not until our tracer spell. And don't even get me started on Adley. The LA Coven didn't notice her shortcomings either. So, no. I don't think we deserve penalties or any punishment."

"Are you sure about that, Miss Merlin?" Leonidas replied, once more raising an eyebrow. He didn't come across as angry anymore. More like impressed. *What the heck?*

"Absolutely," I said. "As soon as Finch was discovered, we moved to neutralize him, but he'd already—by the way, Wade, I suppose we know how the gargoyles got out the other day, right?"

"Yes. Finch had hidden disruptors all over the place," Wade explained. "Some were discovered during multiple sweeps, but not all of them. Preceptor Bellmore helped us with the search, after we contained all the gargoyles."

"So, yeah, as I was saying," I continued. "The San Diego Coven did everything right. We investigated, we cleaned up. I'll bet you folks didn't even know about my apartment and the church incident until you got here." I scoffed when Leonidas, Imogene, and the other Mages all nodded. "My point exactly. And even with what happened two days ago... Our communication channels were down, from what I remember. Everything happened so fast, so violently, and yet, less than an hour later, most of the gargoyles were captured or killed. And Wade tells me the city-wide cleanup operation is going well. We've lost people in this fight. We've suffered enough."

Leonidas sighed, then leaned against the back of his chair. He glanced at his fellow Mages and motioned for Imogene to pass a verdict. She stood, clearing her throat as her gaze wandered across the hall.

"I must say, after all the testimonies and the evidence before us, I agree with Harley on this entire issue," Imogene said. "I believe the San Diego Coven has been through enough, and that there were issues that were simply impossible to avoid. I've felt like that since before she was brought in to speak—despite no one asking her to do that." She chuckled softly, then winked at Wade, and my stomach tightened in response. "I hope the rest of the Mage Council will agree with my requests, which are as follows: Adley de la Barthe is to be tried and convicted as per magical laws; until then, she will be held in this coven's prison."

I looked at Adley and felt her genuine relief. The idea of Purgatory filled her with dread. "Finch Shipton will be taken to Purgatory and will be held there until we find and capture Katherine Shipton and any other accomplices she might have," Imogene continued. "After that, he, too, will be tried and convicted as per magical laws." Finch didn't seem disappointed. In fact, given the grin slitting his face, it was exactly what he wanted—and that really didn't sit well with me. "While I do agree that the San Diego Coven did everything it could to prevent this, I also agree to some form of punishment. I recommend stripping twenty points off, for not notifying the Mage Council of the subsequent gargoyle attacks."

Dismay kicked me in the ribs, followed by painful waves of discontentment. Nobody was happy with losing more points. We had it bad enough as it was. We needed that end-of-year bonus now, more than ever. *Wow, I am really taking this "we" thing seriously. Okay, guess it's sort of settled, but I'm holding on to my trial period, just in case.*

"And last but not least, for their bravery, impressive skill, and speed in containing this tragedy," Imogene added, "I think the San Diego Coven should be awarded up to a thousand points toward the end-of-year prize. Oh, and the Bestiary should stay, too. The Mage

Council will provide an external security detail, though, to assist, in case someone else tries to pull a 'Finch.'"

Gasps and cheers erupted from the assembly hall. Relief washed over me, and I couldn't help but gasp, overwhelmed by how much these bonus points meant for the coven. Most importantly, it felt amazing to know that they were all cleared of any wrongdoing, and that their efforts were fully recognized by the California Mage Council.

I sank into my wheelchair, feeling my cheeks flush as a wave of kind thoughts flowed my way. It was my first time in a crowd where I was actually welcome. It was weird and wonderful, at the same time, making me grin with pride. I'd done something good—scratch that, I'd done something great, and it felt awesome.

Wade's hand squeezed my shoulder gently. I looked up and found him smiling at me, in a way that made my heart perform exquisite somersaults in my chest. *This feels nice…*

Leonidas and the other Mages stood, prompting the assembly hall to tone it down with all the cheering. Silence settled over us once more, and Leonidas nodded my way. "The Mage Council of California agrees with all the verdicts," he said, then glanced at Alton. "I trust you'll secure Ms. de la Barthe's cell accordingly."

"Absolutely," Alton replied. "Preceptors Nomura and Bellmore have devised a tamper-proof mechanism."

"Good. We'll be on our way then," Leonidas said, then snapped his fingers at Finch.

It was then that I realized that Leonidas Levi was a Telekinetic, like me—only infinitely more skilled. Finch shot to his feet, unable to control his body. He looked frustrated and helpless. A part of me enjoyed the sight. He threw me a sideways glance. "I'll see you soon, Little Sister. Like you said, blood is thicker than water."

"In your dreams, a-hole," I said, tempted to flip him off, for good measure. I held back, though, eerily respectful of the Mage Council, not wanting to get penalized for foul body language or something.

With one swift hand movement, Leonidas snapped Finch's chain from the iron ring mounted on the floor, then threw him through one of the rippling mirrors like a rag doll. He then gave me a brief smile, slightly narrowing his eyes. "Keep your nose clean, Miss Merlin. I'll be keeping a close eye on you."

I shrugged in response. "Duly noted."

Imogene graciously waved goodbye, then walked through one of the mirrors, followed by the rest of the Mage Council. Leonidas and Raffe exchanged brief glances, and I felt the promise of a talk coming up soon between them. *Man, there's still so much I don't know about these people, and I nearly got myself killed for them. Sheesh.*

As soon as the Mage Council and Finch disappeared into the seven mirrors, Alton turned to face the crowd, while Preceptor Nomura ordered two security magicals to take Adley away. They removed her charmed chains from the floor, then escorted her off the podium.

"I'm sorry, I didn't know," Adley mumbled as she passed by me.

"Doesn't change what you did," I replied. "Your duty was to the coven, not your lover. Even I know that, and I've been here less than a week. At least help us out in the future, even if you're in prison. If you know anything about what Finch was doing, tell us."

She opened her mouth to say something, but gave up and gave me a soft nod, then let herself get carried out by the security magicals. I could feel her shame and regret, but, with all the lives lost, it was damn near impossible not to be angry with her. She was in love with my murderous half-brother and—*jeez, I have a screwed-up family. I think I was better off as an unsuspecting orphan.*

"Harley, you should rest and stay away from the crowds for a while," Alton said, approaching me with Tobe right behind him.

"Thank you, Harley," Tobe said. "You helped clear my name. Thank you all."

The rest of our Rag Team came over, while the crowd gradually dispersed. I didn't even realize that Wade's hand was still resting on my shoulder until he removed it, leaving a warm spot behind.

Santana, Tatyana, and Astrid took turns hugging me, while Dylan and Raffe shook Tobe's feathered hand.

"Harley believed in you," Raffe told Tobe, then smiled at me, "and we believe in Harley."

Santana was beaming like a midday sun. "You were amazing back there. I hope you'll forgive me, I did put you at risk when I let the Orishas help you. They're highly volatile when they deal with a non-Santeria magical, but it turned out okay. You're strong, and they felt that."

"Oh, it's cool," I replied. "I mean, my voice was the only thing that seemed to work in drawing those gargoyles back, so, yeah, risk worth taking, in the end. Besides, I only did one part of the job. Tatyana kicked major ass, from what I could see."

"To be honest," Tatyana chuckled, "I wasn't sure I'd pull off such a big trap, but, thanks to Wade, Dylan, and Raffe, it all worked out."

"How are *you* feeling?" Astrid asked me, adorably concerned for my wellbeing. "You took most of the brunt."

"Yeah. I'm okay, I think. Just really sore. I couldn't feel my leg back there. Whatever Finch's Esprit can do, it played quite the trick on me when he cut me."

"We don't know much about his Esprit, at this point, but the Mage Council will definitely look into it," Wade replied. "There was a neurotoxin in your system, probably something that the blade was laced with. Adley actually helped with that, before we figured out what she did and detained her. The new physician handled the rest."

"That's enough with all the gushing and congratulations." Alton intervened, smiling gently. "Harley needs to rest. Can you take her back to her room, Wade?"

My heart skipped a beat at the thought of being alone with Wade again. I didn't like to admit it, but he was really growing on me. His ego would probably explode if he ever found out, so I tried my best to stifle my smile.

"Shouldn't she go back to the infirmary?" Wade replied with a frown. He was worried. *Aww.*

"Nah, I'm cool. I'm hungry, though. Really hungry. Like, an extra-large pizza with cheesy crust, two cheeseburgers, large fries, and rivers of Coke on the side hungry," I said, my stomach protesting too much.

Alton crouched in front of me, so we could be on the same level, his hands covering mine in my lap. "Harley, with everything you've done for us, at a time when others would have run screaming, lunch is on the coven. Wade will get you whatever you need."

"I'm not her servant," Wade said.

"It takes a phone call, don't be melodramatic," I answered, without bothering to look at him. Instead, I kept my eyes on Alton, who gave me a soft smile.

"I know you still have three weeks on your probationary period before you decide what you're going to do, as a magical," he said slowly. "I just want you to know that no matter what your choice will be, you will always have a home and a family here. But if you decide to apply for a Neutral position, I will gladly sign your recommendation for the Mage Council, even though we'd rather have you here, with us."

I teared up almost instantly as Alton squeezed my hands, then dropped a kiss on my forehead and got up, motioning for Wade to take me away. I smiled at our Rag Team and Tobe—their affection seemed to heal my broken heart.

Alton was right. I didn't need Hiram and Hester Merlin alive to have a family. I didn't even need that woman I'd seen through the dreamcatcher, maybe my father's sister, an aunt or something. I had the Smiths back in the human world. And I had new friends here, who were ready to stick their necks out for me. *Family isn't something you're necessarily born into.*

My journey as a magical was only just beginning. There were some pretty annoying faults in this magical society, and the elitism and choking rules were a little too much to handle at times, but there was room for learning and improvement. Not just on my end, but on theirs, too.

The coven wasn't perfect, but they were all trying to be better versions of themselves, even when they didn't know which way to go or what to do in order to accomplish that. And I was right there with them, for the time being, aspiring toward the same goal.

A better version of me. Harley Smith was going to stay behind, quaintly attached to her life as a foster kid in a human world.

Harley Merlin, on the other hand, even though she'd been deemed a Mediocre and had yet to find her Esprit, was just getting started. And if this turbulent beginning filled with forbidden charms and bloodthirsty gargoyles was any indication, the ride was bound to get even bumpier in the future.

That's cool. I'll be ready.

Chapter Thirty-Four

I slept through most of the week. Everything that had happened since the first night with Wade at the casino had finally caught up with my body. The Rag Team took turns visiting, with hot coffee and Chinese takeout, mostly. They brought me up to speed on the cleanup operation and arranged private tutoring sessions with all the preceptors.

Wade went back to being his usual pompous jerk self, and I was okay with that. His snark was my emotional anchor—literally. I needed our banter to function properly and process every single detail of my existence, particularly the discoveries we'd made about my family.

The time would come when I'd sit down and comb through the archives, one page at a time, until I learned everything I could about my father, my mother, and, most importantly, Katherine Shipton. She was still alive and extremely dangerous. I had a bone to pick with that witch.

The sun poured through the windows. My last visitor, Astrid, had left the drapes pulled back last night. I'd fallen asleep staring at a starry sky. I sat up, stretching my arms, then scratched the back of my neck. The bandage was really annoying, so I decided to untie it and take it off. My throat wound was almost fully healed, anyway.

I got out of bed and checked myself in the mirror. There were still purplish bruises around my neck, and a stitched-up hole left behind by Santana's button, plus some more bruises on my shoulders and arms. But, other than that, I looked like I was definitely going to live to see another day. That button was going to leave a scar, though.

My bright red hair was a wavy, slightly tangled mess. My sky-blue eyes now reminded me of Finch. I welcomed that, in a way, because it kept me focused on what came next: finding Katherine and throwing her in Purgatory, along with her son. After I scrunched her face up, of course, for what she did to my family.

I exhaled, then fished my father's note from the back pocket of my jeans, and read it, over and over.

Harley, I am so sorry for doing this to you, but there is no other way. Stay safe. Stay smart. I love you. Dad.

What kind of a father would do what he did? He and Katherine burned my mother alive. I swallowed back tears, crumpled the note, and tossed it into the trashcan. It hit the lip and bounced back, then tumbled on the floor and vanished under my bed.

I didn't need that façade of his, that bunch of lies from the man who'd killed my mother. There was a lot I didn't know yet, though. And the one memory I had of him didn't match what the newspapers or even Finch said, not at all. But he'd been tried and convicted.

He pleaded not guilty.

Was I letting my grief get the better of me? Was there, maybe, the inkling of a possibility that my dad had told the truth?

Remorseful to have tossed away a message that had kept me sane for so many years, I got down on the floor and retrieved the crumpled note from under the bed. Only then, upon seeing it again after days, did I remember the box that Alton had given me. I pulled it out and left my father's note on the floor next to me.

I turned the box over a couple of times. The engravings were all symbols I'd seen before, though I couldn't exactly say where. They just felt familiar. The box itself was the size of a regular book, with mother-of-pearl inlays in the form of delicate floral patterns on the sides and on the lid. The engravings followed the petal and leaf lines, like words lost in the image, tucked away and not for everyone to see.

The lock seemed peculiar, cast in sterling silver, with swirling lines leading into the keyhole. My mother's name was elegantly engraved on the lid. Hester Merlin. I tried to force it open with a small Swiss Army knife I kept in my pocket, but it didn't even budge.

Then I noticed the text inscribed on the bottom. I'd been so tired and distraught the last time I'd tried to open it that I hadn't even seen the writing. It was clear, all in capital letters. *Sanguis Crassior Aquae*.

I knew that line. I'd read it before. Heck, I'd said it myself, just recently.

"Blood is thicker than water," I murmured, absently passing my index finger over the keyhole.

A sharp prick startled me, and I gasped, sucking on the bloodied tip. Something had punctured my fingertip.

"Wait," I mumbled, tasting my own blood, then brought the box up to get a better look at the keyhole. "Yep, there you are."

I could see the tiny steel tip of a needle, glazed in my blood. To my surprise, it shot back inside, and the sound of little, mechanical wheels turning emerged from within. Three loud clicks later, the lid popped open.

"Oh, whoa."

The box was lined in black velvet, and there were three objects inside. I held my breath for a few seconds, my gaze darting between my pricked finger and the contents of the box. *Holy crap*.

With trembling hands, I took the first item out. It was a photograph—Hiram and Hester Merlin, long before they had me. They looked young and carefree, elegantly dressed against the backdrop of a sparkling ballroom. My father wore a three-piece suit, his black hair combed neatly on the sides, his sky-blue eyes beaming at the camera. Yup, there was definitely a part of him in me. I could see it so vividly there. The eyes, the freckles, the shape of his nose… all me.

My mother was gorgeous in her black evening gown, her bright red hair caught up in a stylish up-do, with pearl earrings and a smidge of red lipstick. She looked familiar, but I couldn't really tell where I'd seen her before. The shape of her face was mine, as was the hair. Her playful smile echoed in me, too. Maybe that was where I'd seen Hester Merlin before. In the mirror.

They seemed happy and in love, holding each other and smiling as if there were nothing but good days ahead. *Little did they know.*

I wiped the tears from my eyes and put the photo back inside, moving on to the next object—a pack of game cards with a classic design, each meticulously hand-painted, nestled in a thick cardboard box. There was a message on the back. *Knock 'em dead, turtle dove!*

The cards were beautiful, reminiscent of the early 1920s. The queens were sensual princesses depicted in an Art Nouveau style. The kings were dapper and dashing, and the jacks were swanky musicians who winked at me, their beholder. "Knock 'em dead, turtle dove," I repeated the message out loud, slightly amused. "I think my mom was a gambler. Hah."

It was the third object that really had an impact on me, before I even laid a finger on it. It was a stunning ring-bracelet, splendidly crafted in an elegant gothic style, in amber gold. The bracelet held one large, oval black onyx, and the metal was decorated with swirling patterns all around. The ring had a large white pearl mounted on it, and there were four smaller gemstones on the delicate chain connecting the ring to the bracelet—a sapphire, a red garnet, an emerald, and a diamond.

It looked so beautiful, yet so different. I'd never seen anything like it. The moment I touched it, however, my heart nearly exploded. I bit my lower lip, then put the ring-bracelet on my left hand. As soon as I locked the bracelet around my wrist, I found myself smiling. It was a perfect match.

Three breaths later, my body reacted, and my very soul sang. It felt like liquid happiness pouring through me, lighting me up from the inside. It was as though the entire world was right again. A piece had been missing from my very existence, and this was it. I knew it, deep in my heart.

It spoke to me. Not in words, but in a flurry of emotions, as if I was finally aligned with the universe. A surge of power rippled through my skin. *Is this what Chaos feels like?*

I didn't want to rush to a conclusion, but there was one way to put it to the test. I dashed out of my room and ran down the hallway toward the backyard, where the dragon fountain was—that little corner of paradise I'd yet to fully enjoy.

It didn't even matter that I was wearing my slacks and tank top, or that I was barefoot. I ran as fast as I could, thinking I needed some space in case something went wrong.

"Harley!" I heard Wade behind me.

My heart was beating so fast, my vision focused on the path ahead, that I hadn't even seen him. I heard his footsteps behind me. He was running after me.

I made it into the garden, my left arm tingling with what felt like delight. *This is it. I think.*

"Harley, are you okay?" Wade caught up with me.

I lifted my hand in response, my gaze fixed on the fountain. It took him a couple of seconds to respond, after checking out the ring-bracelet.

"Is that—"

"Let's find out," I interrupted him. I didn't even want to hear that word until I was able to confirm it. Light bubbled through me, stretching my muscles and filling my chest with hope. I couldn't bear the thought of a disappointment.

I put my hand out, focusing on the water trickling out of the stone dragon's mouth. The sapphire on the connecting chain lit up in a breathtaking blue hue, and I squealed with joy, wiggling my fingers at the water.

Droplets were pulled from the flow, perfect little balls of spring water that hovered in the air above me. "Oh! My! Days!" I giggled, watching as the droplets trembled and swirled around one another until they combined into a larger blob of water, the size of a soccer ball.

Relief burst through me, and I feared my heart wouldn't take that much happiness.

"This is it! This is my Esprit! I managed to open my mom's box, and it was in there. Wade, meet my Esprit. Esprit, meet my Wade—" I laughed, then instantly realized what I'd just said. "I mean, meet Wade. Esprit, meet Wade."

My face burned as I turned to look at Wade, who was staring at me, all wide-eyed and befuddled. Heat expanded in my chest. He pointed at the water blob. "You might want to keep an eye on that."

"What, why?" I asked, then checked my water ball and stilled. It had tripled in size and was shaking uncontrollably.

One second later, as a burst of energy flowed through me, it exploded, splashing water all over Wade and me.

We stood there, dripping wet and saying absolutely nothing. I was equal parts excited and embarrassed, my Esprit animating me better than six shots of espresso in one chug.

"I'm guessing this is what you meant when you said the Esprit can be highly unstable until I learn how to use it?" I asked, rhetorically, then wiped the water from my face, relishing the subtle jingle of my ring-bracelet. That was a sound I was more than happy to get used to.

Wade needed a couple seconds to respond, his eyes locked on me, as water trickled down the slim blade of his nose and onto his already-soaked shirt. "Think of it as a sports car. You can feel the rush from the moment you get in it, but you still need to learn how to drive it properly, so you don't end up in a lake."

I sniffed, then nodded slowly, lovingly gazing at *my* Esprit.

"I think this belonged to my mother," I breathed.

"That makes it all the more beautiful," Wade replied softly.

I couldn't help but agree. Sure, I had a lot of work cut out for me, plenty of training and reading up on the Esprits, but I'd found it. I'd tossed my father's message away, and it had somehow led me back to my mother.

A tear found its way out, rolling down my cheek and splashing against the cobblestone pavement, where my bare feet and toes were wiggling with delight.

"It *is* beautiful," I murmured.

That road ahead didn't seem as scary anymore. I was a complete magical now, with so much to learn.

But one thing was certain, even before I thought of admitting it to myself.

I was right where I needed to be.

Ready for the next part of Harley's story?

Dear Reader,

Thank you for taking a chance on this book. I do hope you enjoyed it!

I'm excited to announce that Book 2 of the series, **Harley Merlin and the Mystery Twins**, is available now.

Visit: www.bellaforrest.net for details.

I look forward to continuing Harley's journey with you. See you on the other side…

Love,

Bella x

P.S. Sign up to my VIP email list and you'll be the first to know when my next book releases: **www.morebellaforrest.com**

(Your email will be kept 100% private and you can unsubscribe at any time.)

P.P.S. I'd also love to hear from you. Come say hi on Facebook: Facebook.com/BellaForrestAuthor. Or Twitter: @ashadeofvampire

Read more by Bella Forrest

HARLEY MERLIN

Harley Merlin and the Secret Coven (Book 1)

Harley Merlin and the Mystery Twins (Book 2)

THE GENDER GAME

(Action-adventure/romance. Completed series.)

The Gender Game (Book 1)

The Gender Secret (Book 2)

The Gender Lie (Book 3)

The Gender War (Book 4)

The Gender Fall (Book 5)

The Gender Plan (Book 6)

The Gender End (Book 7)

THE GIRL WHO DARED TO THINK

(Action-adventure/romance. Completed series.)

The Girl Who Dared to Think (Book 1)

The Girl Who Dared to Stand (Book 2)

The Girl Who Dared to Descend (Book 3)

The Girl Who Dared to Rise (Book 4)

The Girl Who Dared to Lead (Book 5)

The Girl Who Dared to Endure (Book 6)

The Girl Who Dared to Fight (Book 7)

THE CHILD THIEF

(Action-adventure/romance.)

The Child Thief (Book 1)

Deep Shadows (Book 2)

Thin Lines (Book 3)

Little Lies (Book 4)

Ghost Towns (Book 5)

HOTBLOODS

(Supernatural adventure/romance. Completed series.)

Hotbloods (Book 1)

Coldbloods (Book 2)

Renegades (Book 3)

Venturers (Book 4)

Traitors (Book 5)

Allies (Book 6)

Invaders (Book 7)

Stargazers (Book 8)

A SHADE OF VAMPIRE SERIES

(Supernatural romance)

Series 1: Derek & Sofia's story

A Shade of Vampire (Book 1)

A Shade of Blood (Book 2)

A Castle of Sand (Book 3)

A Shadow of Light (Book 4)

A Blaze of Sun (Book 5)

A Gate of Night (Book 6)

A Break of Day (Book 7)

Series 2: Rose & Caleb's story

A Shade of Novak (Book 8)

A Bond of Blood (Book 9)

A Spell of Time (Book 10)

A Chase of Prey (Book 11)

A Shade of Doubt (Book 12)

A Turn of Tides (Book 13)

A Dawn of Strength (Book 14)

A Fall of Secrets (Book 15)

An End of Night (Book 16)

Series 3: The Shade continues with a new hero...

A Wind of Change (Book 17)

A Trail of Echoes (Book 18)

A Soldier of Shadows (Book 19)

A Hero of Realms (Book 20)

A Vial of Life (Book 21)

A Fork of Paths (Book 22)

A Flight of Souls (Book 23)

A Bridge of Stars (Book 24)

Series 4: A Clan of Novaks

A Clan of Novaks (Book 25)

A World of New (Book 26)

A Web of Lies (Book 27)

A Touch of Truth (Book 28)

An Hour of Need (Book 29)

A Game of Risk (Book 30)

A Twist of Fates (Book 31)

A Day of Glory (Book 32)

Series 5: A Dawn of Guardians

A Dawn of Guardians (Book 33)

A Sword of Chance (Book 34)

A Race of Trials (Book 35)

A King of Shadow (Book 36)

An Empire of Stones (Book 37)

A Power of Old (Book 38)

A Rip of Realms (Book 39)

A Throne of Fire (Book 40)

A Tide of War (Book 41)

Series 6: A Gift of Three

A Gift of Three (Book 42)

A House of Mysteries (Book 43)

A Tangle of Hearts (Book 44)

A Meet of Tribes (Book 45)

A Ride of Peril (Book 46)

A Passage of Threats (Book 47)

A Tip of Balance (Book 48)

A Shield of Glass (Book 49)

A Clash of Storms (Book 50)

Series 7: A Call of Vampires

A Call of Vampires (Book 51)

A Valley of Darkness (Book 52)

A Hunt of Fiends (Book 53)

A Den of Tricks (Book 54)

A City of Lies (Book 55)

A League of Exiles (Book 56)

A Charge of Allies (Book 57)

A Snare of Vengeance (Book 58)

A Battle of Souls (Book 59)

Series 8: A Voyage of Founders

A Voyage of Founders (Book 60)

A Land of Perfects (Book 61)

A Citadel of Captives (Book 62)

A Jungle of Rogues (Book 63)

A Camp of Savages (Book 64)

A SHADE OF DRAGON TRILOGY

A Shade of Dragon 1

A Shade of Dragon 2

A Shade of Dragon 3

A SHADE OF KIEV TRILOGY

A Shade of Kiev 1

A Shade of Kiev 2

A Shade of Kiev 3

THE SECRET OF SPELLSHADOW MANOR

(Supernatural/Magic/YA mystery. Completed series)

The Secret of Spellshadow Manor (Book 1)

The Breaker (Book 2)

The Chain (Book 3)

The Keep (Book 4)

The Test (Book 5)

The Spell (Book 6)

BEAUTIFUL MONSTER DUOLOGY

(Supernatural romance)

Beautiful Monster 1

Beautiful Monster 2

DETECTIVE ERIN BOND

(Adult thriller/mystery)

Lights, Camera, GONE

Write, Edit, KILL

For an updated list of Bella's books, please visit her website: www.bellaforrest.net

Join Bella's VIP email list and she'll send you an email reminder as soon as her next book is out. Visit: www.morebellaforrest.com